PRAISE FOR FRANCINE MATHEWS

"A wonderful new stylist on the mystery scene. Nantucket and its impenetrable, secretive fog and characters come to life in Mathews' capable hands."
—Diane Mott Davidson, author of *The Main Corpse*

AND HER NANTUCKET ISLAND MYSTERIES
DEATH IN ROUGH WATER

"Refreshing island atmosphere, believable villainy, and down-to-earth sleuthing."
—*Kirkus Reviews*

"An enticing read."
—*The Denver Post*

"Mathews offers a nice blend of island lore and contemporary connivers, a . . . twisty plot and a dogged heroine."
—*The Armchair Detective*

"Mathews skillfully incorporates close-knit relationships, small-town gossip and a salty Nantucket flavor as she steers this intricate tale to a satisfying conclusion."
—*Publishers Weekly*

OTHER MYSTERIES BY FRANCINE MATHEWS
FEATURING MERRY FOLGER

Death in the Off-Season
Death in Rough Water

and coming in Bantam Hardcover in June '98:

Death in a Cold Hard Light

and

THE JANE AUSTEN MYSTERY SERIES
BY FRANCINE MATHEWS
WRITING AS STEPHANIE BARRON

Jane and the Unpleasantness at Scargrave Manor
Jane and the Man of the Cloth
Jane and the Wandering Eye

and coming soon in Bantam Hardcover:

Jane and the Genius of the Place

Death in A Mood Indigo

Francine Mathews

BANTAM BOOKS

NEW YORK
TORONTO
LONDON
SYDNEY
AUCKLAND

This is a work of fiction. All of the characters, whether central or peripheral, are wholly the product of the author's imagination, and neither the characters nor the situations which were invented for them are intended to depict real people or real events.

This edition contains the complete text of the original hardcover edition.
NOT ONE WORD HAS BEEN OMITTED.

Death in A Mood Indigo
A Bantam Book

PUBLISHING HISTORY

Bantam hardcover edition published July 1997
Bantam paperback edition / May 1998

Library of Congress Catalog Card Number: 96-48324.

ISBN 0-553-57624-0

Published simultaneously in the United States and Canada

Bantam Books are published by Bantam Books, a division of Bantam Doubleday Dell Publishing Group, Inc. Its trademark, consisting of the words "Bantam Books" and the portrayal of a rooster, is Registered in U.S. Patent and Trademark Office and in other countries. Marca Registrada. Bantam Books, 1540 Broadway, New York, New York 10036.

PRINTED IN THE UNITED STATES OF AMERICA

OPM   10   9   8   7   6   5   4   3   2   1

This book is dedicated with love
to Mo Mathews,
my Ralph Waldo—
in wisdom, if not in years

Acknowledgments

To Ruth Connor, my volunteer researcher on Nantucket, my deepest thanks. My description of Daffodil Weekend, not to mention my knowledge of Sconset off-season, would have suffered in verisimilitude without your zealous pursuit of Truth (and your handy camera).

Michael A. Trudeau, assistant district attorney for the Cape and Islands District, gave generously of his time in the midst of the high season in order to explain the intricacies of the Barnstable DA's jurisdiction and case load. You have my gratitude as a lawyer's wife, who knows what it costs to give up your lunch hour.

Barbara P. Andrews, Librarian Emerita of the Nantucket Atheneum, gamely embarked on some necessary research and forwarded the results in twenty-four hours; while Michael P. Norton of the *Inquirer and Mirror* told me where to look. I owe the entire staff of the *Inky Mirror* a debt, in fact, for the excellence of their wonderful newspaper, without which Nantucket and its people would seem far too distant during the long winter months.

And last, but hardly least—to my editor, Kate Miciak, the most talented and exacting woman in publishing: my profoundest respect, my eternal thanks.

Death in A Mood Indigo

Chapter One

"I could help," Nan Markham said. "I could." Even to her own ears her voice was plaintive and young, the voice of a neglected baby. "I could carry the water for you. In my pail."

Nan lifted a dull-red plastic sand bucket and waggled it tentatively toward her brother's unfeeling back. But Cecil was absorbed in his digging, the castle's trench a widening perfection of scarp and contrascarp, the turrets rising wetly against the blue-black of the surf. He had worked at the fortifications for days—each afternoon when school was over, and now for the bulk of Saturday. What the tide and the weather destroyed in the hours of darkness, Cecil patiently rebuilt, in a determined contest with time and the sands. The two children were always out-of-doors, despite the gloom of the deserted beach, the fitful showers of chill rain. Even immersion in this dispiriting spring was preferable to being at home.

Nan brushed back a strand of bright-red hair and hugged her sweatered arms closer to her body. The wind scoured her cheek with stinging grains.

"Mummie said to let me help."

The last resort of the tagalong: the invocation of Mummie.

Disgusted with herself and her eight-year-old weakness— disgusted with her brother and his silence and his solitary building—she kicked at the nearest rampart. "Stupid. Stupid old castle. I *hate* your castle, Cecil!"

Her wanton destruction left him unmoved. That was Cecil's way. He did not react like other boys—with a shove or a blow or the careful plotting of revenge. He did not offer curses. He merely looked at his little sister, incomprehension and tedium filling his face, and said, "Go away, Nan. There's going to be a battle."

And so Nan turned disconsolately from the rampart she had ruined and trudged off toward her secret place in the dunes, there to sit on a piece of driftwood and arrange a tea party. She used shells for teacups and her thoughts for friends. And Satchmo—her beloved Satchmo, his fur matted from repeated bouts with sand and salt water, his huge body shapeless from lying too long on the kitchen floor, his legs dangerously arthritic as he stepped each morning into the pounding surf—Satchmo settled down in the dune grass opposite her and waited eternally for his tea.

A gull cried from its perch a few feet away, and Nan turned to stare at it: malevolent dark eye, cruel mustard beak. It lifted one reptilian claw and flicked an orange peel her way.

What do the gulls do, she wondered, *when flying is not enough?*

The clouds were lowering on the rain-swept horizon, but before the iron grip of storm closed the sun's eyes forever, a faint glimmer of light shafted across the turbulent sea. Lord Cecil of Trevarre raised a hand to his brow and gazed intently at the enemy fleet and its forest of billowing black sails. In salute to the vanishing sun, a fourteen-pound gun roared from the flagship's bow, a challenge and a curse in its orange flare; and seconds later the ball whistled past Trevarre's noble head.

"Get down, my lord!" his lieutenant cried, and gripped his ankle in desperation.

"We shall not prevail by skulking within doors," Lord Cecil shot back, his expression both proud and bitter. "The castle can avail us nothing now. To the fore, lads, and show a brave face! Or die in the attempt!"

He sprang down from the breastworks, his feet finding soft purchase on the sand below, and raced to the water's edge, his standard raised high. The first of the enemy's landing boats were racing toward shore, filled to their gunwales with scores of men; in a matter of moments his own would be outnumbered. To die, then, and die nobly in defense of what he held most dear—this was his last, his only, destiny.

Gordon, his faithful retainer, appeared suddenly at his side holding the reins of his stallion, Satchmo; the mettlesome beast pawed the ground, his iron shoes ringing sparks— (no, not sparks, since the beach was sandy, not rocky like the beaches in England). *The mettlesome beast pawed deep furrows in the shore's wet sand. Lord Cecil took hold of Satchmo's mane and swung himself into the saddle, his eyes fixed upon the enemy boats. As with one voice, the black-clad invaders cried aloud and jumped into the shallows, their brutal faces intent upon one man and his destruction—Trevarre.*

A wave furled and crashed, mightier than its fellows, racing ahead to storm the beach's heights. But Lord Cecil and his small surviving band stood ready.

Water poured into the gap between Cecil's sneakered feet, foamed and swirled across his shoelaces, licked at the cuffs of his faded jeans. He gave a ferocious yell and thrust out his strong right saber arm, his invisible horse rearing high; then he tore down to the edge of the surf.

The wave retreated in routed terror. Victory was in his very grasp.

Cowards. They had turned tail and taken to their boats, beating desperately against the tide to their black-sailed ships, rather than face his heroic band. Lord Cecil of Trevarre raised his saber arm in scorn and triumph and cried aloud. As if in answer, Satchmo neighed.

"Cecil! Cecil!"

He looked over to the dunes, exhilaration torn by annoyance. *"What?"*

Nan's bright head, crowned with a wreath of the first daffodils, emerged from the fringe of beach plum that fronted the derelict homes of Codfish Park. January storms had swept several houses out to sea, and the remaining few looked likely to follow. Nan had probably scavenged the flowers from some abandoned front steps, like a camp follower rifling a battlefield's dead. As she scrambled up, the dog Satchmo groaned, a sound from deep in his blasted frame. He turned to stare at Cecil, something caught between his jaws, and then slowly, creakily, he trotted in Nan's wake. She ran pell-mell down the beach.

"Look!"

She was offering Cecil what looked like a twig— strange, since twigs came from trees, and there were none so near the beach. He took it from her fingers, his brow furrowed.

"I found it," she said, breathless. "In the sand, while I was digging. There are lots of others if you dig far enough."

And as he listened and turned the twig in his hand, Cecil felt the beginning of an inner excitement—something that seemed to spread from Trevarre's sea-drenched socks until it reached his noble heart.

For what Nan had found was a bone.

The rain that had threatened all morning commenced in earnest an hour after lunch, as Peter Mason and Rafe da Silva grunted and strained over Meredith Folger's dining-room table. It was not that lunch had proved difficult to consume, or required a certain strenuous attention, but rather that the table itself was massive and dense, a veritable monolith in mahogany. And the table was sitting in the midst of Merry's front yard, imperiled by the sudden rain, and obdurately resisting its removal to the bed of Rafe's truck.

"Can I help?"

Merry was dancing around the two men as they strained over her board, feeling useless and very much like a *girl*. "I can get up on the tailgate and help you lift it from there—"

"Get outta the way," Rafe spat between clenched teeth. His perpetually tanned skin was streaming with something other than rain, and the distinctive odor of laboring male emanated from his T-shirt. "*Move.*"

Merry scuttled backward to the doorway of her family home on Tattle Court and felt her grandfather's arm encircle her shoulders. "Be glad you have help," Ralph Waldo Folger told her. "Even if it's as stubborn as the day is long. You aren't going anywhere with that table alone."

"It's not their need for gratitude that galls me, Ralph," she said, and crossed her arms against her damp green slicker. Her fingers were chill and reddening from the raw April day. "I could give them that. It's the female adulation. The groveling, you know? Just to get a lousy table moved."

"And a mattress, and a sofa, and a couple of easy chairs," her grandfather replied cheerfully. "Guess I'll check on that pea soup. You'll be wanting it, I expect, before long. You hardly ate anything at lunch."

Merry looked over her shoulder as he disappeared in the direction of the kitchen, feeling a sharp stab of doubt. Ralph was always worried about how much she ate—and though she would no longer be eating most of her meals in his kitchen, old habits died hard. She knew he would be knocking on the door of her apartment sometime this week, with a pan of lasagna, or a jar of soup, or some corn muffins he'd just whipped up. Another granddaughter might find his attention irritating—but, suddenly, all Merry could think about was that tonight Ralph would be eating without her.

She had dreamed of this day for months—all through the relentless snows of an unusually brutal winter and the rains of a late-blooming spring. Years of careful saving had finally reaped a reward: Merry had signed a year's lease on a small apartment—a guest suite over a neighbor's garage, really—that commenced this very weekend.

January had found her sitting rapt and silent in the glow of Peter Mason's fireplace, browsing linens catalogs; February was dishes and glassware. Did she want teacups, or mugs? Why not both? And what sort of wineglasses? She considered balloon- and tulip-shaped, hefted them in her mind, all but felt the misty beading of a well-chilled chardonnay.

In March, Merry abandoned economy and purchased the Islander's Special—a fifty-dollar round-trip ticket on the local commuter airline—for a weekend of mall hopping in Hyannis. There she bought cheap bookshelves and a small television; two lamps; an iron-and-glass floor vase Peter declared was an escapee from a medieval dungeon; a patchwork quilt handmade in China; and assorted throw rugs of sisal and hemp. She bought a garlic press and hand towels. Three excellently forged pots with steel handles. And a tin of English tea leaves—loose, unfettered, wildly redolent—and a sieve-like ball for steeping them. She ordered everything shipped to Nantucket by the next ferry and boarded her return flight feeling spent and slightly intoxicated. She was moving to her own home at last.

Gone would be the clutter of Tattle Court—the piles of junk mail on the dining-room table, the collection of nineteenth-century blubber-cutting tools from some forgotten Folger's whaling ship; the unfinished portrait of her brother Billy, awaiting her dead mother's hand. And gone, she thought, as she caught a snatch now of Ralph Waldo's singing over the whirr of the kitchen blender, would be all the comfort of wordless love.

Well, not quite gone. She was moving only three blocks away.

"Hey, Mere," Rafe da Silva said.

She emerged from her musings to find the dining-room table safely embedded in the truck, a plastic tarp shielding it from the rain. Peter was slumped on the bumper, his dark hair turning black in the downpour. Rafe leaned by his side.

"We need the keys."

"To the truck?"

"To your apartment," Rafe answered patiently. "There's no way that bed's going in the back with the table taking all that room. Besides, your neighbor's been bugging us to let her out of the driveway."

Tattle Court was grandly but optimistically named: in fact, it was little more than a sandy track divided among three houses. Rafe's truck had been blocking the exit to Fair Street for nearly two hours.

"Let's go," Merry said quickly, as she felt for the keys beneath her slicker and ducked out into the rain.

The flickering light of the ship's lantern, held high in Gordon's hand, threw Lord Cecil's broad-shouldered shadow monstrously across the sand. Trevarre stood silently next to his faithful retainer, his eyes intent on the bent backs of the two navvies grunting and heaving over the open pit. As a shovel lifted its burden of sandy soil, another bone glinted whitely in the fitful lantern flame—bones, the pirate's age-old signal of warning, left to guard a hidden treasure. A menace to the faint of heart; an invitation to the brave. Lord Cecil felt a stirring of familiar excitement. They must be very close now to the steel-bound leather casket, the gleam of jewels too long obscured from the light of day.

A clink of metal against metal—and he fell to his knees, thrusting his men aside, intent upon the smooth surface of the chest's domed lid. A moment of exertion for his prying hands; then the treasure came free—

And Cecil sat back on his heels in the sand, Nan wordless and awestruck at his side. Until this moment it had never occurred to him that the bones might be *human.* And holding the thing like this in his hands—the cracked eye sockets encrusted with damp sand, speaking hollowly of death; the upper jaw devoid of its teeth—the fantasies of Lord Cecil, master of Trevarre, gave way to sudden terror. Cecil threw down the skull and took off across the dunes as though all the imps of hell were upon him, Nan shrieking behind.

Satchmo followed at a more measured pace, his aged limbs stiff with too much sitting in the wind and the damp, a stray bone clamped firmly, lovingly, in his jaws.

"Meredith—"

The voice was Ralph Waldo's, and it held that special evenness that signaled urgency—a holdover, perhaps, from the days when he knew crisis and had run Nantucket's police force himself. "Your father just called. He needs you out in Sconset as soon as possible. Which, by my way of thinking, is as soon as you've had something to eat."

"But I'm off duty!"

"I know."

Merry studied in turn the downpour pummeling the hood of Rafe's truck, Peter's patient face distorted by the streaming windshield, and the bed frame awaiting its place in Rafe's truck bed. Then she stared balefully back at her grandfather. "What is it?"

"Something unique in my experience." Ralph pushed open the screen door and handed her a steaming mug of his remarkable pea soup. "A couple of kids just dug up a skeleton."

Chapter Two

Siasconset—or Sconset, as it is pronounced and most frequently spelled—sits at the southeastern tip of Nantucket Island, facing squarely across the Atlantic some fifty miles north of the dreaming wreck of the *Andrea Doria*, the Italian luxury liner that was rammed nearly amidships in the summer of 1956. It is a charming backwater of a town roughly seven-and-a-half miles from Nantucket proper, known for its grassy one-way lanes of rose-covered cottages; its summer residents of ancient and hallowed pedigree; its small gourmet grocery store where pâté and fresh strawberries and fine cheese may be purchased during the summer season, which ends abruptly in mid-September; and its relative desolation during the winter months, when the sole hotel and restaurant close their doors against the brisk tides, and the summer people retreat, and only a hardy few brave the relentlessly howling winds and the eroding force of the sea. Sconseters firmly pronounce themselves to be *Sconseters*, to distinguish themselves from Nantucket's hoi polloi; and the great mansions sitting high in the shadow of Sankaty Light have a timeless quality, breathlessly posh.

But now, in this wet and chilly April, the town huddled forlornly between the gunmetal sky and the petulant sea, a lost dog curled at the island's feet.

The rain was torrential by the time Merry pulled up in the Gully Road cul-de-sac near the entrance to Sconset beach. Only two cars sat dully in the downpour, hoods streaming with wet, tires half-sunk in the grass at the road's verge. She recognized them both. Clarence Strangerfield's scene-of-crimes van, and Dr. John Fairborn's teal-colored BMW convertible, its canvas top darkened with rain. The rest of her team had made better time from town than she, being unimpeded by the necessity to consume Ralph's split-pea soup.

Merry turned off the ignition of her unmarked gray Explorer, jammed on the parking brake, and tugged the hood of her slicker up over her white-blond hair. Then she thrust open the car door and dashed down to the edge of the sand. Her father had said the kids were waiting in a house in Codfish Park, the small settlement of cottages hugging a few streets between bluff and eroding shore; but the kids would have to wait a little while longer. What interested Merry was the knot of uniformed and plainclothes'd men kneeling around a spot in the wind-tossed scrub just below Codfish Park. And so she began to slog through the wet sand, which was depressingly gray, like everything else about the day. It clung determinedly to her hiking boots with every step.

"Marradith!"

Clarence Strangerfield, the crime-scene chief. His peremptory greeting was flung over one shoulder, and his broad jeans-clad bottom blocked her view of the pit over which he knelt. Merry broke into a trot, fingers grasping the edge of her hood to shield her face. The effort *not* to get wet in the midst of a deluge is a peculiarly human one—as only humans wear clothes, and occasionally mascara—and abruptly, disgustedly, Merry abandoned it. While she closed the distance of five hundred yards between herself and the men, she took a mental census: Clarence; his assistant, Nat Coffin; John Fairborn—and Howie Seitz, his dark mop of curls glinting wetly in the rain. Her father had sent her favorite first-year officer, the one she had trained and depended upon during the scut work of two murder investigations; and Merry's spirits suddenly rose. It was too soon to declare the skeleton a result of *murder*, of course. It might be centuries old—the burial of an Indian, say, or one of the scores of men who first established Sconset as a seventeenth-century fishing colony. But the chief of Nantucket's police was clearly weighing other possibilities, like death by violence. And if he had sent his daughter and her favorite assistant, he might even let her investigate it.

"Hey, guys," she said casually as she came up to them, and laid a hand on Clarence's shoulder.

He grunted and heaved himself to his feet, hands on his bent knees for support. "Careful of the scene, now, Marradith."

She glanced around at the piles of disturbed sand, the torn beach plum, the scattering of small bones. The remains of a cement foundation, its house long vanished in January's waves, lay jagged and broken in what had once been a yard. A wilting daffodil, brilliantly yellow against the sodden sand, had been flung down beside a bruised red sand bucket. "Like there's any evidence to preserve, Clare," Merry said tartly. "These are kids we're talking about, right?"

"Ayeh," the crime-scene chief said wearily. "And a dog. If you'll believe."

"The dog's taken a nip or two from a number of these bones." Fairborn, the Nantucket police's volunteer medical examiner, offered Merry a gnawed gray example. "Look at the damage. Hard to tell what's dog and what's death trauma."

"Great. And you're sure they're human?"

"Well, the skull's a pretty good indication," Fairborn shot back, and took a drag on the cigarette he kept always lit between the fingers of his right hand. How a doctor could so imperil his health Merry never quite understood; but she accepted Fairborn's smoking as a sign that he was somewhat normal. The man usually behaved like a stand-in for God.

"Any idea how recently they were buried?"

"The utter lack of flesh or ligament articulation might be a clue."

"Ligament articulation?" Merry recognized the term from her forensics class—ten years back now, wasn't it? She just couldn't quite remember what it meant.

"Ligaments hold the skeleton together," Fairborn said, with what passed for patience. "These bones lost theirs years ago.. They're completely disarticulated. Which means, in my view, that they weren't killed last week."

"Thanks, Fairborn. You're an immense help. Clarence?"

The crime-scene chief looked at Merry from brown eyes as large and soulful as a basset hound's and shook his head. "Ah've no idea, Marradith. Coulda been heah for yeahs, and the sand just worn away by the tides and whatnot this wintah. No tellin', rally. What we need is a good forensic anthropologist, and I'm not sure we'll find us one o' those at the state crime lab in Boston. But befarh we worry about that, Nat here has an awful lot o' siftin' ahead, don't yah, Nat?"

The youngest of the numerous Coffins raised his brown head and smiled cheerfully. Nat labored over a large mesh sifter Merry suspected was culled from Clarence's beloved garden tools; the crime-scene chief, as always, pursued his mission with precision and efficiency. No bone, no matter how disarticulated or long buried in the Sconset sands, would slip from Clarence's grasp.

Merry surveyed the area silently, searching for the skull. She found it already bagged in plastic and set off to one side—incongruous and ghoulish and inevitably sobering.

"Alas, poor Yorick," Howie Seitz said as he followed the direction of her eyes.

"You never cease to amaze me, Howie. I had no idea you could be a fan of *both* Kurt Cobain and Shakespeare."

"Hey, a poet's a poet, Detective," he protested.

"Particularly when he's dead." Merry blew out a gusty breath—that failed in its object of lifting her sodden bangs—and turned away from them all.

The address her father had given her belonged to a house two down from the corner of Beach and Codfish Park roads—safe, for the moment, from the ravages of storm and tide—with neat lygustrum hedges by the door and the pale golden facade common to the island's newly-shingled. Trellised roses ran the length of the cat-slide roof; a welcoming light shone in the window. No wonder the kids had come here for help.

Merry ran up the crushed quahog-shell path to the sheltered doorway, pushed back her hood, and stabbed the bell.

It was a man who answered her summons—nearly sixty, perhaps, with gnarled hands poking from the ends of a heathery blue sweater, and thinning salt-and-pepper hair. The eyes behind his half glasses held a roguish twinkle that even the vicarious discovery of a skeleton had failed to dim. He peered at Merry through his storm door, nodded twice, then opened it wide.

"Detective Meredith Folger, Nantucket police," she said, and held out her badge.

"Lenny Schwartz." He adjusted the glasses to peer at the police shield, in much the same manner that a man will gaze at the label of a wine bottle he has ordered, at once knowing and ignorant; and then he studied her, his eyebrows raised. "You're a detective," he said.

"Yes."

"I'm impressed. I didn't know Nantucket allowed women to handle murder. How progressive."

"What makes you think this is murder, Mr. Schwartz?"

To Merry's surprise his face creased in a smile. "Well, now—if you don't sound like the star of every police show I've ever seen. Have I just talked myself into being suspect number one?"

"That takes more than talk."

"Thank goodness," he said mildly, and led her into the living room.

"My wife, Ruth." Lenny motioned to a broad-hipped woman in a Shetland sweater sitting protectively close to two young children huddled on an overstuffed sofa. Both balanced Dixie cups of what appeared to be Coca-Cola in their small hands and stared at her fearfully. "And our neighbors Cecil and Nan Markham. This is Detective— Meredith?—Folger."

With the telltale hesitation of one who endures significant back pain, Ruth Schwartz stood up and extended her hand. Merry shook it.

"We're so glad you could come," Ruth said, and glanced at the two children.

"I'm sorry that I have to intrude." Merry swung her leather purse from her shoulder and fished in its capacious depths for her notebook and pen, then felt the square bulk of her reading glasses and pulled those out, too. "I could take the kids home and talk to them there, if that's more convenient—"

"I think perhaps you ought to do it here," Ruth Schwartz interposed, with what Merry read as a significant look. So home was not a congenial place for the young Markhams. "We've called their mother. I'm sure Julia will be along fairly soon."

"In that case—"

"Please, take a chair. Can I get you anything? Soda? Coffee?"

"You know, a cup of tea would be great," Merry said gratefully. "It's really chilly out there."

"Yes. And the Daffodil Festival only a week away—"

"Ruth," Lenny Schwartz said warningly. "The detective's tea."

"I'm going, I'm going." Ruth shot her husband a look, one that acknowledged her garrulousness as it reproved him for censuring it. Then she smiled at Merry and moved stiffly toward the kitchen. An imposing woman, gray hair drawn back in a loose bun, her high cheekbones still markedly beautiful.

"Weather's killing her back," Lenny explained, "and of course she refuses to lay off the gardening this close to Daffodil Weekend. She's got several entries in the show. But that's neither here nor there, right? You want to talk to the kids."

"Yes."

"You're really from the police?" a small voice said. Merry turned and found Cecil Markham's large gray eyes fixed upon her. "Why aren't you in uniform, then?"

Merry was struck by something in his tone—a refinement of accent she couldn't quite place—and she turned this over in her mind as she took a chair near Cecil and Nan. "It's Saturday," she replied, opening her notebook and settling her glasses on her nose. "And, besides, I'm a detective. A lot of us don't bother with uniforms."

"Oh." Cecil was obviously disappointed—and something else. . . . Relieved? Perhaps a *real* policeman would have been too intimidating.

"Which one of you found the bones today on the beach?" Merry asked, looking first at the small red-haired girl and then at her brother. The children exchanged a glance, then studied their cups of Coke.

"I did," the girl said finally. "Then Cecil came and helped. We thought it was buried treasure."

As Merry's brow furrowed, Cecil elaborated. "Pirates always leave bones on top of their jewels. To signal their mates and ward off the curious." There it was again—the unconscious formality, the stilted diction. As though he had learned to speak from reading books instead of listening to the words around him.

"Ah," Merry said. "I see. You kept digging, then, in the hope of hitting pay dirt."

"But then we found the—Cecil found the skull," Nan said in a thin voice. She shivered involuntarily, her red curls shaking. "It was horrible."

Merry nodded thoughtfully and sat back against the chair's needlepoint pillow, studying the Markhams. They did not look like happy children—although any child who found a skull on the beach might be similarly sobered. "Nan," Merry said, "I'd like you to tell me something, if you can. Why did you decide to dig in that spot in the first place?"

"It was Satchmo," she said promptly.

"Satchmo?"

"Their dog." Ruth Schwartz appeared at Merry's side with a steaming mug of tea. "He's tied up out back. A dear old thing."

"Satchmo started the digging," Nan said. "He must have smelled the bones."

"Satchmo's a great digger," Cecil offered, "and he loves bones."

"But why were you sitting near the condemned houses at all?"

Nan's change of expression was swift and formidable. "Cecil wouldn't let me play."

"But there was going to be a battle, Nan!"

Merry turned to him. "And girls aren't allowed to fight?"

"Of course not."

"What about me?" she asked blandly. "I'm a police detective. We have to fight sometimes."

"Can you fire a gun?" Nan's voice was filled with awe.

"I know how to, certainly. But I try to avoid it."

"Gee," Cecil breathed.

"So you were sent off to play by yourself while Cecil

fought his battles," Merry said to Nan. "Why that spot anyway? It's an awful mess right now, with the houses gone and the foundations exposed."

"I didn't start out there, exactly." The girl's eyes narrowed with her effort to remember. "Satchmo and I were having a tea party. And then I saw some daffodils up near the front steps and went to pick them. Satchmo started digging then, I guess."

"And what did you think when he found the bones?"

Nan shrugged—the catchall little-girl gesture of ignorance and indifference. "I thought maybe he'd buried them there himself. Satchmo's got bones everywhere. But then I saw a real little one—like a twig—and I wanted to show Cecil."

The doorbell sang out sharply in the quiet of the cozy living room, and Merry jumped.

"That'll be Julia," Lenny said, and disappeared into the hallway.

"Miss Detective." Cecil's hand was tugging at Merry's sleeve, and his voice had grown oddly desperate. "Please tell Mummy it wasn't our fault. That we found those bones, I mean. Please tell her we didn't mean to do it."

And as Lenny Schwartz ushered Julia Markham into the room, Merry saw just why she intimidated her children.

She was a frail-looking woman, hollow-eyed and darkhaired, with two sharp lines running from her nose to the corners of her mouth. Her forehead was similarly creased, suggesting weariness and unwonted aging, although Merry decided the woman couldn't be more than forty. Julia Markham wore a pair of faded duck trousers and a torn blue T-shirt under a jacket pulled hastily over her shoulders; the clothing hung upon her body. A tide of stale cigarette smoke permeated the room as soon as she entered it.

"Whatever did you have to run to the Schwartzes' for, then?" she asked, her voice deep with irritation as she looked at her children. Merry grasped at the sound of that husky voice, finding in it the explanation for Cecil's oddities—Julia Markham was British.

"Hello, Julia," Ruth Schwartz said.

Julia ignored her and crossed rapidly to her son. She jerked the boy to his feet with one fluid movement of her arm. He hung his head. Nan sank miserably into the sofa.

Merry stood up and extended her hand. "Meredith Folger, Mrs. Markham. Nantucket police."

"You've done with the children, then?" Julia Markham demanded, by way of greeting.

"For the moment."

"Right. Then we'll be leaving. Step smartly, Nan." Julia wheeled for the door, mouth set and black hair rippling snakelike across her narrow back. Cecil dragged at her heels.

"Mrs. Markham," Merry called after her as Nan slid to her feet and took a reluctant step in her mother's wake. "I'd like to speak to you, if I may."

"What is it?"

Merry glanced at the children's averted faces. Nan had given up the battle not to cry. "Could we talk a moment in private?"

A faint, derisive smile flickered across Julia Markham's face and was gone. "Whatever for? You think these kippers listen to anyone?"

"Yes," Merry rejoined evenly. "I do."

Julia rolled her eyes. She turned Cecil abruptly toward the Schwartzes' kitchen. "Go get the dog, mate, and take your sister with you," she commanded, with a slap to his behind.

The children scuttled off without a backward glance.

"Get on with it, then," Julia told Merry.

"It's possible that what happened today on the beach might disturb your children for some time to come. You should expect nightmares at the very least. Possibly an aversion to the entire area. Maybe even an unwillingness to go out alone."

Julia laughed derisively. "With all the violence on the

telly? You think a few bones are going to unnerve my Cecil and Nan? You don't know kippers, Miss Nantucket Policewoman. They're nasty little beggars. Haven't a sensitive bone in their bodies. It takes growing up to teach you pain."

"Then I'd say Nan and Cecil are growing up fast," Merry said softly, and bit back the words too late. Julia Markham's face, if anything, became instantly more closed and unreachable. Nevertheless, Merry reached down to her purse and fished out her wallet. "I'm no psychiatrist. I'm only telling you what I've learned from experience. But I'd like to give you this."

Julia took the small buff card from Merry's extended hand. "What's this?"

"A counseling service we recommend. In case you find your children are more sensitive than you think."

The woman looked at Merry for the briefest second. Then, deliberately, she tore the card in two.

When the Markhams had gone—a silent and fulminating trio blackly outlined against the sodden sky— Merry took her leave of Lenny and Ruth Schwartz.

"You were very good to those children today," she told them. "I'd like to thank you, even if Mrs. Markham won't."

"Oh, we never expect thanks from Julia," Lenny said roguishly. "It's against her creed. She's a confirmed misanthrope. Any spark of gratitude would cause her face to crack."

"Sad, isn't it?" Ruth said a trifle wistfully. "They're such gifted children."

"Are they?"

Ruth glanced at Lenny. "Well, *I* think so," she said. "Not that I'm an authority. Nan is utterly delightful—a budding poet. The child asks the most curious questions— all about the *mentality* of things. Do dogs fear death? Are waves the sea's way of reaching for the shore when it wants to be human? She's absolutely enchanted with flowers, of course, and is always stealing into the garden when her mother's in one of her moods."

"Cecil lives entirely in his mind," her husband added, "when he's not living in his books. A daydreamer. Well, they both come by the imagination naturally."

"From—their mother?"

Lenny snorted. "Not Julia. At least, not that anyone would be able to tell. No, from Ian. Ian Markham. He was a fairly famous sculptor, you know. Sank his boat and drowned in a squall about eight years back."

"*That* Ian Markham!" Merry exclaimed, jolted by memory. A flamboyant British expatriate—known for his charm, his daring work, his high-paying clients, and his sudden, tragic death. Markham had taken the island's art world by storm, if only briefly. "And his wife has stayed here all these years?"

"Kept the studio, the house, the whole artist schtick." Lenny nodded. "Stuck up a forest of No Trespassing signs when the tourists started collecting on the front lawn. You'd think she loved it here in Sconset. Couldn't tear herself away. It's absolutely weird, I think."

"Now, Lenny." Ruth's voice held the mildest reproof. "We've no idea how Julia feels about living here."

"The hell we don't," he rejoined. "You *always* know exactly how Julia feels."

Or do you? Merry wondered as she walked swiftly down the Schwartzes' neat white path in the dissipating rain. Was it antagonism Julia Markham wore upon her face—or a desperate shield against a too-painful world?

Chapter Three

Chapter Three

By Sunday the weather had cleared and offered the islanders one of those spectacular and rare spring days, when the vault of sky arcing from sea horizon to sea horizon is a brilliant blue, presaging the glories of summer, and the notion of wearing light-colored clothing and letting one's hair whip in the breeze is well-nigh irresistible. Meredith Folger rose early, not having anticipated that sunlight would stream so forcibly through her new bedroom window, hitting her squarely in the eyes; and as she turned and stretched and sighed, momentarily disoriented by the strangeness of the ceiling above her bed, which was flat and painted, by the previous renter, an unfortunate mauve (exactly the color and texture, Peter had said, of boysenberry yogurt), she decided then and there to order window shades.

But first she needed coffee.

This presented the second problem of her day, as her new coffeemaker was nowhere to be seen; and so she tumbled out of bed and began a calculated rummaging through her boxes. Unpacking even one of them had felt impossible the previous night. It was as much as she and Peter could manage to set up the bed frame and position the mahogany table. Rafe, after disgorging the furniture from his truck's flatbed and helping them heave and persuade the various pieces up the flight of steps that led to Merry's over-the-garage domain, had gratefully departed to help his wife, Tess, with dinner. A man's work, Rafe proclaimed as he waved good-bye, was just never done these days.

Or a woman's, for that matter.

Merry had left Clarence in charge of sending the Sconset bones by plane to the state crime lab in Boston, as evidence handling was properly his province. Other than securing the site—although how a site exposed to the elements and regularly swept by high tides could *be* secured was an admitted dilemma—little of a police nature was necessary until the bones were dated. If they were several decades or several centuries old, the likelihood of a formal investigation was slight. If, however, they were determined to be fairly recent, Merry's father would have some hard thinking to do. But she doubted that the Sconset skeleton had met its end only a little while ago. The complete disarticulation of the bones and the utter lack of flesh suggested the body had been dead for quite some time. Personally, she suspected an early fisherman—one of the men or women who had spent the eighteenth- or nineteenth-century summers in exile from Nantucket Town, netting the vast schools of cod and blues that had swarmed past the island's southern tip, and living in the small rose-covered shanties that fetched such exorbitant prices in the late twentieth century. Which wasn't to say that murder was an impossibility— for even among fishermen a more orthodox death by drowning or illness would have occasioned the body's removal to town for a funeral and burial in the Nantucket cemetery. Perhaps there had been a drunken brawl, she mused, as she shifted books and turned disconsolately from a case of the coveted wineglasses (balloon-shaped, as it happened). Maybe one cod fisherman suspected another cod fisherman of dalliance with his nineteenth-century wife. Someone was killed by accident. And then there was the hasty digging of a moonlit grave, and perhaps the launching of the victim's boat—to suggest a mishap at sea and a body lost in the depths. But why not send the body to the bottom in that very boat? Merry wondered. Or bury it farther inland, where the eroding storms of later years could never expose the evil?

There was a mystery here, but hardly one she was likely to solve.

Merry paused an instant in her bedroom doorway to survey her new world and smiled exultantly to herself. Even amid the disarray of packing materials and piles of clothing, the three rooms were decidedly *hers*. The bedroom, filled already with her familiar bird's-eye maple; the larger room just beyond the door, which was living and dining and kitchen area at once; and the small bathroom she intended to paint a brilliant red—just because she had always wanted the warmth and comfort of a red, red room.

The humped shape of her coffeemaker cried out from beneath a pile of kitchen towels—which Ralph Waldo had properly thought would protect it in transit—and Merry seized it with a small crow of victory.

Now, if she could only find the coffee.

"Have you ever thought about kids, Peter?"

"Every time I look at your white-blond hair and black eyebrows," he replied, flicking a glance at her sideways. His arms were folded over his handlebars with the expert ease of the perpetual athlete, and though the two of them were laboring up a distinctive rise in the Madaket bike path, his voice betrayed nothing like strain. "I have a growing urge to test whether the combination can be repeated, or if it's a complete fluke."

"You mean freak. As in freak of nature."

"I would never call a child of ours a freak."

Merry slapped his shoulder. "I mean have you thought about how fragile kids are? How easy it is to ruin their lives?"

"No," he said brusquely. "I thought about that too much when I was young myself."

Peter Mason's Greenwich childhood had been privileged in ways that he knew Merry only vaguely understood—the privilege of yacht clubs and private schools and frequent trips to Europe. What it had lacked was something most children recognize and crave, long before they can define it completely: a steady and unquestioning love.

"What do you mean?" she asked.

He did not reply immediately, his brow furrowing, his eyes on the macadam whirling away beneath his tires. "I think I never felt safe. Never felt as if I could relax and just *go* with things; I always had to be on my guard. I figured disaster would strike exactly when I wasn't looking. Like Will Starbuck a few years ago—remember?"

Merry nodded. Rafe da Silva's stepson, Will, had been a bundle of nerves the first time she had met him, over the drowned corpse of Peter's brother. The fact that Will was still recovering at the time from the drowning death of his own father had only made matters worse. "That's why you care about him so much."

"Of course! Will's *me* at the same age. Waiting for the next terrible thing to happen. My father leaving, for instance—I was always afraid Max would simply disappear from our lives. I mean, who would decide to *stay*, with opportunities like his, and a wife like my mother? Who could come home every night, year in and year out, to her incredible coldness? She was a nightmare. She deserved to be left."

"And she has been," Merry said quietly. "By everyone, eventually."

"Except Georgiana," Peter replied. "Thank God for George and her marvelous kids. Once or twice a year my mother can feel as if she has a family again, without having to exert herself unduly or drive George into therapy for weeks afterward."

"I met some kids like that only yesterday," Merry said.

"Like George's?"

Merry shook her head. "Like Will. The kind who wait for disaster. I can't get them out of my mind."

Peter shifted gears, his legs never faltering at the pedals, and glanced ahead along the path. Gulls circled in the bright blue above, which meant they were approaching the open garbage dump that was Nantucket's landfill. Not the most scenic of the Madaket bike path's spots. "These would be the two who found the skeleton?"

"Right. Nan and Cecil Markham."

He snorted. "Their mother obviously hated them from birth. Nan and *Cecil*? They must be hounded at school."

"Nan's not such a bad name," Merry objected. "It's sort of retro. I like it."

"But *Cecil*?"

"They're British."

"Oh, great. So he probably pronounces it *Cess*-ul."

"He does."

"And every kid in Nantucket Elementary calls him Cess-hole. I bet you any amount of money."

"He's a pretty lonely little kid," Merry said. "With a face straight out of *Oliver Twist*. Pale, pinched cheeks and big gray eyes, as though he sees and feels everything too much. Nan's a little younger and a little dreamier—which probably helps. But Cecil . . . he told me he thought he would find a buried pirate treasure when he dug down through the sand for those bones. He really believed it, Peter—I could see the belief, the *hope*, still vivid in his face."

"Good for him," Peter said comfortably. "He's got imagination, at least. It's saved many a desperate soul."

"I'm not so sure." Merry's voice was thoughtful and a little sad. "I'm not sure escape is the answer."

"So what's wrong at home?"

"Oh, everything, I'd say. Their father died in a boating accident about eight years ago—Ian Markham, the sculptor."

"Wow. I hadn't made the connection."

"Neither did I. How quickly we forget."

"You weren't even on-island then, were you?"

Merry shook her head. "I was in New Bedford." Her first posting out of the police academy.

"What about the mother?"

"Pretty spooky. Hair like Morticia's, and enough anger to scare folks a lot older than her kids. Cecil was practically begging me to protect him before she walked into the room. As though finding that skeleton were somehow his fault."

And suddenly Peter remembered that sort of panic—the fear that an accident, a trick of fate, might bring accusation and guilt upon his head. "These kids show any scars or bruises?"

"Oh, I don't know, Peter—do harsh words leave scars? The woman was just so *mean*!"

Peter turned his head to look at Merry's strong legs, pumping methodically a few feet away from his own, and felt a sharp rush of love. She was virtually oblivious to the beauty of the day, the wind tugging at her upswept hair, or the trickle of sweat slowly working its way between her breasts. Her mind was returning, again and again, to the ones she could not save; and it was this empathy, this absorption in the fates and disasters of others, that made her peculiarly fitted to her work. She was a better detective *because* she lived and breathed the tragedies the police force handed her—although her father would never believe it. Chief John Folger was perpetually chiding his

daughter for her emotional involvement in her cases. But
Peter knew that was exactly the source of her strength.

"I don't know, Merry," he said as the end of the bike
path loomed. "Every kid has his agonies, and sometimes
they're not the sort you can bandage and heal. You can't
prosecute a woman for meanness."

"But you don't have to like her for it, either." Merry
swung her leg over the bicycle seat, her gaze abstracted.
She had elected to wear shorts, in tribute to the fineness
of the day; but the wind off Nantucket's western point
was brisk, raising gooseflesh along her thighs, and a bank
of fog hung low over the water. The promise of spring
was transient, as it is the nature of spring to be; and
Merry shivered as she locked her bike and followed Peter
through the dunes.

"And in the end," Peter said as he drew her close and
stared determinedly into her shadowed green eyes, "the
best you can do is declare to God and all the heavens that
your own life will be different. That your kids will be
happy for the right reasons. That they'll never feel anything but safe."

"Sometimes it seems easier to just skip the whole
thing, you know?" she murmured, and he felt her stiffen
in his arms.

The days passed in alternate storm and sun. At home
Merry unpacked her boxes and attempted to arrange
her furniture in varying patterns that actually varied
very little. At work she closed the case on a little girl
found floating in the boat basin one January morning
(rode off the dock on her bicycle and drowned) and
opened a file on a series of burglaries among Nantucket's
restaurant kitchens. (A thief with a fetish for professional
cooking utensils? Or simply a very hungry one?) She
occasionally thought of the Sconset bones, undergoing
analysis in Boston, and more frequently wondered how
Nan and Cecil were doing. Did they avoid the beach

with its staked-out barrier of yellow police tape? Or were they drawn to the place with a child's usual attraction to the horrible? Did they have nightmares? Did their mother care?

But by Thursday, the eve of the Twenty-second Annual Daffodil Festival, she was too absorbed in the logistics of crowd management—a crowd under the heady influence of antique car parades and tailgate picnics and window-decorating contests—to consider much of anything else.

Three million daffodils, by common estimation, bloomed annually on Nantucket. Merry ascribed this to the fact that many islanders were rabid gardeners, and some of them had too much time on their hands. Particularly in the fall, when the revelries of July and August were past, and the weather turned unpredictable, and diversions were few. People took to reading indoors, their lights glowing through the fogs of early afternoon. They browsed nursery catalogs and raked leaves and grew inflamed with thoughts of organic mulch. Their eyes turned from the sea and the horizon to fix upon the good brown earth. By October and November gardeners were everywhere—dotting the verge along the Milestone road, poking among the post-and-rail fences near the Madaket bike path, turning over the soils of Surfside and Tom Nevers. They knelt in supplication by the altars of their bulb bags, or strained at hoes, scrabbling in sacks of bone meal. When accused of daffodil madness, they pleaded the pieties of civic duty.

Merry cursed them one and all. Every bulb planted, in her mind, meant another tourist popping up in the spring.

Ralph Waldo, a prop of the Nantucket Garden Club (and one of its few male members) disagreed. In fact, her grandfather scolded Merry each April when she deplored the masses of daffodils springing skyward at every turn. Ralph, in Merry's estimation, could afford to be magnanimous. He no longer had to police the daffodil hordes during the last weekend in April.

It was then that the first of the tourists descended on Nantucket—a few days' taste of the overwhelming crowds, the traffic, the appropriation of *place*, that would dominate the island throughout the summer months. For most people it was a kick in the pants after the doldrums of January and February, of course, with all the joy of summer and none of its endless burdens, as most of the tourists were gone by Monday. Retailers threw open their doors, restaurants extended their hours, and under the bare-branched arch of Main Street's trees, hundreds of revelers strolled the cobblestones with happy disregard for motorized traffic. Daffodils were everywhere—wreathing women's hair and thrust rakishly behind male ears; strung in dog collars and standing high among the Sconset tailgaters in champagne-bottle vases.

Hundreds of happy, laughing, defenseless people. A pickpocket's paradise. A shoplifter's show time.

John Folger, deprived of the summer police interns who normally accompanied the summer crowds, allowed none of his dozen or so regular officers to take leave during the Daffodil Festival. Never mind that it was a weekend; they could relax on Monday, after the parades and the flower shows and the strolling lovers were gone. And so Merry awoke that Friday morning, nearly a week after the finding of the bones in Sconset, and donned a blue Nantucket Police uniform for the first time in months. The more uniforms these people saw, her father reasoned, the less likely some of them would be to relieve others of their wallets. Merry spent all of Friday afternoon strolling from Main to Broad along Federal Street, and then back up Centre, her flat police hat sitting roundly on her head and her hands clasped loosely behind her back. She nodded frequently and firmly to local and tourist alike. It was part of her personal Daffodil Weekend ritual.

Friday witnessed the window-decorating contest, the Nantucket Inns Tour, and, in the evening, the Nantucket Experiences dinner, an auction to benefit A Safe Place, the island's shelter for battered women and their children. Merry survived these without incident, unless one considers the uniting of several errant children with their lost parents to be incidental. She even stopped by the Nantucket Experiences dinner long enough to witness an elegantly clad Peter Mason bid against a menacing New Jersey stockbroker. Being accustomed to stockbrokers, Peter upheld the Mason family position and outbid the interloper, to the relief of all—particularly Merry, who coveted the object of his upraised hand: an overnight cruise on the beautiful two-masted schooner *Wayward*, the last of the tall ships to anchor in Nantucket Harbor, and theirs now for a weekend's sail to Martha's Vineyard or the Cape.

She slipped away from the auction before Peter could see her, conscious that she was still on duty, and walked the brightly lit streets of Nantucket Town in her authoritarian garb.

Saturday morning dawned misty and cool. From her post on the corner of Federal and Main, Merry surveyed the entrants in the Antique Car Competition, their gleaming flanks surrounded by well-groomed families resplendent in their Easter best, and wondered at the human capacity for ritual. One man had turned his entire head into a flower—face at the center, array of petals from ear to ear— while a similarly spirited damsel gazed benignly at the crowd through a Venetian-carnival mask made entirely from daffodils.

The Most Beautiful Car Award went to a 1966 Mercedes-Benz 250SC convertible; the Most Creative to a '66 Ford Mustang. Apparently '66 had been a very good year.

"Hello, Officer!" a voice boomed in her ear; and she turned to see her grandfather, resplendent in a white linen suit and starched blue shirt, a daffodil-trimmed straw fedora on his head. His blue eyes were snapping, and on his arm was a small, round woman in an enormous navy-and-white straw hat fairly tipping under a burden of yellow flowers. Ralph raised his hand in salute. "Upholding the reputation of the force, I see. You remember Emily Teasdale, Meredith."

"Of course," Merry said quickly, and offered her hand. She had solved a mystery at Emily's Madaket house the previous summer—the sudden, inexplicable disappearance of ten geraniums *and* their pots from the Teasdale deck. "Don't let Ralph talk you into too much tailgate champagne. He rarely knows his own limits."

"My dear," Emily said with a shy glance upward at Merry's grandfather, "I confess that limits seem ill-advised on such a festive day as this."

"Have you got the Ford all gussied up?" Merry asked Ralph sternly. The Folgers' 1959 Ford pickup was Ralph Waldo's pride and joy, a dark-green behemoth, all exaggerated fenders and looming curves.

"Shining from bumper to bumper. She's sitting right over there." He gestured toward the end of Main. "Care to throw your hat behind a bush and join us for the tailgate in Sconset? Emily and I intend to take a prize."

They gave each other a knowing glance, chuckling, and Merry felt suddenly foolish. "Thanks, but no. You two run along. You have my vote for Most Distinguished, Grumpus."

"As I should," he replied comfortably, and walked off with a salute of the fedora.

A nagging worry settled over Merry's thoughts: Was Ralph getting childish in his old age? Or merely lonely? And what did he even *know* about this Teasdale woman— but at that moment she noticed her father shouldering his way through the surging crowds. His expression was dark, and she sensed immediately that he was looking for her.

"Chief!" Merry yelled, and waved her hand.

Her father caught the gesture, found her blue police cap through the crowd, and made his way to her side.

"What's up?" Merry said.

John Folger leaned close to her ear and muttered a few words.

The crime lab's report on the Sconset bones was in.

Chapter Four

Clarence Strangerfield was already waiting in the Water Street station's second-floor conference area when Merry and the chief arrived. He held a large manila file folder in his hands and was flipping through the pages intently. At Merry's approach he looked up and handed the report to her with a flourish, saying, "We've gaht ourselves a murdah, Detective."

Merry had assumed as much from what little her father had told her during the few blocks' walk to the station. As the festival crowds surged around them, John Folger conveyed the gist of the crime lab's findings: from the nature of the pelvis and smoothness of the skull's frontal plate, they had determined that the skeletal remains belonged to a woman, but they were uncertain of her age at death. The hyoid bone in the neck was fractured, which suggested that she had been strangled, but the lab would commit itself to saying only that death had occurred anywhere from two to ten years prior to the bones' discovery.

"That's a pretty wide range," Merry protested. "They must be able to do better than that. What did the pH factors tell them?"

She knew that Clarence had sent along samples of the sandy soil in which the skeleton had lain, as well as adjacent sand for comparative purposes. "You'll have to ask him," John Folger replied. "I let him handle the small stuff. This forensic detail is beyond me."

Merry glanced at her father as he held open the station door for her. Although her chief would never admit it, everything to do with dead bodies positively turned John Folger's stomach. The less he knew about Clarence's "small stuff," the better.

Now, as Merry took the lab's report from Clarence's hands and turned back to the beginning of the file, the crime-scene chief seemed to read her thoughts.

"The pH of those samples hahdly differed, Marradith," he said, "so I'm guessin' we can look to the fahr end of that range o' death."

"Because the tissue decay must have ended some time ago for the pH of both samples to be nearly the same." She looked back at the report, turned over a page. "So we've got an unidentified woman of indeterminate age who died a number of years ago. Talk about a needle in a haystack."

"First place to staht would be our missing-persons reports," Clarence said mildly.

"That's a job for Howie." She reached for her purse and the reading glasses in its depths. Her frustration at the report's vagueness grew. "To my mind, Clare—and I don't know a *thing* about this, admittedly—all that salt water under the Sconset sand should make some sort of difference in the decomposition rate. And that difference should tell us more about when she died. Wouldn't you think?"

"Ayeh. A cahrpse doesn't decay the same way in watery sand as it would in dry soil. Different bugs, farh one thing."

A small breath of disgust brought both their heads around apologetically to the chief, who had taken his customary spot at the head of the conference table.

"Why don't you two hash out the gory details some other time?" John Folger suggested. "Over lunch, maybe, which I'm sure you'd both consider a treat. Right now we have to talk."

Merry grinned and slid into a seat at the table. "This is where I'm supposed to beg him on hands and knees to give me the case, Clare, so that he can do his usual song and dance about fairness among the members of the criminal-investigation division—all three of us—and how it really is my esteemed colleague Matt Bailey's turn to handle a murder. At which point I get angry and remind him that Bailey is a complete chucklehead he's been trying to fire for two years now, whereas I have a homicide case-closure rate of one hundred percent. Then we fume silently at each other, turn on our heels, and slam doors all over the station."

"Ayeh," Clarence agreed. "And speakin' o' that case-closhuh rate, I'm thinkin' it's made you a bit cocky, Marradith. Ya didn' exactly close 'em alone. Relied *pretty heavily* on Yahrs Truly, as I recall. Maybe huntin' through the missin'-persons report is just the sarht o' come-uppance you need."

"I can't imagine undertaking such a task without *Yours Truly*, Clare."

"Now, Marradith—"

"Neither of you is undertaking anything," her father snapped.

Merry and Clarence looked at each other, banter quelled.

"I've asked the crime lab to send the bones on to the FBI for further analysis. They have forensic anthropologists down there in Washington—people who work at the Smithsonian. I've heard they can do amazing things."

"Why the big guns, Dad?" Merry asked quietly.

"The case isn't a case until we put a name to those bones. We have to place this woman, somehow, in the life of the island over the past few years. Otherwise, I for one haven't the slightest idea how to begin investigating her death."

Merry drew breath to speak and then stopped, considering the truth of the chief's words. Whom did you interview, when the victim was faceless? Where were the next of kin? The motives, the opportunities?

"Once we know who, we can think about how," John Folger said, as if she had spoken aloud. "How and why. We can try to fix the time she might have died—a month, a year. Maybe even the place."

"Sconset," Merry objected. "At least we know that."

"We know nothing," her father countered, "except that the bones were discovered there. She could have been killed in Timbuktu, for all we know. And this report from the crime lab doesn't answer any of those questions. With a bit of luck, however, Washington will."

Faintly, persistently, came the blare of trumpets across the old brick buildings of Main Street—and the antique cars, Merry knew, were commencing their parade to Sconset. Ralph and Emily Teasdale were among them, sitting proud and straight in the Folgers' dark-green pickup. The entire town was moving, in fact, toward the splendid lunches arranged so prettily along the streets of the old fishing village, and the judging of the Tailgate Picnic Theme Contest—motoring ceremoniously to the scene of a forgotten murder, and a victim who had once had a name. Her father was right. Without the big guns they might as well file the bones in a storage locker until the end of time, forgotten and unrevenged.

"So what do we do next?" she asked.

"Sift the missing-persons reports, as Clare suggested," her father replied. "And that means *you*, Meredith, not poor Howie Seitz. I need Howie on the street until these damned flower lovers go home."

In recent days the missing-persons reports had been computerized like everything else, but files from as long ago as ten years were stored the old-fashioned way— in boxes. And so Merry spent the bulk of that cloudy April afternoon in the station's attic, an under-the-rafters catchall space with exposed beams and a sneezing abundance of dust, not to mention shelf upon shelf of cardboard boxes. Only a few of the hundreds of files held missing-persons reports, of course, and of these, many could be immediately discounted—the little boy whose dory slipped its mooring in the summer of 1985 and drifted all the way from Madaket to the waters several miles off Sconset before he was found. Or the twenty-eight-year-old woman who left her husband, an orthopedist from Scarsdale, only to turn up in Paris with the man who had painted the exterior of their Monomoy house the previous summer. Or the college kids who, in the midst of a rather wild Labor Day beach party, bundled one of their own onto a USAir flight bound for New York and neglected to include his wallet.

They were all there, the stories ludicrous and maudlin, some with endings, some without, and Merry found herself beguiled by their sheer normalcy. She dallied along the reports' byways and half forgot the purpose of her search.

But it could not be denied—the bones had emerged from Sconset's sands, demanding recognition. The bones of a woman whom someone—a lover? a perverse stranger?— had seized about the neck and throttled to death. Had it been summer, and the night a perfect one for walking under an August moon, the surf gently curling at her tanned bare feet? Or was it winter, and the hour only a little past dawn, as she walked the shore in an effort to banish the nightmares that had disturbed her sleep?

What had she worn?

Abruptly Merry's dissatisfaction with the crime lab's
forensics report resurfaced, and she thrust aside the file
she had been reading. No matter how long ago the
woman had been killed and buried in the dunes near
Codfish Park, some fragments of her clothing should
have been found with the body. Those bones were altogether too clean—unbelievably so. The state crime lab,
Clarence, even her father—they were missing something, all of them. Perhaps the FBI's anthropologist
would find it.

By the end of four hours' work, her eyes and neck
aching, Merry had identified three possible missing per-
sons who might have ended in Sconset. A girl named
Terry Schultz—blond, twenty-two in 1989, a waitress at
the Club Car restaurant—had allegedly boarded the ten
o'clock ferry bound for Hyannis one Saturday, intending
to do some shopping. She had not reported for work the
following Monday morning, and her boss, after stifling
his annoyance for several hours, then querying Terry's
roommates in the group house on Washington Street
over the subsequent two days, had finally become worried enough to file the report. The Nantucket police
talked to Barnstable and sent out a description of the
missing girl—but after months went by without result,
they decided Terry Schultz had simply grown tired of the
island and moved on without notifying anyone. Maybe
she'd met a guy and accepted his offer of a ride to California; or maybe she'd bought a ticket to Las Vegas and
tried her luck as a waitress there. Who knows? The man-
ager of the Club Car protested this notion and mentioned Terry's uncollected back wages; but nothing more
was heard of her, and the file remained unclosed.

The second young woman was a French girl of eighteen who worked as an au pair for the Harcourts, a
wealthy New York family living on Orange Street during
the summer of 1988. Their two little boys were at that
particularly trying age, according to Martha Harcourt,

the mother of Patrick, aged 4, and William, aged 2; Annelise du Pois seemed sadly unable to cope with them. Mrs. Harcourt admitted to having argued with the girl, who went to bed in tears; the next day her room was empty. She had left everything behind. Investigation disclosed that Annelise was enamored of a steward on the private seagoing yacht *Blue Lady*, which was moored in the boat basin that August and left the very morning of the French girl's disappearance.

Strange, thought Merry, how a person can simply drop off the face of the earth—or at least of the official earth. Even in this age of computerized communication, of faxes and E-mail and the World Wide Web, someone who wished to remain unfound apparently could manage it. Was Elizabeth Osborne alive and well somewhere, and snickering at her husband?

Dr. Elizabeth Osborne, née Shaw, a forty-two-year-old Harvard-educated psychiatrist and third-generation Nantucket summer resident, was Merry's third prospect for a match to the Sconset bones—and the most compelling prospect of all, as she had disappeared from Sconset itself. When her husband (who was named Jack, according to the file) awoke in the luxurious Osborne home on Baxter Road that Tuesday morning of September 13, 1988, and found his wife's bed undisturbed (*So they were sleeping apart,* Merry thought, and filed that fact away.), he searched the beach first, as it was Elizabeth's habit to walk the sands at all hours. Jack failed to find his wife— but discovered her sandals and her passport lying near the dunes just above the high-water mark.

Near Codfish Park? Merry wondered. The file did not say.

Though a suicidal drowning was suspected (Jack Osborne admitted he and his wife were experiencing marital difficulties), and a watch kept for bodies surfacing in island waters, no trace of the psychiatrist was ever found. The presence of the passport, however, suggested a different scenario to the investigating detective—that

Elizabeth Osborne had a lover and intended to flee with him to another country. Perhaps her swain had met her in a boat off Sconset beach in the dead of night, at low tide. Perhaps she had stripped off her sandals and waded out to join him, a suitcase held high in one hand and her passport dropping unnoticed to the sand.

"Or maybe Jack strangled Elizabeth and buried her in the dunes of Codfish Park," Merry said to Clarence as they stood in the crime-scene chief's office.

"The little French girl's stewahd could'a done the same. But, personally, ah'm bettin' on the waitress. Girls like her fall in an' outta focus all the time. Barely missed. Pahtickulahly at a summah place like this."

"No mention of a boyfriend," Merry mused as she shuffled through Terry Schultz's file. "I think we should get on the NCIC terminal and verify that none of these three has turned up anywhere else."

"Now, *that's* a job fahr Howie," Clarence said wisely, and Merry smiled. Trolling through the records of the National Crime Information Center could be tedious in the extreme—but an excellent learning experience for a rank beginner like Patrolman Seitz.

"I suppose, too, that it wouldn't hurt to call the next-of-kin numbers listed in these files," Merry continued, "just to find out whether the errant souls ever made contact. I'll volunteer for that."

"And I'll send the medical records on to Washington first thing Monday mahrning," Clarence finished. Dental records were of limited use, as the Sconset skull's teeth were missing and all of Nat Coffin's careful sifting had failed to glean them from the sands; but two of the files had medical records, and these might serve to put a name to the bones once and for all.

Annelise du Pois had undergone a physical that declared her fit for employment before entering the United States; a copy was filed with her international agency's parent office in New York, and several X rays were included in the police file. Merry knew very little about forensic anthropology but recognized the usefulness of the ghostly images of Annelise's lungs. The X ray managed to outline the skeletal structure of the French girl's rib cage, shoulders, clavicle, and neck—all features that could be compared with the Sconset bones.

Terry Schultz's file contained only a local dentist's notation of her teeth. But Elizabeth Osborne's must hold copies of every known medical episode in the woman's life, Merry thought, complete with pictures. Osborne had been, after all, a doctor herself; and meticulous record keeping was clearly her passion. A note in the file proclaimed the medical data to have come from the Osbornes' Sconset home, with fuller documentation available, if necessary, at the psychiatrist's Harvard offices.

"Wouldn't you know," Merry said to Clarence as she scanned the numerous pages detailing Elizabeth's Pap smears and urinary-tract infections and occasional injuries to ankle and elbow. "And she's probably living happily in sin with an unknown houseboy in Bora Bora."

"Not Elizabeth," Clarence replied. "Too bahring after a while. She was a smaht woman. She'd have come back if she were still alive just to laugh herself silly ovah all of us."

"You knew her?" Merry's fingers stilled in their restless page turning. She had been in the midst of her New Bedford assignment when Elizabeth Osborne had disappeared in 1988; but Clarence had barely budged from the island since his birth fifty-three years earlier. An ideal brain to pick.

He shrugged. "Not to speak to. But her reputation preceded her, Marradith. She was quite the toast o' Nantucket, yah know. Beautiful, and rich as all get-out, and smaht into the bahgain. Quite somethin', Miss Elizabeth Shaw. I remembah when she was just a little girl, and come here for the summah from New Yahrk with her nursemaid and her mama. We'd a'bin about the same age, Miss Elizabeth and me. But I doubt she evah noticed

Clahrence Strangahfield in his ovah'alls and striped shuhrt."

"So if she hasn't come back to laugh herself silly," Merry asked, "where is she, Clare?"

The crime-scene chief considered this, and an uncharacteristic wave of sadness washed over his face. "Ah'm guessin' she's dead, Detective."

"At the hands of her husband?"

"Ayeh. It's possible. He kills her on the beach and then goes back to bed to sleep his way through an alibi."

"Not much of an alibi," Merry objected. "Looks like he slept alone."

"Then he discovahs the passpahrt on purpose the following mornin'," Clarence persisted, "and suggests The Abscondin' Lovuh theory."

"And the Nantucket PD kindly obliges. Who *was* this chump of a detective, anyway?" Merry flipped to the front of the report and studied the investigator's name. "Joe Halloran. I never ran into him."

"Yah wouldn't have," Clarence said wisely. "Yarh fathah let 'im go. Little prahblem with the bottle. Couldn't keep his hands off it. But he wasn't the only one working on Elizabeth's disappearance. Musta been fifty or a hundert people combin' the scrub round Sconset for the bettah parht of a week. Coast guahd sent ovah a spottin' plane from the Cape. I walked the beach myself every mornin' at six o'clock for a couple o' weeks ahftah she disappeared, looking for a body washed up by the surf. But there was nothin' to be seen. Poor woman."

"So what's Halloran do now?"

"Don't know."

"Another missing person," Merry said disgustedly, and handed the file to Clarence with a conclusive slap. He had medical data to package for the FBI, and Peter Mason was waiting for his dinner.

The Moona Bar and Grille was a pleasant enough place to wait, however, with its chic lighting and its enticing odors of roasting meat, welcome now as the spring-time chill descended on the darkening island. Peter leaned backward against the bar, one loafered foot rest-ing on its rail, and allowed himself a moment of anxiety. The procuring of a glass of pinot noir had barely won him this spot among the crush of humanity vying for seats and glasses of beer. He had no desire to come to blows over an actual table. Reservations for dinner on a Satur-day in Nantucket were never to be taken lightly. In sum-mer one made them ten days in advance and confirmed them forty-eight hours before service, or one lost them for good. In winter, when so many places closed for the season, one relied upon the good graces curried over the previous season to ensure a place among the hardy few; and now—Daffodil Weekend being neither *quite* summer nor winter—one planned ahead and kept rigorously to schedule, ever vigilant against the invading (and raven-ous) hordes. Particularly when one's dinner partner was unaccountably late.

Peter knew that Rodney Clark, Moona's present man-ager, was attempting to catch his eye. No doubt he would point to his wristwatch in another instant and lift his brow in delicate query. So Peter forced his hand between the elbows of the couple sandwiched against the nearest bar stool and clutched at a spare menu. He would be absorbed in consideration of the evening's fare if Rod-ney Clark pestered him about the time. Better yet, he thought as he debated the merits of venison and black-bean chili with cheddar tortillas, why didn't he just take the table *now* and have a pleasant little tuck-in all by himself?

But at that traitorous thought, Meredith arrived. Peter knew the exact moment she breathed his air, or perhaps he felt her heart beating across the clatter of silverware and dish. His head came up, searching, and found her bending an ear to laugh at something Rodney Clark had just said; then she tapped the manager lightly, playfully, on the arm. She was wearing a dress he had never seen—cut narrowly from some wine-colored stuff, a square neckline that suited the angularity of her face. Deceptively simple. Probably purchased on impulse from one of the island's pricey stores during their ridiculous January sales, the only time Meredith permitted herself to enter them. Peter's pulse quickened. He took an instant simply to stare at her, one hand in his trousers pocket, the other still holding the menu. She had no idea how beautiful she was—did she?—or that it was spring, and Saturday night, and the beginning of all their springs together. He caught her eye then and smiled, and walked to where Rodney was waiting with Merry's chair pulled back from a *very* nice table in the quietest possible corner, given the circumstances and Daffodil Weekend—and prepared to be completely happy.

"I have an idea," Peter said when they had worked their way through Mama's Plain and Simple Green Salad with Prissy's Famous Dressing, two orders of braised lamb shanks, and much more of the pinot noir. "Let's say we avail ourselves of that *Wayward* cruise right now. Call up Patrick"—Patrick O'Donnell was the *Wayward*'s skipper—"grab a change of clothing, and slip our moorings just as the moon comes up. There's nothing like sleeping on the water, or watching the sun rise far out at sea, preferably over mugs of coffee made by someone else."

"Lovely," Merry murmured, her eyes narrowing in the candlelight. "Absolutely seductive. Irresistible, even. Except—"

"Except it's Daffodil Weekend and you're wanted on the corner of Federal and Main."

"Not exactly." She set down her fork, her dreamy expression abruptly fading. "Turns out those Sconset kids found more than a nineteenth-century fisherman."

"You're kidding." Peter leaned back in his chair, his fingertips toying with the stem of his wineglass. "A murder?"

Merry nodded.

He understood then; her life was no longer her own. He felt suddenly tired, as though spring and its promise had been routed by an unexpected snowstorm. Meredith in the midst of an investigation was hard to reach, physically and emotionally. "And your dad's letting you take it?"

"Only sort of," she replied. "He's got me doing the scut work for the FBI's anthropologist. Ever hear of a woman named Elizabeth Osborne, Pete?"

"The psychiatrist. She disappeared off Sconset a while back."

"Bingo. Where'd that come from?"

"Her mother was a friend of my mother's," he answered. "Backbones of the Sconset Golf Club's Ladies' Eighteen-Holers. Why the FBI?"

"Dad thinks they'll be able to identify the bones. I've been reading back files of missing-persons reports all afternoon, looking for likely candidates. Elizabeth Osborne is one of them." Merry's green eyes were intent, and a lock of blond hair swung provocatively from behind her right ear. "So you knew Elizabeth?"

"My dear, I am exactly thirty-six years old this year," Peter said, "whereas Elizabeth, if she were around to celebrate, would probably be closer to fifty."

"Fifty exactly," Merry said. "Shoot. I forgot the age difference."

"Are you trying to tell me that Elizabeth is the Sconset skeleton?"

"Lower your voice, Peter." Several neighboring heads had turned slightly in their direction, with the well-bred attitude of those trying not to eavesdrop. Merry smiled serenely at an approaching waiter. "Two decaf coffees, please, and the gentleman will have the crème brûlée."

"I will?"

"Yes. I mean, no, I haven't the faintest idea whether Elizabeth is the Sconset skeleton. But I'm convinced she got a raw deal, Pete. The guy who handled her case didn't exactly *handle* it, if you know what I mean."

"And you would like to?"

"Yes. I feel *compelled* to. For the honor of the Nantucket PD. For Elizabeth Osborne. For justice."

Peter smiled. "I sense the contempt of the competent for the sins of the totally clueless."

"Something like that."

He raised his glass in salute as the waiter reappeared. "To deals well-done, rather than raw. To the redress of a wrong too long buried."

"To crème brûlée," Merry said avidly, and seized a spoon in readiness.

Chapter Five

On Monday the medical records of Annelise du Pois and Elizabeth Osborne, carefully photocopied and labeled by Clarence Strangerfield, left Nantucket on a plane bound for New York and thence to Washington.

On Tuesday, Clarence was informed of their receipt by the FBI. Howie Seitz continued his browsing through the NCIC computer and learned that the waitress, Terry Schultz, had been arrested for marijuana possession in California three years after she'd left Nantucket. A relatively quick survey of the California Motor Vehicles Administration revealed a driver's license in Schultz's name, issued eighteen months earlier. Merry marked her missing-person report closed and returned the file to the police station's attic.

On Wednesday afternoon the Massachusetts state police attempted to stop an adult male motorist heading

southbound from Boston on Highway 93. He was driving
erratically, and his car's registration sticker was several
months expired; and he made the unwise decision to ignore Sergeant Tony Ramirez's flashing lights and warning
siren, putting pedal to floorboard in so decided a manner
that Ramirez radioed immediately for backup and took
off in pursuit. The subsequent harrowing chase encom-
passed four state-police vehicles and led from 93 down to
Highway 3, almost to the rotary junction with Route 6.
Just before the Sagamore Bridge, the perpetual bottle-
neck that heralded the Cape Cod Canal, the desperate
motorist further endangered his fellow drivers by jump-
ing the rotary curb itself and rolling his Dodge Aspen
twice before coming to rest near the monument in the
traffic round's center.

He was approximately thirty-four-years old, dark-
haired, dark-skinned, of medium build and height, and
his name was Manuel Esconvidos. Ramirez would later
report that Esconvidos appeared to be under the influence of a chemical substance (exact nature unknown
pending the results of urine testing). He was pulled un-
hurt from the car, and roundly, if verbally, abused by
Sergeant Tony Ramirez and his backup supporters, who
threw him roughly against the hood of one of the state-
police cars. He was then handcuffed and searched.

So was his Dodge Aspen.

A ball of twine, a roll of duct tape, a length of plastic
sheeting, and a shovel were discovered on the floor of the
backseat. And in Manuel Esconvidos's right jeans pocket
was a nasty-looking switchblade.

In the trunk, battered from the high-speed chase and
unconscious as a result of the Aspen's final rolling, was a
blond young woman wearing a business suit and nylon
stockings. One high-heeled shoe had been lost, probably
in the scuffle that had ensued when Esconvidos had
forced her into the trunk of his car at knifepoint. Her
hands were bound with duct tape, and a wool sock was
stuffed into her mouth. More duct tape served as a gag.

However, other than these manifold indignities and terrors, a slight concussion, and bruises to the extremities of her body, she was unharmed. Several hours later, when she regained consciousness in a Hyannis hospital, she told police her name was Lisa McChesney. She worked as a commercial real-estate broker in downtown Boston.

Manuel Esconvidos admitted to abducting Lisa McChesney but claimed he had intended only to scare her. The materials found in his car—twine, shovel, plastic sheeting—were meant not for the disposal of a body, he insisted, but for the transplanting of a twenty-year-old oak tree in his brother-in-law's backyard.

When asked *why* he wished to frighten Ms. McChesney, Manuel Esconvidos cast about and finally offered his impression that she was an uppity bitch who never looked him in the eye, despite the fact that she passed him on the street nearly every day. It happened, police learned upon further inquiry, that Lisa's firm was handling the lease of a vacant warehouse in the same block where Manuel worked at a meatpacking plant. She had no memory of having seen Esconvidos before.

But the state police did. They had arrested Esconvidos seven years earlier, on a charge of sexual assault. His previous victim had also been bound and gagged and thrown into the trunk of a car. Terrified of Esconvidos, and in mortal dread of the police, she had refused to testify. But the pattern was there, all the same.

The pattern.

The state police began to think about patterns. To look through their files of cases long gone cold. And as Manuel Esconvidos languished without benefit of bail, the questioning began. Where had he been on this day, and this? Had he ever been to Braintree? To the Charles River bike path? To a supermarket parking lot in Newton, perhaps?

Esconvidos claimed not to remember. So many places, so many dates; and his life was hardly a testament to routine. But as the files assembled—there were five, eventually, over the course of the past six years—the state cops grew increasingly convinced. There *was* a pattern: to Esconvidos's addresses, and the places where certain bodies had been dumped like so much refuse on the city's streets. A pattern to his antagonisms, his trigger points, the things he could not abide—and the profiles of the victims. To the fragmented nature of his replies as the questioning wore on, and the disintegration of a carefully-lived lie. To the unsolved murders of five young women, found in various parts of Boston and its suburbs.

The state police informed Boston's district attorney. She called her colleague, Dan Peterson, the DA in Barnstable. Esconvidos, after all, had been on his way to Cape Cod when his Dodge Aspen had run afoul of the Sagamore Bridge rotary. Were there any cold cases of strangulation in the Barnstable jurisdiction?

The district attorney remembered the bones found so recently on Siasconset beach. He called the chief of the Nantucket PD.

And John Folger was suddenly all ears.

"Detective."

Merry looked up from the paperwork of a Friday morning and found her father's head peering around the doorjamb of her office. "Yes, Chief?"

"You have time to run out to the airport this afternoon?"

"For you? Anything."

"Good." He walked into her office and slapped a pile of paper in front of her. "You're looking for this guy. Dr. Tucker Enright. On the two-thirty Cape Air flight out of Boston."

"Who is he?"

"Somebody from Harvard." John Folger motioned to the pile he'd placed on her desk. "Read that. It's his résumé. Then come by and talk."

Merry glanced at the résumé as her father went on his way, then turned back to her notes. She had occupied her time at the beginning of the week with visiting the residents of Codfish Park, including the helpful Lenny and

Ruth Schwartz, to inquire whether any of them had observed disturbing movements or peculiar activity around the dunes at night. The fact that she was interested in such disturbances and activities at any time in the past ten years made the question fairly ludicrous, but Merry asked it nonetheless. The local people looked at her doubtfully, scratched their heads, mentioned bonfires in previous Augusts and Fourth of July parties that went on until dawn. When she inquired specifically about *digging*, or single lights at odd hours, they were uniformly blank. But she went patiently from house to house along Jefferson and Jackson and Fawcett and Beach, finding that many were shuttered and lifeless during the winter months. Others were occupied by retirees, or by women like Mabel Johnson.

Mabel was eighty-three, black, in poor health, and perched above the eroded shore in a house that she had been forced to evacuate three times in the past four months. Two of the neighboring shingle cottages on Codfish Park Road had already capitulated and washed out to sea, leaving severed pipes and broken concrete behind.

"But I don't worry my head about *that*," Mabel told Meredith in as strong a voice as she could muster. "The good Lord will look after his own. And if he don't, why, the fire chief will."

The house had cost her only fifteen thousand dollars, Mabel confided over a cup of tea. When she had purchased it, way back in forty-nine, Codfish Park was the only area the island real-estate people would *show* to a black woman. Ten years ago Mabel's home was appraised at six hundred thousand dollars, and a swell-looking guy from New York had wanted to take it out from under her. Now she couldn't give it away.

Merry looked appreciatively around the two-bedroom cottage, its simple furnishings, its spectacular view of sand and rolling Atlantic. "So do you wish you'd let him have it?" she asked.

Mabel smiled. She was a small woman, spare and

narrow-faced, her graying hair drawn back in a bun. Her right hand, poised on the head of an elegant cane, was knobby with arthritis. "I won't leave this house until they carry me out, child. And that money's been eaten up by the sea. No one wants Mabel's house now it's been *evacuated*. I tell you, child, I *thank* that Atlantic, greedy busybody that he is, for taking those folks next door, I *do*. He's give me a clear ocean view on every side! Guess they'll leave me in peace, all those money-hungry real-estate folks that couldn't wait to get me fixed here in the first place."

"Speaking of peace," Merry said, "have you noticed any disturbances along your beachfront in the past few years?"

"Disturbances? You mean, like houses falling into the water?" Mabel crowed with laughter. "Back in January, darling, these places were practically running into the surf, yes they were. But old Mabel's house sit tight."

"I was thinking more of people on the beach. Digging, for instance, or moving around in the darkness with flashlights. Anytime over the past, say"—she balked at the word *ten*—"several years?"

Mabel's eyes narrowed. "You talking 'bout those bones what they children dug up, few days ago? You wondering how they got there in the first place?"

"You heard about the skeleton. I guess it was all over the papers."

"Mabel don't need nobody to tell her what she's seen for herself. I watched you standing down there with all those men on their knees, making fools of theyselves, yes I did. Then I talked to Mrs. Schwartz at the post office next day. She's a lovely woman, Mrs. Schwartz. Don't bother looking through you like you was the hired help, and you living here all along and without no mortgage, either."

"Yes."

"I don't know nothing about the past few years," Mabel said firmly, "but I'll tell you that *somebody* was digging at *something* not so very long ago. Middle of January, it was, in the middle of the night, and that terrible snow-storm come the next day, so's I never went down to the beach to look. Your asking just now reminded me of it."

Merry sat up. "Digging? In the middle of the night? How do you know?"

"Well now, child, sometimes it happens that I can't sleep so well at night, and when that wind is howling ter-rible off the water, and I'm wondering whether tonight's the night that old Mabel's going to float off into the Atlantic—why, I just sit up in bed and hold my Bible in the dark, and say, 'Help me, Jesus,' over and over until I fall asleep or the daylight comes."

Merry imagined the elderly woman alone with her Good Book, waiting for the waves to lick hungrily at the steps of her home. She felt an impulse to reach for Mabel and hug her.

"That night before the storm the wind was kicking up terrible, you know. It always *does*, in Sconset of a winter, but this particular night was something awful. I sat there in the dark, holding my Bible, but pretty soon I found that the Lord wanted me on my feet—and so I got up and got myself to the front window, and I looked out at the sea. Not that I had to look too far—it being right up by the dunes, and crashing not a few feet from my house. And then I saw it."

"What?" Merry leaned forward, her eyes riveted on Mabel's face.

"The light. First I thought it was the fire department, coming to check on Mabel—they always does, you know, when the weather's terrible bad—but then it stopped, in front of one of those abandoned shacks that used to be-long to the white folks from Boston, and whoever was holding it must've set it down on the sand."

"You saw the person?"

"Just his boots, child. Mabel's eyesight's not too good in the best of times, and this was *some* night. Black as my Aunt Hattie, and nasty. Anyway, I saw enough to know that this fellah with the light was hunched over and digging."

"You're sure it was a man?"

"I ain't sure o' nothing, 'cept it wasn't a ghost and it wasn't a dog. Whoever it was wasn't there too long. He finished digging, shook a bag of something over the hole, and tamped it down with the shovel. Then he picked up the light and headed back the way he'd come."

"Toward the parking area at Gully Road?"

"Yes indeed, child."

"And you never went down to see what he had been digging?"

"Can't say as I had time. Next morning—and no morning's ever come so late for Mabel, let me tell you—the fire chief came and took me away. Drove me to my cousin LouAnn's house down near the airport, and I stayed there for a week." She licked her lips and moved her palm restlessly along the head of her cane, her eyes on the water beyond her door. "Worrying the whole time whether my house'd be here when I got back."

Merry reached for Mabel's free hand and pressed it. There had been nine houses lining the oceanfront side of Codfish Park Road before that January snowstorm. By the time the storm was over, twenty-four hours later, two had washed out to sea, and the other seven were essentially condemned by town officials. Four had been voluntarily moved by their owners only a few days ago. The others would probably be handed over to the town, jacked up on their foundations, loaded onto tractor trailers, and forcibly removed from the area. What Mabel would do, Merry couldn't think. The cost of a removal— from five to ten thousand dollars—was probably beyond the elderly woman's resources, even if she had a place to put the house once she moved it. Merry asked the question anyway.

"This doesn't seem like a very secure spot for you, Mrs. Johnson. Is there any way you could move your home? To a different lot? People do it all the time, you know. And I hear the house movers are *very* careful."

"Lord, child." Mabel's smile widened. "You got some land somewhere that the rich folks from off-island don't need to buy? 'Cause Mabel ain't found any. Everything she's got is right in this house. And here it will stay."

And thus Meredith Folger frowned as she reviewed her notes this Friday morning. Mabel Johnson had seen a suspicious burial of *something* the night of the brutal snowstorm in January that tore away two houses in Codfish Park. By Merry's reckoning (and she had sifted through back issues of the island's weekly newspaper, the *Inquirer and Mirror*, just to be sure), that would have been January 7 of the present year. But the state crime lab believed the bones that Cecil and Nan Markham had discovered were at least two, or as much as ten, years old. Perhaps the surreptitious digging dealt with another matter entirely. Or had the bones lain *elsewhere* for years and been reburied by the light that Mabel had seen?

She needed more information.

Merry rubbed her temples, feeling the beginning of a headache, and picked up the résumé her father had tossed onto her desk. All she needed this afternoon was a dry run out to the airport in pursuit of some academic.

But *academic*, Merry discovered as she leafed through the twenty-odd pages of his résumé, was hardly the word for Dr. Tucker Enright. He was a Harvard-educated forensic psychiatrist with tenure at Harvard Medical School; and more intriguing still, he had made a career out of consulting for the FBI. Merry was familiar with forensic *anthropologists*—those experts in human development who turned their analytic skills to the identification of human remains—but a forensic *psychiatrist* was new to her experience. Enright, it seems, had a degree in psychiatry but had never practiced; he taught at the university and spent his time attempting to understand the mental forces behind the commission of serious crimes. Serial killers—particularly those much given to bizarre sexual fetishes and immersion in the macabre—were Enright's specialty. He cut his teeth on Charles Manson, and moved on to the Son of Sam murders; he surfaced at the Jonestown Massacre and consulted on the case of cannibal Jim Duquesne. He stood by during a confrontation with antigovernment militia in Colorado and had made a hobby of tracking the Unabomber before Ted Kaczynski was apprehended and charged with the most lethal of those crimes. Enright had trolled the edges of the Oklahoma City bombing disaster, too, tape-recording his observations and paying particular attention to the devastation of the day-care center.

Like a vampire, Tucker Enright seemed to gravitate toward the dark places in human society, Merry thought. He watched among the shadows and sent back bulletins to the living. Evil was his lifeblood.

At the close of the résumé Merry skimmed the list of Enright's scholarly papers. *Alcohol and the Suppression of the Guilt Reflex. The Incest Scar and Homicidal Mania. Panty Hose as Manacles in Child Pornography Films.*

Merry read and was increasingly nauseated. This was a side of law enforcement she was happy to know nothing about. This was the stuff of nightmare, the churning, haunting darkness of the human psyche. Her impulse in the face of it was to turn away, to make the sign against the evil eye, to think instead of summer days and kindness freely given, and the sustaining truth she found in the people she loved. What did someone like Enright turn to, when the darkness became too much? How could anyone—scientist or no—make a *career* from absolute evil?

And what business did the guy think he had on her island?

She pushed back her chair and went to find her father. He was sitting with Clarence Strangerfield in his office, brow furrowed as he read through the weekly duty summary. Despite his best efforts, a number of tourist wallets

had indeed been stolen during the course of the Daffodil Festival. Handblock, a distinctive linens store on
Main Street (and winner of the third-place award for
Most Beautiful Window), reported some missing needlepoint pillows; and Tonkin Antiques had lost no fewer
than three brass door knockers in the shape of lightship
baskets.

"On the upside, however," the chief said as he raised
his head to meet Meredith's outraged green eyes, "both
stores probably racked up more sales over Daffodil Weekend than they did the entire winter. I hope they keep that
in mind, 'cause none of this stuff is coming back."

"Chief," she broke in with a wave of Enright's résumé.
"What's going on? Why is this creep coming to Nantucket?"

"Sit down." He directed her toward a chair opposite
Clarence's. "You both ought to hear this. I had a call from
Dan Peterson this morning."

With a look for Clarence, Merry took the proffered
chair. Neither of them knew Dan Peterson well. He was
simply the district attorney under whose jurisdiction Nantucket fell—and his office was across the Sound in Barnstable. He dealt primarily with the state-police office on
the island, and when the local petty crime escalated to the
level of district court—most frequently for drug possession or sale—Peterson's assistants flew to Nantucket for
the trials.

"He's been working with the state folks on a multi-
jurisdictional case," John Folger continued. "A pattern of
killings around Massachusetts that they think is the work
of one man. They have a suspect sitting in Boston right
now, in fact—a guy named Esconvidos."

"Multiple killings?" A shot of adrenaline raced through
Merry's system. "You're kidding. How many?"

"Five so far."

She glanced at Clarence. From his expression this was
news to him, too. "Five this year?"

John Folger shook his head. "They're saying the murders

are spread over at least six years. Maybe more. The first victim disappeared in the spring of 1990." He searched through a pile of two-day-old newspapers for his notebook, found it, and opened it to the appropriate page. "A nineteen-year-old sophomore at Boston U. Jennifer Morgan. Found her lying under some bushes along the Charles River bike path, right around where it hits the boathouses, you know? She'd been dead awhile."

"How did she die?" Even to herself, Merry's voice sounded remote.

"Strangled." Her father snapped the notebook shut and let the word hang in the air between them. "All five were strangled."

Clarence cleared his throat. "Like a certain unidentified woman from Sconset."

For something to do, Merry picked up a pencil lying idle on the conference table and twirled it between her fingers. She was aware of a persistent pain behind her eyes. Random killings—psychotic, apparently motiveless, brutal killings—honestly terrified her. She liked to think that murder was the last act of a person driven to extremity by a passion so powerful that all control—all submission to social norms and unspoken codes of behavior—momentarily snapped. But murder as pastime, murder as inhuman sport, threatened every notion of order and stability she had come to expect in her world. The Sconset bones could *not* be a part of something so impersonal, so driven by unseen madness.

The last such spate of killings in Massachusetts were the Roadside Murders around New Bedford, between 1988 and 1990—eleven young female victims, most of them involved in prostitution and drug use, whose skeletal remains were found in the tall grass near highway rest areas. Only nine of the women were ever positively identified. The murders were still unsolved. Which might mean that the killer himself was dead, or had already been caught and never linked to the New Bedford murders; or that he was out there now—alive, lurking, killing.

"A serial killah," Clarence added, as if thinking out loud. "Ah've nevah worked on one o' those."

"And you probably won't be working on this one either," John Folger replied. "This is a case for the state police—and from the drift of Peterson's words this morning, I'd say *they're* being preempted by the FBI. If the Sconset bones are part of the pattern, the most we'll be expected to do is liaise."

Merry heard his words with relief. No matter how much she enjoyed the demands of police work, she had no desire *ever* to handle a serial case, but she pushed aside her personal fears and made an effort to be practical.

"We still know so little about our bones," she pointed out, "that it seems premature to say they're part of this pattern. Or does Peterson know something we don't?"

"I doubt it." The chief tipped his swivel chair back against the office wall, legs dangling and arms clasped behind his head. "We know that the bones were those of a woman who was strangled. Period."

"But *our* victim was buried. It sounds as though the others weren't."

"Peterson wasn't entirely clear about the details. The other five women were certainly found and identified more quickly. And that may mean the Sconset murder is the work of a different person. Or it may not."

"This is too weird," Merry said flatly, and ran her fingers through her bangs in frustration. "I mean, this is *Nantucket*, for God's sake. We don't have nutsos here. At least—not homicidal nutsos. Not like that."

"Ayeh, they always vacation on the Vineyahd," Clarence said dryly. "Or hang around Provincetown wearin' turquoise eye shadder."

"You know what I mean, Clare."

"You mean the wahrld just came to Nantucket."

The three of them were silent a moment. Then Merry sighed. "We won't know, will we?" she said finally. "Until we know who she is and have a better idea when and how she might have died."

"Well, Meredith, that's where your Dr. Enright comes in," her father replied, and glanced at his watch. "We're hosting him at Peterson's request. Or the FBI's order, whichever you find more compelling. Maybe you should be heading out to the airport soon."

"Have you read this?" Merry asked Clarence conversationally as she passed him the psychiatrist's résumé. "The man's a psycho himself. He has to be, to do this for a living. Just reading that stuff made my skin crawl."

"Aren't you being a little emotional, Detective?"

Merry rolled her eyes at the sharpness of her father's tone. "What am I supposed to do? Take clinical notes, like Dr. Enright? If he'd ever experienced an emotion in his life, he'd be doing something else for a living."

"He's pretty well paid, you know."

"And that's supposed to make his work palatable?"

Her father smiled. "I think a thousand dollars a day in expenses, and an hourly rate of two hundred, could make just about anything palatable."

Clarence gave a low whistle. "Yahr tax dollars at work."

"Well, Chief," Merry said, "I never thought I'd see the day when John Folger was impressed by a price tag."

"He's put a lot of sick people away, Meredith." There was a warning in her father's voice. "Enright specializes in defeating the insanity defense. It's his primary purpose in working for the Bureau. He's one of the experts they call in to testify that these psychos knew *exactly* what they were doing—that they were completely sane and should be punished to the full extent of the law. In my book that's a service we can all admire."

Merry bit back a retort and took a deep breath instead. Maybe she *was* a little too emotional. "You said the suspect is in Boston. What's Enright hope to accomplish here?"

"The DA says he wants to see the Sconset site. Apparently he's looked over the previous five and has a sense of the killer's MO. He thinks he can determine whether our bones fit the pattern just from seeing where they were discovered."

Clarence snorted, and Merry looked dubious. "Dad—"

"Yes?" the chief looked up, his hard blue eyes expressionless.

"Are you sure you want this guy nosing into our case?"

"I'm not so sure it's our case anymore. If it ever was."

Merry could summon no reply to this.

Clarence pushed himself to his feet. "Thanks for lettin' me in on the loop," he said with a nod to the chief, "but it sounds as though there's too many cooks ahreddy in this pahtickulah kitchen."

Merry watched the crime-scene chief go, feeling irresolute about the whole affair. But all she said was, "I'm on my way to the airport, Chief."

"Good. Don't drive like a maniac. And try to treat Enright with something like respect."

"Promise. Dad—"

"Yes?" His head came up from the shoplifting reports, and Merry could tell from his expression that his attention was already elsewhere.

"Were these women sexually assaulted before they died?"

Her father hesitated. Shielding her, as usual.

"I'd like to know."

"This isn't our case, Merry."

She stood up and made for the door. "If those bones fit the pattern—if such things are really happening here—then it's *everyone's* case, Dad. You must see that. How did John Donne put it? *Any man's death diminishes me, because I am involved in mankind*?"

"You've been listening to your grandfather." John Folger sounded amused. "I've heard that one more times than I can count."

"Ralph passed it on the day you gave me my first case, and I've never forgotten it. It's the reason I come in to

work every morning—but you know that." Merry drew
her hand across her eyes. Her headache was intensifying.
"I can't stand around watching while the tragedies happen, like your precious Dr. Enright. I think I'd dislike him
less if he managed to *prevent* a few murders, instead of
descending like a vulture to pick among the bones."

"You don't even know the man, Meredith. You can't
possibly dislike him."

"I assume the other women were sexually assaulted."

"Talk to Enright about it," her father replied with his
first expression of distaste. "It should be a real icebreaker."

And so, sustained by an unhappy mixture of contempt
and anger, Meredith Folger stood in the Tom Nevers Airport that afternoon holding a square cardboard sign with
Tucker Enright's name printed in strong block capitals.
The plane was on time, and Enright was listed as a passenger, thereby quenching Merry's lingering hope. No
mishap in Boston had detained the consultant unavoidably; no Atlantic fog descended of a sudden to prevent his
plane from landing. Merry considered this punctuality,
this adherence to plan, to be of a piece with Enright's entire résumé. Perhaps because he was so absorbed in de-
viance and perversion, he kept rigidly to the straight and
narrow. She peered grimly at the deplaning passengers,
searching for a man in a dark suit with the aspect of a
hungry buzzard; and so missed Enright entirely.

"Hello," someone said at her elbow. "You looking
for me?"

She turned in surprise toward the slight man beside
her. "*You're* Tucker Enright?"

"Yep." He extended a hand in greeting.

He was probably around fifty, Meredith knew, from his
year of graduation at Harvard Medical School; but he
looked much younger. A compact, athletic body in jeans
and a wool sweater the color of the sea; Birkenstocks and
socks on his feet. Receding blond hair, a narrow Irish
face with a prominent nose; cool and assessing eyes a

pale shade of blue. His smile belied the expression in those eyes, being easy and warm—a smile that instantly engaged Merry and made her complicitous in Tucker Enright's life from the very moment of meeting him. He held a small black leather bag in one hand, and a furled magazine in the other. *Golf Digest*.

She took his outstretched hand and said, "Detective Meredith Folger, Nantucket Police."

"Ah. You're the one who oversaw the skeleton's removal. The police chief's daughter, right?"

"How did you know?" Merry asked, surprised.

Enright shrugged. "I spent an hour this morning in Barnstable talking to the DA. He filled me in on the local force. He has only good things to say about you—I guess you handled a pretty major arson case here last summer. Shall we go?"

"Of course. My car's not far. The arson thing was really the state police's problem—"

"Until you stepped in and saved their asses, right?"

"Well, I wouldn't put it *that* way."

"No. You wouldn't." Enright's tone was as teasing as a kid brother's, and Merry flushed.

She led him to her car, conscious not to help him with the black bag, or to be too solicitous for his comfort. She was a fellow law-enforcement officer, not a female acolyte, and it would be helpful to make the point early. "Where did you want to go first?" she asked.

"Siasconset," Enright replied, pronouncing it correctly; and Merry obliged.

Cecil and Nan Markham did not avoid the beach forever, although Merry was correct in thinking it was several days before the children ventured back to their familiar haunts. Cecil, at least, had tossed and turned for three nights running, his sleep banished by a familiar dread, a persistent sense of anxiety that had been his constant companion since infancy. When sleep did come, it brought only nightmares. In one of them he was hard at work on his castle's battlements, when bony fingers reached up out of the sand to suck him down. He woke up screaming, trapped in a snare of blankets, his mother's face looming palely over his own.

"Cecil," she had whispered fiercely. "*Do* shut up, you silly sod. You'll wake Nannie." Her face gleamed like a skull in the moonlight.

The oppression of the Markham household was a poor rival for the strengthening spring calling from beyond the window, and a love of the sea is impossible to thwart for many days together. The two children returned to the beach that Friday after Daffodil Weekend—returned in some trepidation, although neither expressed their fears to the other, and Nan forbore reaching for Cecil's hand as they made their way along the shore.

The sea, happily, is a great renewer; and the freshly washed sands, kneaded and smoothed by a week's worth of tides and several intervening storms, looked untouched by grief or memory. Only a fluttering yellow square of police tape around what had been an open pit served as reminder of the gruesome discoveries two weeks earlier.

Cecil swallowed hard to summon his tenuous courage. "Should we go look, Nan?" he asked, as though *she* were the elder; and Nan glanced at him scornfully.

"You're such a baby, Cecil," she said. "I'm much braver than you." And she took off across the sand.

After a moment Cecil followed.

They crouched under the yellow tape and peered over the edge of the pit, Satchmo at their rear, his tail wagging, and noticed how little remained of the pirate's grotesque treasure. A protective tarpaulin had been thrown over the hole, but despite this Cecil could see that salt water had poured in and out of the pit. The marks of their digging, and the police's subsequent sifting, were blurred.

"There's a full moon tonight," Nan observed. "The tide will be nearly up to the road."

Cecil nodded and looked out at the sea, which was heaving and curling under the influence of a brisk May wind, sunlight glinting whitely on the crests of the waves. He stood and brushed off his pants, then ran pell-mell down toward the water. Satchmo came after him more slowly, and where the boy halted at the surf line, bending down for a striated scallop shell upturned in the wet sand, the aged dog walked on. Head up, tongue out, thick matted coat turning dark with the wet, he breasted the incoming waves purposefully until the sand beneath his feet dropped away, and he was swimming.

Satchmo in particular had missed their daily walks to the beach.

"Cecil!"

He turned and looked for his sister, who was calling and waving from beside the pit. Two adults stood next to her. Cecil narrowed his eyes, shading them with one downturned palm. He recognized the detective; but who was the man in the faded jeans, his sparse hair whipping in the wind?

Chapter Six

"There's not much to see, is there?" Tucker Enright straightened up from the pit. He glanced around at Cecil Markham and smiled. Cecil looked doubtfully back, although the detective had made a proper introduction of her doctor companion and he should be all right. Cecil still wasn't sure whether he wanted this man on his beach—but there was the problem. It wasn't exactly *his* beach. He could tell that Nan felt equally uncertain. His sister stood stirring the sand diffidently with one red-sneakered foot. This spot in the dunes had been her special place, after all; and now the whole world came to gawk at it. Cecil watched her sneaker, which was making a careful pattern of curved lines like the arcs of a rainbow, and saw that she had a hole in the canvas right above her big toe.

"No," Detective Folger said now, in answer to Enright's question. "Certainly nothing worth a flight out to Nantucket."

"Oh, I wouldn't go *that* far."

"You've found something?" Her black eyebrows lifted.

"What is it you're looking for, mister?" Cecil crouched down once more at the edge of the shallow hole. The protective tarpaulin had been shoved aside by the detective and her companion, and Cecil noticed how the sand was several colors at once, and how the fragments of scallop and quahog shell gleamed with a separate coolness.

"Nothing you can see with your eyes," Enright replied. "I'm looking for what *isn't* here."

"The curious fact of the dog in the night," Merry said.

"Exactly."

Cecil looked from one to the other, knowing that they were speaking the way grown-ups so often do, confident that their words flew over a child's head; and so he said, somewhat defiantly, "That's from Sherlock. Only you've got it wrong. It should be 'the curious *incident* of the dog in the night*time*.' "

"Bravo." The thin man looked at him then, rather intently, with his pale-blue eyes. "And in what story did he say that?"

Cecil thought for an instant. " 'Silver Blaze.' "

"Got it again."

"I've read all the Holmes stories exactly seven times," Cecil told him proudly.

"Are you going to be a great detective when you grow up?" Detective Folger asked.

Cecil shook his head and looked away. Should he tell them? Or would they laugh? "I'm going to be an explorer."

"If there's anything left to explore," Enright said, his eyes meeting Merry's. "We're running out of world at a spectacular rate." He was being exclusionary again, as though a conversation with Cecil was meaningful only if it operated on two levels. Laughing at him, in fact.

"Oh, I wouldn't go *that* far," Cecil said airily, quoting

Enright from memory. "I don't intend to explore *this* world."

"What about you, Nan? What do you want to be?" Merry Folger had seated herself several feet from the yellow-taped police square and was letting warm sand run through her fingers. She was pretty, Cecil thought, with her blond hair and green eyes, the crisp way her khaki pants met the striped cotton sweater. Not like his mum, who wore the same things almost every day and never seemed to notice how awful they smelled from cigarette smoke. And at that thought he looked around instinctively for his sister. A few months earlier Cecil's class had discussed secondary-smoke inhalation, and the dangers it posed to everyone; and Cecil worried about Nan. She coughed sometimes at night, waking him, but his mother never seemed to hear. Nan was like some fairy sprite—heedless and vulnerable as she danced on the sunlit sand; and, watching her, Cecil saw with relief that her memories of the buried bones were gradually wearing away. He hoped they never returned to trouble her nights, as they haunted his. But if they did? He couldn't really help Nannie. He couldn't even help himself. It was only as Lord Cecil of Trevarre—the powerful knight, the intrepid post captain, the stalwart chief of a desperate band—that he managed to combat his nightmares.

Nan turned now, flopped down onto her stomach near the detective, and said matter-of-factly, "I'm going to be an artist, like my daddy. Did you know that he was a great artist? Only he's dead. Or I'll be a gardener like Mrs. Schwartz. She let me plant some seeds in a corner of her backyard, because I promised not to tell."

"Not to tell?"

"Mummy. If Mummy knew, she wouldn't let me."

"Were you gardening here?" the man called Enright suddenly asked. "When you found the bones?"

Nan's cheerfulness faded. "It was Satchmo, not me."

"Their dog," Merry Folger supplied. "The one in the water. Satchmo's got a nose for bones, it seems."

"We were having a tea party," Nan added. "With sand for tea. Only Satchmo wouldn't play. He was too busy digging."

"Do you always play here?" Enright hunkered down to Nan's level, quiet and purposeful.

"Sometimes. Sometimes we go down to Low Beach," she added, gesturing in the opposite direction, "when Cecil's pretending to be a commander in the Royal Navy. Or sometimes we stay close to Gully Road."

"And yet your dog never smelled the bones before. He just happened to find them there that particular day. I suppose stranger things have happened."

"I'm not sure they were here all that long," Merry Folger objected. "But we can talk about that later."

Cecil heard the signal the detective was sending Enright—*not in front of the children*—and looked uncomfortably out toward the water. Satchmo's black nose lifted gallantly above a wave, his forepaws churning. A woman Cecil did not recognize was walking along the shoreline, and as he watched, she stooped and clapped her hands. Satchmo struggled out of the surf, a stick triumphant between his jaws, and padded up to her. He dropped the stick at her feet and, after a fractional hesitation, shook out his coat roundly, showering the stranger with icy salt water. She laughed and patted his head.

So *that* was what kept the dog in the water so long today—the age-old game of loss and retrieval.

"What did the bones look like, Nan?" Enright asked.

"Like twigs," she said. She was avoiding Enright's gaze, intent upon furrowing the sand with a razor clam's shell, and Cecil could feel her distress from several feet away. "I didn't know they were bones until we found the skull."

"And they were just—loose?"

Nan nodded.

"You didn't find anything else?"

"Like what?"

Enright shrugged. "Oh, I don't know. A ring, maybe, or a piece of clothing."

"Nope." Nan said it flatly. "But you know, I was pretty scared once we found the skull. Cecil screamed and ran away, and I ran after him. So we didn't look too hard for anything. Maybe Miss Folger knows. She looked later."

Of course, Cecil thought irritably. Didn't this man know what he was doing? He should have checked with the detective first. The detective knew everything. Or did he think that Nan had stolen something?

"I'm done here," the psychiatrist said, rising from the sand and nodding at the detective, "if you are."

"Of course." Merry stood, too, brushing at her seat, and looked at Cecil. "It was nice to see you two again," she said. "I'm glad you're back out on the beach."

"So'm I," he replied. "It's almost summer, isn't it?"

"Yes." And at her glad expression of hopefulness as she turned her face to the sun, Cecil felt a surge of something unfamiliar—something like joy. He reached out and took his little sister's hand. "Come on, Nan. Let's go throw Satch's stick."

"Well," Merry said as they settled into one of the Second Story's small tables, "what do you think?"

Enright took a moment to answer, his eyes caught by the line of blue beyond the window. He had requested food and a water view—something more difficult to provide in the off-season than it seemed. Most of the tourist places on the wharves had yet to open for the summer, or served dinner only on weekends; and this was a three P.M. meal they were calling lunch. But the Second Story's food was great, and from its upstairs room the waters of the boat basin were just visible, curling serenely around the bright hulls moored at the Nantucket Yacht Club.

Enright turned back to Merry and smiled. "I'm sorry. I've never been able to resist the Atlantic. Must've been a sailor in a past life. You were asking?"

"About the Sconset scene. What you thought. Whether we're part of the serial pattern or not."

"It's probably premature to say, but if you back me to the wall, I think I'd have to go with no."

"Really? That's a relief." The slight tension that had been gripping her since the morning eased and dissipated.

"Is it? You've still got a murder victim. That body didn't bury itself." The psychiatrist sounded amused.

"True," Merry conceded, "but there's something unavoidably nasty about the notion of a serial killer. Particularly on Nantucket."

"Why?"

"Why? Because this is my *home*, that's why. Not to mention my professional turf. Besides, things like that don't happen here."

"Things like—strangulation?"

Merry hesitated. "Okay. The woman in Sconset was strangled, I grant you that."

"So it *was* a woman."

"Yes. Didn't you read the forensics report?"

Enright shook his head and reached for a roll. "I haven't even read a copy of the file. The state police got in touch with me in Braintree and asked if I'd come right over here. Said they had a case that fit my pattern. So I assumed the victim was female; I just didn't know."

"I wondered why you were grilling little Nan about the bones."

Enright's face crinkled with mock remorse. "Was I grilling her? And I tried so hard to be fatherly! I've never had the right practice, I guess."

"No kids?"

"No kids. No wife, no lover, no alternative orientation. Just an altar to Old St. Andrews in my hall closet and a fortune in golf balls lost on two continents. So tell me about your bones. Is what Nan said true? Nothing at all was found with them?"

"Right. And they were completely disarticulated, not

to mention scrubbed clean. It was as if they had been hanging in a sophomore biology class. Weird, huh?"

"Decidedly." Enright's eyebrows shot up, and he reached again for the bread basket. "Have you checked with the local high school? Maybe some teenagers are yanking your chain."

"I wish they were. There's the slight matter of the broken hyoid bone."

"Ah, yes. In an adult woman, undoubtedly strangulation."

"However," Merry amended, "I do think it's possible the Sconset grave is fairly recent. A woman who lives nearby claims to have seen someone she can't identify digging in that spot one night last January. She says the person dropped something from a sack into the hole and then refilled it."

"And yet she never went to look?"

"She's fairly elderly, walks with a cane, and was evacuated from her house the next morning in the middle of a blizzard."

"January," Enright mused thoughtfully. "The storm that shut down the whole East Coast? Just after New Year's?"

"Yes. It tore off a piece of Sconset's beach, not to mention two houses. By the time it was over, all memory of the late-night digger had gone completely out of Mabel's—that's my elderly lady—head."

"Until you brought up the subject of digging."

Merry nodded.

"This is great," Enright exclaimed. "Forget the serial murders—give me a midnight burial any day! I hope the grave digger had a sinister profile and carried a flickering lamp." He grinned.

"Laugh all you like," Merry protested, smiling, "but you see the problem. The bones might have come from anywhere. Until we get an identification, we're lost."

"Yes," Enright said. "That *would* be a ticklish problem."

"I just hope the FBI's people can help us."

The psychiatrist's head came up from his bread, and he looked at her intently. "You sent them to the FBI?"

"To the Smithsonian, actually. Their forensic anthropologists sometimes help out the Bureau with random remains. But you know that, I'm sure."

"I know some of the anthropologists," Enright said frankly. "Good people. Well, I see why the DA spoke so highly of you, Detective Folger. You've got a head on your pretty shoulders. If anyone can help you, the Smithsonian will. You tried dental records, I guess?"

"No teeth."

"No teeth?"

"Either they were deliberately removed by the murderer to prevent identification, or they were lost when the bones were moved. *If* they were moved. Regardless—"

"There's no help in dental records." Enright's expression had turned inward, and he was crushing some bread crumbs absently with his thumbnail.

"I wouldn't be surprised if the rest of the bones proved equally unhelpful," Merry added. "By the time our scene-of-crimes chief and the medical examiner got out to Sconset, some were chewed, some were missing, and any hope of an intact scene was pretty much out the window."

"Only natural," Enright observed, "when one considers the dog. More heinous acts have been suddenly exposed by a helpful canine with a bone. But it's a rare day, Detective, when I get to work an intact scene."

"I suppose you wouldn't," Merry said, considering the nature of serial murders. "But, then, you don't exactly *work the scene*, do you?"

"Only mentally." Enright took a sip of ice water. "I work everything mentally. Then I retrace the killer's steps. If there's a suspect, I talk to him. Intensively."

Merry shuddered.

"It's not as bad as it sounds." Enright's blue eyes met hers gently. "Most of these guys are quite friendly.

Unassuming. The underdogs of the modern world, in fact. And they love to talk about their work."

"And they're all *guys*, aren't they?"

"Generally. Sometimes a particular woman—wife, girl-friend, mother even—will serve as assistant. Pick the victims. Deliver them up."

"That's sick."

"I know. Although that's not exactly the word I use."

"And they tell you all this?"

"Most of the time. I'm a good listener. I know the right questions to ask."

"But isn't it possible," Merry countered, her black brows furrowing, "that they're just feeding you a line?"

Enright chewed his bread for a moment ruminatively, his gaze fixed on a boat coming into the yacht club's moorings. "There's something about the patient-analyst relationship, Meredith. It isn't as linear as you think. A good analyst listens to the purpose *behind* what is said. To what isn't there, as well as what is. Truth is variable, you know. It's partly the process of the telling that reveals the subject's soul."

"Okay," Merry conceded. "I'll take that one on faith, since I have no training whatsoever in psychology."

"Of course you do. You've been listening to suspects for years. Playing out the rope and leading them gently into the noose. The art of conversation is a detective's sharpest weapon." Enright looked over his shoulder toward the boat basin again and then glanced around the empty dining room. "Are there waitresses in this place, or are we expected to live on the view? I'm famished."

"She's probably waiting for us to open the menus," Merry pointed out. "We haven't even looked at them."

"Oh—*right*." Enright flipped his open and scanned it. "You see? You're such a good listener I'd have talked us both to death."

They took only seconds to decide, and then Merry slapped her menu shut. Her earlier distaste for Enright's profession was dissipating. His approach to it was undeniably compelling. "So then what do you do? After you've interviewed the killers?"

The psychiatrist's features stilled, and he paused an instant before answering. "Then comes the curious part. The alchemy."

"Incantations and appeasement of the gods."

"Almost." Enright folded his hands on the table and leaned toward her, as though he were about to share a secret. "I practically become the man myself—his habits, his routines, what he eats for dinner, the way he dresses. I figure out what his buttons are—the ones his victims push. Then I push them too. I watch how he reacts. And in the end, I visit the scene. Or scenes, as in this case. I force myself to see what happened there. To feel the karma. And then I know."

"What, exactly?" Merry asked, in almost a whisper.

"Whether the guy is sane. Whether he planned the killings meticulously. There's the kernel of the nut, if you'll forgive the pun—in the planning and execution. Only a sane person can deliberately set about the extinction of another life. And then repeat that process, over and over again."

"And the scenes tell you this?"

"The scenes, and everything I feel around them."

"But how do you know? About Sconset, for instance? You've only been there twenty minutes, and you've ruled it out entirely."

"It's hard to define," Enright answered slowly. "But I've seen all the other places where the bodies were discovered, and this one doesn't fit." He looked up at the waitress as she approached. "You know what I'm dying for? Really? A lobster roll. It's not on the menu, but could you do that?"

"Of course," the woman said, responding to Tucker's smile the way that Merry assumed most women did; and then she looked at Merry herself, one eyebrow raised.

"A bowl of quahog chowder for me."

The waitress moved off wordlessly. Merry slid her

water glass one inch to the right, and one inch back to the left, aware of how little she knew about the pattern of murders. She felt uncharacteristically hesitant to invade Enright's turf. "*How* doesn't it fit—or aren't you able to tell me?"

"Too pastoral." Enright unfurled his napkin. "Too end-of-the-world. Maybe it's the fact that your bones were moved—that Sconset isn't really the scene, if you see what I mean. There's no trace of violent horror about it."

Merry debated this mentally. "But wasn't the first body found on the Charles River bike path? That's kind of pastoral. And there's a similar element of water."

"Yes," Enright replied, "but the atmosphere is utterly different. The Back Bay victim was strangled and thrown under a bush near the boathouses—and the sensation of public scrutiny is intense. I still don't know how the killer managed it. There are lights on the path, and occasional dog walkers, even in the dark. He must have run an incredible risk. Personally, I'm betting he strangled her somewhere else and brought her to the path later."

"In the trunk of his car, for instance. Like Lisa McChesney."

Enright studied her appraisingly. "Maybe. But I'm not sure yet whether Manuel Esconvidos is our man."

"You're kidding." Merry sat back in surprise.

"He gives me no impression of an alternative life. Esconvidos doesn't move in the shadow of his fantasies, he doesn't seem controlled by them. He may be a rapist—or have impulses in that direction. He may suffer from resentments, intense hatreds even, particularly of women. But he is hardly in thrall to his mental demons. At least not in my estimation." He shook his head.

"And is that what it takes? That sort of . . . possession, if you will?"

"Yes. These people—the ones who kill repeatedly, out of a lust for the act of taking a life—they live and breathe in the maw of their passion."

"And yet you don't call that madness."

"No."

Merry frowned. "I don't understand. I really don't. In my view anyone who decides to kill another person must be insane. Even if only for a moment."

Enright laughed. "By that definition, Detective, we're all slightly mad. Don't tell me you've never been angry enough to murder someone."

"But I've never acted on it."

"And if you did," the psychiatrist countered, "I would probably tell you that you had made a definite choice. Particularly if you first went about obtaining a murder weapon, observing your victim, and constructing a plausible method of the body's disposal." He tempered the grimness of his words with a small smile. "I would be particularly interested to learn that you took a stiff drink before committing the act—because that would tell me you *knew* it was wrong and needed some Dutch courage to ignore your conscience."

Merry's green eyes narrowed. "The state police thought Manuel Esconvidos was on something."

"He tested positive for PCP," Enright said. "Very unpredictable stuff."

"So you think he'll argue he wasn't in his right mind?"

"Probably. And rape juries being what they are, he'll probably get off. But look at the contents of his car—it's a walking escape vehicle. Everything you need to commit and conceal a crime. He plotted the abduction and was in a fair way of carrying it out. And PCP or no, that sort of clear-headed mental activity is completely incompatible with insanity. It suggests—it proves, by a simple chain of decision making—that Esconvidos acted by choice. With intent. *Mens rea*, to phrase it in legal Latin."

"But sane or not, you don't think he's your multiple killer."

"I'm not entirely convinced, no."

Merry's thoughts were rife with objection and counter-argument, but this foray into the mentality of killers had little to do with Enright's conclusions about the Sconset bones. "The body on the Charles River bike path wasn't buried," she said. "What about the others?"

"Two were found in shallow graves. The Braintree body, however—1993—was similarly exposed. Thrown into a Goodwill pickup Dumpster sitting right out there in a supermarket parking lot. The victim *had* to be dead before the killer left her body. The third—Charlestown, ninety-five—was found in a trash Dumpster. And if you notice, both those women were meant to be found. All of the sites, in fact, have some aspect of publicity about them. Whereas in Sconset the effort seems to have been one of *hiding* the crime. That's true whether those bones were moved or not."

"Which we'll probably never know."

"Oh, I wouldn't say that," Enright replied. "Any forensic anthropologist worth his salt should be able to tell you if your bones were moved. They would show the presence of two different soils, for instance, or of irregular bleaching where parts of the bones might have been exposed to sunlight in a way that was impossible under all that sand."

"If the bones were moved, it would solve one of my problems," Merry mused. "I've been wondering why no clothing was found. It seemed too improbable that it had entirely disintegrated."

"Unless she was buried in the nude."

"Well, of course. I'd ignored that possibility."

Enright signaled the waitress. "Could I get a beer? One of those Nantucket Amber Ales? The real point, Detective, is that regardless of whether your bones began or ended in that spot on the Sconset beach, I doubt they fit the pattern of my killings. My killer isn't the type to leave a corpse hidden long enough for himself—or someone else—to rebury it. The element of secrecy your witness is describing is utterly lacking from the serial pattern. Why bury the body at all? Why not just leave the Sconset victim sitting on a lifeguard chair with a whistle around her neck? You see what I mean? Oh, great—" Enright broke off as the waitress approached with their food and the beer. "I'm starving. They didn't even hand out peanuts on that plane."

Merry waited while he tucked into the lobster roll, her spoon toying with the chowder and her eyes flicking up to the psychiatrist's face. Weathered and tanned, probably from too much golf; but oddly youthful, all the same. Enright was nothing that she had expected. A warm man, and a rather modest man, considering his achievements; but something in his eager rush of conversation, the sharing of his theories, suggested he was also a lonely man. Working too hard to have time for a life.

"So were these women sexually assaulted?" she asked finally.

"Oh, yeah," he replied, swallowing. "Most of them, we think, were strangled in the act. And the killer took a trophy—a hunk of hair cut off at the scalp. But that sort of thing is par for the course."

A golf metaphor, Merry thought.

"How do you do this?" she asked abruptly. "Visit murder sites and then chow down on lobster?"

Enright paused, his blue eyes on her face. "The same way you order soup, I guess."

"That's not what I meant."

He toyed with a half-eaten french fry, then set it back on his plate. "Everyone in law enforcement has to cultivate a certain distance from his or her work. That must be something you've learned over the years—particularly living here, where every victim could be someone you know."

"Or nearly."

"And when something awful happens to one of them," Enright posited, "a wall comes down, right?"

"No," Merry said, thinking of her friend Del, murdered the previous summer. "A wound opens. But I suppose your work is very different from mine."

"Not at the moment." Enright looked slightly puzzled.

"This murder aside," Merry said, searching for the

right words, "Nantucket is utterly distinct from most places in New England. Probably from most places in the world."

"It's caught in a time warp, I'll tell you that." Enright was looking for the ketchup. Merry placed it wordlessly next to his plate. "Thank you. I mean, all these gray-shingled cottages straight out of the last century. The cobblestones. No traffic lights, even. It's like living in Disneyland. How do you stand it?"

Merry laughed incredulously. "I wouldn't live anywhere else. There's a civility here that goes bone-deep."

"Particularly in Sconset."

"Oh, *very funny.*" She set down her soup spoon. "I suppose it's difficult for you to understand—because you choose to immerse yourself in an utterly different world. Different values."

"I do?" Enright looked at her coolly, with the faintest suggestion of derision. "And how would you know the slightest thing about my values?"

Merry felt her face flush. "I'm sorry. You're right, I don't know you at all."

"But you've made some pretty strong assumptions. Based on what—my clothes? My hair? My curriculum vitae?"

Merry tugged her blond bangs testily. "All right. *Yes.* Your curriculum vitae. I've never read a worse litany of perversion and smut in my entire life. How do you exist in the midst of so much evil? How do you *immerse* yourself in it, every day, and stay sane?"

She had spoken with more heat than she'd intended, and there was an awkward silence.

"Forgive me," Enright said slowly, "but I'm not entirely sure how to answer that. I'm struggling not to find it naive."

"Naive?" Merry bridled. "I think it's an honest question."

"But for someone working a murder investigation in the 1990s, it's rather singular." He pushed his ravaged plate aside. "I spend my life trying to put some very nasty people away for crimes I know they committed. And murder isn't nice, Meredith. It's ugly. It's unforgettable. It's the jagged line between the animal and the insane. And it brings people like us closer to the horrific in ourselves than most people will ever go. If you haven't learned that, I'd say you're not working hard enough."

"Now who's making assumptions?"

"I don't have to. I'm a psychiatrist. I know how your mind works just from talking to you."

Merry's mouth tightened. "Are you trying to scare me?"

"No. I'm trying to explain myself to someone who thinks I speak a different language." Enright threw up his hands in exasperation. "Look. Maybe I do. I live in the city, and I face the darker side of human existence every day. You grew up *here*, right?"

"Yes," Merry said grudgingly.

"Aside from a few years on the Cape and at the police academy, a stint in New Bedford, you've been working for Daddy and the neighbors for most of your life."

Apparently the DA had told Enright more about Merry than she had realized.

"You go to the beach, buy attractive clothes in expensive shops; you eat at great restaurants with million-dollar views. You'll probably marry some sweet guy with a trust fund and set about having little blond kids. Somewhere inside, I think you've probably got a lot of strength—you're a police officer, after all—but in a way, Meredith Folger, you're living in fantasyland. How many murders happen on this island, anyway?"

"There have been only two in the past three years, thank God," Merry said evenly.

"Right! And you probably knew both victims!"

"Is that a sin?"

"It's nothing like reality," Enright said, grimly. "Reality is a Mack truck careening out of control. And playing *Let's Pretend We're Safe and Happy* is not going to help you in the slightest when you're right in the middle of that truck's path."

"Okay." Merry crossed her arms as though she felt a cold draft. "That's one view. It doesn't happen to be mine. You're welcome to focus on the harsher aspects—the violence, the loss, the inexplicable ruin. I prefer to think about the vast majority of people who lead ordered, uneventful, and, yes—*happy*—lives. That's what I aspire to."

"What are you so afraid of, Meredith?" Enright asked her gently. "Why is it so necessary to stick your head in the sand?"

"Dr. Enright—"

"Tucker."

"Tucker." Merry drew a deep breath, torn between resentment and the need to explain herself. "Call it fear, if you like. Call it avoidance. The fact is that violence disturbs me deeply. Violence, and the wanton ruin of human life. But I don't think that affects my work as a police officer—if anything, it makes me more dedicated."

"Does it?" Enright's expression was sardonic. "A dedicated woman wouldn't have left New Bedford. That's where dedication is needed."

"Bullshit," Merry said succinctly. "There have been Folgers on Nantucket for over three hundred years. I live here because it's my home. But you have to look beyond the gray-shingled cottages, Tucker, to understand the life of the place. A seasonal economy makes for some tough times— and that means drugs, domestic abuse, petty crime. And occasional nasty incidents—like the teenager who burned down our AIDS hospice. But we get over them. We hold a fund-raiser and rebuild the hospice. We volunteer at the battered women's shelter and the retirement home. That's involvement, not escape. And it's nothing I'm ever going to apologize for."

"Okay." Enright sat back in his chair, his hands spread in truce. "I'm probably out of line. You go on fighting your way, and I'll fight mine."

"I would think you'd say *fighting* doesn't pay," Merry shot back. "That it doesn't do any good."

"Oh, no," Enright said softly. "It's the only thing that makes life bearable. I like to see the suckers pay. And pay, and pay, and *pay*."

The vehemence behind the muted words silenced her. Merry looked down at her chowder, cooling unattractively now, the small squares of potato and leek bobbing whitely against the cream.

"There is evil in the world, though we've forgotten to call it by its name," Enright continued softly. "*Evil*. And it grows more unmanageable, Detective, the further we stray from the natural world."

"And yet you indict me for living here," Merry said wearily, "one of the most natural places on earth."

Enright exploded. "Oh, for heaven's sake! You call designer showplaces and antique shops *natural*? You're not even *trying* to understand. Nantucketers think they can recapture the past, when in fact it's irretrievably lost. You hide in a replica of the nineteenth century here, driving a car without the benefit of a traffic light. I recognize that for the ridiculous compromise—the futility—it is."

Merry studied him quizzically. "What could Nantucket's building codes possibly have to do with serial killers, Tucker?"

"Look at us." Enright's voice had risen slightly, so that the idle waitress started and turned her head in the direction of their table. "We're on the threshold of the twenty-first century. For hundreds of years we existed in a world lit only by fire. A world where good and evil contested daily for the souls of men and women. Where salvation was possible, yes, but damnation was understood. Where crimes had a terrible retribution. Where to be *cast out* was to lose one's identity." He balled up his napkin and thrust it toward his discarded plate. "Now if you commit a crime, you simply trade one community—the street— for the same community behind bars. There's no loss involved in evil. No stigmatization, no mantle of shame, no setting apart. And so evil has become banal."

"Are you talking about religion, Doctor?" Merry asked.

Dismissively, Enright waved a hand. "We've worked the notion of God and the Antichrist out of our vocabularies, Meredith. I don't feel strongly one way or the other about that—but I recognize its effect on the human psyche. We think now almost solely in technological terms. We *expect* order from our existence. But evil—evil is utterly chaotic. No amount of technology can suppress it. Because it comes from *within*."

"I think that's why it terrifies me," Merry said slowly. "The thought that such demons are part of us. That, and the very randomness of violence . . . the way it strikes without warning, without reason."

"Some would argue that we only *perceive* it as unreasoning," Enright observed, and his body relaxed, his vehemence fading. "I'm sure our serial killer, for example, has a very clear idea about his visitations of violence, and his choice of victims. It's anything but random to him. But that wasn't your point—you were really talking about yourself. And I think you know yourself rather well: your desire for control, and your panic when it's taken out of your hands."

He signaled the waitress for the check, and with something like relief (had the woman been listening to them, Merry wondered?) she hurried over to place it in Enright's outstretched palm. Before he could take it, Merry handed the woman a twenty-dollar bill.

"Of course," he continued, smiling, "it's only an illusion that we ever *have* control in the first place. All of us like to pretend."

Merry swallowed and looked away, exhausted by the psychiatrist's probing; abruptly, she felt very much alone. She closed her eyes, and Peter Mason's face rose clearly in her mind.

"You remind me quite strongly of my sister, as she was just before she died," Enright said quietly.

Merry's eyes flew open.

"The same hair. The same openness and fear."

"I—your sister—died?"

"She was murdered, actually."

"I'm so sorry." Inadequate words, as always. Any antagonism Merry might have felt—any defensiveness at Enright's too-penetrating brain—faded and was instantly forgotten. "When?"

"Years ago, when I was a kid. She was about twenty."

"May I ask what happened?"

He looked at her, looked away. "Someone stabbed her thirty-three times and left her in the tall grass down by the river of the town I lived in. Paterson, New Jersey. You know it?"

Merry shook her head.

"They say it used to be a nice town. That must have been in the last century." He glanced out at the water. "One night Jen went to work—she dished ice cream at Howard Johnson's—and she just never came back."

"How awful," Merry murmured.

Enright shrugged. "My dad figured she'd left us and run off to New York—my mother had done the same thing a few years before. He didn't look for Jen very hard. But I did. I was never done looking. Every blond head on every street corner might have been her."

"When was she found?"

"Over two years later. In the spring. A fisherman and a dog—the canine with the bone again." A faint smile flickered over the psychiatrist's face. "Nothing of Jen at all, by that time. Just bones in a blue-and-orange-checked uniform."

Merry was silent a moment. "Was anyone ever charged?"

Enright's gaze shifted from the sea beyond the window, found Merry's face. "Oh, no. No. I said I'd never stopped looking, didn't I?"

Chapter Seven

Chapter Seven

As she drove Tucker Enright to the airport for his return flight that afternoon, Merry was surprised by a sensation of regret. She hardly knew the man, and given his conclusions about the Sconset bones, their paths were unlikely to cross again. But something about him—the swift intellect and the unstudied charm, the way he had seen distinctly through her—had caught her off guard. Perhaps she had affected him the same way. She doubted that he confided the nature of his sister's death to every casual stranger. And so they said their good-byes awkwardly, with an enforced lightness, and the psychiatrist hurried across the macadam to the waiting plane, his golf magazine furled under one sweatered arm.

At the rotary, Merry glanced at her watch, considered the approaching weekend and the heaviness of her mood, and turned her Explorer resolutely away from town. She needed to see Peter.

She drove back along Milestone Road toward Sconset, then turned abruptly into the moors, following a half-hidden sandy track that led to Altar Rock. At ninety feet above sea level, this was one of the higher points on the island; but Merry did not stop tonight to perch on the flat monolith, or search for a distant water view. Instead, she followed the bumpy road until she came to a three-way fork, and chose the right-hand turning to Mason Farms.

The scrub oak and pine, the humped shapes of rose-bush and bramble, the low-running heather and beach plum, were all touched with the first gentle brush of green—a color so transparent and vivid, it seemed almost superimposed on the twisting stems. Every March, Merry found it hard to believe spring had ever existed, or could ever come again; and like a miracle, each May the colors stole over the moors and the gardens of town, sprang up in the marshes and the pines along the roadsides, as inevitable and quiet as the breath of Life itself.

Did Tucker Enright enjoy the onset of spring? Or did it bring to mind unspeakable thoughts, the ghost of the long-dead Jen?

She pulled her car to a halt before the Mason Farms gate, remembering as always her first sight of Peter's domain, in the early-morning fog of a Labor Day weekend two years past. The body of his brother had lain dead in the cranberry bogs already flooded for an early harvesting. Now the sturdy vines branched tentatively green in the spring sunlight. In another month the sunken fields running along either side of the drive would be aflutter with pinkish white, those wind-tossed cranberry blooms so reminiscent of a crane's dancing head. Merry loved this spot almost more than any other on the island—more than Tattle Court, or the empty track of Madaket beach, or the jumble of houses that marked the comforting closeness of town. Peter's world was one of privilege and peace, an oasis of natural perfection; and she refused to apologize to Tucker Enright for choosing to bury herself in it.

Tucker Enright again. She was *not* going to obsess about the man for the entire weekend.

But he was a curious personality—complex, challenging, and ultimately disturbing, both in the darkness of his vision and the brutal truth that lay behind it. His thoughts were like bulletins from another country, a place she had never seen; and for a moment Merry gave way to restlessness. An islander, after all, no matter how fulfilled by her island, lives a life defined by its limits.

She jumped out of the car and pulled open the gate, careful to close it behind her once the Explorer had negotiated the entrance. A few of Peter's sheep might still be lambing, and though the dog Ney was alert to the hazard of strays, even he was a poor match for an expectant ewe determined to bear her young in private. An open gate was an invitation to wander.

Peter was nowhere in sight as Merry pulled up to the old saltbox's door. But Rafe da Silva called to her from the neighboring barn and emerged into the long afternoon sunlight with a bandaged arm and chaff in his dark beard.

"What happened to you?" Merry asked, concerned.

Rafe shrugged. "Hooked myself on a hay fork. Don't ask." He leaned forward and hugged her briefly. "How're things?"

"Let's just say I could use a drink. Where's Peter?"

"Gone into town. Which I was just about to do myself." Since his marriage to Tess Starbuck the previous July, Rafe had worked Peter's farm only during the day. He lived now in town, over Tess's restaurant, The Greengage.

"I thought you were stuck here," Merry said. "Until the sheep are done lambing."

"They are. The last one dropped yesterday afternoon—and hallelujah, Mere. I'm ready for a weekend."

"Is Peter on call, then?"

"Pete's always on call," Rafe replied, grinning, "and he's always on vacation. I've got Will coming out in the morning to tend the sheep—earns the kid a few bucks and gives the rest of us a break. Peter's spent more nights in the lambing pen lately than either of us cares to think about."

"Then I'm glad I kept to my rule." The one that forbade her to see Peter during the work week.

"Why don't you head inside? Door's open," Rafe said with a wave toward the saltbox. "Get Rebecca to uncork a bottle of wine. Make her join you. She'll be scandalized—and she does so enjoy that."

Peter's Quaker housekeeper, Rebecca, was an island native like Merry and Rafe. Rebecca adored Merry, but she never drank.

"I'll do that," Merry said, smiling, and as Rafe turned to walk away, she called after him, "Give my love to Tess and Will."

"Come by The Greengage over the weekend," he shot back over his shoulder. "It's high time Pete took you out to dinner."

"Is Tess open for business?" Merry asked, surprised.

"For you? Always." Rafe swung himself into the driver's seat of his truck and waved. Merry waved back and wondered at the elasticity of the human heart. There was a time when the thought of Rafe returning to the home of another woman—and that woman his *wife*—would have been the source of unbearable pain. But Peter Mason had overlaid every other passion in Meredith's life; she recognized and accepted that, though she feared its ultimate effect. The possibility that Peter would tire of her ordinariness—her island background, her lack of education, the disparity in their experience—was a constant shadow in the corner of her mind. She dreaded Peter's loss the way she feared the death of Ralph Waldo, or of her father, or the sudden intervention of violence.

As she had begun to explain to Tucker Enright.

Rafe roared off down the driveway; Merry pressed her

closed eyelids with a forefinger and thumb. Tucker Enright seemed to find fear degrading. He seemed, in fact, not to comprehend it. And so, Merry decided, he must never have loved anyone deeply; for love was a prerequisite to the kind of fear Merry felt. Love made possible the devastation of loss. Or perhaps that devastation had touched the psychiatrist too closely—his sister's brutal murder?—and he had decided that pain was stronger than love could ever be. Hence the absorption in golf, to the exclusion of kids, wife, lover, or alternative orientation. A mistake he was long past remedying.

Merry had known enough tragedy—her brother's death in Viet Nam, her mother's suicide a few months later, the murder of her childhood friend Del Duarte only last summer—but every loss left her more thankful for the people who remained to sustain her. Was that merely a fantasy? A way of living a lie?

The sound of approaching tires pulled her head around, and with a quickening of her heart Merry saw Peter's red Range Rover rocking its way along the drive. She raised one arm in greeting, and he thrust an answering hand from the driver's window. She shivered slightly and glanced skyward. Clouds were gathering to the east; they would have a day of rain and fog tomorrow, not altogether a bad thing for a lazy April Saturday. Because the lambing was over, Peter would be catching up on sleep. Perhaps she would stay here tonight, and spend the morning reading on the sofa before a good fire, and take a long ramble through the bogs with Ney in the afternoon, holding Peter's hand. They would eat Rebecca's chowder. Or her bean soup, if she had made it this week.

The vision was rendered more wistful, more compelling, because Merry knew it was completely out of reach: her Saturday was preordained. She would be in the station attempting to make sense of the Sconset murder.

The fact that the case was hardly a case until the bones were identified had never really mattered. And now there was Mabel Johnson's testimony to consider. Merry could hardly prove that Mabel had witnessed the bones' reburial, but neither could she ignore the possibility. She would send her interview report to Bill Carmichael, the head of the state-police force on Nantucket, tomorrow morning. Tucker Enright might still have doubts that Manuel Esconvidos was the serial killer, but the state police were unlikely to free the suspect on the basis of gut instinct. And they might want to check Esconvidos's whereabouts on the night of the big blizzard, January 7.

The Rover came to a halt next to Merry, and she smiled.

"Hello, stranger," Peter said, switching off the ignition. "I was hoping you'd materialize out of the moors and the mist." He jumped out of the car and enfolded her in a hug, one hand still clutching a brown bag full of groceries. "Take-out," he said in answer to her inquiring look. "From The Greengage. Which means it's anything but take-out."

"I'm famished." Merry grabbed his arm with both hands like an eager child, suddenly aware of a bottomless hunger.

"Let's see," he said, unfurling the bag's edge and staring into its depths as he steered her toward the cottage door. "Sliced warm duck breast and chèvre over baby greens. Scallops with cherry tomatoes, corn, and bacon; roast rosemary potatoes on the side. Apple crisp. I'm afraid you'll have to do without the usual toppings of cinnamon ice cream or crème fraîche; they don't travel well. And a nice little bottle of sauvignon blanc. Tess sends her love."

Merry had barely tasted the Second Story's chowder a few hours earlier, so engrossed in conversation had she been; and her spirits rose now at Peter's recitation of the evening menu. "Not bad, only you're supposed to preface it all with 'Good evening, I'm Peter, and I'll be your waiter tonight.' And where's the bow tie and butcher's apron?"

"In the car," he said contritely. "Only it's a little French maid's outfit, complete with garters."

Merry stepped into the dusky foyer and heard the sounds of a fire crackling in Peter's study down the hall; and without quite realizing it she gave a sigh of happiness. "I was dying to be coddled tonight, which is of course why my car brought me here."

"Bad day?" Peter said over his shoulder as he disappeared through the door to the kitchen.

"Let's just call it challenging."

Peter reemerged almost immediately, with the aforementioned wine, a corkscrew, and two glasses. "Rebecca's got the food in hand, so let's head for the fire. It's still winter out here when the sun goes down."

"Can we eat in front of it? Please?"

"We can eat *in* it, if that's likely to help." He threw himself into his favorite armchair and brushed a hand through his dark hair. The gray eyes, which had been dancing as he'd ticked off The Greengage's menu, were steady now and somber as they took in Merry's face. "So you had a lousy day. Those bones again?"

"Sort of." Merry sank into the chintz sofa and kicked off her shoes. "God, this is wonderful. I know I probably spend too much time retreating, Peter—I've made a habit of sticking my head in the sand, I suppose—but it's such a relief, sometimes!"

He snorted. "You're the last person in the world who retreats, Detective. Who's been handing you that nonsense? Not your father, I hope?"

"Hardly. Peter—I don't know what I would do without you." The words sounded more plaintive, more tinged with regret, than she had intended. Tucker Enright's shadow was a little too long.

"And is that suddenly a bad thing?" he asked quietly.

"Oh, I don't know." Merry shrugged elaborately, as though all her tension and doubt lived in her shoulders, and looked away from him, toward the flames. "I spent hours today with an FBI expert, a psychiatrist, in fact—

and he told me some things I probably didn't want to hear. About the way I live."

The cork came out of the wine bottle with a delicate *pop!* and Peter reached for a glass. "And is it because he's an FBI expert, or a psychiatrist, that you took his opinions so seriously?"

"Maybe it was the tenure at Harvard Medical School."

"He sounds formidable."

"He was . . . very interesting."

Peter's eyes narrowed. "And what was so august a personage doing on Nantucket?"

"Visiting Sconset. To see if it fits the serial pattern."

"What serial pattern?"

"Peter! I almost forgot!" Merry took the glass from Peter's outstretched hand. "The Barnstable DA called this morning. Boston thinks they have a suspect in custody responsible for the murders of five women. The bones in Sconset may be a sixth. So Enright flew over to look at the scene. Only he thinks that probably it *doesn't* fit the pattern, so we're right back where we started."

"Enright is the psychiatrist?"

"Right."

"Since when are psychiatrists attached to law enforcement?"

"The FBI, actually."

"FBI? On Nantucket?"

"I know. We've hit the big time."

"If that's the big time, I prefer my times small."

"Peter," Merry said tentatively, "do you ever think of moving to the mainland?"

"Never. I grew up there."

"I know. Don't you miss it?"

"Only at Christmas. Department-store windows, and the tree at Thirty Rock, the bustle of crowds bundled up against the snow." Comprehension dawned on his face. "Is that what this is all about? A yen for a Manhattan weekend?"

"More escapism." Merry set down her glass impatiently.

"Sometimes I wonder if my life is too safe. Or too comfortable. If I consciously avoid the edge. You know?"

"No," he replied. "I don't. I think you manage to walk the knife quite steadily in your pursuit of sundry murderers. But this psychiatrist clearly made you think otherwise."

"Well—" She hesitated. How to explain Tucker Enright to Peter? It was Peter, after all, who had once tried to heal a wounded heart by retreating to the moors for ten years. He was hardly the type to recognize avoidance when he saw it. "Enright spends his life in the study of serial killers," she attempted. "He takes on a terrible load of darkness, I think, in order to put these killers away. And he saw that his way of life scared me. He challenged me to ask myself *why*."

"I see." Peter was still frowning. "And what did you answer yourself?"

"That I'm something of a coward," Merry admitted grudgingly. "I call myself a police officer, but I'm so happy in my life that I'm desperate to keep violence completely out of it."

"Any sane person would be."

"There's sanity, and there's sanity. I learned that today."

"From Enright." Peter snorted. "Merry, Merry. You care about your work. And you work hard. The fact that this island isn't a welter of violence and pain is irrelevant. You help maintain the quality of life for a lot of good people."

"But don't you think it would be more admirable to work in a place that *really* needs me? New Bedford, for instance . . . or Fall River?"

"Or Sarajevo. Right. You're hitting yourself over the head for nothing. But that's completely like you."

She looked at him, considering, and then sighed deeply. "Now I've got you depressed. I guess we know it's Friday. The one day of the week I unload all my troubles."

Peter reached for her right foot. "Drink your wine," he

said, "and try to relax. Those bones may have nothing to do with the serial pattern."

"Enright *says* they don't. Will you rub my feet?"

"I will. But first I have a proposition for you."

"Oh, goody." Merry's face lit up.

"Let's slip off to the *Wayward* after dinner. Head heedlessly out to sea. You could do with a break."

"I could?"

"Trust me."

"And is this a break," Merry argued, beginning to smile, "or mere avoidance of life's pressures?"

"It's avoidance only on Monday morning."

"I seem to remember your propositioning me in a like fashion just last weekend," she observed.

"You turned me down, if you recall."

"And I'm turning you down again," she said, with rather more disappointment this time.

"Don't tell me you think it's going to rain," Peter protested. "I have it on good authority. The coast guard says these evening clouds are exactly that—*evening* clouds—and that by morning we'll have a fair wind and bright sunshine. Perfect spring cruising weather." He leaned forward in his chair and gripped her toes. "You can bring bulky sweaters. Foul weather gear for the spray. We'll drink hot soup out of a thermos and roar into the troughs of the waves. I'll make Patrick let you hold the wheel. Come on, Mere."

"Where do you want to go?"

"Anywhere you like. Just name your destination. The *Wayward* is standing by in the harbor."

Merry hesitated. All at once the allure of escape seemed overwhelming; it drowned out the voice of Dr. Tucker Enright and his admonitory words. What could she *really* do with Mabel Johnson's information? Once she passed on the fact of the midnight burial, dubious though it was, to the state police, her obligation ended. A message for Seitz would be adequate; he could send over her witness report the next morning.

The mingled smells of duck and scallops and bacon filtered into the room. Rebecca was very busy. And the fire was very bright. Merry thought of the swift plunge of a seagoing vessel, the creak of the canvas as it got under way, past the harbor's jetties and its dangerous shoals; and she stretched her arms high over her head with the deepest of sighs.

"Let's head south," she said decisively. "Block Island. Shelter Island. Something like that. The waters of your childhood."

"Done." Peter raised his glass in salute. "And Dr. Enright be damned."

Saturday, as Peter had predicted, dawned brilliantly sunny. Merry awakened early, her thoughts only slightly befuddled by the strangeness of the teak cabin bunk, the sloping walls of the hull, and the *Wayward*'s pendular rocking. They were cocooned in blankets in the triangular space at the bow, and Merry raised herself on one elbow and eased open the cabin door to peer aft into the boat's interior. Patrick's cook—a young woman named Alice—was bent over the oven. The smell of coffee was tantalizing, and from the deck above, someone was whistling disjointedly. A slight breeze rattled in the rigging.

Merry crept over Peter's sleeping form, shrugged herself into her sweats and a windbreaker, and found her way to the coffeepot bubbling quietly on the stove.

"Sleep well?" Alice discarded a pot holder and brushed a strand of loose blond hair up into her neat bun.

"Like a log. I'm still groggy."

"It's the waves," the girl replied. "That cradling motion. Like being back in utero." She reached for a mug and poured Merry some coffee. "Milk is in the fridge."

For an antique boat the *Wayward* had a remarkably up-to-date galley. It showed the effects of love and money. Patrick had lavished both on his sloop, having lost his wife—the previous claimant to Patrick's expenses and affections—in a nasty divorce four years earlier. From Peter, Merry had learned that the skipper had spent his first life doing mergers and acquisitions in Manhattan. His second life had begun when Shelley had walked out the door. Now for nine months of every year Patrick O'Donnell lived as his wife would never have allowed him—on the *Wayward*. From January to March, he did contract work long-distance for his old law firm, sleeping in a one-room guest cottage attached to a Cliff Road mansion.

Peter had also told Merry that the Cliff Road house once belonged to Patrick. Now it was Shelley's summer home.

Merry found the milk, lightened her coffee to a pale brown, and tore herself away from the banana-walnut scent of the muffins Alice was baking. With her free hand, balancing the coffee mug carefully in the other, she pulled herself up the gangway and through the hatch.

"Cap'n O'Donnell!"

"Grand morning, isn't it?"

The sunlight dazzled Merry's eyes, but the air off the water was rather more brisk than she had expected. The *Wayward*'s skipper sported a ski hat on his blond head, and the hands wrapped around his coffee were reddened by wind and sea. She took a sip from her mug and sighed appreciatively, huddling near the wheel.

"You're up early," Patrick said. He was gazing southwest, toward the low outline of houses on Tuckernuck Island. Most were uninhabited in winter. In summer the homes were reachable only by boat or plane. Looking at the distant faces of the quiet cottages basking in isolated sun, Merry thought incongruously of fire. Tuckernuck's houses were a constant worry for the Nantucket fire department. If a blaze broke out, the chance of ferrying an engine and men across the watery gap in time to save anything was dicey at best.

The *Wayward* had not progressed very far the previous evening, Patrick being less than easy about the portent of the clouds, and his passengers more than happy to drop

anchor off Muskeget Island, the small fishhead of land
trailing sandily beyond Tuckernuck. They had donned
warm sweaters and placed a ship's lantern near the
wheel, opened a bottle of wine and listened to twenty
years' worth of Patrick's sailing stories.

"You were up even earlier," Merry said to him now,
"and had the good sense to get Alice baking."

"I never miss watching the sun rise over the water," the
skipper replied. "Too much of a gift, on a day like this. Alice
is the same way. BJ, now"—BJ was Patrick's first mate—
"he'll be snoring until I call him to up-anchor."

Merry nodded, feeling herself a part of the swell as it
lifted the ship, and studied the choppy blue-green water.
She licked her finger and lifted it to the wind, as she had
seen countless mariners do; but the gesture told her
nothing.

"Wind's blowing from the west," Patrick said, observing her, "but it'll shift to the north in another few hours.
We'll have a stiff breeze to our backs by the time we head
for Rhode Island."

"How do you know?" Merry asked, impressed.

"Listened to the weather report on the radio," he
replied cheerfully, and ducked down the hatch in pursuit
of muffins.

A few hours later—perhaps eight-thirty or so—Peter
and BJ and the rest of Patrick's five-man crew had joined
the companionable group in the cockpit and consumed
the last of Alice's superb breakfast. The anchor was
weighed, the multitude of sails unfurled in the tall ship's
complicated rigging, and the *Wayward* came around and
headed into the wind. They slipped south past Tuckernuck and Madaket, the sunlight rippling in a wide band
of brilliance before them, as though laying a carpet for
the ship to tread. Merry's hands gripped the starboard
rail, and her knees were slightly bent, anticipating the
Wayward's pitch; but the schooner's keel was slicing

cleanly through the waves. The port rail was breathlessly low to the water.

"You were right," she told Peter, who sat close beside her, his dark hair ruffled by wind. "I needed to get away. This is marvelous."

"And you can feel *good* about it. We purchased Patrick to benefit a charity. No escapism there. Civic duty. The grim reality of domestic abuse. Your friendly psychiatrist can rest easy."

"I suppose," Merry said doubtfully, "but I feel rather bad for Patrick all the same. Here he is, paying his crew and losing his weekend, and he's not getting a dime." Patrick had donated the *Wayward* trip to the Nantucket Experiences Auction.

"Tell you what," Peter said. "We'll hire him properly for another weekend when we get back. At exorbitant summer rates. Happy?"

"No." Merry shook her head firmly. "That would *definitely* fall into the category of self-indulgent fantasy seeking. Tucker Enright would *not* approve."

"Hey," Peter said, shrugging his shoulders. "Your fantasy is Patrick's livelihood. The more we escape, the more likely he is to keep body and soul together. Not to mention hold on to this boat. Consider it charity of another kind."

"I'll consider it," Merry replied, "after I consider Alice's cooking. I'm ravenous."

"It's only nine o'clock."

"Some of us—the ones who awoke responsibly early— ate breakfast three hours ago."

"Poor planning. If I know Patrick, we're not stopping for lunch. You'll have to sneak below and rifle that fancy fridge."

"Ralph Waldo has a theory," Merry mused, "that the only true way to avoid seasickness is to eat constantly while on board."

The tip of Nantucket was just appearing off the port side, but Merry ignored the sight of Sconset on a

Saturday morning and pulled herself into a crouch. Holding the starboard rail for support, she eased herself along the deck, intent upon food.

"Go ahead and sneak," Peter said remorsefully. "Me, I have an iron stomach."

"Peter!" Merry gripped his arm suddenly, and he swung around anxiously to follow her gaze. She was shading her eyes with her free hand, an expression of amazement on her face. "Those are *kids* in that boat!"

"What boat?"

"That little dory! Don't tell me you can't see it—look!"

Peter narrowed his eyes and looked.

The small craft was painted dark green, the color of the waves tossing at its bow and tripping up its stern; a dory, as Merry had said, with no motor in sight and what, at this distance, seemed to be only one oar. Two tiny figures huddled together amidships, featureless across five hundred yards; but despite the intervening stretch of rough water, Peter could see they were underdressed for the coldness of the wind and the spray. Were they indeed children? Or simply nautical innocents bowed down by the terror of their drifting oblivion? As he watched, a particularly high whitecap tore at the gunwales, drenching the forlorn crew. They were headed for the shallower water over Old Man Shoal, but even there the sea was too deep to ground the hull of their little boat. Without assistance they might drift for days.

"Patrick!" Peter called into the wind. The skipper, whose eyes were trained on the horizon, looked up inquiringly. O'Donnell had exchanged the wool hat for a broad-billed swordfisher's cap, but his cheeks were chapped red with wind. He held a hand behind his ear in a mute appeal for more sound.

Peter jumped down and worked his way carefully to the wheel. "Looks like we've got an emergency to starboard. There's a dory out there with a lost oar and a pretty sorry-looking crew."

"They're not sorry-looking," Merry protested. "They're kids."

"You're sure?" Peter asked her. Merry's eyes were better than his.

"Positive," she answered. "I'd know them anywhere. It's Cecil Markham and his sister, Nan."

Chapter Eight

Lord Cecil of Trevarre—rear admiral of the Royal Navy's Mediterranean Fleet—had never been in quite so precarious a position.

He tore his gaze away from the battered remains of his crew, the tattered remnants of his sails, and stared out over the roiling waves. His sleek frigate Victory *had braved her fortunes in battle and triumphed after three nights and a day; but the cost was high. The foremast had fallen to the last wild shot of an enemy cannon, as the broken French ship sank beneath the waves; and now, too many leagues from a friendly—*

"Cecil," Nan said faintly, "I think there's a ship."

"A ship?" He stared about him wildly and saw it: a shining wooden vessel, like something straight out of Nelson's navy, with its square-rigged sails hanging slackly now that her captain had turned her out of the wind. The worried faces of several adults were craning in the bow. But was it French or English?

"Cecil! Cecil Markham!"

The voice was a woman's, and as Cecil stared up at the approaching schooner, which seemed to be approaching somewhat *quickly* for his ungovernable dory, he recognized her. The detective lady, Meredith Folger. Relief—unspoken, half-acknowledged, and so overwhelming it brought tears to his eyes—swept upward from his very toes. It was followed just as swiftly by fear. If the police were here in their special boat, his mother must already know.

"Miss Folger!" Nan cried out beside him, leaping up with a glad wave of her hand; and at that moment the dory pitched into a trough. Nan lost her balance and toppled overboard under Cecil's nose. He lurched toward the gunwales, his mouth open in a despairing wail, as pandemonium broke loose on the approaching ship.

Nan's bright-red head rose briefly above the swell; the horrified watchers saw her bewildered eyes; and then a crest broke over her and she was gone.

Cecil reached toward where his sister had been. There was nothing but water.

Pure terror rushed over him with sickening force, and he fell back into the bottom of the boat. Nannie would die, just like his dad, and it would be all his fault. He ought to save her—ought to throw himself into the churning waves—but the sight of the ocean, heaving and deadly, paralyzed him. He forced himself into a crouch by the oarlock, scanning the water for a glimpse of Nan's head. Only a chaos of green water. It had sucked her down, gasping and choking, frantic for the salvation of air—and he had done nothing. He *must* move. Must go after her, whether it killed him or not. Cecil closed his eyes and drew a quick breath, steeling himself for the dreadful plunge.

"Cecil!" Merry Folger's voice cut through his feverish thoughts. "Don't move! We're coming!"

There was a loud splash, and Cecil looked over his

shoulder. A dark head was plowing through the waves toward his dory.

"*Peter—*"

It seemed a thousand voices cried the name, as all the adults strained over the larger boat's rail, their faces taut with apprehension. A diving arc, like a dolphin's, at the spot where Nan had gone under; and then, for what felt like an endless interval, nothing more.

"That water has to be freezing," Cecil heard the detective mutter anxiously. The boat, which had the name *Wayward* painted flamboyantly along its bowsprit, was drifting toward Cecil's port side. In a few moments he might even touch it as it slipped serenely past. But he barely registered this. For the expression of mingled dread and anguish on Merry Folger's face confirmed his worst fears for Nan. The detective knew it was Cecil's fault, too.

"Pete's got a few minutes." This from a man Cecil did not recognize, a blond-headed, stern-looking sailor whose hands gripped the *Wayward*'s rail. Cecil's stomach clenched. *A few minutes.* And Nan—

But at that moment the curling waves broke more whitely than ever, and Nan's rescuer surged skyward. His lips were the color of a bruise, and he was shuddering visibly from the cold—but his arm was locked around Nan. At the sight of him the blond sailor at the rail called out and heaved a life preserver into the water. Nan's rescuer ignored it, however, and made quickly for Cecil and the dory. The swimmer thrust Nan over the gunwale. Cecil reached for her, terrified that she was dead; and as he did, Nan coughed up a mouthful of seawater and opened her eyes.

"Throw me a line!" her rescuer called to the *Wayward*.

"Get out of the water, you idiot!"

"Just throw me the goddamn line!"

The blond man shook his head but tossed a coil of rope toward Cecil. The dark-haired man caught it and quickly tied what even Cecil knew was a pretty good sailor's knot around the iron ring in the dory's prow. "Hi," he said, looking up at Cecil. "I'm Peter. Take your sweater off and wrap it around your sister, okay?"

Cecil simply stood like a statue, unable to speak or move. Disaster filled his lungs and throat with an aching, fluid pressure.

"Now, pull the dory in!" Peter called, and like everyone, the blond sailor obeyed him. Hand over hand he hauled on the painter, and within minutes the dory bumped against the bigger boat's side. Cecil had just enough presence of mind to fend it off with his shaking hands. Then strong arms reached to pull him aboard, and he sobbed from weakness and relief.

Below him he heard the dark-haired swimmer's labored breathing as he crawled toward safety through the cold springtime Atlantic.

"What did you think you were doing?" Merry Folger asked Cecil, in some exasperation. "Replaying Trafalgar?"

They were sitting companionably in the *Wayward*'s main cabin, making all possible sail for Nantucket Harbor, with cups of steaming hot chocolate prepared by the wonderful Alice. Merry had helped Nan remove her sodden clothing and had wrapped the child in her own oversize sweatshirt, with a pair of thick socks and a blanket for good measure. Cecil still felt peaked and spent; but Nan was holding her mug contentedly enough, as though her brush with a hypothermic death had been nothing more than an August dip in the waves.

"We were running away," she piped up now, oblivious of Cecil's warning look.

"My sister and I did that when we were about your age." This from Peter, who sat across the table. "There was a house we loved across Oyster Bay—we called it the Sultan's Castle, because that's what it looked like—and one morning when we were feeling particularly unappreciated, we took some sandwiches and our dory and set out to join the harem. We had a vague idea they would take children."

"But weren't you really *scared*?" Cecil asked. Fear had seized him from the moment he'd lost the oar, only a few hundred yards offshore; and fear still fluttered like an unquiet bird in the pit of his stomach. He pushed his hot chocolate aside.

"Not at first," Peter told him, "but after a while, when we realized that rowing was hard work and we couldn't quite control the current, things began to seem a bit more complicated. We kept our oars, though, and got farther than you did. It took our folks a couple of hours to catch up with us."

"Were they mad?" Cecil dreaded facing his mother's anger. When it reached a breaking point—as it would when she heard what he'd done—she turned bitter and silent with fury. As though she hated him. As though her life and all its unhappiness were entirely Cecil's fault. One look was like a stab from a knife. *Maybe,* he thought, *if she never wants to see me again, I can stow away on the ferry tonight. Get off when it's safe in Hyannis.*

"They were furious," Peter answered comfortably, bringing him back to the present, "but in that respect, my sister and I weren't as fortunate as you two."

"How come?"

"We faced our parents alone. You, on the other hand, have us." He looked at Merry and smiled.

"Good," Nan said. " 'Cause Mummy's going to *kill* us." And, remarkably, she giggled.

Cecil swallowed hard and looked down at his hands. He'd gnawed his fingernails to the quick. "Maybe she won't have noticed," he suggested faintly. "That we were gone, I mean. Do we have to tell her?"

"I think we do," Merry replied. "I think she ought to know that Nan fell into the water, for one thing, in case Nan gets a bad cold. And I'm sure your mom will have noticed you're missing by now."

"No." Cecil said it decisively. "She never notices anything. 'Specially lately. She just sits in her chair, playing her record and smoking cigarettes. One after the other, like she's eating potato chips. That's why we left," he added falteringly. "She's stopped hearing us when we talk to her. She never answers anymore."

Peter and the detective once again exchanged glances; and Merry gave a small shake of her head.

"Cecil," she asked thoughtfully, "where did you think you were going?"

"To England. To make my fortune."

"Don't you know how far away that is?"

"Of course," he snapped. "I know all about England. I'm English." His shoulders squared and his head came up. "I was looking for a ship. A British one. To pick us up and sail us there."

"I see. So we're taking you in the wrong direction."

"That's okay." Cecil's burst of confidence flagged, and he looked away. "After we lost the oar, I started wondering if it was such a good idea. We were pretty cold and scared. And then when Nan fell in—" He shuddered. "I used to have dreams about it. Drowning. Because of my dad."

"Weren't you very young when he—sank his boat?" Merry asked.

"Three," Cecil replied. "I don't really remember him, except when I'm asleep. Then I see him so clearly, and he's terrible. Sinking, with his hands out like Nan, and I can't reach him. Sometimes he pulls me in after him." He glanced up at Peter, abashed by his own weakness. "You were wonderful out there today. You didn't even think. Or at least you didn't *stop* to think."

"No," Peter said, amused. "Sometimes I manage to do two things at once. But it takes practice."

Cecil studied him with a painful concentration. "And does practice make you brave, too?"

"It doesn't seem like you planned this very well," Merry interposed. "No extra clothes, no food."

"Oh, we *had* food," Nan said. "We just ate it right

away. But I'm glad you found us. I miss Satchmo. Cecil says dogs don't like to travel on boats, so we had to leave him. But he was sad. He came out into the water after us and barked."

"We didn't want to take the clothes in case our mum noticed," Cecil explained. "We told her we'd be playing on the beach."

"What made you decide to take this boat? And *where* did you find it?"

Cecil looked at Nan. "It's been sitting in the dunes at the foot of the bluff for a while," he said in a small voice, "like nobody loved it. So we thought they wouldn't mind."

"I see." They had stolen the dory, probably one belonging to the large summer houses sitting high on the Sconset bluff. "We'll have to make sure the owner gets another oar, okay?"

Cecil nodded. "I was going to pay him back once I made my fortune," he said solemnly.

It was nearly noon by the time they moored the *Wayward*, shipped the dory that had been trailing in its wake, and loaded it onto the roof of Peter's Range Rover. They bundled Nan, still wrapped in her blanket, into the car and headed out of town toward the Milestone road.

The Markhams lived not far from Lenny and Ruth Schwartz, as it happened; on the corner of Jefferson and Codfish Park roads. It was a house, Merry decided, that deserved to sail out to sea in another season's storms, so neglected was its air; but the building was set back far enough on the corner lot that it would probably survive. Merry wished, suddenly, that Mabel Johnson could exchange places with Julia Markham. The elderly woman would have known what to do with the gift of this house, as Cecil's mother clearly did not.

Weeds had submerged what had once been a garden. No Trespassing signs were tacked to the garden gate. The picket fence enclosing the property was dingy with years of exposure to the salty wind and weaved precariously up the path like a misstepping drunkard. At the door climb-ing roses still wrapped a sheltering trellis close, but their canes were dead and lifeless. The house itself might once have been charming—a traditional one-story Sconset cottage, hugging the ground and shingled in gray; but the windowpanes were clouded with dirt, and a number of slats were missing from the shutters.

The haunting strains of a jazz melody filtered from somewhere at the rear of the house. What was it? Famil-iar as an anthem from a vanished age, and yet Merry could not place it.

"Sleeping Beauty," Peter murmured. He was holding the swaddled Nan in his arms, as her tennis shoes were too wet to wear and he refused to let her walk in her bare feet; and for a moment Merry thought he referred to the child. But after a look at Peter, who stood studying the lines of the house wistfully, Merry understood. The Markhams' cottage seemed to have died nearly a decade ago with its owner.

Julia took several minutes to answer Merry's knock. The four of them stood listening to the plaintive record and waiting uneasily.

"Someone sure likes Duke Ellington," Peter observed. "That's 'Mood Indigo.' "

"My dad's favorite song," Cecil offered. "He named his boat after it. Mum plays it over and over until it runs through your head all day long."

Merry knocked again, more forcefully.

"Maybe she's out," Cecil said, despite the music; but now they heard the unmistakable sounds of stirring from within. Cecil edged perceptibly closer to Merry. She took his hand.

"Yes?"

The opening between door and jamb was a matter of inches. Julia stood concealed behind it, as though unwill-ing to admit her existence.

"Mrs. Markham?"

"What do you want?"

"It's Meredith Folger, Nantucket Police."

"Oh, God. The children aren't here." Julia moved as if to shut the door, but Peter's free hand thrust hard against it, forcing it open.

"I'm surprised you have any idea where Cecil and Nan might be," he said harshly. Merry reached involuntarily for his arm, as though to restrain him. Peter rarely lost his temper—but when he did, it could be ugly.

Julia stepped backward into the dimly lit hallway, her hand still firmly on the doorknob, and scowled. "Who the bloody hell are you?"

"Peter Mason. And in case you've forgotten, these are your children."

"Don't tell me you've gone and got yourselves into trouble again!" Julia exclaimed, and clutched at Cecil's shoulders. The boy's pale face drained a shade whiter, and he bit his lips convulsively. "What have you done?" his mother demanded. "Broken a window? Taken something you shouldn't have? Well? Out with it!"

"They were adrift in a borrowed dory," Merry cut in, "about a mile off the Sconset shore."

Julia's face went blank. "How—?"

"We happened to be sailing by and towed them into Nantucket Harbor." Peter said, his anger dissipating. "But your little girl here fell into the Atlantic before we could get to them. She's had a shock and a drenching in water I'd guess to be right around fifty degrees."

At that Julia seemed for the first time to take in her daughter's bedraggled condition—her snarled red curls, the pallor of her face, the unfamiliar blanket Peter held close to her small body.

"Nan!" she said with a rare note of tenderness. "Dear baby Nan!" and she reached out to take the child from Peter's arms. He seemed to give her up unwillingly.

Julia clutched her daughter close, swaying back and forth as she murmured unintelligible words, a strangely agonized expression on her face. And then, as they watched, she crumpled and slid to the doorstep itself, her black head bowed over Nan's shoulder.

"She's all right, Mum," Cecil interposed anxiously. His eyes were enormous in his tense little face. "It was all my fault, but Peter saved her."

"She's not all right," his mother replied bitterly. "We're none of us all right, then, are we?"

Later, after Julia had opened a can of soup and set the children to eating it in her cluttered kitchen, she stood stiffly in the cottage's living room, glaring at Merry and Peter. They had not bothered to take a chair, as there was none available; the room's seating was filled to capacity with stacked books, discarded clothing, and ashtrays brimming with crumpled cigarettes. Many, Merry noticed, had barely been lit before being stubbed into ash. The smell of stale tobacco was overwhelming.

"Tell me what they thought they were doing," Julia said to Merry. "In that boat. Having a lark?"

"They were running away."

Julia's lips tightened. "That bloody Cecil," she said, beginning to pace rapidly in front of her sofa, "and his headful of nonsense."

"I don't think he understood what he was doing," Merry began.

"I did the same thing as a boy," Peter added, "and I can tell you I hadn't the slightest idea of the gravity of my actions. I might have killed my sister, too."

"Oh, my Cecil knew *exactly* what he was doing," Julia spat viciously. "He was getting out. Getting as far away from me as he possibly could. I can't even find it in me to blame him." She came to a sudden halt and looked blankly around. "Now, where the *hell* are my cigarettes?"

"Mrs. Markham—"

"I know what you think." Julia shoved aside a magazine and scrabbled beneath the sofa cushions frantically. Her hands came up with a plastic lighter and a crumpled packet of Camels. "You think I'm an unfit parent."

"I didn't say—"

"You bloody well didn't have to." She wrestled a ciga-rette from the packet and shoved it between her lips. "It's written all over your sanctimonious faces."

"Children don't attempt to run away for no reason." Peter spoke evenly.

"Oh, really? The voice of bloody experience. And what was *your* reason, Mr. Mason? Unhappy at home? Parents at each other's throats? Or was your mother a certified looney, like Cecil's?"

"Insane—or indifferent, Mrs. Markham?" Peter's voice was very quiet, a warning Merry instantly recognized.

"Sometimes I think they're the same," she said curtly, and flicked her lighter. She took a moment to inhale deeply and blew forth a cloud of smoke. "You'd have to be bloody insane to be indifferent to children like mine."

They stood silently for a moment after that.

"Can't we—help you?" Merry asked at last. "Isn't there something we could do?"

"You've done it," Julia replied, with the briefest of smiles and a nervous flicking of her ash. "You've brought my children back when they could be dead in the ocean, like their father. It's a sharp slap across the face when I least expected one." She turned away, as if burned by the flame of her own intimacy, and crossed to the door.

"Now, get out, please," she said as she opened it, and jerked her head to the street. "I feel an almost desperate need to be alone."

"What a bizarre woman," Merry said thoughtfully as she settled herself next to Peter in the Range Rover and glanced back up the path toward the Markhams' door. "She knows what she's doing to those kids, doesn't she?"

"And yet she seems incapable of change," Peter replied. "She's a strange mix of anger and self-absorption."

"And despair. Don't forget the despair. As if she's con-tinuing to exist only through force of habit. Did you no-tice? The house?"

"How could I do otherwise? My God, the way some people live!"

"That's not what I meant."

"I'm forgetting. Tattle Court is hardly a model of order."

"Peter!" Merry exclaimed, hurt. "Tattle Court is absolutely lovely."

"When you've managed to step over the back issues of the *Atlantic* and the *Inky Mirror* stacked in the doorway," he teased.

"At least it's scrupulously clean," Merry argued, "and there's not an ashtray in sight. But I was talking about what *wasn't* there."

"Ah. The curious fact of the dog in the night," Peter said.

"*Incident*, not fact, and it was in the night*time*," Merry said absentmindedly. "There wasn't a stick of sculpture anywhere in the place."

"Sculpture?" Peter's brow knit.

"*Ian Markham*. The man was a fairly significant talent, from everything I've heard. So where's his oeuvre? Where's the shrine to a great life tragically cut short? I didn't even see a snapshot of the happy couple perched on a convenient piano."

"Much less a piano," Peter pointed out helpfully.

"Do you think she's had to sell it all? Could they be that hard up?"

"If she did, she probably made a fortune." Peter downshifted as he slowed to take the Pleasant Street turnoff. They were bound for Tattle Court and a Saturday-night dinner with Merry's family. "Enough to get the house trim painted, at least. There's nothing like death to send an artist's reputation sky-high."

"I wonder how we could find out," Merry mused.

"Nothing easier," Peter said as they drove gingerly through the narrow passage of Hiller Lane. "Just drop by the Markhams and have a spot of tea with Julia."

"Very funny."

"I'm serious." He pulled up before the entrance to Tattle Court off Fair Street. "I know you'll want to check on those kids. Make that an excuse. And then profess an interest in their father's work. Julia's starting to like you."

"Oh, yeah. About as much as she likes a visitation of the plague," Merry shot back, and thrust open the car door.

The scent of roasting chicken wafted down the hallway as they stepped into the house (being careful to avoid the stacks of newspaper at the entry), and Ralph's gruff voice was lifted in a refrain. Merry smiled as Tabitha leaped from the stairs and curled her length around Peter's legs. He lifted the cat quickly and buried his nose in her tortoiseshell fur.

" 'Bout time you got back," John Folger called over his shoulder from his favorite living-room chair. He didn't bother to look around, being absorbed in the previous Thursday's *Inky Mirror.* "We found Dr. Elizabeth Osborne."

"You're kidding!" Merry instantly forgot the Markhams and their problems. "Was she in Bora Bora after all?"

"Nope," the chief said. He folded the newspaper deliberately and removed his reading glasses. "Never left Sconset beach, after all. Or so the FBI are telling us."

Chapter Nine

The identification of the Sconset bones, Meredith learned as she read over the FBI report at the Water Street station in all the quiet of a Sunday morning, had come from a forensic anthropologist named Natalie Prescott. Prescott worked in the anthropology department of the Smithsonian National Museum of Natural History; but on occasion, for a small fee, she dabbled in crime. The FBI was happy to pay her, as were the police forces of several states, simply to examine a miscellany of bones. Natalie Prescott invariably saw something in them that mere police examiners did not. And so it was with Dr. Elizabeth Osborne.

Prescott, unlike some scientists, was a fluent and elegant writer. From her report Meredith learned about the human frontal sinus, which sits above and behind the brow bone of the skull, its butterfly shape as unique as a fingerprint. Prescott had X-rayed the Sconset skull and compared it to an X ray of Elizabeth Osborne's cranium taken thirteen years earlier—and found that the frontal sinuses matched.

"That simple," Merry murmured, and unconsciously touched the flat surface of her middle brow.

The Smithsonian anthropologist further noted what she considered to be a bleaching of the bones, as though they had been exposed to sunlight or a chemical agent; she gave it as her opinion that the skeleton had lain somewhere other than the shallow sands of Sconset for some years before its discovery. The tantalizing words left Merry eager for more; but Prescott declined to elaborate. Perhaps she was comfortable only with certainties.

And of certainties there were plenty. The occipital bone in Osborne's neck was indeed fractured, confirming the crime lab's diagnosis of strangulation. From the lack of distinctive scrapings on the interior of Osborne's pelvis, Prescott determined that the dead woman had never borne a child. And most intriguing, to both the anthropologist and her reader, was the fact that the skeleton revealed an unusual degree of wear and tear. Osborne had suffered a fractured arm some time before her death. Bone chips were missing from her left tibia and right femur, as though she had been kicked. Several of her fingers and ribs also showed healed fractures, and most disturbingly, Prescott noted, so did her facial bones. At one point in her life not long before the fatal strangling, Elizabeth Osborne sported a broken cheekbone and eye socket. It was remarkable, the anthropologist wrote, that the woman had escaped reconstructive surgery.

Prescott had rifled the assembled medical data for some sign of a severe car accident, or a significant fall, and found nothing. No record of emergency care or hospitalization, even, from a victim who was herself a medical doctor and kept scrupulous records.

Merry frowned and reread the paragraph. But she had interpreted the words correctly—the injuries Prescott noted were not received from a brutal beating at the time of Elizabeth Osborne's murder. The chips and fractures were acquired earlier, and mended in quiet, all details of their existence obliterated from Osborne's official memory.

Absent a significant accidental trauma, Prescott noted dryly, the fractures were consistent with a pattern of sustained abuse. From a domestic partner, perhaps.

And there we have our motive and means, Merry thought. What had the Osborne missing-persons report said? That the marriage was in trouble?

It was high time to make a call to Jack Osborne and inform him that his long-lost wife had been found.

"I think we owe Elizabeth Osborne this one, Dad," Merry said, and set down her coffee cup. The chief had agreed to meet her for Sunday-morning Scotch oat cake at the Downy Flake's small branch bakery near Children's Beach. They sat outside, staring meditatively at the yacht club's slips (mostly empty) and at the coast-guard cutter moored just beyond.

"Won't be long, now." John Folger nodded toward the jumble of summer houses on Brant Point and the squat bastion of the lighthouse. "Few weeks, and the season will be upon us. We'll need every officer we've got. This might not be the time to take on a decade-old murder, Meredith. Why not let the state police handle it? Jack Osborne lives in Boston, after all. If he's guilty, it's out of our jurisdiction."

Merry frowned impatiently. "Come on, Dad. It happened *here*. In Sconset. And there's no statute of limitations on murder. We bungled the first investigation. That guy—what was his name?"

"Joe Halloran."

"Right. Good old Joe. Did he have his head up his ass, or what?"

"Meredith," her father said wearily, and his expression

was pained. "Your language is appalling. What would your mother say? Or Peter, for that matter?"

"Everything I know I learned from you, Dad," she soothed, and patted his arm. "But I'm curious. Why did you drop the Osborne investigation? From the file I've read, nobody even bothered to fly to Boston. Nobody talked to her colleagues at Harvard. It's like you just *quit*."

"Well," her father said irritably, "our funds for off-island travel have never been ample, as you well know. I'd have had to ask the district attorney's office to pay for the trips to Boston, and the DA at the time—Wes Stanley—"

"Was a tightfisted SOB."

"He'd never have approved the expenditure."

"Yeah, but *Dad*—"

"I know, Meredith, I know. There was another reason, I'll admit. I'd heard some rumors."

"About her having a lover."

"Over fifty people searching the bluffs and the golf course for four days. Coast-guard planes flying overhead. Clarence walking the Sconset shore every morning at dawn. We even brought over special tracking dogs. Elizabeth Osborne wasn't there." John Folger looked bleakly at Merry. "Halloran and I talked about it. Then I called off the search. To his credit, Halloran put up a fight. But when the lady's body never surfaced, he seemed to take it personally. Started hitting the bottle on weekdays. Passed out once, after lunch. By Christmas he was gone."

"Best decision you ever made, firing Halloran," Merry said. "Now, let me have this case. I'm not doing a thing."

"You will be." Her father took a gargantuan bite of Scotch oat cake and chewed ruminatively. "Crime always picks up around now. It's a sure sign summer's coming."

"You mean that theft of the necklace out in Monomoy last week, which may actually have been 'borrowed' by a relative? Or the entire *hedge* that Mrs. Quinley reported missing?"

"It is," her father protested. "I sent Matt Bailey out to

the Quinleys' just yesterday. Poor woman got back on-island in time for Daffodil Weekend and found nothing but a bunch of holes and a brown patch in the grass where the boxwood used to be."

"Like Emily Teasdale's geraniums."

"Exactly. You caught that guy, right?"

"Yes. And it was a fifteen-year-old, not a guy. Found him selling the pots along with some roses he'd stripped from somebody else's place, beneath a beach umbrella at the intersection of Main and Centre. A young entrepreneur, that one. Speaking of Emily Teasdale, Dad, did you know Ralph has taken to squiring her about?"

"Has he," John Folger replied neutrally. "Well." They were both silent a moment, uncertain how to proceed. Ralph's love life was something neither had ever been forced to discuss in the past.

"Shame about that boxwood," John finally said. "Stuff takes forever to reach a useful size. And you know how expensive it is?"

"I mourn," Merry said. "I truly do. And I suggest that Bailey check out some of the island nurseries, which would be in keeping with his low intelligence and obvious train of thought, since no nursery worth its reputation would consider wholesale stealing. Meanwhile, someone will have broken up the hedge, trimmed it, planted it in clumps around the property, and sat back on the deck with lemonade and a touch of gin to admire his handiwork. Case closed."

"You really don't like Bailey, do you?"

"Not in the least. However, his absorption in the Affair of the Burgled Boxwood is a type of salvation. At least you won't assign *him* to the Osborne case."

"What makes you think Dan Peterson will give it to us?" her father asked. The Barnstable DA had the final word on the disposition of all murder cases.

"Tucker Enright," Merry answered, and her green eyes were alight with satisfaction.

The chief took a long draft of coffee, then pushed

back his chair. "Did you ask Enright to put in a good word for you? Is this guy sweet on you or something?"

"*Dad.* Of course not. But I think the fact of Tucker Enright—and this serial-murder case that has the state guys tied up in knots—will make our offer to handle the Elizabeth Osborne matter extremely attractive to Dan Peterson."

"You're probably right. And having you look into the matter might ease my conscience. I can't help thinking that if I'd been a little less cynical eight years ago, we might have caught a killer." Her father stood and adjusted his newsboy cap—a Christmas gift from his daughter. He looked surprisingly natty, Merry thought. "I'll tell you what. Get going on the preliminaries while I fax a request to Peterson's office. He won't be there, of course, its being Sunday, but at least we'll have followed procedure."

"Has anyone informed Osborne of his wife's identification?" Merry asked.

John Folger shrugged. "Don't know, m'dear. The state crime lab sent the bones on to the FBI, so the state police probably saw a copy of the forensics report around the time we did. I wouldn't be surprised if Osborne has been told. And by the way, the state folks may have stolen a march on you. We'll have to check with Peterson tomorrow morning."

"I'd appreciate it if you'd do that, Dad," Merry said briskly. "I'll call in for the information."

"Oh, really?" Her father's eyebrows shot up. "And just where will *you* be, Detective?"

"In Boston," she replied. "Asking Jack Osborne how his beloved wife got that fractured cheekbone."

If Merry had learned anything from her previous investigations, it was the truth of the old adage that knowledge is power. Criminal detection is really an elaborate process by which the ignorant (the police) persuade the knowledgeable (the murderers) to share their information. This requires the ignorant first to identify the knowledgeable, a somewhat difficult process that wastes a great deal of both parties' time. In Elizabeth Osborne's case, Merry hoped to skip that stage by assuming her husband, Jack, was the guilty party until proved otherwise. But first she intended to arm herself with details. The man, after all, was a Harvard law professor.

She sat at her desk that Sunday morning, memorizing the essence of Natalie Prescott's forensic report. She rehashed Jack Osborne's discovery of his wife's shoes and passport in the dunes below their home on the Sconset bluff, the morning of September 13, 1988. She studied the shoes themselves, which were held in eight-year-old sealed plastic evidence bags—hot-pink patent-leather sandals, sexy against tanned skin. *Not* the usual footwear for a walk on the beach in the dark. She donned plastic gloves and flipped through the passport, noting stamps for entry and departure from several European countries and one each from Japan and Kenya. She stared, fascinated, at the official Department of State eagle that spread its wings beside Elizabeth Osborne's face. The wanly-colored image that stared back from the inside cover was probably like all passport photos—an injustice—but nonetheless Elizabeth Osborne was arresting. Dark, glossy hair; wide, dark eyes; a strong chin; a look of intelligence. A perfection of a nose. The one thing, apparently, that had escaped being fractured.

Merry herself had never bothered to apply for a passport, as she had never succeeded in leaving the country. These were two facts she kept to herself whenever Peter Mason spoke casually of a favorite boulevard in Paris, or a building in Prague, or the summer he had spent in Dorset. At such moments she fell unusually silent and soon changed the subject. She was embarrassed and cowed by her parochial life. She planned secret trips, designed for the sole purpose of conversational one-upmanship, that she never found the time to take. But it occurred to her now, as she fingered the raised printing and the stiff blue cover of the dead woman's passport, that what she really coveted was the document itself. The dispensation, the official imprimatur, of the world traveler.

And finally, putting Elizabeth's belongings aside, Merry read and reread Jack Osborne's statement.

I awoke at six A.M. My wife was not in her room. Her bed was either undisturbed from the previous night or had been slept in and already made up. She was not in the house. I decided to see whether she was on the beach and so left the house by the back porch. I took the stairs down to the beach and began walking in the direction she usually chose—toward Gully Road. I came upon Betsy's sandals about five minutes later. Her passport was lying near them. I shouted her name, but there was no answer; and thinking she might be visiting in one of the neighboring houses (at six A.M.? Merry thought), I returned to our place and had breakfast. When she had not returned by ten o'clock, I walked back up the beach. I saw that her things were still lying where I had first seen them. I gathered them up, returned to the house, and called the police.

Just below this signed paragraph, which Merry thought inspired more questions than it answered, the pathetic Joe Halloran had recorded Jack Osborne's answers to several questions. *I do not know where my wife might have gone. If I did, I wouldn't be asking you to find her. No, I don't think Betsy had any reason to commit suicide. We were about as happy in our marriage as most people are—I mean, how happy is anybody, really? We had our problems. Most of the time we worked them out. Of course I loved my wife. That's why I'm here. The question you should be asking is, Where is she?*

Merry stared into space, considering Jack Osborne. Then she pulled his telephone number out of the next-of-kin information in Elizabeth's file and dialed it. A machine answered the call.

"Professor Osborne," Merry said, after a moment's hesitation over the proper title for a doctor of jurisprudence and settling on the student's fallback, "this is Detective Meredith Folger of the Nantucket police. I have

new information regarding the disappearance of your
wife and would like to meet with you in Boston as soon
as possible, preferably tomorrow afternoon. Please return
my call"—and here she almost left the Tattle Court number out of habit, summoning her new one from memory
with considerable effort.

All that remained now was a visit the next morning to
the Nantucket Atheneum. Their microfiche files *must*
have something on the celebrated Osborne case.

"So you're flying to Boston," Peter said from his loung-
ing position on her sofa. "Tomorrow. Just like that."

"Yes," Merry replied. She shook some excess water
from a head of lettuce and dumped it into her salad spin-
ner, intensely happy in the compactness of her own
kitchen.

"And this gentleman lives *where*?"

"Back Bay. Three hundred block of Marlborough
Street."

"*Where even the man / scavenging filth in the back alley
trash cans, / has two young children, a beach wagon, a
helpmate, / and is a 'young Republican.'* "

"Really?" She lifted a satiric brow.

"Sorry." He swung his legs to the floor and began sifting through the scattered sections of the Sunday *Globe*.
"You triggered a memory. I had a vicious Robert Lowell
phase in high school."

"Wasn't he a nut?"

"Merry!" Peter looked hurt. "Lowell had bouts of madness, yes. But he was an absolute genius."

"I see the vicious phase is not quite over."

"I can recite the rest of the poem, if you like," Peter offered grinning.

"I'll wait and let Jack Osborne do it. He probably had
a Lowell phase, too. It's the male equivalent of every
teenage girl's absorption in Sylvia Plath."

"You really think Osborne killed his wife?"

"Let's just say it makes sense." Merry slid her new

knife through a tomato with a frisson of satisfaction. It was the first time she had used it. "The forensic anthropologist who made the identification is willing to guess he beat Elizabeth systematically for years—beat her badly enough to break bones all over her body. In nine cases out of ten an abusive husband would be my pick for murderer."

"And your plan is just to ask him about it."

"Uh-huh."

"Do you think that's wise?"

"Look." Merry slid the tomato off the chopping block and licked her fingers. "I'd rather you didn't tell me how to do my job. I don't come around your place at harvest time and criticize the way you're deploying your beaters, do I? I don't analyze the crop and wonder whether you'd have done better with chemical fertilizers instead of insisting on organic. I don't presume to tell you about merino-sheep breeding, either."

"No, you don't," Peter agreed. "But cranberry farming isn't hazardous to my health."

"What are you trying to say?"

"That you might want to take Howie Seitz with you." He made an effort to sound lighthearted, when in fact he was somewhat concerned. "From what you've said, this man didn't hesitate to throw a punch or two in his day. He may even have strangled his wife to death. And you've made an appointment to visit his home alone."

Jack Osborne had called not half an hour before Peter's arrival for dinner, and agreed to make some time available for Merry.

"I'm flying to Boston and I'll probably stay overnight," Merry argued. "My father made a point today of reminding me how tight our off-island travel budget is. I can't justify the expense of adding Seitz to the bill."

"You could add me," Peter said. "I'd pay my own way."

Merry stiffened. "That would be mixing business and pleasure in a decidedly unhealthy manner. Besides, I don't need a bodyguard. I'll take my gun, if it'll make you feel better. Frankly," she said, reaching for some Parmesan, "I doubt a Harvard law professor is likely to murder a police officer in his own home."

"Why not? He's got a bunch of colleagues ready to defend him. But, seriously, Merry," Peter said, "you have to let me come. Tomorrow's May sixth."

"So?"

"So it just happens to be *May sixth*."

"And should that date mean something to me?" Merry turned to the oven and pulled open the door. A wave of heat and rosemary wafted into the room. The lamb chops were not quite done. "Obviously it should."

"Obviously."

"Let's see . . . it's not a national holiday. Or a religious one, as far as I can remember. Could it be the start of the Nantucket Looms preseason sale?" Her face lit up at the thought, and Peter took a brutal satisfaction in extinguishing her joy.

"No. You missed that one in March, if I recall."

"It's not our anniversary."

"Do we have one?"

"Which means—oh, lord, Peter, your birthday! It's your birthday, isn't it?"

"You missed that, too, I'm sorry to say, way back in November. I sulked for a week." He lifted a section of newspaper and waved it emphatically. "Think, Meredith. May sixth."

"I can't think. I'm cooking."

Peter sighed deeply and got to his feet. "All right. You give up. May sixth is the New England Genealogical Society's open house, from five to seven P.M. I intend to go. I want to learn more about my roots."

"Your roots are deeply embedded in green," Merry said acidly, "the kind that buys and sells empires daily. Your family founded Nantucket along with mine. Those histories were written long ago."

"I realize that," Peter said mildly, "but most of them happen to be stored on the society's open shelves. I intend to browse. To wander among the landscape of my forebears. To find out which Masons married what Folgers however many years ago. I'll take notes on Newbury Street while you ask questions on Marlborough. Then we'll meet halfway between and have dinner. At the Ritz, perhaps."

"The Ritz is not halfway between."

"But it has a view of the Boston Public Gardens. We can gaze out at them while comparing my newfound knowledge of Great-great-aunt Letitia and your suspect's appearance of guilt."

"I don't know," Merry said. She leaned across the counter that separated her kitchen from her living room and took the genealogical-society ad from Peter's hands. "It's breaking our rule. I'd be seeing you on a weeknight. And it's hardly the most professional thing I'll ever have done. . . ."

"Consider it a birthday present," he replied, "and long overdue."

The *Inky Mirror*, Merry discovered, had devoted quite a bit of column space to Elizabeth Osborne's strange disappearance. It was Emily Teasdale, the object of Ralph's Daffodil Weekend gallantry, who steered Merry in the proper direction. Emily was a volunteer—a librarian emerita, in fact—who spent numerous hours each week in the reference section of the newly-renovated library.

"Elizabeth Osborne," she murmured thoughtfully. "Yes, yes, my dear. We have any number of requests for information about *her*. Quite a Nantucket mystery."

Emily left Merry sitting in a chair before the reference desk and returned a few moments later with several squares of microfiche. All were issues of the newspaper from eight years back.

Merry began with the issue immediately following the report of Elizabeth's disappearance. Because the *Inky Mirror* was a weekly, and appeared every Thursday, this was two days after the events of September 13; but the time lag had a hidden advantage. The reporter had profited from his leisure by turning the story into several articles. One detailed the specifics of the doctor's disappearance—the shoes, the passport, the husband's distress—and the other profiled her life as a third-generation Nantucket summer resident.

It was the last that held Merry's attention. For there, dramatic and stark in the microfiche's black and white, was an image of Elizabeth Osborne. She leaned forward, laughing, her arms folded across a tablecloth in the midst of what appeared to be a riotous party. Four other people huddled with her, smiling for the camera.

One of them was Julia Markham.

A younger, prettier, lighthearted Julia Markham, with a highball glass clutched in the same hand as her cigarette. Her eyes were flashing, her mouth was parted in laughter, and her free hand gripped her neighbor's affectionately.

Merry scanned the lengthy caption below. *Marked for misfortune?* it read. *Elizabeth Osborne and Ian Markham in happier days. From left: Osborne, Markham, Jack Osborne, Sylvia Whitehead, and Julia Markham celebrate* A Mood Indigo's *win in the 1988 Opera House Cup. Markham was presumed drowned in the sinking Monday night of* A Mood Indigo, *a thirty-six-foot single-hulled wooden boat.*

"Whew," Merry said aloud, and did a mental calculation. Ian Markham's boat sank the same night that Elizabeth Osborne disappeared. Coincidence? Disaster? Or murderous design?

She studied the photograph again, looking with renewed interest at the man to Osborne's left. He was laughing with her, his eyes narrowed and his teeth flashing whitely in a deeply tanned face. A blunt-fingered hand, callused like a laborer's, trailed in the picture's foreground; the other rested on Elizabeth Osborne's sleek shoulder. And across the distance of time and death, Merry Folger sighed. Ian Markham's personality leaped off the microfiche negative. A powerful force, without question; sensual, abrupt, not to be denied. What currents had swirled among the people joined in victory? And why had death swept them apart so irrevocably?

Perhaps Jack Osborne could tell her. But *would* he?

Chapter Ten

"It should feel like a relief," Jack Osborne said to Merry, "but, oddly, you know, it doesn't." He gazed toward the corner of his elegant office, at approximately the level of the egg-and-dart ceiling cornice, and stroked his neatly trimmed beard. A professorial gesture, Merry thought, entirely in keeping with the house and Osborne's gray flannel trousers, with the atmosphere of academic calm. Only the occasional blare of a horn from Marlborough Street intervened to break the stillness. "If Betsy has been lying in the Sconset sand all those years, it raises more questions than it answers."

"How so?"

"Well—" Osborne uncrossed his legs, smoothed his trousers, and looked directly at Merry. "It shoots *my* theory of what happened completely to hell, now, doesn't it?"

"I don't know, Professor Osborne. What *is* your theory? It appears nowhere in our files."

He laughed sourly. "No, I don't suppose it does. I was very careful about what I said to that idiot—pardon me, to your colleague—from the Nantucket police."

"And do you intend to be equally careful with me?" Merry asked. "I'd like to know at the outset."

"So you can change your tactics?"

"So I can catch the last plane back to the island. I'm not particularly fond of wasting time."

"Neither am I—one reason I was so annoyed with your colleague. He was the very last person likely to find my wife, and I knew it."

"So did you seek outside help?"

"Hire an investigator, you mean?"

Merry nodded.

"No," Jack Osborne conceded. "I never did."

"I'm surprised." The impassive comment hung in the air between them, rife with implication.

Osborne looked away again, as if suddenly uncomfortable with Merry's steady gaze, and again his hand went to his chin. The beard was a goatee—distinguished on this man, where it might appear subversive on one half his age. Jack Osborne looked the very picture of breeding, and intellect, and measured behavior—an unlikely person to strike a woman in anger. "Because a husband *should* do everything to find his wife, right?" he said finally.

"A husband who hoped his wife was alive, yes." Again Merry let the unspoken question hang in the air.

"Are you suggesting I *murdered* Betsy, Detective?" The law professor's voice was quietly amused. "I'm not sure that would be wise."

"Wisdom isn't really at issue, here, is it?" Merry replied. "It's the truth that concerns me."

Osborne sighed. "You're rather young, aren't you? Do you even remember the late eighties on Nantucket? You must have been in high school."

"Just out of the police academy," Merry corrected him, "and watching a good friend's trial for rape and double murder in New Bedford. None of which he'd committed." That episode in Rafe da Silva's past was one everyone tried to forget; but Merry never saw Peter's foreman without the most vivid memories rising unbidden before her eyes.

"And was he acquitted?" Osborne sounded intrigued.

"Yes. But, you know, sometimes that doesn't really matter. A man's reputation can be tainted by crime, whether he's responsible or not. Take yourself, for instance, and this disturbing business with your wife." Merry looked at Osborne deliberately, letting him feel the weight of her stare. To judge from his placid expression, it was none too heavy. "Have you ever returned to Nantucket, Professor Osborne?"

"No. I shut up the house and practically threw away the key. Too many memories, I guess—and, eventually, too much work for me to spare the time."

"Really. And yet you've never sold your house. That's a valuable piece of real estate sitting idle. The taxes alone must be considerable."

"Fifty thousand a year," Osborne said easily, "but it's Betsy's house, Detective, and until yesterday I thought it was just possible Betsy might come back one of these days and want that key."

"There must have been a lot of talk on the island after Dr. Osborne disappeared. About your marriage, for example."

"I'm sure there was." This man would be adept in a deposition, Merry decided; he said only what was necessary, and very little that was helpful.

"I notice Halloran—the detective assigned to your case—believed suicide was a possibility," she prodded.

Osborne smiled thinly. "Never. With Betsy, never. Unless, of course, she discovered that she had a terminal illness—pain was something my wife found difficult to bear. But I'm not surprised by talk. Talk followed Betsy wherever she went, Detective. She ignited it like a match brings a flame."

"How did you feel about that, Professor Osborne?"

"I understood it." His expression did not alter.

"*Understood* it—no anger? No jealousy? No—desire to strike out?"

Another laugh—supercilious, condescending, to Merry's ears. "I'm not a terribly possessive man. And marrying Betsy was like purchasing a coveted objet d'art. Ownership is merely an *idea* in such cases, Detective; a temporary state at best. You probably never saw Betsy—but she was beautiful in the way that only very intelligent women can be. Her features were always alive with some emotion, the force of thought, an impulse awaiting action. Simply by breathing, she compelled people to notice her. She never waited for life to come to her: she went forward, always, to meet it."

"So you're saying you didn't much care how she lived, or what gossip followed you both." Merry peered at Osborne over her half glasses, her pen suspended above her notebook.

"What are you driving at, Detective?"

"Did you love your wife, Professor?"

"Does love presuppose jealous possession?"

"I don't enjoy the Socratic method," Merry said easily, "and I'm not, after all, one of your students."

"Very well," Osborne conceded tightly. "Yes, I loved my wife."

"So, tell me. What *do* you think happened the night Elizabeth disappeared?"

He studied Merry's face an instant, apparently debating within himself. Then he shrugged slightly. "What can it matter? They're both dead, after all. I thought my wife had run away with her lover, Detective. And that they had come to a disastrous end."

"Because Ian Markham sank *Mood Indigo*."

Osborne started, as if surprised by the extent of her information, or perhaps her leap of faith. "Exactly. I thought it probable that Elizabeth was on Markham's boat when it went down."

"Why? Had she given you any reason to think she would leave you?"

Osborne tilted his head wordlessly from side to side, in the age-old expression of ambivalence. "Not explicitly, no. But I had already left *her* in a way, Detective. I spent the 1987–88 academic year in Paris, as a visiting professor at the Sorbonne. Teaching American constitutional law. Betsy chose not to accompany me. She pleaded the demands of her own position at Harvard—but when I got back to Boston and saw what was going on, I knew that it was Markham who had kept her here."

"So you assumed she had simply left."

"Yes. And there were the things she'd left behind. They suggested flight, rather than death."

"The shoes and the passport."

Osborne nodded. "That morning, when I heard about *Mood Indigo* sinking, Elizabeth's absence suddenly made terrible sense. The passport dropped carelessly, the shoes discarded on the beach . . . she might have slipped them off to wade out into the water, to meet Markham in the boat, perhaps. Maybe they intended to head for the Caribbean. Her money would have made it possible for both of them to start a new life. Only they hit bad weather and worse water fifty miles south of the island."

"Why wouldn't she have driven into town with Markham and boarded the boat at the dock?"

Osborne lifted his hands in supplication. "I don't know. I admit that would have made more sense."

"And you never shared a word of this with the police. Not to Halloran or anyone."

"No. I probably should have. In retrospect, I *know* I should have. But I felt that the fact of Ian's drowning was enough for Julia to bear. Why burden her further with the public examination of her husband's affairs? The woman was eight months pregnant at the time. It seemed inordinately cruel."

"Despite the fact that your wife was missing, and possibly drowned as well."

Osborne did not reply.

"And you never requested divers in the area—to attempt to locate the boat, look into the cabin, find out whether two bodies were on board?"

A faint smile played around the law professor's lips. "Do you know where *Mood Indigo* sank, Detective?"

Merry shook her head. "My information about Markham's death is confined to a few phrases in articles about your wife's disappearance. I didn't have time to research the story of the boat's sinking."

"I see." Osborne clasped his hands around his knee, the picture of calm. "From a distress call Markham made just before the boat keeled over, we know that he went down beyond the edge of the continental shelf, not far from where the *Andrea Doria* lies. That's roughly two hundred fifty feet below the surface of the Atlantic. The effort to send divers in pursuit of *Mood Indigo* seemed excessive, especially given the possibility that one or both of the passengers might have been washed overboard as the boat sank. In such cases searching for two bodies is rather futile."

Merry merely nodded, as though unimpressed by his level of certainty. She made a show of adding to her notes, letting the silence build. "And now we know that Elizabeth wasn't on board anyway," she said finally, fixing Osborne in her green stare.

"Yes." He unclasped his hands and stretched his fingers, as if easing some tension. "She was lying there all the time, as those fifty-odd volunteers walked the beach calling her name. You see what I meant when I said this news raises more questions than it answers."

Merry might have told Osborne that she doubted his wife's bones *had* been buried in the sand all those years—their bleaching surely suggested otherwise—but she refrained from sharing the information. If Osborne had indeed killed Elizabeth, there was no point in furnishing him with the precise degree of police knowledge about the crime.

"I've been wrestling with those questions for days," she said with an air of frankness. "Perhaps you can help me answer them."

Jack Osborne glanced at his watch. "I've a class in a little over an hour, and I'm afraid traffic between Back Bay and Cambridge forces me to leave forty-five minutes ahead of time. I can give you twenty minutes."

"That should be more than adequate. When did you first meet the Markhams, Professor Osborne?"

He pursed his lips and frowned, as if lost in thought. "It must have been through Sylvia Whitehead." The third woman in the newspaper photo. "Sylvia owned a gallery that showed Markham's work, and Elizabeth collected art. It was her passion. She simply extended it to the artist, in this particular case."

"And you knew them how long?"

"Four or five years. I got Markham hooked on sailing, in fact—and helped him barter for *Mood Indigo* before he bought it. We won the Opera House Cup together. Do they still run that race?"

"Yes," Merry said shortly. The Opera House restaurant, the original sponsor of the wooden-boat cup, had been an island landmark for over forty years. The restaurant's doors had closed by the time Ian Markham had won his race, as she was certain Osborne knew. But the professor's association with the Opera House Cup and the wooden-boat sailors symbolized a rarefied world for Merry, one of off-island money and privilege and free hours spent near the sea. Peter's world. Not hers. She was instinctively wary of it, and she felt now that Jack Osborne was using his familiarity with that world—his charm, his ease, his elegant handling of conversation—to divert her questions.

"Four or five years," she repeated, forcing his attention back to the Markhams. "And how well would you say you knew them?"

"We were very good friends," he said quietly. "Which made Betsy's behavior all the more appalling."

"Betsy's?"

"Yes. Betsy's. She bent Ian to her will, Detective, with single-minded precision. My wife was an only child, you know. And a psychiatrist. Something of a deadly combination. Betsy knew exactly *why* she was selfish, and exactly *how* to manipulate the people around her. That summer she wanted Ian."

"And, in your opinion, she succeeded?"

"Absolutely. Markham was head over heels in love with her, and his poor wife pregnant. A hideous spectacle we all tried to ignore."

"All of you being—who?"

"Me. Julia Markham. I *hope* her toddler remained in ignorance. Our friends knew, of course. A few others, who were mere social acquaintances, probably suspected."

"And everyone simply took the affair in stride? Continued dining and dancing together as though nothing were the matter?"

A faint expression of irritation crossed Osborne's face. "We've established that my wife was not on *Mood Indigo* when it went down, Detective. What possible interest can her involvement with Ian Markham now hold?"

"Two people died that night under suspicious circumstances."

"I beg to differ. Markham, at least, died from his own stupidity."

The first suggestion of spite. Never mind that Ian Markham's boat might have been deliberately sabotaged—by the man who helped him buy and sail it. "Perhaps you were angrier than you're willing to say," Merry suggested impassively. "Perhaps Markham's wife was less understanding than you believe. Perhaps someone *else* in your circle decided to exercise some outrage on your behalf. The connection is there. The double tragedy. You choose not to make a link, Professor, but I have to give it some consideration."

"It was so long ago," Osborne said wearily, "and Julia can't have had anything to do with it, because she was off-island at the time. You must know that. Markham had sent her back to Boston to be close to her doctor. And conveniently out of the way of his amorous affairs."

Merry *hadn't* known. "That would have been after the Opera Cup?" she asked, remembering Julia's smiling face in the victory picture. Hardly the expression of a long-suffering housewife.

"Yes. The Cup was usually held around the third week in August, and Julia left about Labor Day, I think. No pun intended, of course. Markham drowned a week later."

But Julia might have returned to Nantucket long enough to murder your wife, Merry thought, *while you took care of Ian's boat.* She made a note to verify Julia's alibi. "Have you kept in touch with Mrs. Markham since the tragedy?"

"No."

A one-word answer. Suggesting sensitivity to the question, perhaps? "Not even a Christmas card?"

"Not even."

Merry changed tack. "Any idea why the boat went down?"

Osborne shrugged again. "Bad weather, shoals, an overly confident skipper. Might have been anything."

"But wasn't, in fact, *specifically* anything?"

"As I've mentioned, the boat was never recovered. Any theory as to the sinking must remain conjecture."

Convenient. "And your wife, Professor Osborne—how long would you say she 'bent Ian to her will'?"

Osborne shifted in his chair. "I have no idea how long the affair had been simmering. I was gone the entire winter, if you will recall. But I don't think it had begun before I left. A brief interlude, at best. Wasn't destined to prosper, I suppose."

"How fatalistic. You wouldn't have lent Fate a hand?"

He snorted. "Since you've asked—no, I would not."

Merry snapped her notebook shut. "Then you would be a very unusual husband, Professor Osborne."

Osborne's head shot up, and he looked narrowly at Merry. "What are you implying?"

"That you're not being perfectly honest."

He laughed bitterly. "I've been nothing *but*. It's you, Detective, who's holding your cards close to your chest. There's a lot you're not telling me."

"Isn't there always, in a conversation between the police and a suspect?"

"So now I'm a suspect."

"Of course you are, Professor." Merry removed her half glasses and searched in her purse for the case, deliberately casual. "I can't imagine that a tenured member of the Harvard law faculty wouldn't have assumed as much. You're suspect number one, in my book. I hope you're lining up a lawyer."

There was a moment of silence, and when Merry glanced at Osborne's face again, she read disbelief and shock in it. But nothing like consuming rage. She felt a mild pang of disappointment.

"We now know that your wife was strangled," she persisted. "And you admit to a troubled marriage. She was sleeping with your friend. All your acquaintances knew it and were laughing up their sleeves at the idiotic figure you made. 'Poor Jack, he's so tied to Betsy's strings he can't even stand up for himself when she's cheating on him.' I bet they were even snide enough to wonder if you needed your wife's money. *Something*, after all, must have made you stay and turn such a blind eye."

The man seemed to digest this in silence. The expression on his face did not alter. Merry waited. Finally she prodded, "Did you ever confront your wife about her affair with Markham?"

Osborne folded his arms across his chest, as though to contain his antagonism. "No."

"I'm surprised you weren't beside yourself with jealousy and anger."

"Would it make you *less* suspicious, Detective, if I admitted to a murderous rage?"

"It might, at that," Merry retorted. "At least then I could consider your reaction normal. Because, frankly, Professor, *nothing* that you did in the wake of your wife's disappearance eight years ago looks that way. You find out Ian Markham's dead, leap to the conclusion that Elizabeth was with him, and make no effort to prove the fact. You leave Nantucket and apparently"—here Merry glanced with calculation around the comfortable study in the expensive Marlborough Street row house—"live off her money until someone unfortunately trips over her bones."

"I couldn't touch Betsy's money, Detective, because she was never declared dead—which you'd have known if your understanding of law was somewhat better than the minor idiocies you learned by heart at the police academy," Osborne said. The words were sharp, but to Merry's frustration and intense interest, he was completely in control of his anger.

"Funny," she mused. "At the police academy they taught us you can declare a missing person legally dead after seven years. By my reckoning, your wife has been gone nearly eight."

Osborne smiled thinly. "I probably would have got around to all that paperwork this summer. But your Sconset discovery saves me the trouble. Why is it, Detective, that I have the impression you're deliberately trying to make me angry? To see if you *can*? If I manage to govern my emotions better than the average man—I can only plead *superiority* to the average man."

"Of course you would." Merry's voice was heavy with irony. "I doubt you've ever known much about the guy in the street, except when you were swinging at your wife." A comment she expected would make Osborne apoplectic.

But the professor merely looked bewildered. "Swinging at my *wife*?" he said.

"Well—at her arm, her cheekbone, her rib cage, her femur, her tibia, and her eye socket, to be specific. The FBI's forensic anthropologist found healed fractures all over Elizabeth's body. The report suggests a sustained pattern of abuse. From a domestic partner, perhaps."

"Who might then have gone on to strangle her, is that it?" Osborne said acidly.

"Exactly."

"The O. J. Simpson influence."

"Oh, I'd guess it predates *him* by several thousand years."

"I can tell you categorically, Detective, that I never struck my wife." Stiffly, Osborne rose, as if to steer her immediately from the room.

"Then you can offer a reasonable explanation for her injuries? You must have witnessed their effects. I notice"—and here Merry flipped backward through her notes—"that pain was something your wife 'found difficult to bear.' Strangely enough, your wife removed any record of treatment for these particular pains from her medical files. Was she shielding *you*, Professor, or someone else?"

Osborne hesitated, his mouth hanging open, and then abruptly snapped it shut. "Whatever Betsy's injuries, Detective, they must have occurred while I was absent in Paris. I'm afraid I can't tell you a thing."

"A lot seems to have happened while you were conveniently elsewhere."

"Are you done with Betsy's bones?" Osborne asked, with an effort at casualness that utterly failed. "Could I arrange a decent burial, I mean?"

"Of course." Merry scribbled a number on a piece of paper and passed it to him. "They should be released by the state police at your request. It's best to have an undertaker of some kind accompany you, for the actual transferral."

Osborne glanced at the paper, his face blank. "Thank you."

"Where were you, Professor, the night of January seventh?" The night Mabel Johnson saw someone burying what might have been Elizabeth Osborne's bones.

His brow furrowed. "This *past* January seventh?"

"Uh-huh."

"I have no idea. What does that have to do with anything?"

"I'd appreciate it if you'd check your calendar. It has a bearing on your wife's case."

"But I thought you only just found—"

"Your calendar, Professor."

He wheeled around and pulled open the top drawer of an antique desk, rifling among some papers. A black leather daytimer appeared, and he flipped through the pages.

"January seventh. That was a Sunday night, wasn't it?" He looked up and met Merry's eyes. "I think I must have been sitting here at home. There's no record of an engagement."

"Alone?"

He smiled faintly. "I take it that would be a mistake."

"Just curious. Whether anyone else could verify you were at home."

"There isn't much of anyone else *in* my life at present, Detective," he replied, and dropped the calendar back into the drawer.

Merry followed Jack Osborne to his door, grudgingly impressed by his poise and self-control. The professor was too intelligent not to discern the case she was building against him, and yet he betrayed neither anxiety nor fear.

"Just one more thing," she said as he pulled open the door and gestured, as if to usher her through it. "That money of Elizabeth's. If you can't touch it, who does?"

"Morgan Guaranty Trust. A fellow named Bromwell.

Martin Bromwell." He spelled the name for her helpfully and ushered her to the street. "And, Detective—"

She looked back over her shoulder, quick enough to witness Osborne's odd smile.

"Now that Betsy has been declared good and dead, I should be coming into some of that fortune, shouldn't I?"

"If you don't land in prison first, Professor," Merry said, and walked away.

Chapter Eleven

Merry walked briskly down Marlborough Street to Exeter, resisting the impulse to glance around and check whether Jack Osborne was staring after her, then turned out of sight toward Newbury Street, feeling something akin to relief. Her pulse was singing, her cheeks were flushed, and she experienced all the adrenal surge of a challenging interrogation. It was like chess, she supposed—although chess seemed too passive a game in comparison to her conversation with Osborne; perhaps fencing was better. Something swift and sharp and punctuated by abrupt reversals of fortune.

It was a glorious Boston afternoon. A brisk breeze stirred the first leaves of the maple trees lining Back Bay's streets. Tulips nodded behind black wrought-iron grills, and the first geraniums were already springing up in row-house window boxes, vivid against the aged brick. Merry drew a sudden breath of exultation; her steps quickened. Dr. Elizabeth Osborne was dead, of course, and had been for years; but the world that had been so much a part of the dead woman's days—this genteel neighborhood, this hurried passage of street fair and student life—was Merry's to enjoy. She felt extraordinarily *alive*: her work was done for the afternoon, however incomplete it might still be, and Peter waited somewhere in the chic huddle of shops and restaurants and skateboarders and businesspeople that made up the charm of Newbury Street.

She had agreed to meet him at the entrance to the Boston Public Gardens, where the ornamental ponds, drained all winter, were slowly filling; but between Exeter and the Ritz were dozens of dazzling shop windows. Left side of the street, or right? On the corner she hesitated. Armani was on the right, but Merry thought she remembered a particularly enticing home-furnishings shop on the left—and now that she was in possession of her own home, of three *entire* rooms, housewares won out over fashion every time. She turned decisively to the left and embarked on the oldest entertainment known to man— the fathoming of the bazaar.

"You seem predisposed to believe Jack Osborne murdered his wife," Peter observed as he reached for his wineglass an hour and a half later. They were sitting in the dining room of the Ritz Hotel—without, as it happened, a view of the gardens. Merry no longer cared, having strolled the gardens' length arm-in-arm with Peter, attempting and failing to name every type of bulb springing skyward from the beautifully tended beds. She was tired and happy, in possession of an excellent pear-and-endive salad, and looking forward to the prospect of a duck browning nicely somewhere in her name.

"Don't you consider his behavior rather suspicious?" she asked.

"Most behavior can seem that way, if you work hard enough."

"All right." Merry set down her fork. "If you persist in thinking you can do my job for me, I might as well take you to the cleaner's while I'm at it. Bet me whatever you please. I'm willing to go out on a limb and say that the man tampered with *Mood Indigo*, causing it to sink, and then strangled and buried his wife. Somewhere. And for some reason he was forced to rebury her a few months ago on Sconset beach, which led to his downfall."

"You're on." Peter held out his hand.

Merry studied him. "You don't agree with me. You refuse to see the plausibility of the act."

"I admit he *could* have killed his wife and Markham," Peter said calmly, "and that he may have had prodigious motivation, being cuckolded and embarrassed and possibly abusive to boot. But I think you're very far from proving it."

"He did nothing to search for her after the boat went down! Because he *knew* she was already dead. He trusted the public nature of her affair would place her, in most people's minds, in *Mood Indigo* with Markham. He probably left her shoes and passport on the beach for himself to find. And Peter"—she raised a forkful of endive and shook it for emphasis—"he can't come up with one single excuse for those healed fractures. The man was married to Elizabeth for fifteen years. He *should* remember a broken arm, or the facial injuries, or the taping she must have had around her ribs."

"Fine," Peter rejoined, "I'm not arguing that things don't look black for the distinguished professor. He may have killed them both, as you say. But consider the contingencies! How could Osborne possibly *know* that Ian Markham would take his boat out in a storm?"

"Maybe he lured him out."

"Prove it. Then tell me how he got his friend to sink the thing just beyond the continental shelf. If Osborne tampered with the boat, and it was *retrieved*—or if Markham somehow survived to explain the disaster"—Peter snapped his fingers—"there goes Osborne's happily widowered life."

Merry looked crestfallen. Peter pressed his advantage. "I won't even go into the unlikely series of events that are required to bring Osborne back to the island this January, reburying his wife's bones in a snowstorm."

Merry brightened, inspired. "What if Julia was in on the murders with him? And *she* reburied the bones in January for reasons we haven't discovered?"

"Possible," Peter conceded. "But if she plotted to murder her husband, why has she remained in Sconset with the kids all these years, slowly going mad? Why not make a new life with his insurance money—return to England, for instance?"

"Guilt. Guilt, guilt, guilt, guilt, guilt."

Peter shook his head in protest. "Seems to me that if you're going to knock off your errant spouses together, you should at least get to enjoy the fruits of your crime. Instead, as far as you can tell, Julia Markham and Jack Osborne haven't been in touch."

"So Osborne would like us to believe."

"Seems odd, doesn't it?"

"Maybe they hoped to divert suspicion from one another. That would explain Osborne's avoidance of the island."

Peter drank the last of his wine and reached for the bottle. "For eight years? You've got to do better than that."

"Okay," Merry said thoughtfully through a bite of pear, "I agree there're a few holes."

"And how do you propose to fill them?"

"With talk, for one thing."

"Talk."

"Yep. Everyone who knew the Markhams and the Osbornes was talking about that affair, by Osborne's own admission. Some of them must remember it well enough to share their impressions with me. Ever hear of a woman named Sylvia Whitehead?"

"No. Sounds like she should write the *Inky Mirror's* bird-watching column."

"She's an art dealer. Or was. I thought you'd know all those sorts of people."

"I don't deal art. I inherit it."

"Snob."

Peter's sharp-boned face softened with amusement. "Talk to everyone you like, Meredith. Talk until you're blue in the face. But talk won't amount to diddly in a court of law."

"Fine." Merry lifted her glass defiantly. "What're the terms of your bet?"

"If you win," he said, reaching for her hand, "you force me into marriage at the soonest possible date. If I win, I get to do the forcing."

Merry snatched her hand away as though it had been burned. "I didn't think you'd joke about something like that."

"I'm not joking. Heads I win, tails you lose. It's the oldest bet in the house." Peter was smiling, but Merry saw how narrowly his gray eyes watched her. When had she lost control of the conversation? When had this corner come up against her back?

"I'd never make a wager about the rest of my life," she rejoined, deliberately light, and took a bite of salad; but her stomach clenched, and she found she could no longer meet Peter's eyes.

"What is it?" he asked quietly.

"What's what?"

"What's the yawning gulf that opens at your feet every time I tell you how much I love you?"

Merry sat back in her chair, as carefully as though it might collapse suddenly beneath her, and saw that she was gripping the edge of the table. She laced her fingers together and placed them safely in her lap. "Fear," she said softly, with utter honesty. "Fear yawns."

"I don't understand why." He turned the stem of his

wineglass slowly between thumb and forefinger, studying it as if his life depended on it.

"Because of the possibility of failure."

"Failure? Us?" The gray eyes came up to hers.

"Me. *Me.* One of these days—and it won't be very long now—you'll wake up and realize I'm nothing like your sort of woman."

"What in God's name does that mean?"

"It means I'm not Greenwich," Merry said desperately. "I was never a debutante. I don't speak French. I went to a community college, not the Ivy League. I majored in criminal justice, not philosophy. I've never played hostess to a brilliant affair. I've never ridden in a limousine. I don't speak your language, Peter, and you know it."

"My language apparently being French."

"I've never even"—Merry took a deep breath, as though on the brink of a terrible confession—"been out of the country." She threw her hands over her face in mortification. "And you talk so casually about Le Toilet—"

"That's L'Etoile," Peter said helpfully.

"—and growing up with a housekeeper, and that summer school in Switzerland, and I'm *absolutely terrified* of meeting your mother. Much less the people you grew up with."

"Then don't," he said gently. "I can't stand my mother, you know that. You'd be marrying me, not her."

"It doesn't matter," Merry insisted. "She's a dragon and she'll hate me. I'm surprised she hasn't *arranged* a marriage for you by this time."

"This being the Middle Ages, and I a pawn in some dynastic game. I could tell you none of that mattered to me, but I'd be lying. I *do* recognize that we're profoundly different. That you had a relatively happy childhood, aside from losing half your family to the Viet Nam War, and that I didn't. That you love your father, and Ralph Waldo, and that your relationships are the envy of most people on the island. I could worry about whether Ralph considers me fit to take the hand of his only grandchild—"

"He thinks you're wonderful, you know that!"

"—or whether you'd grow tired of being married to a gentleman farmer who tends to delegate his work and spends too much of his time training for the Nantucket Ironman. I happen to be afraid of loss, too, you know. And of failure. I'm not very good at either. But you give me something, Merry, that I can't live without—something stronger than fear or doubt."

Yes, Merry thought. *I know. That's what terrifies me. The thought of living again without you.* But she could not say even so much—because one day, when he realized his mistake and left her, it would hurt to remember having opened her soul. It was enough to live in this moment, and to live it fully, without her familiar dread of the end.

"I can't think about it now, Peter," she said, avoiding his eyes. "There's too much going on. We'll talk about it when all this is over."

Peter did not reply, but his expression was troubled; and a blight fell over the remainder of their dinner that no effort at conversation could ease.

Evening seemed to fall more slowly on Nantucket that night, unheralded by candle flame or the spark of faceted crystal; and Emily Teasdale, alone in her Madaket cottage after a long day at the Atheneum, lingered by her living-room window. It gazed west, over the dunes, toward the last orange rays of a sun blazing slowly into the sea; and though she had witnessed this miracle a thousand thousand nights in the span of her long lifetime, she was awestruck by the day's final moments, as ever.

"Look at that, now, Mack," she said to her dead husband, twenty-three years gone; "look at that. One for the record books, isn't it? *If only I were a camera-carrying man*. Isn't that what you used to say? Something like it, anyway."

Emily wondered for an instant whether Ralph Waldo Folger were a camera-carrying man and then decided he was not. His blue eyes took in too much.

She was a frail-looking woman from the waist up, with her narrow shoulders and thin face; but her hips were wide and sturdy, and her stocky legs were accustomed to mounting the Atheneum's step stools with a ballast load of bulky books. The newly renovated library—still imperious as ever behind its Greek Revival columns, on the one bit of rising ground at the center of town—demanded a great deal of work, and Emily was tired. Her back ached, and her neck was stiff with craning toward the shelves. She reached one gnarled hand to her shoulder and rubbed, remembering how easily Mack had worked the tension from her limbs. No one ever touched her that forcefully now, not even her granddaughter, Roxanne—who seemed content with air-brushed kisses, cheek to cheek, as though Emily might shatter at a touch.

The Atheneum had been closed for nearly a year, and all the books held in the twilight must of cellar boxes were still being restacked on gleaming new shelves. Emily, as one of the library's mainstays, volunteered for everything— ushering the winter lecture series, attending the readers' discussion group, helping to rejacket old books whose plastic covers were torn and peeling. She loved the work, loved the feel of the volumes sitting solidly in her hands— hardback books with their tough paper and delicate type-faces. Paperbacks she avoided, as she did all things of temporary convenience, much to her granddaughter's surprise. She should, perhaps, have taken to collecting first editions. But the Atheneum was her treasure trove, her hoard.

The sun slipped without warning below the horizon, and the glowing color seeped from the sky. Soon Roxanne would be home from the elementary school; and maybe Ralph would call. Emily pulled her Shetland cardigan closer and moved away from the window. In a little while, perhaps, she would draw the shade, when the sky had turned to gunmetal and the water churned blackly under the gathering dark. But not yet. Not while the memory of Mack and their summer days lingered in the last light of evening.

Chapter Twelve

Fool, fool, fool, Peter said to himself the next morning as he watched Merry standing in front of the glittering windows of Shreve, Crump, and Low. Before he had ruined their evening by saying too much too soon, he had intended to bring her to this venerable Boston jeweler to search for a diamond ring. Now she seemed absorbed instead in the study of Bernardaud china. *Perhaps she simply can't love me enough,* he thought. *It happens sometimes, this blindness of mine. I never understood it with Alison, all those years ago. Until she left.*

Merry's blond hair, falling just to chin length and held back from her eyes now with one upswept hand, was fluttering in a light May breeze. She wore a pale-green cotton sweater that managed to slide away unexpectedly from her collarbones, which were as sharp and modeled as the planes of her face. He loved the slope and jut of her

bones—from hip to shoulder blade to the knobby curve of
one wrist, falling delicately from the sweater's sleeve; and
of a sudden he thought of Elizabeth Osborne. Had someone looked at *her* this way, never thinking those beloved
objects—the knee, the ankle, the hinge of a shoulder—
would end in an anonymous pile?

And with a sharp stab of knowing, Peter knew then
that Merry would die. One day, someday, unforeseen and
inexorably, she would vanish from the earth. The sense of
loss was so swift and absolute that he felt a lump rise in
his throat. She turned and smiled at him, one dark eyebrow raised, and said, "I know. We've got to get going,
don't we?"

"I want to be with you for as long as you live," Peter
said, and touched her hair lightly. "And don't make me
regret that I've said so. Let me be foolish and maudlin
and deathless when I must. It's what I have to do, if I'm
to cope with loving you."

She pressed her hand against his cheek. They walked
to their taxi without a word.

All such deathless questions were banished from
Merry's mind, however, within minutes of her return
to Nantucket. She and Peter drove separately from the
airport—he to Mason Farms, and she, after a stop for
gas, directly to the police station. She felt a creeping
anxiety whenever she was absent during the work week,
an inborn sense of guilt that she might be enjoying herself too much on the taxpayer's dime. The fact that most
of the enjoyment of the past twenty-four hours—like
most of the tension—had been on Peter's dime didn't
lessen the anxiety one whit. He caused her thoughts decidedly to stray; and there was a murder to investigate.
Learning the facts about Elizabeth Osborne's money, particularly now that the woman was officially declared
dead, was Merry's first priority.

Or was until she dashed up the steps to her office on
the station's second floor and interrupted a conference in

progress. Her father sat at one end of the table, his chair tipped back in a deceptive attitude of relaxation; at the other, pointer in hand and easel pad at the ready, stood Dr. Tucker Enright.

At the sight of him, Merry's heart began a slow, painful thumping. She had hardly expected to see him again, much less so soon; and if he was standing here . . . if he had come back so quickly . . . had he changed his mind about Elizabeth Osborne and the serial murders?

"Detective Folger," Enright said, pausing in what was clearly midsentence. He smiled briefly. Eight heads swiveled toward Merry. She recognized most of them: Clarence and Howie, and Dr. John Fairborn; Bill Carmichael and Dave Otis, from the state police. The other three were actually wearing name tags. *Where did Dad dig those up,* she thought, *and what in hell is going on?*

John Folger's head craned over his shoulder to meet her inquiring eye; and then he brought the precariously tilted swivel chair abruptly back to earth.

"Welcome home," he told his daughter. "How was the trip to the U.S.?"

An old Nantucket joke, that the mainland was another country. Oddly hollow today, given the strain on her father's face.

"Fine. We can talk about it later."

"Why don't you take a chair, Meredith, and we'll let Dr. Enright get back to his briefing."

She did as she was told, walking halfway around the table to the only empty seat, which a redheaded woman in a gray business suit offered politely. Merry glanced at the woman's name tag as she slid into the chair. *Special Agent Dana Stevens,* it said. *FBI.* Merry swallowed and found that her mouth was dry.

"Just to bring you up to speed, Detective—" Tucker Enright said, and Merry looked over at him swiftly. He was in a dark suit and tie today and seemed somehow diminished—slighter of build, more nondescript, and wearier than a few weeks earlier. "We've invaded your station because a woman was found strangled last night in the area of the island called"—he glanced down at a yellow legal pad on the table before him—"Madaket. Which I guess is to the west of the place where you folks found those bones."

"Strangled? Who?" She turned toward her father and heard the echo of her own voice as though it came from someone else in the room—someone detached from all emotion, someone she was watching carefully. Meanwhile, the real Meredith was thinking to herself, *It's not possible.*

John Folger cleared his throat. "Roxanne Teasdale. Emily's granddaughter."

"*Emily* Teasdale?" The name fell on Merry's ears with all the force of a blow. *Ralph,* she thought. "I didn't know she had a granddaughter."

"Roxanne is—was—right out o' college," Clarence supplied. "Taught third grade ovah at the elementary school."

"Oh, my God—poor Emily," Merry exclaimed, and started up from her chair as if to go in search of the white-haired woman that very moment.

"Meredith," her father said, his voice low and tense, "Dr. Enright is in the middle of a presentation."

Merry hesitated, glanced at Enright, and then sank back into her seat.

"Right." Enright turned to the easel and flipped up a page—revealing an enlarged photographic print of what must be Roxanne. The girl's face was turned away from the camera, but Merry could see the bruised impression of a pair of hands on her long white neck, obscenely stark in the glare of police lights. She had been wearing jeans; they were still pulled down around her ankles, along with her underwear, and her shirt was rucked up, exposing a length of rib cage. Her arms were drawn over her head and bound, unable to cover her nakedness; and for some reason it was this—the casual horror of that nakedness,

and all the violation it presaged—that utterly appalled
Merry. She closed her eyes, sick to death.

"I've only had a preliminary look at the corpse and the
scene, but every indication—the characteristic ligature at
the wrists, the killer's use of his hands for strangulation,
and of course the sexual assault and the clipping of a lock
of hair"—at this Enright's pointer described an arc over
Roxanne's tumble of auburn curls, and Merry, opening
her eyes, saw that a section of the hair had been raggedly
severed—"suggest that the killing falls into our pattern.
I'm particularly struck by the disposition of the body,
which, as you know, was left draped over a discarded sofa
in the middle of the landfill."

"The landfill?" Merry burst out. "Jesus Christ! Who
found her at the landfill?"

Enright studied Merry for a wordless moment, a faint
crease in his forehead. "I'm sorry, Detective. We've all
had some time to digest the facts of this case. It's a bit
different for you. Perhaps you'd like to get a drink of water or something, and learn the details in private."

He was inviting her to leave. Merry flushed, instantly
humiliated, but when her voice came, it was tolerably
controlled. "I apologize for the tenor of my words, Dr.
Enright, but I think the question is a legitimate one. At
this time of year the landfill closes early—around three in
the afternoon. It's just not a place most people visit at
night."

"She was found by a construction worker," Enright
said, "and, yes, he was dumping after hours. Probably trying to avoid paying some fees—I'm not sure how your
system works here—or getting rid of some paint he was
supposed to recycle. Whatever it was, he forgot about it
when his headlights picked up this baby."

"This *baby*," Merry said tightly, "happens to be a member of our community. She's the granddaughter of a woman
we all know."

"Meredith," the chief said warningly.

"I'm all right, Dad. I'm sorry, I—" She hesitated, took a

deep breath, and looked back again at Enright. "Have you considered the possibility that this construction worker might have murdered the girl?"

Enright ignored the question, and in the silence that followed Merry's words, Bill Carmichael, the most senior of the island's state police, cleared his throat. "It was Casey Ambrose, Meredith," he said. "Getting rid of some paint. Missed the quarterly collection day for toxic substances."

"Oh." Merry's voice was subdued. Even she could see that Casey—a carpenter in his midfifties and a fixture on the island—was unlikely to have murdered Roxanne.

"We questioned him and all," Bill continued. "Wanted to know if he'd seen anybody coming or going from the landfill area before he found the girl. Couldn't tell us much."

"Parh fellah was pretty shook up," Clarence added. "Saw him tippin' back a few in the Rose and Crown just before closin', and his hands were tremblin' like my old granny's."

"Understandable," Tucker Enright said grimly. "It's not a pretty sight." He snapped his pointer shut and dropped it next to the yellow legal pad. "There's no point in prolonging this. You folks asked for my opinion—did the man responsible for the previous five murders also kill Roxanne? I think so. And that man is clearly not Manuel Esconvidos, since he's safely in jail in Boston."

"What about a wanna-be?" asked Bill Carmichael suddenly. "A copycat killer? Esconvidos has been splashed all over the papers. Any nut could decide to copy his MO."

"Possibly." Enright nodded. "But as you may know, I'm not convinced Esconvidos is guilty of anything other than attempted rape. I'm wondering now if we've been following the wrong man. Maybe the right one—the one responsible for *all* the murders—just hit Nantucket."

Merry sighed in frustration. "You're wondering, we're wondering—doesn't anybody have a clue? I mean, it's all very well for the FBI to juggle theories, but women are *dying* out there." Enright's blue eyes were fixed on her face, and the concern Merry read in them encouraged her to go on. "This is a very small town, you know? And one that survives on tourism. People are going to panic. The ones who can will catch the next boat to the mainland, and the ones who can't will be lined up outside the police station's door. Wanting answers. Wanting to know they're safe. And it's my father's head that'll be on the block."

"It won't be sitting there alone," said a voice at Merry's side.

She turned toward the redheaded FBI agent. The woman extended her hand. "I'm Special Agent Stevens. I'll be remaining here for the duration of the investigation into Roxanne Teasdale's death."

"In effect," John Folger added, "we'll be working for Dana, along with Bill and Dave here, liaising on this part of the entire case." He nodded to the state police, who looked down at the cups of coffee and swiveled their pens between awkward fingers.

Merry glanced from Dana Stevens to her father, then reached a quick hand to shake the FBI agent's extended one. There might be *some* good to be found, Merry decided, from a situation that forced her father to work for a woman.

The FBI had certainly descended on the island in what, to Merry's unaccustomed eyes, looked like force. Besides Enright and Agent Stevens, two forensics guys had attended the meeting, and their assistants were still working out at the landfill, sifting through the garbage surrounding the area where the corpse had been discovered. Even the sofa on which Roxanne Teasdale was found had been bagged in plastic, for shipment to Washington.

"They might as well do us all a fayvah," Clarence Strangerfield observed as he settled into a chair in Merry's office, "and take the landfill itself." Despite her oppression of spirits, Merry smiled. Clarence was partly in awe of the FBI, she knew. She guessed he would be spending much of the day looking over their shoulders and assessing the equipment they used so effortlessly. He had already witnessed one operation Merry was certain he was itching to try at home—the attempt to lift finger-prints from Roxanne Teasdale's cooling body.

Unlike the previous five victims, Roxanne had been dead only about an hour when Casey Ambrose picked up her tortured form in his truck's headlights just after eight P.M. The marks of her killer's hands were still vivid upon her neck, as Merry had observed in the photograph of the scene. Latent prints could be retrieved from human skin for up to twelve hours after an attack, and the FBI forensics team, seizing the opportunity, made it from Boston to the island by midnight. Clarence had told Merry what had happened next: every inch of the dead woman's exposed skin was examined with a magnifying glass as she lay, still sprawled on the shabby couch, under the police lights. The forensics team concentrated on areas of her body that appeared to be chafed or bruised—her hips, thighs, upper arms, rib cage, and neck—assuming that her killer had touched her there. Then they applied small squares of photographic paper firmly to the spots. When the squares were lifted from the skin, the FBI dusted them—revealing a disappointing array of blurred markings. The killer had, of course, worn gloves.

And now, Clarence confided, they were searching the surrounding landfill for the gloves themselves, in the faint hope that the killer had tossed them aside when his work was done. It was nothing to the FBI to lift prints from the interior of a latex glove; and then, the crime-scene chief told Merry grimly, they might just have him.

"I wish it were that simple," Tucker Enright said from the office doorway. "He probably threw them into the sea. This is not a stupid person we're dealing with."

"Hello, Doctor," Merry said.

"Am I interrupting? Or do you have a moment?"

"I should be getting out to the landfill anyway, Marradith." Clarence rose creakily to his feet. "I'll just offer up my chair."

"Thanks." Enright watched Clarence amble down the hallway. "Nice guy, isn't he?" he asked Merry.

"The best," she said fondly. "A Nantucketer through and through. And he's an institution on the force. What can I do for you?"

Enright hesitated, then slid into the chair before her desk. "I wanted to apologize, I guess. For upsetting you."

"Don't bother." Merry shifted uncomfortably and looked down at the pen she was turning in her fingers. Before the influx of guests she had been editing her notes from Jack Osborne's interview. All that seemed remarkably trivial now. "My dad says I have a tendency to be overly emotional. I guess I just proved it. My behavior wasn't entirely professional."

"Well," Enright said with an effort of lightness, "you *did* warn me at lunch the other day that violence was not one of your favorite things."

"So what were you supposed to do? Shield me?" Merry flung her pen down in disgust. "I think I've had enough shielding, Doctor."

"I asked you to call me Tucker," he said quietly.

There was a fractional pause. "I'm not sure that would be a good idea, now that you're here on a case."

"Too . . . unprofessional?"

"Something like that."

"I see." Enright sighed. "I see all too well. How unfortunate. I enjoyed our conversation very much, you know. I don't connect that way with people at the drop of a hat. I thought of nothing but you all weekend."

Embarrassment swept over Merry in a wave. She attempted to ignore it. "And did I improve your golf game?"

"Not in the slightest," Enright replied cheerfully. "It's beyond improvement. But I hope you spent your time better. I gather you were on vacation."

"Not exactly." Merry thought guiltily of Peter. "I just

got back from Boston, but that was work. The Sconset bones."

"Really? Can you tell me about it?"

"We have an identification. I was breaking the news to the husband."

"Who lives in Boston."

"Back Bay."

He seemed about to inquire further; and then something—a natural delicacy, an awareness that he might be invading her case—persuaded him otherwise. He said only, "Congratulations. Now you have to solve the murder."

Merry smiled faintly. "Not very important, in light of what happened while I was away."

"No," Enright said. "I suppose not. Although why one woman's strangulation should seem more awful than another's is beyond my understanding." His eyes flickered over her face with the same gentle concern. "I just wanted you to know that I'm not entirely a monster. I understand that this is troubling for you."

"In a way that it's not for the FBI?"

"Right. We've become inured to this sort of thing. The flip charts and the photographs tend to obscure the lives involved. I realize that."

"But you must feel something—outrage, anger."

He stood up, his lips compressed. "I learned long ago that if I didn't push the anger out of my mind, it might threaten to take over. Jen taught me that."

Merry had no words to answer this.

"And, too," Enright added, "you knew this girl. That would have to make a difference."

"Not the girl," Merry corrected. "Her grandmother. And I know her only slightly, of course. But it's enough to make me feel horrible. This—*obscenity*—should never have happened to Emily."

"Dana's heading out to interview her," Enright said casually. "Maybe you should go along."

Merry's head came up. "You think? She wouldn't mind?"

"She'd be a fool not to find it helpful. And Dana's no fool." He smiled and turned toward the hall.

"Thanks, Doctor," Merry called after him; and at his offhand wave she felt her heart skip a beat.

Chapter Thirteen

"Enright's a remarkable guy," Dana Stevens said. Her face was turned toward the passenger window, seemingly absorbed in the passing landscape. "Most people burn out on the sort of stuff he has to handle every day. Enright just keeps going. It's his passion, I think. What everybody else finds completely draining is *his* reason to exist."

"You've known him a while?"

"Eleven years. Since I first joined the Bureau. He taught part of the forensics unit at Quantico when I was in training." She laughed suddenly. "All the women idolized him. And he knew it."

"And yet," Merry said carefully, "he lives alone. Or so he said when we had lunch the other day."

Dana studied her narrowly. "Don't tell me the famous Enright charm is already at work! Be careful—he's a pro!"

"Don't be silly," Merry said, more abruptly than she had intended. "I'm just curious, that's all."

"Yeah, well, the good doctor excites a lot of curiosity," Dana Stevens observed. "Probably because he's so visibly alone. How can a man do what he does without a safety valve at home? It defies understanding, in a way. That he could be so self-sufficient. But, you know, despite the eleven years I can't really tell you much about him." She paused, considering. "He shuttles wherever a case takes him, hovers on the edge of investigations, watches everything without saying much—until the chips are down and the perp is caught. Then he's the one person you can count on to put a real creep away. If you've got to have an expert witness, it better be Enright, and your side better be paying him."

"So I've heard," Merry said. "This is Madaket, by the way."

The two women were on their way to Emily Teasdale's cottage; and though Merry had elected to accompany Dana Stevens, she frankly dreaded the interview. Emily was in her seventies, a widow. The loss of her granddaughter would be devastating, and Merry hesitated to intrude on the woman's grief so soon after Roxanne's murder. It was Dana, however, who would do the questioning. Merry's role in the FBI–state police investigation appeared to be limited to ferrying members of both forces to various points around the island.

"How big is Nantucket?" Dana asked. "I thought we were driving *away* from the water, and yet here it is again."

"It's about fifteen miles long by four miles wide."

"That small? How do you stand it?"

Merry looked sideways at the FBI agent. "Where are you from?"

"New York."

"State or city?"

"Both. Born in Westchester, lived in Manhattan, and stationed now in the FBI's Boston field office."

"A city girl."

"Yep. Don't get me wrong—I'd love to come out here for the weekend. But it's so isolated. What's it like in February?"

"*Gray.* Gray sky, gray sea, gray-shingled houses. Gray car," she said, patting the Explorer's wheel. "I wear a lot of bright colors in February." Involuntarily, Merry thought of the fire in Peter's sitting room, and the comfort of the hand-loomed throw wrapped around her legs as she settled into his sofa with a good book. "There's a perpetual wind roaring over the moors that makes you hunker down inside. It can be absolutely wonderful in winter. And very far from anywhere else."

"These are the moors?" Dana tilted her head toward the window.

Merry nodded. "The only native North American heath. More of it is going under the construction knife every year. I don't know what people are thinking of, when they throw up those plywood palaces. Or how they talk their way past the building inspector and the zoning commission."

Dana studied the massive summer "cottages," gabled and shingled and dotted with fake Palladian windows, that sat grandly on the rolling hills of scrub pine and beach plum, and nodded slowly. "This is really your home, isn't it?"

"It's my country," Merry said quietly, and sped up as they passed the landfill, its barricaded entrance lost in a knot of reporters and screaming with yellow tape.

Emily Teasdale's house sat on Smith Point, at the far end of unpaved Massachusetts Avenue, so Merry abandoned the Madaket road and crossed over Hither Creek, sparing a glance for the boats moored quietly in its marshy pools. The Teasdale house looked south, toward the Atlantic, rather than east to Tuckernuck Island. It was a lonely view of choppy green water made bleaker by the cloudy day. Like Sconset, Madaket was very much a summer community, and those who hugged the island's extremities in all seasons were a hardy breed.

Emily Teasdale was no exception, as Merry tried to explain to Dana Stevens.

"She's lived here forever," she said, "which is unusual for an off-islander."

"You still call her that?" Dana asked, amused.

"Of course. She's from New York originally. Came up here in the summers while her husband was alive, and when he died, she sold the New York house and took up residence. It still surprises me when an off-islander does that, although more and more of them do."

"So only people born here are real islanders."

"Well," Merry said with a smile, "it depends who you ask. You asked *me*. My ancestor was one of the first to settle Nantucket in the 1670s, so I take a somewhat longer view of things."

"Understandably," Dana said, smiling back at her.

Merry pulled up before Emily Teasdale's door. "I'd like to hear more about Enright," she told the other woman, "when you have the time."

"Sure." Dana grabbed her briefcase and pushed open the car door. "Has he mentioned his sister's murder yet? That's one of his sure-fire openers. It establishes his credentials as a caring guy."

Somewhat unsettled by this last remark, Merry led the way to Emily Teasdale's front door.

She was waiting for them behind the screen, and at the sight of Merry her soft, wrinkled face crumpled and became featureless with grief, the way a full-blown rose will dissolve at a fingertip's touch. To Merry's surprise Emily threw wide the door and enfolded her fiercely in her arms, as though the touch of another young woman was necessary to fill Roxanne's void. She said nothing; and if she wept, she wept in silence. There was something terrible about that stillness, and Merry's throat constricted even as she looked her apology to Dana over Emily's sweatered shoulder.

"Merry Folger," Emily said, releasing her at last. "The

very person I wanted to see. You'll find this vicious man. You *will*. For my Roxie. I know it."

"We'll do our best, Mrs. Teasdale," Merry said gently. "This is Special Agent Dana Stevens, from the FBI. She flew in from Boston this morning to help."

Emily Teasdale may have moved into the very maw of grief, but she had hardly taken leave of her senses. She looked at Dana shrewdly. "Why is the FBI interested in Roxanne?" she demanded.

"That's what we'd like to talk to you about," Dana Stevens replied. "May we come in, Mrs. Teasdale?"

"I thought the worst moment was hearing about it, last night, from that policeman." Emily was holding Roxanne's picture, which probably dated from the girl's senior year in high school, and her eyes were on it, bright with grief, as she spoke. "They figured out who she was when they found her purse lying somewhere in that landfill. He left her there—did you know that, Detective? Like she was garbage. My Roxie. But I was wrong." At this she glanced up and away from them, out the window to the sea. "The worst moment was looking at her at three o'clock in the morning, at the hospital, once those police had finished with her. Saying her name out loud, and knowing she would never hear. Because then I knew there was absolutely no mistake. It wasn't someone else's girl they'd found. Until I went into that room, and they lifted the sheet away from her face, there was always a chance."

"I'm so sorry, Mrs. Teasdale," Merry said, and felt immediately and profoundly inadequate.

"Did you expect Roxanne home at any particular time last night?" Dana Stevens asked.

Emily nodded. "Yes. I thought she'd be back around eight or so. She was working on the third grade's spring pageant after school—making scenery and so forth—and called to say she was having dinner with Lily. When the doorbell rang, I thought maybe Roxie'd lost her key, you see. That she was standing on the doorstep. But instead it was the police."

A shudder racked her narrow body. She covered her face with her hands.

"Whom did you say she had dinner with, Mrs. Teasdale?" Dana asked.

Emily searched distractedly in her pockets for a tissue. Merry reached in her purse and pulled out a packet of them. She pressed it into Emily's hand. "Here. Keep it."

"Oh, thank you, dear." Emily blew her nose tidily and tucked the used tissue into her sleeve. "She was going to the Brotherhood with Lily Olszewski. Lily teaches the fourth grade. The two classes were sharing the skit, you see, and most of it was Lily's idea. She's a little older than Roxie, maybe twenty-four, and has been at the school longer."

"I understand. Do you know where we could reach Ms. Olszewski?"

"At the school, I guess—though I wouldn't be surprised if she didn't go in today. I called her this morning and told her about—about Roxie. Lily was quite devastated, poor girl. Well, she *should* be. You *all* should be," Emily finished, looking sharply from Merry to Dana. "Someone out there is preying on young women, and none of you is safe. I never thought I would live to see the day such things happened on Nantucket. I still can't believe it."

"I can't either," Merry said grimly. "Mrs. Teasdale, did you notice any strangers in the Madaket area in the past week?"

"Looking in the windows to see who's home and who's not?" the woman replied. "No, can't say as I have. But the summer folks are starting to trickle back—ever since Daffodil Weekend—and sometimes a stranger's nothing more than a new neighbor. You know how that is."

"And you saw nothing unusual yesterday?" Dana asked.

Emily shook her head. "I was in town myself until about six. I volunteer at the Atheneum."

"The library," Merry supplied sotto voce to the benighted Dana.

"I came home, let myself in, took Roxie's message off that fool machine"—Emily gestured emphatically toward a distant room. "I hate it, you know, but she brought it with her and insists on using it. Personally, I hang up whenever one answers *my* calls. If someone won't take the time to answer, why should I take the trouble to leave a message? But there was her dear voice. Her *dear* voice. Just as happy and carefree—she never knew. Of course not. Never knew what was in store for her." Emily's hands gripped one another so fiercely, the knuckles shone white beneath the skin. She met Merry's eyes steadily. "You've lived too long when you've seen as much death as I have, Meredith."

Merry reached out and took Emily's hand between her own.

"How long has your granddaughter lived with you, Mrs. Teasdale?" Dana asked.

"Almost a year now." Emily's gaze shifted to the FBI agent. "She came out in June and did some waitressing before the start of the school year. She'd been out the previous spring, of course, to interview when the third-grade spot went vacant."

"And before that?"

"At school. In San Francisco, where my son Paul and his wife, Kathy, live. Can you imagine how I felt last night," she appealed to Merry "calling them to say their only girl was gone? They have three boys, and then Roxie. She's the youngest. The baby. The others are all married. Poor Paul figured she'd be safer here than anywhere on earth. To hear him cry—"

"It came as a complete shock to everyone."

"Of course."

"There was no intimation," Dana said, "that your granddaughter had been stalked, for example, or was the target of violence before her arrival on the island?—From a jealous boyfriend, or a spurned acquaintance—even a complete stranger? Someone who might have followed her here to Nantucket?"

"Absolutely not." Emily's lips pinched together in irritation. "Roxanne never knew those kinds of people."

"And Mrs. Teasdale," the agent continued smoothly, "whom did she associate with here on the island? Did she date anyone?"

Emily shook her head. "I got the impression she was carrying the torch for some young man away in medical school," she said. "He called or wrote occasionally. When I asked Roxanne about him, she always laughed and said they were just friends. So many young women have men for friends now—it comes of going to school together. But all that's foreign to me, you know. In my day you were either seeing someone or you weren't."

"I understand. Do you know his name? Where he lives?"

"His name is Michael," Emily said after a moment, "and he's someplace in New York, I believe."

Dana pressed her lips together, to stifle frustration, Merry thought, and looked down at her notebook. "And Roxanne's Nantucket friends?"

"I suppose Lily would know best."

"Could you give us Lily's number, Mrs. Teasdale?"

"Of course," Emily said, and rose immediately in pursuit of it.

"At the very least she'll know when the two of them said good-bye last night," Dana said to Merry, "and where Roxanne was heading."

"Here it is." Emily reappeared in the living room with her reading glasses perched on her nose. "I'm sure she'd be happy to talk to you." She paused. "Now, tell me why the Federal Bureau of Investigation is meddling in island business."

"We think Roxanne's death is part of a pattern," Dana said gently.

"And that this *animal* has killed someone before. Where?"

"Throughout Massachusetts, but primarily in the vicinity of Boston," Merry replied.

"How many girls have died?"

"Six now," Dana Stevens said, "over roughly the past five years."

"Five years. Five years, and you've never caught him." The expression on Emily's aged face was scathing. "You had to wait for him to kill my Roxie. Well, let me tell you something, Miss FBI Agent from Boston. You're working with Merry Folger now. And nobody knows her business better. She's an *island* girl, after all."

As they drove away from Emily Teasdale's house, Dana picked up the car's cellular phone and dialed Lily Ol-szewski's number. Merry heard the faint buzz of repeated rings. No answer.

"Maybe she went into school anyway," the FBI agent said.

Merry shook her head. "I doubt it. Probably just ignoring the phone. Try again and let it ring a bit longer."

Dana clicked the phone's power button and redialed. "Ever run into her yourself, Merry? You seem to know everybody."

"Unfortunately, no. Fourth-graders and their teachers are rare among my acquaintances."

"Hello, is this Lily?" Dana's head turned slightly away from Merry, as though she were searching for privacy. Merry kept her eyes on the road.

"My name is Dana Stevens, and I'm with the FBI," Dana continued. "I'm sorry to trouble you, but I'd like to talk to you about Roxanne Teasdale."

Even Merry heard the burst of weeping that met this simple statement, and she winced. Dana merely waited a moment patiently, her eyes trained on the passing landscape, and then said, "Would it be possible to stop by your house this afternoon?"

A hesitation, as of dead air on the line, and then a woman's muttered assent, electronically distorted.

"Okay. So that's—that's 176 *Sewer* Bed Road, in Surfside?" Dana's head swiveled toward Merry's, one eyebrow raised. "We'll be there in—oh, about . . ."

"Fifteen minutes," Merry offered. She came to a rolling stop at an intersection. Dana said good-bye to Lily Olszewski and turned off the phone. Then she looked at Merry.

"How do you feel about all this?"

"About the murder?"

"No. I *know* how you feel about the murder. I haven't seen so much emotion in a conference room since the Kennedy assassinations."

"You must have been four around then."

"Four exactly—for Bobby's," Dana rejoined cheerfully. "Same age as yourself, I'll bet."

"Five," Merry admitted.

"Regardless. I find your level of involvement with this case rather admirable. In our line of work it's too easy to forget that real lives end every day, sometimes in horrible ways."

"You think so?" Merry mused. "That's the one thing that keeps me going. The sense of those real lives."

"Not me," Dana replied after a moment's thought. "For me it's the puzzle. The chase. The matching of my wits against a killer's. When I'm really honest, I have to say that's why I joined the Bureau."

"And what about Tucker Enright?" Merry asked her. "Why's he working for you guys instead of taking clients on Madison Avenue?"

"Probably because we pay him more. And because Tucker's the same as all of us. He gets off on the excitement. The hunt. You can see it in his eyes when he's really working." Dana shifted in her seat and turned her body slightly toward Merry's. Employment with a large government agency had its disadvantages, Merry decided, however glamorous it seemed; Special Agent Stevens was trapped in stockings, high heels, and a slimly fashionable skirt, while Merry was comfortably casual in the same cotton sweater that had carried her through Shreve, Crump, and Low.

"It may even be intensified for Enright," Dana continued, "because he's so *mentally* involved with these killers, you know? He's matching wits with them, literally. It becomes such a personal battle."

"I suppose." Merry downshifted and turned right into Surfside Road. "But who's getting into the minds of the victims?"

"I'm sorry?" Dana asked, as though she had misheard.

"The victims. Who's thinking about *them*? About why they might have fallen into the hands of this killer? Is there any pattern to the women he's killed, other than their age and the way he's killed them?"

"I'm sure someone's looked at that," Dana said vaguely. "But I'm relatively new to the investigation. They threw me onto it when Esconvidos was caught, and I've spent most of the past two weeks checking his whereabouts on key dates over the past five years. The broader picture's being handled by my chief's deputy, a guy named Kinkaid. He's the one who decided these seemingly unconnected killings fell into a serial pattern."

"And does Kinkaid have any thoughts about where Roxanne matches the pattern?"

"Well, there's the way her body was left—two of the others were found in or near trash Dumpsters, you know, so there's that element; and then there's the hunk of hair cut from her scalp—"

"All well and good," Merry broke in, "but you're telling me about the creep who killed her, not about Roxanne."

There was a silence. "I don't know much about her," Dana said quietly.

"Or in what ways she may be similar to the other murdered women."

"Right."

"Or even whether there *are* any similarities among them, other than their age."

"You start there, don't you?" Dana said. "With the victims. It's a police thing. I'd forgotten that, working so many years at the Bureau. By the time we get involved in a case, it's usually so much bigger than the people who've been killed."

Involuntarily, Merry gripped the wheel. "How strange," she said evenly.

"That's why I asked how you felt about all this," Dana continued. "About the FBI's involvement. About the scale of this investigation. And the fact that you're—well—"

"Reduced to ferrying people around the island?" Merry shrugged helplessly. "I work for my dad. He asked me to drive today. Maybe tomorrow I can get back to my case. Who knows?"

"You're working another case?"

Merry nodded. "An eight-year-old murder. A couple of kids dug up some bones on a beach not far from here."

"Wow. *That's* not going to be solved anytime soon."

"Thanks for the vote of confidence."

"I'm sorry—" Dana reached out a manicured hand in swift remorse. "That wasn't a comment on your skills, merely an observation about the passage of time. How can you expect to follow a trail that's gone so cold?"

"By looking at the victim," Merry answered quietly. "By looking at who she knew, and who might have hated her enough to bury her deep in Sconset sand."

"So you know who she was?"

"A Harvard-educated psychiatrist with a taste for charming men. Too many of them, perhaps."

"This gets better and better. Was she young?"

"Young to die, or young in the reckoning of the world?" Merry cut right into the unfortunately named Sewer Bed Road, an unpaved lane flanked by imposing summer homes, most of them showing the blank and unloved windows of seasonal disuse.

Dana laughed. "It does make a difference, doesn't it?"

"This woman would have said so. She was forty-two when someone strangled her."

"And a Harvard-trained shrink, you say? Then I think you definitely need to warm up to Enright."

Merry was busy peering across the FBI agent's shoulder, in search of Lily Olszewski's house number, but now she glanced over at Dana in surprise. "Why?"

"Sounds like they're roughly the same age, and that may mean they were classmates. Or at the very least, within a year or two of each other. I'll bet he knew her. And if Enright knew your victim, Detective, you can be certain he knew *everything* about her."

Number 176 Sewer Bed Road was one of the few that appeared to be inhabited in early May. A typical summer rental, Merry decided as Lily Olszewski opened the door to the two women—what the realtors termed an upside-down house, with the bedrooms on the lower floor and the upstairs reserved for an open living-dining-kitchen area with sweeping views of the sea. When they had introduced themselves, and followed the blond Lily up a staircase to a comfortable sofa clad in blue-and-white-striped mattress ticking, Merry's suspicions were confirmed. Lily was house-sitting for some off-islanders, due back around the Fourth of July. The house was rented before and after the absentee owners' two-week vacation, and Lily was vacating the premises Memorial Day.

Dana appeared slightly bemused by this islander's dilemma, but Merry immediately recognized a kindred soul. The survival tactics of the people who formed Nantucket's backbone—the teachers, firefighters, postal workers, and shop clerks—were all too familiar. It had taken Merry years to achieve the status of independent living herself. None of them could afford a rented home during the summer months. Lily was simply lucky she had won a coveted job as caretaker and saved herself eight months' rent.

"I can't believe what happened to Roxanne," she said

now, tucking one bare foot under her and sitting upright as a dancer on her sofa cushion. Lily Olszewski was supposed to be twenty-four, a few years older than her friend Roxanne, but to Merry's eyes she might have been in high school. Her platinum-blond hair was pulled back severely into a ponytail, and her fair skin, puffy and blotched from weeping, was free of makeup. She wore torn jeans low on the hip, and a shapeless sweater over a narrowly striped T-shirt several sizes too big. For the thousandth time Merry wondered about the appeal of grunge. Was there so great a gulf between twenty and thirty? Apparently so. Lily was, Merry realized with a sense of shock, of an utterly different generation from her own.

"I know it was terrible of me, but I couldn't face going in to school today," the girl began, lighting a cigarette and inhaling deeply. She reached up with her free hand and brushed back an invisible strand of hair. "All those questions. All that false sympathy. I mean, I was the last person to see her alive!"

"Other than whoever killed her," Dana observed, and pulled out her notebook. Lily's eyes hardened. "We were hoping you could tell us what time you said good-bye to Ms. Teasdale."

"Around seven. I can't tell you anything, I'm afraid."

"You'd been having dinner?"

Lily nodded. "At the Brotherhood."

To Merry's infinite respect Dana noted the name with complete insouciance, as though she were all too familiar with Nantucket's restaurants. No doubt Merry would be driving the FBI agent to the Brotherhood of Thieves in another hour.

"And Ms. Teasdale said nothing about plans to meet anyone later that evening?"

"She was wiped," Lily answered earnestly. "Absolutely *shot*. It's bad enough to manage sixteen kids all day, much less sit for hours cutting out a bunch of trees from construction paper. We both needed a beer and a cigarette and some downtime desperately. And then we were planning to take baths and go to bed early. And that's what I did. I mean, it's all so incredible—"

Merry studied the girl's face. It was ugly with grief, the eyes red-rimmed. How well had Lily known Roxanne? Did she mourn her loss deeply? Or was her sense of mortality—that knife edge we all walk so blithely— suddenly heightened by Roxanne's murder?

"There but for the grace of God go I," Merry murmured, and Lily turned to her searchingly.

"Yes," she said. "That's sort of what I'm thinking. That's why I haven't been able to step outside today. What if this maniac was watching us at the restaurant? What if he just *picked* one of us to follow home and killed Roxanne as easily as killing me? Why not me? I mean, why am I alive today? Tell me that!"

The FBI agent cleared her throat. "That's what we're hoping you can tell *us*, Ms. Olszewski."

"Oh, for Christ's sake, call me Lily," she retorted, and took a drag on her cigarette.

"Mrs. Teasdale suggested you might be the person who knew Roxanne best on the island. Can you think of any reason why someone might have wanted to kill her?"

"No."

"Please try to think. Did Roxanne seem frightened of anything? Did she mention any weird phone calls, or people who might be following her, or letters she had received?"

Lily, to her credit, seemed to consider each element of the question before finally shaking her head. "She was just like anybody else. If you're looking for a *reason* why she was killed, ask her killer. I'm sure Roxie didn't have a clue. I certainly don't."

Merry cleared her throat. "You say she was just like everybody else. What does that mean, exactly?"

Lily looked at her with annoyance. "She was basically normal. She ran three miles every morning, hated her thighs, and snitched cigarettes from me maybe once a week. Loved her grandma, but didn't really want to be living with her anymore. Too confining. We were talking about getting a place to house-sit together next fall—I was going to move in with Roxie at her grandma's in Madaket for the summer months. It'd seem kind of weird to do that now."

"Don't rule it out," Merry said. "Mrs. Teasdale might like the company."

Lily shrugged. "I've never really been around someone her age."

Again, Merry felt that distinct sense of alienation, of confronting a different breed.

"How did Roxie feel about her job?"

Lily grinned at Dana Stevens. "She *hated* teaching third grade—called it glorified baby-sitting. It was as much as she could do to keep from screaming at those brats all day long."

"How did your colleagues react to that?" the FBI agent asked.

"Our *colleagues*? We have no colleagues." Lily laughed. "We've got a bunch of old hags who've been doing this and nothing else for most of their lives. And believe me, Roxie and I aren't going to let that happen to us. We're getting out." She stopped, apparently brought up short by the irrelevant present tense. "I'm moving to Boston as soon as I've got enough cash. I want to check out the local club scene—play guitar," she explained. "Roxie was going to take the LSAT."

"Was she?" *Ambitious. Or casting about for a quick fix,* Merry thought. "Did she want to end up in Boston, too?"

Lily shrugged. "Probably. That's where Jack is, after all."

"Jack?"

"Her latest. He's a lot older guy. Teaches law at Harvard. I don't think Roxie could've gotten in *there*, but she wanted to be near him."

Merry stiffened with an instinctive excitement. "Not Jack Osborne?"

The girl's blond head came up. "What, you know him?

Did her grandma tell you? I thought Roxie wasn't talking about Jack at home."

Oh, baby, Merry thought. *Jack Osborne. The man's fingers are in every pie. Or around every throat, as it happens.*

"How did Roxanne meet Jack?" Merry asked, ignoring Lily's questions.

The young woman drew on her cigarette and narrowed her eyes, thinking. "At DeMarco's. Or was it Company of the Cauldron? She worked at both."

"When?"

"Last summer. She came out a couple of months before the school year started. I didn't know her then, but I guess she ran into Jack sometime around August. He was staying out here with some friends, and she waited on his table. The rest, as they say, is history. She was crazy about the guy, but, man, was she keeping the thing quiet. I've never even met him."

"He's come to see her here?" Merry's finger tightened around her pen.

Lily nodded. "He takes a room at the Harbor House. You should hear Roxie talk about *that*."

Jack Osborne, back on Nantucket repeatedly in the past year and a half. Jack Osborne, who insisted he'd never visited the island since his wife's disappearance. Jack, who might actually have buried Elizabeth's bones the night of the January blizzard, when he claimed he sat innocently at home.

Dana was looking at Merry intently. "You know this guy." It wasn't a question.

Merry nodded and shot the agent a warning glance.

"Right," Dana said, her lips pursed. "Now, let's talk about last night. Did you notice anything unusual while you were eating dinner, Lily? Did anyone attract your attention?"

Lily leaned forward to tap her cigarette into a quahog-shell ashtray. "No. I don't think so."

"Close your eyes," Merry suggested, "and think. Where were you sitting? At a table? Or the bar?"

"One of the tables. Against the wall. The fourth—no, the third—from the door."

"Were you sitting with your back to the wall?"

Eyes shut, Lily shook her head. "Roxie was. I was facing her."

"So you didn't see much of the other people in the room."

"No. Just the ones to the left and right of us."

"Anybody eating alone?"

Again Lily shook her head. "All couples. Older, tourist types, nobody I knew."

"And what did you order?"

"We both had salads. No—I forgot. Roxie started to order a salad and then had a cheeseburger. She's the sort of girl you love to hate, you know—eats all day long and never gains weight."

"Really?" Dana interjected in an interested tone.

"And who was your waiter?"

"That guy Mickey, the scalloper. Mid-thirties, looks older. He's working a night job to pay for his alimony."

"How do you know?"

Lily colored. "Why do you think we went to the Brotherhood?"

"Mickey's a friend of yours?"

"I'm working on it."

"Does—did Mickey know Roxanne?"

"No. She was looking him over for me."

"And?"

"She said he was a Total Baldwin."

Merry looked inquiringly at Dana, who seemed equally stumped.

"That's a really cute guy," Lily prompted impatiently. "Like Alec Baldwin, you know? Or one of his brothers. I can never keep them straight." She laughed abruptly, a sound that turned suddenly to a sob. "Oh, God. If I hadn't been such an idiot, she might be alive now."

"Don't think that way," Merry said gently. "You couldn't have kept Roxanne alive last night. None of us could."

"But there's nothing," Dana Stevens said, "that you can remember? No last-minute incident that sticks in your mind? As you said good-bye to Roxie, perhaps? Was there anyone standing in the street? Anyone sitting in a parked car?"

Lily hesitated.

"You didn't walk her to her car, did you?" Merry leaned forward. "You finished your salad, you ordered coffee, maybe, you toyed with the idea of dessert. Looking for a way to keep talking to Mickey. And Roxanne decided she needed to go home. Is that what happened?"

Lily nodded and dived for her cigarette, a picture of misery. "She got up and said really loudly—just to let Mickey hear—that she was heading back to Madaket now and she hoped I had a good time alone in my bathtub. Then she looked around the room with that grin of hers, as though she had a secret, and snapped her fingers. 'Waiter! My friend needs another beer. Maybe you could help her drink it.' "

"And then she left?"

Lily flicked some more ash into the shell. The cigarette had burned almost to her fingers, but she didn't seem to care.

"Did anyone follow her?"

"I don't know," she said miserably. "Mickey came back right around then. With my beer. Can you believe it? Roxie walks out and gets raped and strangled while I'm tossing them back with a jerk ten years older than me, who's already paying alimony on his first wife." She ground her cigarette to nothing. "Now, tell me I couldn't have kept her alive last night. Just try to tell me."

Chapter Fourteen

"Seitz!"

Patrolman Howie Seitz looked up from his desk in the Water Street station's 911 response area, where he was manning the glowing panel of electronics. "Detective Folger. What's up?"

Merry surveyed him hurriedly. Lily Olszewski's casual knowledge of Jack Osborne had changed the rules of her murder investigation in midstream. If Osborne was a far more vicious killer than she had ever imagined—if indeed he was linked to the FBI's investigation of the brutal strangulation of six young women—then it was Merry's duty to hand over her information immediately. And by way of reward for her cleverness and collegiality, she would undoubtedly be taken off the case first thing to-morrow morning.

But she had no intention of giving up the goods on

Jack Osborne before she talked with her father. Dana Stevens, fortunately, had failed to probe her obvious recognition of Osborne's name, being lost in the possibilities presented by Mickey the Total Baldwin. The waiter might have noticed a single man eating in the Brotherhood of Thieves, watching the two girls and following quietly in Roxanne's wake. Roxanne's Boston professor could wait for another day. And so Merry dropped Dana near the Brotherhood's wooden sign and tore down Broad Street for a powwow with her chief.

The station's main door was surrounded by press—not just the local newspaper types, but camera crews flown in from Boston. Two vans, plastered with brightly colored call signs and topped with satellite antennas, were illegally parked on Water and Chestnut. It was Merry's misfortune to be recognized by Suzanne Martel, a freelancer for the *Nantucket Beacon*, who whispered in her companion's ear as Merry approached; and before Merry knew it, a microphone and a camera were thrust in her face.

"Detective Forger," the television reporter cried, with all the vigor of a home-team cheerleader. "Marilyn Trilby, Channel Five News. Are there any leads in the Teasdale murder?"

"No comment," Merry said brusquely, "and it's Folger, not Forger."

Marilyn Trilby stepped bluntly in Merry's path, forcing her to a standstill, and a pack of her brethren strained and bayed beyond her shoulders, their microphones held high. The woman's was leveled like a spear.

"Is this another of the vicious serial killings that have swept Massachusetts? And is Manuel Esconvidos likely to go free?"

Merry's control snapped. "God knows. Don't you people get fed on a regular basis? You're as hungry as piranhas. We've had a brutal murder. A young woman—beautiful, intelligent, and terribly unlucky—has died a death no one deserves. You may have time to stand around talking, but I don't. And neither does anyone else on the Nantucket force."

She shoved Marilyn Trilby firmly to one side, cutting a path to the door.

"What would you tell Nantucket's women tonight, Detective?" the reporter called in her wake, undeterred.

Merry swung around. "The same thing I'd tell you, Ms. Trilby. Roxanne Teasdale was alive yesterday afternoon. Tonight she's dead. It could happen to anyone. It just has."

She slammed the door behind her, ran her fingers through her hair, and shot a rueful look at the patrolwoman, Laura Berry, who sat behind the entryway's small desk. "Don't those people ever go home?"

"Not when they're getting such dynamite material. Bet you're all over the ten o'clock news." Laura's eyes were fixed on her book, her constant companion whenever she drew reception duty, but Merry felt the reproach in her words. She walked meekly by the desk, her mind intent on her notes. Just inside the door she found Howie.

"How long have you been sitting here?" she asked him now.

"All day." Howie turned his wrist to glance at his watch. Nearly six o'clock, the end of his shift. "Some day to draw *this* duty, huh? When anybody with any sense is working the Teasdale murder."

"At least they let you into the conference this afternoon." Merry turned for the stairs to her second-floor office. But something in Howie's stooped shoulders, the defeat in his large frame, held her back.

"Yeah, well—" He looked away, as though embarrassed. "That's because I took the call the night before."

"*You?*"

Howie's normally cheerful face was taut and colorless. "You know what, Detective? When I saw her, I puked. All over my shoes." He lifted a foot for her inspection. "In front of Clarence, too."

Merry swallowed. "That's a pretty normal response, Howie."

"I guess. I've just never seen anybody I knew in that situation before."

Such careful language, Merry thought. How else to describe the atrocities visited upon Roxanne Teasdale's body, except as a *situation*? She perched on the edge of the 911 station and looked down at Howie's bent head, his familiar tangle of dark curls. He seemed intent upon the cuticle of his left thumb, worrying it with his right.

"You knew Roxanne Teasdale?"

He nodded. "But not well. Or not as well as I'd have liked."

"Where'd you meet her?"

Howie shrugged. "Around. The beach maybe, last summer—or it could have been at one of the Rose and Crown's jazz gigs. I can't remember. And it doesn't really matter, does it?" He looked up then, and Merry was struck by the pain in Seitz's eyes. She had grown too used to dismissing him as a baby fresh from Northeastern's criminal-justice department.

"She was only two years younger than me, you know?" Howie persisted.

"I know." A thought came to Merry—a dangerous thought. Until she revealed Osborne's link to the Teasdale murder, she was technically still in charge of his wife's case. And could thus pursue whatever leads appeared in her path. "Listen," she said. "You're finished here, right?"

"Just about."

"When your relief shows up, come over to my office. I've got a job for you. Buy you dinner afterward."

And in the meantime, Merry thought, she'd type up her notes from the Osborne interview. Her father would need them whenever they had that powwow; and she was the last person in the world to hand him an unorganized flood of illegible handwriting. When Howie appeared, they'd start working the fax machines. There was no one like Howie, after all, for digging up the dirt in other people's backyards.

Reading through the course of her interview with Jack Osborne, Merry felt a pang. All the lost opportunities, the questions unasked. What if she had waited a day and marched into the Marlborough Street house armed with the knowledge of Roxanne Teasdale's murder?

You wouldn't have been allowed anywhere near Boston, a small voice inside her admonished. The FBI would have dealt with Jack Osborne. As undoubtedly they would sometime in the immediate future.

"I want you to work the computers on this guy," she told Howie now. She handed him a piece of paper with Jack Osborne's name and birth date. She had found the latter conveniently noted in his wife's file. "Shut the door."

Howie obeyed her and sat down in the one free chair, his eyes alert.

"I know you're coming off a shift, and you're probably worn out, but I think I've got a lead in the Teasdale case, and I want to work it from this end before the FBI gets their paws all over it."

"Great," Howie said. "Could I be fired for this?"

"Oh, probably."

"Excellent. Living on the edge."

"After you've searched his records," she continued, "check into the financial end of Elizabeth Osborne's estate. It's supposed to be handled by a man called"—a quick look at her notes—"Martin Bromwell, at Morgan Guaranty in New York. Then call around the local hotels and find out whether Osborne's been here in the past year or so. Get the dates, if you can. You've done this sort of thing before."

"Damn straight," Howie agreed, and then caught himself. "I mean—that is—"

"Give me whatever you can find before tomorrow morning, okay? I need it before I talk to the chief."

"Osborne." Howie's brow crinkled as he looked at the paper. "This'd be Elizabeth's husband, right? What's he got to do with Roxie?"

"Ask the hotels," Merry said, her voice more bitter than she had intended. "I'm sure they'll remember her. Anybody shacking up with a man old enough to be her father has got to spark some talk, don't you think?"

Howie just whistled.

The FBI forensics team—two men and a woman, dressed in medical scrubs and wearing plastic caps on their heads—were still up to their knees in garbage, searching for the killer's missing gloves. They had been searching all day; large bags of refuse, carefully labeled, were stacked to one side of the spot in the landfill where Roxanne Teasdale's body had been found. If the gloves were here, Tucker Enright thought, this team would find them. But he knew in his heart that the gloves were long gone.

He breathed deep, unaffected now by the foul miasma that rose from the shifting hills of garbage. Over the years his olfactory threshold had risen, until he could endure almost anything—sights and odors that would propel another person from the scene, hand over mouth, body bent double with retching.

He crouched low, oblivious of the forensics people, his eyes narrowed as he studied the couch on which Roxanne Teasdale's corpse had lain. She had been so beautiful, he thought, even in her violation. Her killer had certainly seen her that way. Enright closed his eyes. He willed himself into the heart of darkness. What had Meredith Folger called it? *Incantations and appeasement of the gods?*

The man had watched for her from the darkness of a shuttered shopfront on Broad Street, one of those closed during the long months of the off-season; and when she emerged, with her youthful stride and glowing hair, and turned toward the side street and her desolate car, he had

run on swift and silent feet across the road to the opposite curb, throwing a glance over his shoulder, looking for
hostile eyes. He saw none. A weeknight in early May, and
the streets of the town were deserted in darkness. His
right hand was on her mouth, his left closing over the
keys she had been about to insert in the door's lock, before thirty seconds had elapsed.

And where did it happen?

They would have to leave town, of course—Roxanne
driving, terrified, pleading with him, his knife at her
throat. The car's headlights had carved a trail through the
Nantucket darkness. They would have headed west from
Broad, up Cliff Road toward Madaket, the emptiness of
the moors unwinding beside them.

Her killer's heart keeps time to the cadence of the exe-
cutioner's dull ax. He cannot sit still; he twitches, curses,
looks continually over his shoulder. Roxanne darts tremu-
lous glances from the corner of her eye, her fingers gripping the wheel with a painful concentration, as though
driving well might still save her. She does not think of the
obvious—of careening the car into a ditch, fighting him
tooth and nail as they roll and roll into beach plum and
scrub pine, the sandy soil smearing softly along the grill.
She has no notion it is her death he really wants. So she
drives obediently, at once fearful and hopeful.

There is not a patrol car for miles. There will be no
one to rescue her.

And probably, Enright thinks, somewhere near the
wetlands that bisect the Madaket road, he forces her to
stop and hauls her stumbling into the grass. His heart is
pounding faster now, the obscenities rapidfire, the rape a
mere incident, a trifle on the predator's path.

And when it is over—when his hands have crushed
her throat and his knife has torn from her the trophy of
her hair—he loads her body into the car and drives back
to the landfill, passed a few hundred yards earlier on the
road. Finds the sofa, which he'd spotted hours ago during
a survey of this place, so perfect for his needs. Arranges

her loose-limbed and vacant-eyed, a pillow for her head. And drives away in a matter of minutes, to leave the car—where?

The car had still not been found. Probably sitting in some supermarket parking lot, unnoticed among so many others. Dana Stevens would have thought of that, of course.

Enright expelled a shaky breath. This was his talent and his curse—this seeing through a killer's eyes. Over the years he had charted path after path into the belly of the beast, felt the blood lust and the careening madness, and called it by a different name. *These are calculated choices,* he would say in the courtroom's hush, his voice measured, his words deliberate. Say it so simply that even an idiot—the sort of idiot perpetually placed on juries—would understand—*This insanity they claim is nothing but a sham. We must kill them, or be killed ourselves. We must tear the evil from our very souls, or be consumed by it. This, too, a choice.*

The judge's black robe, the awesome stillness. The flashing of bulbs beyond the courtroom door.

"Dr. Enright!"

His fingers clenched, and Tucker Enright rose swiftly, brushing at his knees. Like the forensics people, he wore a plastic cap and scrubs; only these known fibers were allowed in the proximity of the dump, for purposes of exclusion. Not that it truly mattered—the landfill was such an eyesore of garden refuse, discarded furniture, rotting food, auto parts, and sundry rags that nothing, in Enright's opinion, could be conclusively linked to the perpetrator. Except perhaps the fibers found on Roxanne herself.

"Dr. Enright!"

He looked toward the police barrier and its jostling band of reporters and saw the last person he expected— Meredith Folger. Her face was pale and her eyes were shadowed. She was a sensitive soul. "Don't cross the line," he called in warning, and moved toward her.

"Of course I wouldn't cross the line," she yelled back,

annoyed, and Enright felt a smile twitch at his lips. Sensitive *and* prickly.

"What can I do for you, Detective?" He stopped short at the yellow tape's limit. "I'm afraid we're terribly busy at the moment."

"I'd like to talk to you."

"I'm all ears."

Meredith glanced around uneasily. Ears, in fact, were in oversupply. "I'd rather discuss this in private."

"Then I suggest we go in search of dinner," the psychiatrist said, with a look at his watch. "It's nearly seven o'clock anyway. Where should I eat?"

"*Can* you? Face food, I mean, after all this?"

"Don't hate me," he said, "but I'm starving." He added gently, "At the very least, have a drink. You look like you could use one."

They wound up at the Brotherhood, because Enright asked to be shown where Roxanne Teasdale had spent her final hours. These visitations were part of his method, Merry knew. So she forced herself to remain detached and to learn something from the psychiatrist. Fortunately, Dana Stevens was nowhere in sight. Merry liked the FBI agent already—she was even somewhat in awe of Dana's status—but she firmly intended to keep this particular interview with Enright to herself.

Enright chose a table with a view of the entire room. "Habit," he explained as he politely pulled out the aisle seat for Merry. "I like my back to the wall. I want to see everything before it sees me."

"Were you trained as a spy?" she inquired lightly.

"Of course. Every psychiatrist is born one, after all."

"That's actually what I wanted to talk to you about," Merry began as Enright shook off his windbreaker and flipped open the menu.

"What's good here?" he asked, scanning the small cursive print with a furrowed brow.

"The burgers."

"Of course. That's about all they serve. *Which* burger?"

"Depends who you talk to. Friend of mine eats nothing but the Bostonians—those are the ones with blue cheese— while, personally, I tend to go for the ones with bacon and cheddar. Side of barbecue sauce on the side."

"That cannot be good for you."

"Probably not," Merry said. "If that's a concern, I suggest you try the one with avocado and sprouts."

Enright caught the amusement in her voice, and his blue eyes flicked up to hers, suddenly dancing. "Not exactly a seaside place, is it? No seafood."

"Well, not much to speak of. Few restaurants on-island can make it as straight seafood places."

"Why not?"

"Too touristy, frankly. Particularly in the winter. For those of us who live here year-round, an occasional dinner of fish is just fine, but we'll cook it ourselves. When we go out, what we want is a really good burger."

"For some reason I find that tragic."

"Because it smacks of waste."

"Exactly. Wasted opportunity, wasted experience— ignorance of culture. Of what it means to live on a seafaring island."

"You could always order clam chowder."

"I could do that in Cambridge."

"But you'll never find a burger there to equal the one you're about to order. So I suggest, Dr. Enright, that you decide to be happy."

"Tucker," he amended, and studied her face. "Do you find it so easy? To decide to be happy?"

Merry shrugged delicately and looked away from his probing eyes. "Yes. I suppose I do. I have very little time for people who wallow in the tragic."

Enright grinned. "That could be a sentence from my very own mouth. With the exception that *I* would be speaking the truth, and *you*, my dear, are ferociously pretending."

"No, I'm not," Merry objected, surprised. "I may feel

for poor Emily Teasdale. I may even cry when I think of Roxanne, although I never knew her. But that's altogether different."

"From wallowing in the tragic."

"From deciding to be happy. *Yes.* Happiness has to do with compromise. With balance. With knowing that life may be difficult today—no seafood—but that tomorrow you could order swordfish for breakfast if you wanted it enough."

Unexpectedly, Enright threw back his head and laughed. "So simple," he said. "Such an innocent." He reached for her hand, and to Merry's discomfort, raised it to his lips. "A burger it is."

Merry drew her fingers away and salvaged her composure while a waiter—Mickey the Total Baldwin?—jotted down their orders.

"I wonder which one Roxanne Teasdale had," Enright mused.

"And if we knew, would you order it yourself?"

"Probably. Now, tell me why you dragged me out of that dump."

"Elizabeth Osborne," she said over the neck of her beer. "A woman I think you may have known. She was a Harvard-trained psychiatrist."

Was it her imagination that the air between them suddenly grew heavier?

"Betsy O," Enright murmured, his face suffused with an old sadness. "So-called because of her resemblance, as we callow youths discerned it, to Jacqueline Onassis. That would have been in the late sixties, when we were all young and Camelot was our lost country. When Betsy had been married to Jack for too little time to dream yet of infidelity, and our longings could remain inchoate. Betsy O, of the breathless carriage, the silver laugh, the endless wardrobe, the mortgage-free house on Marlborough Street. Our Betsy of the Forlorn Hope."

"You knew her."

"Oh, yes," Enright said. "There was a time when I believed I had invented her. But she's been missing for years. Where did *you* run across her?"

"On Sconset beach," Merry said. "Remember? You visited her grave."

It was dramatic, perhaps, as a means of telling him— but Enright was equal to anything Merry could offer.

"I wondered," he said slowly, "if the bones were hers."

"You're kidding."

"No. I'm not. It was a very famous disappearance, you know. And standing over that shallow grave on your beach, I couldn't help but think of Betsy. I'd seen her there so often in life."

"But you never said—you never even told me you knew her—"

"Her name didn't come up. And until you had an identification, it seemed ridiculous to speculate. Particularly about a case beyond my province." Enright took a sip of water, sighed deeply. "To be honest, I'd rather have kept hoping she was alive. Laughing at us all somewhere. She was too vivid for death."

"How long did you know her?" Merry resisted the impulse to reach for her notebook and glasses.

"We were first-year medical students together. She was still Betsy Shaw, then." Enright unfurled the breadbasket's napkin and plucked out a roll. "We went through the entire drill in lockstep. Did our residency at the same hospital—McLean, the psychiatric adjunct to Mass General. I went back to teach at Harvard, got tenure. So did Betsy, eventually."

"Is that common?"

"No," he said brusquely. "You might say we were the best and the brightest. I often have."

He was in love with her, Merry thought. The knowledge made her next question more difficult. "When did she marry?"

"In our third year."

"Wow. Despite her workload and the prospect of a residency?"

"She had an excellent mind," Enright said quietly.

"So how did she meet Jack Osborne?"

The psychiatrist's shrewd blue eyes probed Merry's own. "Did he kill her?"

Merry didn't answer him.

Enright nodded and looked down at his hands. Apparently he had lost his appetite for bread. "They met at the VA hospital where she was volunteering. Viet Nam virtually destroyed Jack."

"So he was—a psychiatric case?"

"Yes, the poor bastard. Anything—the pop of a cork, the backfiring of a truck outside the window—and he'd fall to the floor screaming. Betsy took him in hand, day after day, after her classes were finished. Got him somewhat stable."

"Was that usual for third-year students?"

"No—but this is Betsy we're discussing, Meredith. Everyone said she was gunning for a clinical performance prize at graduation . . . until she married him."

"That's some story." Merry looked at the psychiatrist thoughtfully. "The Smithsonian anthropologist found healed fractures all over Elizabeth's body. A pattern of sustained abuse, she said."

"Abuse?" Enright frowned. "You're suggesting Jack beat her?"

"Did he?"

"I don't know. Not for certain. But it's possible, I suppose. And it's possible he didn't even mean to hurt her."

"Oh, come on—"

"Wait," Enright said gently. "Hear me out. Jack was a shell-shock case. He got trapped on the ground when his patrol called in a strike on its own position. I gather he relived that half-hour of his life for two years following his discharge. When a man thinks he's under mortal attack, and is screaming and thrashing about on the floor, swallowing his tongue and tearing at his eyes, actually *feeling*, in his own mind, the sting and the cut of shrapnel—he's beyond reason. Anyone reaching to soothe or to save him is the enemy. He will lash out. He will do serious injury. And never intend to hurt a fly."

"I see," Merry replied. "Of course."

They were silent a moment in consideration.

"Do you see Jack Osborne now?" she asked Enright. "You're both at Harvard, after all."

The psychiatrist shook his head. "We're in very different worlds. Utterly different. And, frankly, I can't say I ever liked Jack Osborne, Detective."

"Why not?"

Enright's eyes slid away from her. He shrugged. "Not my type. He seems to prefer the adulation of his female students to adult male company. He always has one or two starry-eyed girls floating on his arm."

As did Tucker Enright, if Dana Stevens was to be believed. Merry's hand tingled suddenly at the memory of Enright's touch, and she wondered: *Does he see me as an adoring acolyte?*

And did his contempt for Jack Osborne betray an old wound?

"This wouldn't have to do with Elizabeth, would it?" she asked him.

"It has everything to do with her," he replied with a faint smile. "I lied the other day at lunch, Meredith, when I said I lived alone. The truth is, I live with Betsy's ghost. I loved her madly. Still do. No other woman has ever come close."

An awkward silence. Meredith felt the impulse to look away from Enright's pained eyes, and fought it. "Did you see them socially in Boston?"

"Yes. And I saw them socially here. I saw them whenever I could, though I knew I was just another one of Betsy's faithful—the entourage. She held court, like a Renaissance princess." Enright leaned across the table, his blue eyes intent. "So, tell me, Meredith. What are you ginning up in that beautiful little head? That Jack strangled his wife because he was jealous of me? Don't bother.

Betsy knew how I felt about her. She probably enjoyed it. But she never gave it a serious thought."

"I'm sorry," Merry said, and meant it.

Enright shrugged. "I got over it."

Liar.

"When was the last time you saw Betsy, Doctor?"

Enright answered her without hesitation. "June twenty-fifth, 1988. We had a clinical session together at a local hospital. I remember she was leaving the next week to spend July and August here."

"Did you hear from her over the summer?"

He shook his head, lips compressed. "I was consulting on a case for the Bureau. Flying in and out of DC. And that year Betsy pushed the envelope. Lingered on Nantucket longer than usual. Skipped her normal prep work for the school year. I wondered about it—" He stopped short, threw up his hands. "I figured she was just taking some time off."

Or had a new lover. "Tell me what you really thought about her marriage," Merry said.

Enright fixed his eyes on the restaurant scene before them, unseeing. "I think it ultimately bored her. After a while Jack didn't need her in the same way. He went on. Got a law degree. A *brilliant* law degree. Got tenure at Harvard himself."

"Did you ever have any sense that Jack *hadn't* gone on?"

"What do you mean?"

"Any . . . sudden outbursts of violence?"

"Physical, you mean?" Enright shook his head. "Not a hint. Certainly not from Betsy; and I was working fairly closely with her then. We came at our projects from opposite ends of the spectrum, of course—she believed in rehabilitation, while I plumped for eternal damnation—but we always ended up in the same police interrogation rooms."

"Really." Merry digested this and realized she knew too little about Elizabeth Osborne's work. "And she never confided in you about her marriage? Never mentioned any desire to leave her husband, or any . . . fear of him, for example?"

"No. If anything, Betsy was the sort who would hang on longer than Jack, I think." Enright turned over a fork, aligned it precisely with the edge of his napkin. "For whatever reason, Betsy needed to see herself as a savior."

"Long after her projects were saved."

"Exactly. She specialized in lost causes, you know—behavioral therapy for criminals, and so forth." The corner of his mouth lifted in amused memory. "She once went so far as to stage a rape, with a convicted attacker playing the role of victim. Betsy believed that it might have a therapeutic effect."

"My God."

"She only did it once. Too controversial. And too useless."

"Hence the nickname," Merry observed.

"Nickname?"

"Our Betsy of the Forlorn Hope."

"Yes. If you're going to hunt for her killer, even if you think it's Jack Osborne—I'd like to help."

Merry nearly winced at the savagery in his eyes.

"You're pretty busy already. But thanks."

"It might be a way of putting her ghost to rest. I need to do that."

"I know."

The waiter materialized at their table, two platters held high. "Bacon and cheese?" he inquired of Enright.

"Avocado," the psychiatrist said abruptly, "with happiness on the side."

Chapter Fifteen

May 7, 1996, Ralph Waldo Folger inscribed on the notebook's clean page, in his copperplate hand. *Walked three miles into conservation land near Mason Farms, off the Milestone road, and took up position fifty feet from Altar Rock. Waited approximately thirty-five minutes before sighting quarry.*

His white head lifted at a slight noise from the foyer— or perhaps he merely sensed, from long habit, that he was no longer alone. In the stillness he heard the distinct click of a turning doorknob and the strident creak of the front door swinging open. "That you, son?" he called, and stood up slowly, thrusting his hands against the armchair for support.

But it was Merry who appeared in the doorway, her eyes ringed darkly with exhaustion. "Hey, Ralph," she said, and slumped against the jamb.

"Working overtime, Meredith Abiah?"

"Unfortunately."

"Saw you on the television tonight," he offered. "You certainly gave those reporters what-for."

"I shouldn't have lost my temper," she said, annoyed. "They really ran that tape? They must be desperate for news if that's all they can dredge up."

"Oh, they managed to make a story out of it," Ralph said consolingly. "Suggested you were so prone to lose your temper because the police are baffled. No leads to speak of, and worried the killer will strike again."

"Great." Merry sighed. "That's all the FBI needs to hear."

"Eaten anything?"

She nodded. "Burger at the Brotherhood. With Dr. Tucker Enright. Has Dad told you about him?"

Ralph set his notebook on the seat behind him and placed his pen on the open page. "He has. An unpleasant sort of life for anyone to lead, seems to me." He surveyed his granddaughter's form—one part weariness, nine parts dejection—and adopted a brisker tone. "You look done in, burger notwithstanding. How about some tea and carrot bread in the kitchen?"

"I really just want to talk, Ralph." She moved toward the pool of light his reading lamp threw on the worn red fabric of the armchair, looked idly at his notes. "What are you working on?"

"Birding," he said shortly. "*Inky Mirror* reported a snowy owl sighting out near the bog. I went to look for it myself."

"And found it, I see. Do you realize how much your years of report writing have affected your prose?"

"Just the facts, ma'am." His smile was wintry. "Old habits die hard, especially when you're as old as I am."

"You'll never be old, Ralph." Merry threw herself onto the sofa and kicked off her shoes. "As long as the snowy owl can get you out into the moors. That's what the

Tucker Enrights of this world lack. The quickening to the natural world."

"You sound more like Peter Mason every day," Ralph observed, and reached a hand to smooth her golden hair. "Not that I'm criticizing, mind you. Peter's a good man. He has achieved a hard-won peace. That's rare among the men of your generation."

"He asked me to marry him yesterday."

Ralph was silent an instant, observing her averted head, the absence of joy in her form. "And?"

"I avoided the issue. Do you think I've spent my life avoiding issues, Ralph?"

He reached behind him for the arm of his chair and eased himself into the seat, hoping his granddaughter would ignore the increasing stiffness in his back, the disconcerting weakness of his legs. He felt very old tonight, and Merry's questions only deepened the sensation. There had been a time when anything she asked seemed to pull at his first youth; but lately he was at a profound loss for answers.

"I don't think so, my dear," he said now, "but perhaps some issues beg to be avoided. When it's right for you to marry Peter—and I believe it will be, one day—you will know."

Her eyes were on his face, and he saw the first wrinkle of concern—for himself, not for her own cares—etched between her black brows.

"Are you okay, Grumpus?" Her childhood name. The use of it showed him how much he had already betrayed to her. And so Ralph willed himself to smile.

"I'll do for the moment," he replied. "I'm just feeling my eighty-four years. I vowed once never to admit the impact of age, but in the evenings especially it overtakes me."

"There's something else," she probed. "You're *sad* tonight."

"I went to see an old friend this afternoon, Meredith, and to my distress and concern she would not open her door." Ralph capped his pen for something to do and closed his birding notebook.

"Emily Teasdale?"

He nodded and went on nodding rather longer than was necessary, as though to convince himself of the truth.

She came to him then and put her arms around his neck and her cheek against his trim white beard. "I'm so sorry, Ralph. I forced the FBI on her earlier, and she had already been awake for most of the previous night. I imagine she just couldn't face another person."

"And there is the awkwardness of condolence," Ralph mused, holding Merry at arm's length. "Sometimes it's better to assume it's all been said than to endure the expression of it. I've always been fond of Emily—she's a good soul, an active sort of woman, an intelligent mind. Few people remember or notice her until they need someone they can trust. But I confess to you, Meredith, that I went there for another reason."

"What, Ralph?"

"To ward off evil. To keep it from the door—*your* door. If Emily's granddaughter was taken, then you might have been just as easily. I went to see Emily out of superstition. I lost your brother, my dear, and I cannot bear such a loss again."

She smiled falsely, affecting a careless ease. "Me? What could possibly happen to me?"

Ralph shook her slightly by the shoulders. "That young girl in the middle of the landfill—for this moment, and from this day onward, she is all of our daughters. She is all of *us*. Don't tell me you don't feel that as strongly as I do.

"When you've seen the turn of seasons as often as I," Ralph said, thinking aloud now as much as he was talking to her, "the snowy owls in the midst of the moors, the renewal of the daffodils, the passage of the last whales in August—you know that life, the long progression of years, is too precious for words to express. Roxie Teasdale has been denied all that. Her time ravaged for a caprice. It tears at my heart, Meredith, and I don't mind admitting it."

"I know," she said, and turned away from him. "I *do* see the same things, or feel them in the same way. But everyone else is running around talking about *investigation*, and *patterns*, and the *serial mentality*, as if that girl is just a cog in a very large machine. I fight it, Ralph, and I can't get used to it."

"I hope you never do," he replied stoutly. "Is that why you had dinner with Dr. Enright? To learn how to get used to it?"

She shook her head, the lamplight firing the depths of her blond hair. He watched her weighing what to tell him.

"I'm on the verge of committing professional suicide, Ralph," she admitted reluctantly. "I thought you ought to know."

For a moment he did not respond. Then, "And your father? Will he be allowed to know?"

Merry closed her eyes and slid back into the sofa cushions. "Let me pose a hypothetical, okay?"

"Okay."

"Say I had a piece of information about a possible suspect in the serial killings, a piece the FBI and the state folks don't have."

"Then I assume you do."

"And say that I've withheld this information because it stems from another case—one I'm currently working on—that would probably be taken out from under me if the connection to the other murders was known."

"The Elizabeth Osborne case."

Merry's eyes flew open. "Exactly. Elizabeth's case becomes a low, low priority once her killer—or the man I believe is her killer—is fingered for these crimes. It's too old. It gets lost in the shuffle."

"And that bothers you." A statement, not a question. It was the sort of thing that would bother Ralph too.

"Elizabeth Osborne had just as much life denied her, Ralph. Only worse: for eight years she's had people thinking she was living the high life on some tropical island, while her body slowly decayed in the Sconset sand. Or wherever it was buried. Her killer has gone free. Maybe he *was* just practicing on her—maybe she *was* the first in a long line of murders that ends with Roxanne Teasdale. But somehow, Ralph, I'm not buying it. There's another story behind Elizabeth's death—levels upon levels, meanings within meanings."

"This information you're withholding—it's the key to the deeper story?"

"No." She leaned forward, as intent as though he were judge and jury. "This fact, if anything, suggests there *is* no deeper story. And that's why I can't bear to give it to the FBI. Because they'll clap a guy in jail before I can unravel the truth."

A pause, pregnant with doubt and consideration.

"Are you being selfish, Meredith?" Ralph asked at last.

"Selfish?"

"Yes. Wanting the thrill that comes with the control of a case. Wanting to be the one who breaks it."

She mulled this over. "I just want to know, Ralph." Her head came up, all weariness banished. "I just want to know who Elizabeth Osborne really was. And why someone decided to kill her."

"So what you're telling me is that Jack Osborne hasn't touched a penny of his wife's money in eight years."

"That's it," Howie agreed, shoving a sheaf of papers across Merry's desk, "and here's the documentation to prove it, straight from the investment banker's mouth. Got a fax this morning."

"How'd you convince him to give up the goods?"

"Told him we'd subpoena the information if we had to."

Merry's eyes widened. "I'm not sure that's legal, Seitz. It sounds like a threat."

He shrugged. "None of this is particularly smart, is it?

I mean, you're already walking a tightrope. I just jiggled the wires a little."

"And he fell for it. I suppose all these years of insider-trading investigations have taught them respect."

She flipped rapidly through what appeared to be a trust's balance sheet for the previous calendar year. Elizabeth Osborne had been a wealthy woman. "Where did all this come from?" she asked Howie. "Hardly the fruits of a professor's salary."

"She was born into it. Only child of a Boston Brahmin and his socialite wife. The Brahmin's uncle was governor of Massachusetts in the twenties. Elizabeth's parents died when she was a senior at Radcliffe—died here, interestingly enough, when their private plane crashed in the fog at Nantucket airport that June—and left her a fortune in trust. She lived off the income."

Merry whistled. "Some income. And to claim it, all Osborne had to do was have his wife declared legally dead. Which he could have done over six months ago. I wonder why he hasn't?"

"You're assuming she left her estate to him," Howie pointed out, "and we've yet to see the will. It's filed in Boston, and I've requested a copy. They should be faxing it soon."

"I hesitate to say this, Seitz, but you're damn near the best. For an absolute rookie."

Howie grinned. "Rookie I accept. Absolute, I refuse."

"Now, what have you got on Osborne?"

"Nothing you're going to like. That's why I left it for last."

Merry lifted her brows. "What, no dirt?"

"I searched his records. I must point out, Detective, that the Massachusetts State Bar examiners have done most of our work for us. If Osborne were guilty of so much as a speeding ticket, he'd have had to explain it when he applied for admission to the Bar fifteen years ago. So I called the Bar Association."

"And?"

"And they were far less amenable to talking to the police than their brethren in the investment-banking profession. I got passed around the offices at least a gazillion times before somebody decided to demand the name of my chief and threaten to end my career. So I casually mentioned that the FBI was in charge of this investigation, and if they wanted verification, they could call Washington. I also referred ever so delicately to the legislation to curb trial lawyers that is constantly under consideration in Congress, and suggested that perhaps if local Bar associations, which are, after all, heavily controlled by trial lawyers, showed a greater interest in assisting their law-enforcement colleagues in combating violent crime—"

"You didn't! *Seitz*—"

"That got them talking," he rejoined with immense satisfaction. "*Boy* did it get them talking. Not to mention working the fax machines. There was a lot of hoo-ha as well about the Mass Bar's good-faith effort to assist the federal law-enforcement agencies to their utmost extent in prosecuting criminals, etcetera, etcetera, and anxious efforts to bend even further backward than they already had."

"But you said there's nothing good."

"Osborne's pretty clean."

"—For a man we think may have systematically beaten and strangled his wife," Merry shot back caustically. "No citations for domestic violence? No restraining orders?"

"Not even a friendly visit from his neighborhood patrolman."

"So what *did* you get?" she exclaimed, exasperated.

"The Bar application had a lengthy description of his mental illness following his discharge from the U.S. Army in 1969. Don't read it before bed," he advised, passing her three sheets of single-spaced typewritten paper. "Poor guy was pretty messed up. And then there's the testimonial of his sanity from his doctors. Elizabeth

Shaw—that's her maiden name—and this guy Kahn. Her supervisor at the VA hospital."

"Anything else, Seitz?"

"Yes. There's the matter of the part you're not going to like."

"Let's have it."

"Jack Osborne was supposed to give a talk last night before the Massachusetts Bar Association, as they so helpfully mentioned, on First Amendment rights and censorship on the Internet."

"So?"

"He never showed. I've tried the law school and the house in Back Bay. No dice. Jack Osborne has disappeared, Detective."

Chapter Sixteen

"Detective Folger."

If the harshness of the woman's voice wasn't enough to bring Merry's eyes up from her copy of Elizabeth Shaw Osborne's will, fresh off the fax that afternoon from Boston, the British accent did.

"Mrs. Markham." Merry rose hastily to her feet, shoving the documents under a yellow legal pad. "Please come in."

She motioned to her one free chair—a Naugahyde captain's seat in faux walnut—but Julia Markham seemed to hesitate.

"I'm not interrupting, then?"

"Of course not. I'm happy to see you. Are Nan and Cecil well?"

Julia glanced uneasily over her shoulder, as though the hallway might have unwelcome ears. Then she made her decision. She stepped into the room and closed Merry's door.

"I've come to ask for that card you gave me."

"Card?"

"Right." Julia stood awkwardly in front of the desk, as though summoned before a school principal, in a faded salmon-colored T-shirt darkly stained at its midsection—blueberries or spilled ink?—and faded jeans threadbare at the knees. Her hands were clenched tightly around the strap of her purse. "Someone for the kids."

Merry's confusion cleared. "The therapist. Of course. So you think your children need help?"

Julia shrugged. *Don't we all*, her gesture said.

Merry pulled open her center desk drawer and fished around inside it. "This woman's quite good. Sally Winthrop. Her office is on India Street. She's been in practice for years. I went to her at one time myself."

"*You?*"

Julia's expression of incredulity was almost laughable. "Is that so surprising?"

The woman blushed and hoisted the derelict purse, the better to scrabble within. "You just don't look like you need any help, is all. Where the *hell* are my cigarettes?"

"I'd rather you didn't smoke, if you don't mind."

"Well, what if I do?"

"Then I'll ask you to leave."

Green eyes met black; and green held steady. Julia dropped the purse to the floor and slumped into her chair, legs crossed and swinging furiously.

"I lost my brother in Viet Nam when I was nine," Merry said, conversationally. "Six months later my mother walked into the Madaket pond in a pair of boots weighted down with stones. She could have done it another way—sleeping pills, a plunge off a boat—but she wanted to control the situation. To be certain she achieved what she set out to do. Too many suicides are failures, from lack of conviction; and my mother was hardly an indecisive person. She was an artist—though not like your late husband—a painter in oils. Forty-two years and seven months old, give or take a day, the morning she killed herself."

There was a silence.

"Sally Winthrop helped me get to ten," Merry finished.

Julia Markham bent down abruptly and upended her purse onto the office carpet. A crushed pack of cigarettes slid out with her checkbook. She shook the pack with trembling hands and drew forth a cigarette. "I won't smoke it," she said defiantly. "I just need the feel of it between my lips."

"Okay. So do you mind my asking what's going on with Cecil and Nan?"

"It's Nan, really. Oh, hell—maybe it's both. I don't know." She turned the crushed pack between her hands, brooding. "Cecil is always lost in the clouds, anyway. It's impossible to know what he feels, or doesn't. I've never been very good at just talking to him, you know? We're as different as chess and cheese."

"But something is worrying you about Nan."

"It's that teacher of hers. That Miss Teasdale, what they found in the dump the other day."

Merry groaned. Of course. Nan was eight years old, a third-grader. She hadn't made the connection.

"All the kids are nattering on about it. . . . Well, the story's been everywhere, hasn't it?" Julia shoved the cigarette viciously into her mouth, then removed it and worried it between her fingers, bending it this way and that. Flakes of tobacco drifted to the floor. "Nan asked a few questions at first, questions I probably didn't answer as I should. Now she's gone all quiet on me, playing with her doll under the kitchen table, like a bomb's about to drop and she'd better seek shelter. I don't like it." Her black eyes cut across Merry's gaze, and as rapidly slid away. "It's not the season for Nannie to be indoors. And last night she woke up howling."

"Between the bones on the beach and the loss of her

teacher, she'd have to be confused and upset. Hasn't the school brought in a counselor?"

"Oh, the class've had talks, of course." Julia spoke disparagingly. "All about trusting no one and running straight home to Mum. And how Miss Teasdale is gone, but they'll all have happy memories of her forever." She laughed. "As if that were bloody likely. They're all terrified her ghost'll come and get them when the lights go out, so Nan tells me."

"I think Sally will help," Merry offered. "And school is almost over for the year. Have you thought of taking your children away this summer? Giving them a change of scene?"

"Now, where would I be likely to go?"

Merry shrugged. "Boston, maybe. Or have you any friends in England?"

"If you want to know the truth," Julia said, rising to her feet, "I haven't a friend anywhere."

When Julia Markham had fled from the station, black hair streaming and bent cigarette dangling from the corner of her mouth, Merry sat for a moment, brooding. About Sally Winthrop and the difficult winter they had endured together over two decades ago; and about little Nan hiding beneath her sordid kitchen table. What went on in a child's mind? More than most people assumed; more surely than they could ever remember from their own lost days. But what was it that prevented Julia Markham from reaching toward her children? What wall had she slowly built over the years since her husband's death?

And had Elizabeth Osborne laid its foundations?

With a sigh Merry turned once more to Elizabeth's will. The blunt truth of its clauses had defied even her creative speculation: for Elizabeth Osborne had left her entire fortune not to her husband, or to Ian Markham, or to an unknown shadow who might hold the key to her past—but to an organization called Art in Mind, based in Cambridge, Massachusetts.

The will established a charitable trust from Elizabeth's inheritance, to be invested in perpetuity with solely the income reverting to Art in Mind. What was more, both the Marlborough Street house and the Osborne home in Sconset, along with all their contents, were to be donated to the organization for its exclusive use.

But what intrigued Merry the most were the trustees Elizabeth had appointed.

There were five in all: Jack Osborne, who was to act as the trust's attorney; Martin Bromwell of Morgan Guaranty; Sylvia Whitehead, the Nantucket gallery owner photographed with Elizabeth at the Opera Cup celebration; Ian Markham; and last but not least *"my good friend and colleague Dr. Tucker Enright, in the hope that a closer involvement with Art in Mind may contribute to his professional development."*

Well, well. Tucker Enright. She'd have to talk to him about this. But first she had some unfinished business with Jack Osborne.

Merry reached for her phone and buzzed Howie. He picked up immediately.

"Seitz."

"Detective Folger," he said. "What can I do for you?"

"I'd like you to think about something."

"Not my greatest talent."

"Oh, come on, Seitz, don't sell yourself short. I've seen you think at least twice a day. You looked at Elizabeth's will, right?"

"Didn't get past the *whereases* and *wherefores*. Too much fine print." Howie's chair creaked in the background, and Merry imagined him kicking back, heels on his desk, seat upended on two legs.

"Never mind. The gist is this: Jack Osborne gets nothing. Zilch. He didn't touch her money—we've established that—but he continued to live in the Boston house. He's about to lose it."

"One reason he never had her declared dead," Seitz said with satisfaction.

"Could be. Find out whether he has the means to set up a place like that on his own."

"Got it. Hey, Detective—"

"Yeah?"

"You ever gonna have that conversation with your dad? About Osborne's bad luck with women?"

"Why?"

"Just wondered if this was official business or moonlighting. And you still owe me that dinner."

Cambridge could provide no listing for an organization called Art in Mind. So Merry pulled out her Nantucket phone book and leafed through the white pages. It was high time to talk to Sylvia Whitehead, if indeed she still existed; and there in the center of the page was an S. Whitehead, of 30 Federal Street. Right smack in the heart of the historic district, across from Merry's favorite restaurant, 21 Federal, and only a stone's throw from her office on Water. Merry turned for the phone, then stopped her hand in midair, staring at her watch. Four-thirty was arguably close to the end of the workday. She glanced wistfully out the window at the slanting light of late afternoon, the dancing pattern of the first pale-green leaves—and thought: *Why not?*

The sky was turning from cerulean to ultramarine, a color she had inexplicably left at home; and in disgust Sylvia threw down her brush. After nearly thirty years of painting the Nantucket landscape, she *should* have been able to anticipate anything—the shift in wind that sent the dune grass shivering in exactly the opposite direction from the one represented on her canvas; the emergence of sudden cloud; the disappearance of all light and texture as fog rolled inland from the sea. She had even painted that fog—a ghostly scene of matte gray, relieved by a single pinpoint of light: The tip of a ship's mast? A beacon at the roofline of a friendly home? But today her heart was not in the process. It failed, somehow, to comfort or engage. She was lonely today, the light was fading, and her painting buddy, Irene, was unlikely to appear now.

She wiped her brush on a turpentine-soaked rag and laid it carefully in the tray of her painter's box, then, with a grunt, thrust herself to her feet. Years ago the hours would have passed like minutes, the changing life of the moors flowing over and about her, compelling her brush, ringing exquisite changes in vermilion and rose madder. But today time hung heavy. Sylvia was bored and restless from too many months becalmed on the island. The search for something to do had sent her out with easel and paints, the small folding stool ill-suited now to the demands of her aging back. Perhaps, she thought as she closed the paint box and stood looking out over the marshes of Polpis, sharp green and black in the still light of late afternoon, she should start painting directly from still photographs, in the comfort of her own studio, where tea was at hand, and the latest edition of *American Artist*, and a thousand other things to keep her from picking up a brush at all. Her eyes were not what they had been. Objects failed to come into focus, merged at will with other things, a dreamscape always just beyond reach.

Time to slip into her Monet period, she thought, with an acid bubble of mirth. Impressionism being a myopic sort of passion.

The crunch of a footstep made her turn, and with the sound came an involuntary chill of fear. That girl in the dump—*what a fool you are Sylvia, standing here alone in the middle of the marsh—no one aware—a palette knife, perhaps, just to be safe—*

"Are you Ms. Whitehead?"

The voice, low and strong, was both a surprise and a shock. Sylvia hadn't heard its like in years, and a small sensation of pain gripped her at the sound. But the words had come from a young woman with pale, bright hair and dark eyebrows, a tall and lanky girl she failed to recognize.

"Sylvia Whitehead," she corrected, "the *famous* Sylvia Whitehead. And who are you?"

"Meredith Folger, Ms. Whitehead." The young woman approached her and held out her hand. "I stopped by your place on Federal Street and found you were out. I'm afraid I read the note you left for your friend Irene. You gave excellent directions."

"Too bad Irene didn't read it," Sylvia said dryly. "I imagine she's drinking again. Never gets up at all on her bad days, but she insists on setting a date to paint just the same." She folded the stool and then turned to pull the canvas from her easel, unwilling for Meredith Folger to see her work. "Bad habit of hers. Never shows. Lets everyone down. Has somebody died, then?"

"I'm sorry?"

"You're the police chief's daughter, aren't you? The one who solved that murder last year. The harpooning. I remember. I've followed your work."

"I'm flattered."

"Don't be. I promised your mother I would."

"My . . . *mother*?"

"Of course," Sylvia said briskly. "I was one of her friends. One she didn't share with the family, I'm afraid. And if the police have come looking for me, I assume there's bad news to tell. What is it? Is Irene a *dead* drunk this time?"

"I wouldn't know," Merry replied, and Sylvia saw the effort it cost her to recover her poise. "I've come to talk to you about something quite different. About two people you used to know—Elizabeth Osborne and Ian Markham."

She was in the act of collapsing the easel and covered her surprise with a small expression of annoyance as her cloak snagged in a hinge. Freeing the woven mohair fabric gained her another few seconds. And then, finally, she looked at Meredith Folger and said evenly, "Elizabeth and

Ian? They died long ago. What possible haste could have sent you out across the island to me?"

"A wild desire to be out of doors," the policewoman replied, with a grin that turned her strong features impish; and that quickly, Sylvia warmed to her.

"Don't be surprised you never heard my name," she said now, over steaming mugs of tea. They were sitting companionably in her apartment, one floor above the space that had once been her gallery. She had lost it, so she told Merry, to the soaring rents on Federal Street. The walls that had once displayed some of the island's most daring talent were now papered in pink and white stripes. An expensive chocolate shop. As if Nantucket needed another chocolate shop. Sylvia gave it two seasons.

"Come here," she said now. "I should show you these, I think."

Obediently, Merry rose and followed her down the hallway behind the small kitchen. Sylvia was standing in what must be her studio—or her storeroom, perhaps, filled with the effluvia of a painter's life. Canvases were stacked willy-nilly against the walls, their faces turned inward; mayonnaise jars filled with turpentine held fat brushes on every counter and shelf. Arrangements of fruit—unsuccessful efforts at still life, a form Sylvia admired and failed to master—fought for place with vases of flowers, most of them withered to dusty, rigid shadows. The place, Merry felt, had the life seeping out of it, as though Sylvia Whitehead were tired unto death.

"All your mother's painting pals were her secret, and she struggled to keep us that way." Sylvia bent to one of the canvases and peered at it, then pushed it to the wall once more. Another was pulled out for inspection, and another. "Painting was the only thing that seemed to be *hers*—Anne shared everything else, including your father, who was always as much the town's as her own. The people she knew—the gallery owners, the other artists—saw her alone. We weren't exactly asked to dinner at Tattle Court."

"I didn't know," Merry said. "I thought of painting as something she just did on the side, the way other women garden or work needlepoint."

"Very foolish of you. Here it is."

A canvas, like the others. The portrait of a little girl—eight or nine—with her legs tucked up under her and a book propped in her lap. The green eyes stared brutally out at the artist, accusing, unconsoled.

"How I hated sitting for that," Merry said softly. She hunkered down to gaze at herself, her heart turning over. "It seemed such a waste of time. Such a bore. You never think, when you're a kid—" She stopped short. "I wondered where this went. Thought about hunting it up when I moved out of Tattle Court. All this time you've had it."

"She gave it to me. The week before she died."

"So you *knew*?"

Sylvia shook her head. "Oh, no. It never occurred to me that things were so bad. I knew about your brother, of course. But not how deeply his death had gone. It ate away at Anne. We saw only when it was too late." She set the canvas down, facing outward this time. "You seem to have grown up quite admirably."

"Well, I've had enough time. I was only ten when she died. I wonder sometimes if I even knew her."

"Then I will tell you what you should never forget, my dear: Anne Folger had a fierceness in the soul that cried out to be named. You're nothing like her."

"How good of you to tell me so," Merry retorted, nettled.

Sylvia smiled. "I always tell people the truth. Be thankful."

Merry gave a last look at her portrait. It was crudely done, and vivid in its rawness. But perhaps *fierce* was the proper word. Her mother had used a palette knife rather than a brush, she remembered.

Sylvia sighed. "Anne's fierceness killed her, Meredith.

Don't you remember the moods? The volatile days? That *must* have made an impact, even at nine."

And for the briefest moment Merry did remember. How her mother could move through the house like a wraith, silent and unapproachable, her eyes always focused on some invisible horizon. Questions left unanswered, thoughts incomplete. The way she would shut herself in her attic room, where John Folger had cut a crude skylight, chasing the changing light as it swam across the ceiling.

"Yes," Merry said finally. "I do remember. It was something we weren't supposed to talk about, Billy and I— something we worked around. We got quite good at it."

"And so you worked around her suicide, too, I imagine."

"What else was there to do?" Merry countered defensively. "I didn't even have Billy to help me by that time."

Sylvia ran a fingertip along the edge of her easel. It came away thick with dust, and she frowned. "I don't know. Go headfirst into it, I suppose. Not at nine, mind—at nine you simply needed to recover. Go on. But *now*, perhaps. Do you ever think of Anne?"

Merry flinched. "Of course."

"I wonder. I rather imagine you try *not* to think of her." Sylvia glanced again at the nine-year-old Merry staring at them from the canvas. "Would you like to have it back?"

"Yes," Merry replied impatiently. "I want to frame it and hang it on my front door, announce to all the world that this is who my mother was! She usually painted landscapes, didn't she? There are only a few of people."

"Your brother's is unfinished."

"Still propped on an easel in our living room."

"Tell you what," Sylvia said. "I'll have this one framed and send it over to your place. It's no trouble," she said, raising a hand as Merry started to protest—"I have too many old frames lying about, and one of them is sure to be perfect. I'd consider it a favor to Anne."

They were silent then, both awkward, and finally

Sylvia turned away. Merry followed her back to her living room.

"Look," she said apologetically, "I should really be discussing Elizabeth Osborne."

The barest fraction of a pause. Then Sylvia said, "You've found her, I gather."

"Her bones were discovered in Sconset a few weeks ago and only recently identified."

"The bones on the beach? The ones those kids dug up?"

"Yes. Ian Markham's kids, as a matter of fact."

"Good lord." Sylvia dropped to the sofa as though her legs had collapsed without warning, her mouth gaping in mingled horror and delight. "I imagine *that* sent Julia up into the rafters."

"You imagine correctly. Are you still friendly with her?"

"Julia? Heavens, no. She hated my guts. Said I tried to bilk her out of Ian's money. When in fact he owed me more than she could ever repay. I sold his last pieces for what I could get and absorbed the loss."

"Ian Markham was in debt?"

"Up to his eyeballs."

"I thought he was famous."

"*Is* famous. Probably because he's dead," Sylvia said dryly. "But Ian in life wasn't the sort who made good decisions. He always speculated, and he always lost."

"The stock market?"

"That. And ponies, of course. Forays into gambling during his quarterly Vegas debauches. And then there were his charitable causes—his hundred dearest friends, who made even worse decisions than he did." Sylvia shook her head in fond amusement. "Ian was like Mozart, Detective. He could never catch up. He did piece after piece to repay his loans and lived on borrowed money. His work was mortgaged for years to come. But that was Ian. Poor man. If he'd lived, the world might have caught up with him. His pieces command a fortune *now*, of course, when none of us has any. They're all in the hands of museums and private collectors, and traded on a very exalted plane."

"I wondered," Merry said. "Julia Markham looks as if she lives hand-to-mouth. And there's not a stick of her husband's work anywhere in the house."

"There wouldn't be," Sylvia agreed. "Aside from the fact that she's had to sell them over the years, there's the malice at work. I should think she couldn't bear to have the stuff around."

"What do you mean?"

"Julia positively *hated* Ian by the time he died, Meredith. I mean, wouldn't you?"

"Because of Elizabeth?"

"Oh, my *dear*." Sylvia shook her head. "Elizabeth was only the latest and last. Think of the hundreds *before* her. And Julia swallowed them all whole. Waiting it out for the moment Ian made his fortune and she could profitably sue for divorce. Julia specialized in endurance."

"You don't like her."

"She's never given me any reason to."

"Did you like Elizabeth?"

Sylvia considered this, her eyes narrowed shrewdly. "Most women didn't, you know," she said finally, "but I did. Betsy was selfish and controlling, she went after what she wanted without apology; but she made everyone around her feel glorious, a member of the elect. She was smart and honest, and she had taste—three things I can't do without. But I considered her a fool for most of that final summer, once she lost her head over Ian. You found her bones on Low Beach, you say?"

"Codfish Park. Buried in the sand."

"Then she was less of a fool than I thought. I always assumed she died with him on *Mood Indigo*."

"So did most of the world."

"Which may be exactly what her killer hoped."

Merry made no response; none seemed necessary. But it occurred to her that if she talked with Sylvia Whitehead very much longer, nothing about Elizabeth's murder investigation would remain a secret. Time to turn the tables, perhaps.

"Did you know that Elizabeth appointed you a trustee of her estate?" she asked.

"No." The other woman's eyelids flickered, but she betrayed no greater sign of surprise. "Does that mean I come in for some money?"

"Mostly work, I'm afraid."

Sylvia's wrinkled face registered disappointment. "Damn. I thought I might actually get the gallery opened again. What sort of work?"

"Elizabeth's lawyers will probably contact you with the details."

"But you know what they are."

Merry shrugged. "Basically."

"Then drat it, woman, tell me!" Sylvia gripped her hand painfully, demandingly. "I've never been so intrigued in all my life! Betsy leaving *me* in charge of her money? Who'd have thought? Shouldn't she at least have *asked* first before she stuck me in such a position?"

"You're not in it alone," Merry replied, and freed her hand from Sylvia's gently. "You'll be working with Jack Osborne, and a guy named Bromwell who handled Elizabeth's investments, and one of her colleagues from Harvard."

Sylvia's eyes widened. "Not that Tucker Enright!"

"You know him?" Merry asked, interested.

"Only slightly. He came over for a party or two the summer before Betsy disappeared. Madly in love with her, of course, but weren't they all. Tucker Enright." Sylvia's voice was thoughtful. "A challenging fellow, but engaging. He saw through one rather too clearly."

"I know."

"So he's a trustee! I suppose I'd better get used to being seen through."

"Elizabeth named Ian as well, but that's rather irrelevant."

"Not to our Betsy," Sylvia retorted, amused. "Think what she intended! Tying Osborne and Enright and Markham together—her male harem—with myself thrown in for . . .

what? A sense of humor? Gender differentiation? Oh, Betsy, you were a nasty piece of work, weren't you?"

Merry studied the woman across the table. Was the amusement feigned, or a cover for deeper shock? "Don't you want to know about her beneficiary?"

"I'm all ears, my dear."

"It's something called Art in Mind. I haven't been able to contact them yet. She left them the Sconset house and all its contents."

"And all its contents?" There was a sharp edge to the question.

Merry nodded.

The artist shifted abruptly, eyes averted, and reached once more for her tea. It must have been cool by then, but she sipped at it distractedly. "I haven't been near the place in years, of course," she murmured. "But it was once absolutely lovely. Taxes through the roof."

"And Art in Mind? Does it ring a bell?"

Sylvia looked at her speculatively. "For that, my dear, you really must consult with Julia."

"But she's not even named as trustee."

"No," Sylvia said steadily. "I don't suppose she is. It's not usually the thing, is it, for a beneficiary to serve as her own trustee?"

Merry sat up. "You're saying Julia Markham is somehow connected to Art in Mind?"

"Well, she *was* its director, after all."

Chapter Seventeen

"Art in Mind," Julia Markham said as she slammed the refrigerator door, "no longer exists. End of conversation."

"But you *were* involved with it," Merry persisted, holding out her glass for the iced tea Julia was offering. "Sylvia seemed so certain."

"Sylvia bloody well always does. Lemon?"

Merry eyed the forlorn slice of citrus aging on the kitchen counter and shook her head. She took a sip from her glass. Lipton instant. Maybe she'd had too much tea today, anyway. She set it down. "Where are the kids?"

"Gone, thank God. On the beach. But they'll be back soon for dinner."

"Then I won't keep you long. Just tell me what Art in Mind *was*."

Abruptly, Julia thrust herself away from the counter and strode into the cluttered living room. After an instant

Merry followed. The smell of stale tobacco was more overwhelming than she had remembered.

"I'll find it in a moment." Julia was rummaging through a huge stack of old paper piled behind a forgotten desk in the room's corner. "Goes back a hell of a long time, it does."

Merry waited, her eyes drifting over the objects in the room. Everything was worn, stained, shabby with dust and neglect. Scattered pieces of the children's toys were abandoned amid the seat cushions; books with their covers bent backward lay facedown on the floor. Was it simply a lack of money? She had visited homes where the means were slight and found them neat and spotless. Something else was at work here. A heartsick, brooding pall of defeat. Or self-loathing, even. *Julia's* self-loathing. And with this realization came another: there was not a mirror in evidence anywhere in the house. Could Julia not even bear the sight of her own face?

"Here it is. Got my exercise for the day," the woman said, and shoved something at Merry. A photograph.

She studied it, black eyebrows knit. A color photo turning yellow with age, of three rows of kneeling men and women, their hands outstretched. And before them, potter's wheels.

"Ceramics?" Merry said, puzzled.

"Clay *therapy*," Julia corrected. "Art in the service of the Mind."

"I don't understand."

"There's Betsy." Julia thrust a blunt finger at the image of a woman, half-turned from the camera's lens, her dark hair shielding her face. She wore a white physician's coat and her head was bent, her arms folded tight across her chest, as she studied a young woman who was throwing a pot.

"You're saying these people are mental patients?" Merry asked, intrigued.

Julia shrugged. "Call 'em mental, if you like. I've never understood what normal is, myself. But yes. They were all people sent to Betsy from the state welfare folks. Criminals, some of them. Referred by the hospital and the police. Though the police didn't think much of art therapy. Bleedin' liberal hearts, they called us. I've always thought that's why they didn't search too hard when Betsy disappeared. Probably figured she got just what she deserved."

Merry reached behind her, eyes still fixed on the photograph's image, and cleared a magazine from a chair. She sat down. "What did you have to do with all this?"

"I ran the center."

Their eyes met. "You're an artist, too?"

Julia shrugged. "Ceramics never gets much respect. Unless you electroplate it and call it sculpture, like Ian did. It helps to be a man, as well, if you want to be taken seriously."

There was more than a note of bitterness in her voice, and Merry felt an unexpected kinship with this sour woman. She knew what it was to be accorded less respect than her male colleagues.

"Is that how you met Ian?"

"Oh, no. We grew up in the same town—little place called Trevarre, near Leeds, actually—and came to America together. Years ago. Seventy-three."

"And you lived in Boston then."

"New York at first, and then Ian got a teaching spot at Boston University, in their fine-arts department." She lifted her shoulders and smiled for the first time in Merry's experience—a disarming smile, though the teeth were stained with nicotine. "It paid the rent."

"So when did you buy the Nantucket house?"

The smile disappeared; her face darkened. "Later. After we met Betsy. Betsy thought it would help Ian's career to move in a more moneyed set." A bitter line to Julia's mouth, and a short laugh. "That was Betsy all over. 'Let me lift you out of your terrible condition of contented poverty, my beautiful boy, and make you my tame pet.' Particularly if she could do it in the name of art."

"But it was you she met first. Jack Osborne thought it was your husband. He told me Sylvia Whitehead had introduced Ian to Elizabeth."

Julia's face clouded with an undefined emotion—regret? self-doubt? She shook her head. "No. *I* brought the two of them together. Bloody stupid, wasn't it? Our relationship *began* as a professional one. Then Ian stopped by the center one day, and Betsy spotted him, and the sparks flew, and suddenly she was coming by the house to see his work, and telling Sylvia Whitehead about him—" She stopped, as if to contain her anger. "It was a year later that he bought this house. With the money he made on some public-works commission—a sculpture for the entryway of a new branch library. We'd expected to live on it for months. Never even saw the check."

"So you gave up the Cambridge place?"

"Oh, no," Julia replied. "We were only here summers. But Ian *did* seem to work better in the studio than he did at home—"

"Studio?"

She gestured toward the front of the house. "The shed across the way. It's practically falling into the ocean now."

"And so you moved here permanently."

"I did, yes." Julia paused. "Ian died that September. The same night Betsy disappeared."

Merry looked at her searchingly. "Did you think she was on the boat, too?"

Julia's eyes slid away. "I don't know. She could have been. Or not. Frankly, I was too busy having Nan to think about it." The answer was implausible at best, but Merry saw the warning signs posted on Julia's face as clearly as though they were cut into her skin.

"Explain all this to me," she proposed, shaking the photo. "Art in Mind. I'm fascinated."

Julia eased away from her, the flood of reminiscence momentarily diverted. "Tell me why you want to know, first," she demanded. "What's the sudden interest in Art in Mind? It hasn't been up and running for years."

"Eight years?" Merry asked quietly.

Julia did not reply.

"Now that Elizabeth Osborne has been declared dead, her will comes into effect. She's left everything in trust, including her Boston and Sconset houses, to Art in Mind."

"You're bloody shitting me! That *bitch*." Julia shot to her feet, black hair raging about her head, and paced furiously back and forth. "After all these years! After all the mess! And if she'd only been found—"

"Yes?" Merry said. "If she'd only been found?"

Julia came to a standstill and took a deep breath. The rage slowly faded from her face. "She was never satisfied with just helping, you see. Even though I started the center long before she heard about art therapy and became its principal goddess. She had to *own* everything she loved—control it completely—and take the credit for its success. It was the same with Ian. Wanting to lock him up tight and bring him out on Sundays, to amuse her guests." The black eyes flicked up to Merry's, awash in misery. "And now this. . . . She thought she could buy my world from the very grave. As if she hadn't already done enough damage, with all her money."

"I think I'm beginning to understand," Merry said gently, "but it will help if you tell me a little more about the center itself. What was the point?"

Julia hesitated, her mind still worrying at Elizabeth Osborne and her malice; and then she flung herself into the chair opposite Merry's.

"Have you ever worked with clay? Thrown a pot?"

Merry shook her head.

"It's an extraordinary medium." Julia's voice was quieter now, her tearing breath almost under control. She reached for a cigarette and lit it before she continued, drawing strength, it seemed, from her addiction. "To work with clay is to understand the nature of creation and de-

struction. You pound and pummel the stuff. You force it
into compliance. You can scream and tear at it if you like,
and it always returns to a comfortable ball, no hard edges,
nothing integral lost. But at the same time, it's the clay
that sets your boundaries. How you mold and shape it,
how you control the wheel, determines whether your final
result is worth the firing. No one else—not the therapist,
not the artist teaching you where to place your hands, not
the police who've sent you there—is responsible for the
pot's success. Only *you*. You place it on the wheel and begin. And then the work—the healing, actually—starts."

It was the longest speech Julia had ever managed in
Merry's hearing. Such passion, Merry thought, for a life
she had discarded.

"These patients actually *made* things?"

"It depended on the person, naturally." Julia shook ash
into a soiled mug adrift on the coffee table. "Some of
them had such low self-esteem, such inner doubt, that
they refused to try. It takes practice to throw a pot, you
know, even a simple pinch one. For some of them the risk
of failure was too great. And that refusal—that shrinking
back, or the lack of it—told Betsy a great deal."

"So she was actually observing how they treated the
clay?"

Julia nodded. "She studied the shapes they made, and
the emotions expressed in them—anger, fear, violence,
hurt. Then she made them decide whether to keep or destroy their work. Smashing the symbol of your fear can be
very renewing, you know."

"All that from a lump of clay," Merry said doubtfully.
"Makes you see a three-year-old's Play-Doh somewhat
differently, doesn't it?"

"It's not just the clay," Julia protested, sitting straighter
in her seat. "The *process* is as important as what is made.
Any artist will tell you that. Look at this one." Julia
pointed to a man bent over an elongated bowl that
seemed almost to spin off the wheel. "Throwing a pot is
all about control, isn't it? The *potter* determines the

outcome. And of course, for some of these people, control is exactly what's missing. They learn to shape the clay, to direct its final form, and eventually they manage to do the same with their emotions."

Merry frowned. "Isn't that hoping for a lot?"

"I don't know." Julia's momentary enthusiasm had vanished. "Betsy was convinced that it helped. She believed the act of creation gave a conquering power to the creator—and that empowerment was all that these people needed."

"I'm afraid," Merry said wryly, "that I'm beginning to favor the police view of things. For every challenged artist finding power in clay, there's a psychopath finding it in the infliction of pain."

"That's pretty much what Enright said."

"Tucker Enright?"

"Yeah. Chum of Betsy's from Harvard. He came to watch us at the center from time to time. Not that he thought much of our work." Julia stubbed out her cigarette and pushed her black hair behind her ears.

"Betsy named him as one of your trustees," Merry said. "From the language of the will I got the sense she thought it would be good for him."

"Betsy always knew what was good for other people," Julia retorted, "and it was usually what was good for Betsy. So now I've got bloody *trustees*? What am I to trust them for? The center's gone and dead."

"What happened to it, Mrs. Markham?" Merry asked, setting the photograph to one side. "Why did you stop your work?"

There was a silence.

"I didn't much want to return to Cambridge," Julia said finally. "After Ian died. I thought we'd be better off here."

"Really?" Merry let the question hang. "You like the island so much?"

"It's as good as anywhere else. Aside from the bloody tourists. Tramping all over the lawn. Hanging around

Ian's shop. I actually found one taking a bit of shingle from the wall, if you can believe!"

"Hence the No Trespassing signs."

"For all the good they do."

"I'd have thought the memories would be burdensome."

"Try living with the ones in Cambridge."

"But you seem to have loved your work," Merry persisted. "You speak of it with such passion. Do you still throw pots?"

"No," Julia said curtly, her eyes on her knees.

Merry changed tack. "You weren't here, were you, the night Ian sank *Mood Indigo*?"

In her chair, Julia moved restlessly. "I'd gone back to Boston, what with Nan on the way. We thought it was best, in case she came suddenly."

"There are perfectly good babies delivered every day at Nantucket Cottage Hospital."

"But that's not where my doctor was. Are you trying to pin me for something?"

"I just think it's unfortunate," Merry observed deliberately, "that you were apart from your husband on the last day of his life." *Unless,* she thought to herself, *being apart was vital to establish an alibi. But why? Why? Simple jealousy, that oldest of motives? She doesn't seem to have gained from either death. Not with Elizabeth missing. But perhaps that was never a part of the plan—*

"It's not like I planned it," Julia interrupted caustically. "You meddlesome bitch. It's not like I *knew* he'd sink his bloody boat while I whiled away the hours in a stinking flat alone, eight months pregnant and as huge as a house. What're you trying to say? No—" And here she stood up, fast as a cat, and grabbed for Merry's wrist. "Don't tell me. Just get out, thank you very much, and remind me never to open my mouth in your presence. You're a sneaking bloody cow, Detective Folger, and I don't know why I let you into my—"

She stopped short, her fingers still gripping Merry's

wrist, her eyes on the doorway. "Cecil. Nan. Come in and have your tea, loves."

"Miss Folger!" Nan cried, running with a face transformed to throw herself at Merry's knees. "You came to see us, like you promised!"

"How are you, Nan? All better after that dip in the ocean?"

"We found a piece of sea-glass," Cecil said, holding high a clouded green shard, its edges smoothed by Atlantic tumbling. "For our collection."

"It's like a jewel, isn't it?" Merry turned the glass between her fingers. "There's your pirate's treasure, Cecil."

"That's what Mummy always said." Nan's tone was gleeful. "Before she stopped going to the beach. Why don't you like the beach anymore, Mummy? Was it mean to you?"

"Nan," Julia Markham said warningly, "the detective has to be leaving. Wash your hands now, there's a love. Tea's on in half a tick."

Her eyes challenged Merry's over the children's heads, remote and defiant. Further discussion was pointless.

"I'll just show myself out," Merry said, and went.

Chapter Eighteen

As she drove away from the Markham house in the failing light, her headlights picking out the gray length of Milestone Road, Merry felt overcome by an aching weariness. She longed to turn the car toward Mason Farms and stretch out on Peter's sofa while he smoothed her hair and listened to the tale of her day. There had been too much talking, and far too much confusion; revelations and disappointments; a tangling of the threads. But it was only Thursday, and Merry kept to the strictest of internal rules. No visits to Peter in the middle of the work week.

She drove steadily past the familiar turnoff to Altar Rock, promising herself a dinner of pasta, a hot bath, and an early bed. It was not to be.

When she turned into her driveway from Fair Street, the car loomed blackly in her headlights. Solid and undeniable:

a rented Toyota from the Nantucket airport, parked squarely in Merry's space. Dana Stevens leaned idly against the hood, ankles crossed and eyes lifted to pick out the stars. The agent's face gleamed whitely in the cruel flood of light.

Merry shut off the ignition and climbed quickly down from the Explorer's running board. "Hey," she said. "I haven't seen you around much lately."

"Not surprising," Dana replied. "I went over to Boston yesterday afternoon."

"Picking up a few things for the long haul?"

"That," Dana replied, uncrossing her legs and strolling casually toward her, "and trying to break the news of Roxie Teasdale's death. To her law-professor lover. The one you think murdered his wife—or so Enright tells me. Jack Osborne. Amazing, isn't it, the bad luck one man can have? Every woman he touches ends up dead. We'll have to start calling him Typhoid Jack. Or maybe it should be Jack the Ripper. If we can even find him."

"Dana—"

"Can we have this conversation somewhere else? Like inside?" She held high a brown paper bag. "I brought us take-out Chinese. From Chin's. I hear it's the best."

"Or maybe just the *only*. Come on in."

Merry unlocked the door by the side of the garage and thrust it open, catching the jamb in a pile of mail. She stooped to gather the scattered envelopes and then switched on the stairway light. "I live above."

"So your dad said. I went to Tattle Court first, since that's the address in the phone book."

"I'm sorry," Merry said.

"About the extra trip?" Dana asked casually as they mounted the steps. "Or about lying through your teeth? Wait—I didn't mean that. What I should have said was 'withholding information.' "

"Did you discuss that with my dad, too?" Merry turned to face the FBI agent on the landing.

"No. I just thanked him and went on my way."

"He doesn't know that Roxanne Teasdale was seeing Jack Osborne."

"Just as I didn't know that Jack was married to your skeleton on the beach. Keeping the cases separate, huh? No matter how they might be linked?"

Merry turned to unlock her door, then motioned Dana inside. "You have every reason to be angry."

"Yes. Except that I expected something like this. So I got angry in private yesterday. Tonight I'm just tired." Dana stepped across the threshold and glanced around the room. "Nice place. How long have you been here?"

"About three weeks. Look, I know I've behaved badly."

"Where do you want the food?" Dana asked. "Here on the counter?"

"You don't have to stay." Merry dropped her purse onto the floor and slumped into a chair, feeling defeated. "And I'll understand if you read the riot act to my dad."

"What are you trying to do?" Dana was pulling white cardboard containers of Chinese food from the brown bag. "One-up the Bureau? Or the state guys? Or just me?"

"Is that what you think?"

"Well, I *am* the person nominally in charge of the Nantucket end of this investigation. Where are your spoons?"

Merry crossed to the cabinets and fished out some silverware and plates. "We'll have to use paper napkins."

"This is take-out, for Pete's sake."

"I wasn't trying to one-up anybody."

Dana reached across the counter and took a spoon from Merry's hand. "It's happened before, believe me. Half my time in every investigation is spent soothing the feelings of the local force. I saw it coming when you got so emotional in that conference Tuesday afternoon."

"And do you always build bridges with Chinese food?"

Dana's eyes were tinged with amusement. "Call it the feminist management style of the nineties. A guy would have hauled your ass before the assembled ranks of the state police and the forensics teams, not to mention your father and fellow detectives. I prefer to talk to you first."

"Thank you," Merry said. "I know I've broken every rule in the book by not telling you about Jack Osborne. I just wanted to buy some time."

"At the risk of losing a serial killer? He could be in Brazil by now."

"If Jack Osborne is our man, he's not going anywhere. He's sitting tight. Watching."

Dana nodded grudgingly. "For what it's worth, Enright thinks the same thing. But I've put out an all-points bulletin on the guy anyway. He hasn't left Nantucket or Logan under his own name—we checked the airports and ran a description by the ferry people."

"For whatever *that's* worth. There are a lot of distinguished-looking fifty-year-old men with beards passing through the steamship authority."

"I will not deny that I'd feel better with Osborne in custody. And I lay the mess entirely at your feet."

"I admit it was selfish of me."

"Very. Not to mention the case time it's wasted. While I was chasing back and forth across the Sound, our killer's been happily getting away with the Teasdale girl's murder. That, my dear Detective Folger, is what really has me pissed."

Merry did not reply. There was nothing, finally, for her to say.

Dana pulled up a stool to the kitchen counter and kicked off her shoes. "You know what I hate most about working? The stockings. The heels. Even though I go for short ones most of the time, I have a constant ache in the arch of my foot. Want some sesame chicken?"

"In a minute. Thanks."

"So why was it so necessary to buy yourself time?"

Merry picked up an egg roll for something to do. It was already cooling and greasy. She dropped it back onto the plate. "When we left Lily Olszewski's house, I debated telling you about Jack right away—that he had a bad track record of losing his women in violent ways. But I knew if I did, the Bureau would be all over him. Elizabeth Osborne's death would be just another statistic. His first kill. The case would be lost in the serial pattern, merely routine. I figured Elizabeth deserved better than that. I think she died for different reasons."

"So you went solo."

Merry nodded.

"Checked out his alibi."

"Actually, I had Patrolman Seitz do it."

"Thereby endangering *his* reputation within the force," Dana observed tartly. "That's completely inexcusable and can only stem from an inflated sense of your own importance. But worse, in my mind, is what it says about your law-enforcement skills. You're behaving like a rank beginner."

"Thank you," Merry retorted. "If the FBI says so, it must be true."

"Look." Dana set down her fork and reached for a napkin. "I've never worked for a local force. I know you deal with cases differently—you have a feeling for your community, you sense an obligation to the people you see every day, and the stakes can look a bit higher to you than they might to someone from a federal agency. Our constituency is more diffuse. So are our objectives. They can become abstract. But I think you have something to learn from us."

"And that would be?"

"Teamwork."

Their eyes met.

"The subordination of the self to the needs of the whole."

Merry looked away.

"Because of you," Dana continued, "I can fairly say that our investigation into these serial murders has lost some valuable time. I chased after a red herring and lost a day and a half. I'm not happy about that. Could I have a glass of water, by the way?"

Merry started and slid off her seat. "There's wine. . . ."

"Water's fine."

"So what are you planning to do? Have me fired?"

Dana took her time answering. "That would hardly be in keeping with feminist nineties management, now, would it? Not to mention a complete waste of time. You work for your father, not for me." She patted her lips delicately. "No, Merry, I've got a better idea. I'm putting you on the case."

"What?"

"I can't stay on this island forever. The state guys are reporting to their superiors and trying to fit the Nantucket piece into the larger puzzle. I intend to ask your father for the loan of your services, with the understanding that your work on the Elizabeth Osborne matter will take equal precedence. It's probably connected to the serial pattern anyway. But I'll expect you to spend a good part of every day on the Teasdale killing. Nobody's assessing the Teasdale girl herself."

"Looking at the victim," Merry said slowly.

"Yes. It occurred to me yesterday—once I calmed down—that however much you needed to learn teamwork, *we* had something to learn from *you* as well."

"Really?"

"Sure. You brought it up yourself, that first afternoon while we were talking to the girl's grandmother. *Who's thinking about Roxanne?* you said. Well, I'll admit that I'm not. It's my penchant to think about the perp. When did he get here? Is he a local? If not, why pick an island? Why pick that girl? What's the bit about the garbage all the time? And the hair? Where's the chink in his armor? Enright's the same way, for all his brilliance.

"But you think differently. You know how to work the island. It's bred in your bones. And if you're willing to lend that to this investigation, I think we'll be able to nail the guy—Osborne or whoever—that much sooner. What do you say?"

Merry felt as though her feet were rooted to the floor,

and found she was blushing furiously. "What can I say? You're treating me far better than I deserve."

"I'm just trying to salvage the situation. In the most useful way."

"Of course I'll do anything I can to help," Merry said. "Want some tea with your fortune cookie?"

You are the object of someone's obsession, Merry's fortune cookie declared; and so when Dana Stevens had left and the dishes were clean and dry, she tumbled into bed and dialed Peter's number.

"You've been out all day," he said accusingly. "I've tried and tried to reach you. I had the best intentions of subverting your hard-won resolve, and sweeping you off to dinner."

"But it's Thursday."

"Of course. What is forbidden is always more enticing."

"That sounds like you read it somewhere. In the Koran, for instance. Something eloquent and archaic, from an age that understood original sin."

"Perhaps I did."

"How would you describe your feelings for me, Peter?"

There was an instant of silence. "Probably as though I'd read it somewhere," he said.

"No, seriously," Merry protested, sliding deeper beneath her covers and reaching for her mail. "Would you call yourself obsessed?"

"Does this have to do with the unfortunate question I asked you at the Ritz the other night?"

"Not in the slightest."

"And would obsession be a good or a bad thing?"

"I don't know. We'll have to study the Calvin Klein ads."

"What are you doing? Eating paper?"

"Opening envelopes. In bed."

"Stop! You're driving me wild!"

She turned over a manila packet and frowned at the typewritten address label. *Detective Forger,* it read. The news media, again? "And I'm using my fingernails to do it," she said for Peter's benefit. The envelope had no return address. She shrugged and slit it open.

And gasped.

"Speak to me of love, my darling," Peter said, amused. "What *are* they putting in the electric bill these days?"

"*Peter.*" Merry's voice caught in alarm. "Peter, do you think you could get over here right away?"

"On the wings of desire, my pet. How do you want me?"

"Fast." Merry sat up, her entire being chilled, and stared at the length of red hair coiling around her fingers, sinister and gleaming. "Our killer just made contact."

Chapter Nineteen

Dear Detective Forger, the killer's note read, *After seeing you last night on television, I simply had to write and tell you that you have very beautiful hair.* John Folger's eyes flicked to the right-hand corner; it bore yesterday's date. *Like spun silk, actually, and so striking against your dark eyebrows. At first I thought it might be bleached—those eyebrows being somewhat confusing—but from the play of the camera light and the shine of the strands, I determined it must be natural. You are good and true and honest, not a slut like so many others. You have Nordic blood, don't you?*

It's a weakness of mine, beautiful hair—in fact, I'm something of a collector. I offer the enclosed as a token of my esteem. You know from whose head it comes. I obtained it at great cost. I thought that she was good and true and honest, like you; but I was wrong. Her hair no longer has the power to move me.

*And so I am searching again, searching high and low,
for something silken against the darkness. And I think I've
found what I truly need.*
Perhaps you'll find her, too.
But which of us will find her first?

There was no signature.

John looked up at Merry and Peter. They were leaning
uneasily against the scarred countertop in the Tattle
Court kitchen, trying not to stare at him. The old ship's
clock next to the stove told him it was nearly ten-thirty,
well past his bedtime. Ralph had been asleep for hours.
They had decided it was better not to wake him.

"This gives me the creeps," he said. "Don't even think
of going home, Meredith. You're sleeping here tonight."

Merry's expression was troubled. "That's putting you
in danger, Dad, and Ralph too. I can't do it."

"Nonsense. We'll sit up with our service revolvers if we
have to. Make some strong coffee. Play cards. Nobody's
going to hit on you with all the lights in the house blazing."

"But we can't live that way indefinitely."

"No," her father conceded. "We can't."

There was a heavy silence.

"I have another suggestion," Peter offered. "I could
take her to Greenwich. To my sister George's house.
She'd be safe there, and nobody the wiser."

"That's not the point," Merry objected. "Do you really
think this guy is interested in me? It's not *my* head he's
hoping to scalp. He's playing cat and mouse. He wants
me to come after him."

"Quit the cockiness," her father retorted. "You're *good*
and *true* and *honest*, remember? He said so. And he's got
a thing for your hair."

"So I'll dye it black," Merry argued.

"You're being ridiculous." Peter's voice had gone terribly quiet, as it always did when he was in the grip of
anger. "This isn't a test you have to take."

"If I go to Greenwich, where does that get us?"

"It gets *you* out of danger."

"And throws away our one opportunity to learn something about this psycho. If I cut him off, another innocent person dies a needless and terrifying death."

"That will probably happen anyway," John Folger replied gently. "We can't hope to stop him in his tracks. We know too little. And when it does happen—when we find some poor girl abandoned in a trash bag—you're going to feel responsible. It's what he wants. To make you carry the burden of his guilt."

"I already do," Merry said. "We all do. And going to Greenwich isn't going to solve the problem."

Neither John nor Peter answered her. Their eyes met, equally clouded with worry.

"So here's what we do," Merry declared, pulling out a chair and facing her father squarely across the table. "We dust this letter for fingerprints. He'll have worn gloves, of course—he's shown us that he's intelligent—but it'll give the FBI guys something to do. I'll move back home for the duration and promise never to stir without a companion by my side. Ralph, Peter, Howie Seitz, whoever. I'll get cracking on the case files, and we'll wait for another letter. If he's written once, he'll write again."

"I don't like it, Meredith," her father said heavily.

"I personally hate it," Peter added.

"Good. So we're agreed?"

Merry lay awake a long time that night, curled in a protective ball beneath the mounded covers of the spare bed. Her knees were drawn to her chest, her arms clasped around them—a position learned long ago in Girl Scouts and life-saving classes, so that the hypothermic might hold on and the drowning ones float forever. Every fiber of her body was tensed for the sound of an intruder, every muscle poised to spring. She had even placed her Smith & Wesson beneath the neighboring pillow.

It felt strange to be back in the Tattle Court house, and yet not in her childhood room; but *that* was empty

now. The walls smelled clinically of the fresh blue paint
Ralph had rolled across their surfaces the weekend after
she'd moved. She had stood a moment tonight in the
echoing bareness, listening for—what? The girl she had
been? And heard only the moonlit wind stirring the
maple leaves high above the garden.

How many noises the ancient house made! Three centuries of sun and weather, the heating and cooling of wood;
all snapping in the house's bones tonight, as though it
turned and settled restlessly before sleep. Every creak and
rustle caused her charged nerves to twitch. Was that a footstep? The turn of a doorknob?

Merry took a deep breath and stretched her toes down
to the chilly bottom of the bed. She must admit what she
had been denying for most of the evening; she was afraid.
Sharply and deeply afraid. She stared fixedly at the outline of a clock shining dimly from the bedside table. Past
two, and the digital numbers were marching on inexorably. She wished, at that moment, for Peter's dog Ney—his
comfortable shifting from side to side, the slight groan
and whiffle as he coursed through the fields of dream-
land. Ney's very normalcy might have lulled her to a fitful
dozing. As it was, she was too afraid to blink, much less
close her eyes and sleep. It was a pact she had struck
with herself: as long as she was watchful, and wary, no
murderous hand could reach from the depths of the
rustling night.

She turned and buried her head in the pillow, sighing
deeply. Things could not go on like this.

Peter Mason thought something similar, from his
hunched and uncomfortable position in the Range Rover
parked in Fair Street, not far from the Tattle Court turning.
He had driven halfway home before the idiocy of the attempt hit him squarely between the eyes. He turned the car
around, his headlights sweeping too brightly across the
denseness of the moors and breaking the peace of some
nocturnal beast, whose eyes gleamed yellowly an instant in

the path of the beam; and then he drove purposefully, if too fast, back to Merry's door. If he had to suspend the workings of his life for the length of this investigation, he would. He'd get nothing done until he knew she was safe, anyway.

But tomorrow night, he decided, hugging his jacket closer against the chill of the wee hours, he'd bring a thermos of coffee.

"Is it possible to learn anything from the typeface?" Tucker Enright inquired of Stan, the FBI's Nantucket forensics chief. Stan glanced morosely around the faces assembled at the station's conference table and ducked his head to his notes out of habit.

"Just your basic Courier ten, probably from an ink-jet printer—I'd say a Hewlett-Packard or a Canon offhand, but I've faxed a copy of the note to Washington for analysis and identification. We should have their answer in an hour."

"And the prints?" Dana Stevens interposed. "Anything?"

Stan shook his head. "Aside from a few smudges, and Mary's latents, the letter's clean. He wore gloves again."

"Must carry a box of 'em wherever he goes," muttered Bill Carmichael, of the state police. There was a belligerence to his eyes that Merry recognized. Bill was not pleased, she thought, that the spotlight had shifted away from the statewide serial investigation. *Fine, Bill. You take the sleepless nights, if you're after all the glory. It's not like I sent the letter to myself.*

"And yet the note tells us something about our perpetrator all the same," Enright observed. "The postmark is Nantucket, two days ago. He was on the island that recently—and as I doubt he left on Monday evening only to return on Wednesday, I think he probably remained here after killing Roxanne. In fact, he's probably with us still." Enright's blue eyes swept the length of the table; they fixed on Meredith. She was almost undone by the concern she read in the psychiatrist's face. "He watched us find the body, watched us sift the dump for the gloves he knew were never there, watched our colleague Detective Folger on the evening news. He's been eating in our restaurants, walking our streets, feeling the same breeze we feel as we turn in our sleep."

"We should be searching the hotels for recent customers," Merry said to Dana Stevens.

Her father sat up alertly. *This* was something he could understand.

"But what if he lives on one of your quiet country lanes?" Enright proposed. "What if he's always lived here and is laughing up his sleeve at our collective blindness?"

Merry shook her head. "No. This killer is an urban animal. Not an islander."

"How can we be sure?"

"What *can* we be sure of?" Merry asked impatiently. "What does the letter tell *you*, Doctor? What do you see in *this*?" She tossed him the plastic bag holding the length of woman's hair. Roxanne Teasdale's hair—though only a comparative analysis from the crime lab would be conclusive. Clarence Strangerfield had already packaged and sent strands of the severed lock to Boston that morning.

Enright turned the transparent parcel between his fingers. They were shaking ever so slightly; a departure, Merry thought, from the psychiatrist's usual detachment. He looked up and met her eyes. "It's the habit of such killers to keep a trophy of their attacks—a body part, an organ even, in a refrigerated jar, for example. Or a particular belonging that signifies the act itself. One man will keep the high-heeled shoes of the women he has destroyed, another their underwear. This man has a fetish for hair, as we've seen time and again. He keeps the lock of his victim, turns it between his fingers, imagines himself killing her repeatedly, relives the ecstasy of domination." He paused. "But with every successive victim, his threshold of stimulation is pushed higher. The trophies lose their impact more quickly. This particular lock of hair, for example, has done next to nothing for our murderer. He *gave it away*, and only a few days after he strangled Roxanne Teasdale."

John Folger shifted uneasily in his seat.

"In fact, I'd say our killer is in search of stimulation. We can expect him to strike again very soon."

A tense silence descended upon the table; none of the assembled officers seemed capable of speech. Only Dana Stevens looked unmoved. She reached for the note itself, already labeled and bagged.

"Fine," she said dismissively. "We've assumed that from the outset. He basically trumpeted his intentions in this note to Meredith."

Enright shrugged. "He threw out a challenge. I'm saying he's likely to make good on it."

"You get that from this note?"

"I get many things from this note, yes."

"Like what?"

"It's almost lyrically phrased. Quite sophisticated. He backs into the notion of competing for Detective Folger's esteem—in fact, he lays his challenge at her feet. It brings to my mind the precepts of courtly love, the slaying of a dragon for one's lady fair. I've underestimated the guy. I thought he was a cruder sort of fellow."

"Like Manuel Esconvidos?" Bill Carmichael asked, with the hint of a sneer. "So our pen pal got through high school. That's a pretty big slice of the population."

"Except," Merry broke in, with a warning glance for Bill, "that the dragon lives only in his mind, and I'm not his lady fair."

"I hope that comforts you for a few hours, Detective," Enright said gently, "but I wonder if our murderer agrees with you. I think he almost certainly means to pursue you, if only as the last and greatest attempt of his career. In my book, he's *already* pursuing you."

"Are you trying to frighten her, Doctor?" John Folger asked.

"She's already frightened. We all are."

"Merry," her father said in an undertone, "I think you

should get off the island. In fact, I'm ordering you to take leave."

"Not a chance."

"Detective—"

"We'll talk about this later, Dad," Merry whispered fiercely.

"So," Tucker Enright said, with renewed energy. "The challenge is out there. He's delivered terms. How do we answer him?"

"In the medium he understands," Merry replied. "With a televised press conference at noon today."

Heads turned along the table.

"We'll be showing our hand. Is that wise?" Enright asked.

"You tell me. Isn't that your job? What should we be saying to this man? What's likely to keep him from killing again? To buy us time?"

Enright pressed his fingers against his eyes and drew a deep breath. "Don't ask the impossible, Meredith. If I were able to sit down and probe this man's mind for several days on end, I could give you a reasonable picture of his motivation and impulses. I can't do that from a string of deaths and one letter."

"They must tell you something," Merry argued.

"All right," Enright said, looking up with an air of finality. "If you force me, I'll give an opinion. This man uses fear as a means of dominance. He's hoping to manipulate the police the same way. Why else send such a thing to *you*? Because you're the chief's daughter, a woman police officer, and, in his eyes, that much more vulnerable. *He sent it to your house.* He wants to hit you where you live. He's hoping you've already left town. And if I'm any judge of character, my dear, he's considering catching the next bus after you. Stalking a nervous policewoman must be ten times more exciting than killing Roxanne Teasdale, elementary-school teacher."

A silence.

"That's it, then," Merry said flatly. "We show him I'm still here. And that I'm not about to back down."

It was as they were filing out, a somber group of bent heads and restless eyes, that Merry pulled Enright aside. "I'd like to talk to you sometime when you have a minute."

"Gladly. How are you, *really*?" He grasped her shoulder gently and shook it. "Holding up?"

"Doing a reasonably good imitation of calm, yes. I have to. My dad'll hustle me off to Connecticut if I'm not careful."

"Connecticut?"

"A friend's house," Merry said, her eyes sliding away from Enright's.

"A friend's. I see."

There was an awkward pause. Merry studied her toes, feeling Enright's hand still warm on her shoulder. He took a half-step backward and slumped against the conference area's doorway. "What do you want to talk about?"

"Your friend Betsy Osborne."

"You're still working on that? I'd have thought this mess would have pushed it to the back burner."

Merry shook her head. "Tell me about your involvement with Art in Mind, Tucker."

"Art in Mind," Enright said thoughtfully. "Now, *that's* a name I haven't heard in years. It can't be still running. I'd have known about it."

"Julia Markham shut it down after her husband's death," Merry said. "But Elizabeth Osborne left everything to the center, and now that she's officially deceased, her estate will be probated and Julia will inherit. I read a copy of her will yesterday." She paused. "Did you know that you're named as a trustee?"

"No!" Enright exclaimed. "I had no idea. God, I *hope* Julia Markham has no intention of reviving the place. It was pointless anyway, and I have no time to spare for the business end of it. What was Betsy thinking of?"

"I wondered the same thing."

"Who else did she appoint?"

"Jack Osborne. A guy from Morgan Guaranty. And Sylvia Whitehead. You know her, don't you?"

"Do I?"

"Well, she knows *you*. She's a painter and art dealer. Used to sell Ian's work in a now-defunct gallery."

"*Sylvia*," Enright said, slapping his forehead. "A large woman. Opinionated. I'm surprised she remembered me."

"She said something about having seen you that summer, before Elizabeth died."

"Really." He frowned. "Then she must have. Well. What a delightful crew."

"I'm not finished," Merry added, amused. "There's Ian Markham. But he's largely irrelevant."

"The dead hand of the law," Enright quipped. "Betsy and Ian united in death. Well, well. Can I get out of it?"

"You'll have to talk to the lawyers. Is ceramic therapy really so bogus? Julia Markham didn't seem to think so."

"Julia Markham has never had a firm grip on reality, Meredith," the psychiatrist replied gently. "Or at least not when I knew her. She had a wicked problem with depression."

"Maybe she still does. You never kept in touch?"

Enright shook his head. "Felt too much like the Spurned Lovers Club. Betsy's faithful lackey, calling Ian's discarded wife? No. And what would be the point?"

"I don't know," Merry admitted. "I just wondered. No one kept in touch with Julia."

"She wasn't the easiest personality, even on our good days."

"She still isn't. So why don't you believe in therapy?"

"Oh, I believe in *therapy*," Enright objected, "just not in the kind of therapy Betsy and her followers espoused. It was a little too touchy-feely for me, and I could never be entirely certain the patients had found a cure. I mean, what happens when they get tired of clay?"

"In Julia's case the recurrence of the symptoms," Merry said thoughtfully. "She stopped throwing pots, and her whole life seems to have fallen apart."

"There you go."

"Could it ever be—*dangerous*, actually?"

"Dangerous?" Enright paused to think. "I *do* have questions about the wisdom of releasing certain emotions. Betsy was very big on catharsis—on letting out violent feeling. I suppose it proved beneficial among the Viet Nam vets she had worked with. But it was also a philosophical current of the time, Meredith. The dawning of New Age approaches to mental health. The healing of old wounds, or the inner child, whatever you want to call it. But I wonder sometimes if it's a wise technique. What the mind buries is sometimes its dead—things that are *past* all healing."

"Julia said that Betsy taught people to express their emotions in clay—and then symbolically destroy them."

"She also thought that success in making a pot might lead eventually to self-control," Enright agreed. "I'm not so sure. Taken together, the 'therapy' process looked dangerously to me like a license for emotional violence. And I thought that might lead to physical violence, in the end."

"To self-destruction, or the destruction of others."

"Yes."

"Could that be true of Jack Osborne? He was one of Betsy's first patients, after all."

Enright smiled faintly. "I've never seen him touch a lump of clay, Meredith. But maybe he uses a tennis racket in a similar fashion. He's famous for throwing them over the net in a fury. That tends to break the racket's neck."

They looked at each other as the sense of his words sunk in. "But that doesn't mean—" Enright said quickly.

"—that he broke his wife's. I know." Merry studied

Tucker Enright quizzically. "Why didn't you tell me all this about Art in Mind?"

He shrugged and stuck his hands into his jeans. "I've learned to avoid the memory. I got involved with the center because it was one of Betsy's passions—and she was one of mine."

That simple.

"But, you know, with the perspective of eight years," Enright continued, "I see how dishonest that was. I never believed in the therapeutic effect. I never credited Betsy's work. I just wanted to be near her. So I volunteered."

"I see," Merry said; and, in fact, she did understand. There were memories in her own mind that caused her to wince every time they floated to the surface—incongruities, embarrassments, dishonesties. Too vivid in the recollection, and enduringly painful. Enright's avoidance of the past was just one more sign that he was human.

Despite the tension that filled the station—or perhaps because of it—there seemed to be a premium on sharing confidences. When Merry had parted from Enright and ducked into her office to work up her notes a bare half-hour before the press conference, it was Bill Carmichael who surfaced like an unquiet ghost.

"Hey, Mere," he said, looking distractedly over his shoulder as he stood in her doorway. "Can we talk for a minute?"

"Of course." Merry set down her pen and motioned him inside. "What's up?"

"It's this serial-pattern thing," he said testily, and practically fell into her visitor's chair. "I'm not buying it."

"You don't think these killings are connected?"

"It's not that." Bill ran his hands through his thinning hair, disturbing, in his irritation, the sparse strands doing camouflage service for his male-pattern baldness. "It's Esconvidos. You know they're thinking of releasing him today? Letting it go at a charge of attempted abduction. Five thousand dollars bail."

"I guess the Teasdale murder makes it hard to do otherwise."

"Not to mention the press. All they can ask is, *Is Manuel Esconvidos innocent? Why are you still holding him?* You heard those guys the other day—shoving their cameras in everyone's faces. It's bad enough here at the station, but you should *see* the idiots camped out at our office."

An impulse toward laughter worked its way upward from somewhere deep inside Merry's stomach, and she nearly said, *I have, Bill—believe me, I have;* but he had enough on his mind without a gratuitous ribbing. Bill might be long-suffering, and he might be incongenial; but he was certainly no idiot. He managed the other two state police assigned to Nantucket from a few rooms on North Liberty Street, taking care not to invade the Nantucket PD's turf, and paying homage to the DA in Barnstable far more than John Folger thought necessary or wise. He was a seasick sailor and a nervous flyer forced to endure several trips monthly on planes traveling to and from the mainland— and his greatest desire, he had once confided to Merry, was to be reassigned somewhere in the western part of the state. Someplace like Williamstown—so far west, it might as well be New York, and remote enough that the criminals got lost before they ever got there.

"Have you seen any of the files on the previous victims?" he asked Merry, his hands coming to rest in his lap.

She shook her head. "That's on my agenda this afternoon. I take it you have?"

"I've looked at nothing else since Roxanne's murder. I'm telling you, Mere, that girl's death has me up nights. It's one of the senseless ones. One you can't reconcile. And if it's that bad for me, what's it like for her grandmother? Or her parents, for Christ's sake? I can't get those people out of my head. They're flying into Boston today, did you know that?"

"No," Merry said, subdued. Roxanne Teasdale's body had been flown to the state crime lab for immediate autopsy Tuesday morning and would be released the next day. "So the funeral will be where?"

"California. The grandmother is going out to meet them, and they're all flying back together. I think it's good, in a way—gets Emily off the island, gives her a change of scene. Some closure. If she has any sense, she'll stay out there permanently. Every time she drives the Madaket road between town and her home, Mere, the poor woman's got to think of it."

It was true; the only road from the Teasdale house ran directly by the landfill. Merry made a mental note to call Ralph Waldo; he would want to know that Emily was leaving.

"And what have the files told you, Bill?"

He hesitated. "Where do I start? Maybe I should talk to you after you've seen 'em."

"But you're upset about something. Manuel Esconvidos."

"Look, I know I'm just a law-enforcement grunt, Mere. I'm not a fancy shrink from Harvard or a special agent or anything. I've got three years at U Mass and a stint at the police academy. No other letters after my name. But you ask me, this business stinks. Esconvidos is all over it."

"You think he fits the pattern?" Merry's forehead wrinkled. "But we know he's not responsible for—"

"Roxanne Teasdale. Right. I'm not saying he is."

"But you think he killed the other women."

"It's mostly gut, Mere, but I do. Somebody else decided to copy the crime. Roxanne was just unlucky."

Merry sat back, considering. "What have you got?"

Bill spread his hands. "The man moves around. No address fixed for more than four months at a time. And he always picks dives—sort of apartment hotels, flophouses we used to call 'em—and no bank accounts that anybody can trace. He changes jobs just as often. Specializes in menial labor—roadwork, meatpacking, the odd landscaping stint. No family ties. No wife. Not even a buddy to drink his beer with."

"But does he have blood on his hands?" Merry said. "Where's the evidence trail, Bill?"

The state policeman exhaled gustily. "You smoke, Mere?"

"Sorry."

"Figured. You're the wrong age. Have to be thirteen or fifty these days to carry a pack of lights." He reached for a pencil and stuck it between his lips, working it with his teeth as he spoke. "Esconvidos has lived in every place where a body was found. Braintree. Newton. Charlestown, close enough to Back Bay for the undergrad's murder. You name it, that guy was somewhere around. And he lived in each of the towns at roughly the time that these victims disappeared. Moved on about ten days to two weeks afterward. The first bodies were buried—took a while to find—but the later ones showed up in the trash Dumpsters and whatnot so soon after they were killed that Esconvidos was still living in the vicinity."

"So what are his alibis?"

"Sketchy. Very sketchy. Has a memory problem, our boy, particularly for specific dates. Swears he was in a bar on the evening in question but can't remember which one. I mean, come on, they're asking him to go back five, six years. No wonder he can't come up with the goods."

"Any evidence?"

"After they busted him with that girl in his trunk, they searched the last place he lived."

"And?"

"They found a lot of tools of his trade. Shovels that might be used for landscaping, or not. Butcher's knives. Pickaxes. All of them open to a pretty nasty construction. But no snippets of women's hair. No trophies, as the shrink would call 'em, to speak of." Bill paused. "I figure by the time he'd decided to pick up Lisa McChesney— the girl in the trunk—he'd grown tired of the last victim's hair anyway. Probably tossed it out."

"What about DNA tests? They must have collected fluid and hair from the victims' bodies. Does it match Esconvidos's type?"

"That's where things start to get weird," Bill replied. "The whole DNA thing is like a hot potato for the force these days, ever since the Simpson trial. Everyone's worried about contamination. And because the first victims were found months after death, not much physical evidence could be collected. Because the later ones were found sooner, the crime-lab coroners got what they could—but the debate over whether we can use it has been kicked upstairs. To no less than the attorney general of the Commonwealth of Massachusetts, if you can believe."

"Why?"

" 'Cause nobody wants to look like officer Mark Fuhrman, holding a bloody glove two sizes too small, that's why," Bill shot back. "Esconvidos is Hispanic. Or Latino, depending on who you're talking to. I don't have to tell you that relations between the state police and that sector of the population are hardly good. And what jury of Esconvidos's peers is gonna believe we got firm evidence from a five-day-old corpse we found in a trash Dumpster at the local Finast? Hire all the experts you like. The guy'll walk, I'm telling you." Carmichael spit out his pencil in disgust.

"Speaking of experts," Merry said, "didn't your people in Boston bring Enright in to talk to Esconvidos?"

The malevolence in Carmichael's eyes spoke eloquently of his opinion of experts. "The FBI sent Enright, yes. And since the state police are working with the FBI—which is to say, since the state police are completely under the FBI's thumb—they showed the shrink right into the psycho's cell. With pleasure. I heard it from a buddy works in Boston. They figured Enright'd come out with a diagnosis of murder one, five counts. No dice."

"I remember something about that from Tuesday's

conference. Enright thinks your guy lacks a killer's mentality."

"And in the FBI's mind that's enough, Mere, to set the guy free on bail this afternoon. Particularly if he's clear on Roxanne Teasdale."

"Enright has that much clout?"

"You got it." The antagonism in Carmichael's face deepened. "If Esconvidos *confessed*—which, believe me, I hope he does—the feds would still go with Enright's expert opinion. Sometimes a confession is just an attention grabber, he says."

Merry sat back and let her desk chair swivel slightly, her mind turning over Carmichael's information. "If Roxanne Teasdale's murder is distinct from the previous five—if we've got two murderers on our hands—then we can actually explain a few things," she mused, her eyes focused vaguely on Carmichael's bald spot. "Why Nantucket, for instance. I was finding it hard to believe a serial murderer would just show up on-island and embark on his usual spree. It didn't make sense. Particularly off-season."

"Ted Bundy went everywhere in search of his victims," Bill objected. "Ohio, Florida, you name it. That's what made him hard to catch."

"But as far as we know, *this* killer didn't. He stuck pretty close to Boston. And, as you say, if the killer is Esconvidos, his parochialism may have been his downfall."

"I *know* the killer is Esconvidos."

"So what's next?"

Bill shrugged. "Watch him hit the streets once they release him. Wait until he kills again. Hope we can make a case."

A chill moved up Merry's spine, and she shuddered involuntarily. Bill met her eyes, his own blank with defeat. "The stupidity of it all makes you want to call in sick on a permanent basis, doesn't it?"

"There has to be a way, Bill. To keep him there. We'll find it." She glanced at her watch. "I've got a press conference, I'm sorry to say, in approximately fifteen minutes. But we'll talk again, okay?"

"Okay. I'll be standing beside you at the microphones. For form's sake. Hope you got your speech prepared. Those journalists have no mercy."

"Bill?"

"Yeah?" He turned in the act of opening her door.

"Why did you come to me? Why not take this to Dana Stevens?"

"She has to work with Enright," he replied. "I saw that and knew what it meant. I trust you, Mere. Gotta trust somebody."

Chapter Twenty

John Folger had decided that Meredith would meet the press in front of the Town Building on Broad Street, its red-brick facade and shaded lawn serving as an appropriately official backdrop. Flanking her were Dana Stevens and Bill Carmichael, representing the federal and state forces to which the Nantucket police were nominally subordinate; and behind them, slightly to one side, stood Tucker Enright. At least twenty television and print journalists were gathered in a tight knot, their faces expectant and determined, their muscles tensed like sprinters. A gang bang, as such a conference was informally called by news personnel, yielded little to the shy and retiring.

The chief stepped forward to greet them all.

"Good morning. I have with me Special Agent Dana Stevens of the FBI, Lieutenant Bill Carmichael of the state police, and Sergeant Meredith Folger of the

Nantucket police. Detective Folger would like to offer a few remarks updating the Teasdale case, and then all three officers are available for a few questions." He looked at Merry.

She swallowed, throat dry, and ducked her chin toward the microphones.

"As you are aware, the combined federal and local forces arrayed before you today are engaged in the pursuit of a vicious killer believed to be responsible for the murders of at least six young women, one of them Roxanne Teasdale, whose tragic death has touched all of us on Nantucket."

Tucker Enright cleared his throat. Merry hesitated fractionally, resisted the impulse to look over her shoulder, and went on.

"Last evening I received a letter from a person claiming to be Roxanne's killer." Involuntary gasps and the sudden popping of camera bulbs as the journalists jostled for position. "Enclosed in the letter was the severed length of a woman's hair. Although we are currently shipping a sample of that hair to Boston for comparison with the deceased's, we think it is possible that it was cut from Ms. Teasdale's head. From the tenor of the note we believe her murderer is deliberately engaging law-enforcement officials in a contest of wills. Accordingly, we would like to take this opportunity to warn him directly."

Merry looked up from the microphones for the first time. Her eyes were instantly dazzled by exploding white light, and she blinked, momentarily off balance. Then she found her voice and went on. "You have attempted to challenge the police in a game of cat and mouse," she said deliberately. "The police do not play games. We play to win. Thank you."

"Detective!" A strident cry from a woman Merry recognized as Suzanne Martel, the *Beacon* reporter. "What exactly did the note say? And was it handwritten or typed?"

Dana Stevens leaned toward the mikes. "The FBI believes the note was printed on a Canon ink-jet printer. There is no way to trace the machine that printed it."

"But what did it say?" Martel persisted.

They had all agreed that no good could be gained from releasing the killer's threat to strike again. Panic would be the result. So Merry simply said, "He challenged us to find him. Next question?"

"Can you determine from where the letter was sent?" called an unfamiliar man in a brown canvas vest. He looked, Merry thought, for all the world as though he were reporting from a war zone.

"We're not releasing that information at this time," Dana Stevens said smoothly.

"What about Manuel Esconvidos?" Merry recognized the voice and face of Marilyn Trilby, her televised nemesis.

"Mr. Esconvidos will be released on bail today," Stevens said. "Thank you very much. I'm afraid we all have work to do."

Merry glanced at Bill Carmichael. At the mention of Esconvidos, the state policeman's scowl had deepened. He was staring fixedly at Marilyn Trilby.

"One more thing," he barked suddenly into the mike. "The state police are in no way convinced that Manuel Esconvidos is cleared of the responsibility for the previous five murders. Despite his release the investigation into his movements remains open."

Dana Stevens shot Carmichael a look of surprise. Behind her Tucker Enright's mouth hardened and his arms came up tightly across his chest.

"What are you saying?" The man in the brown canvas vest again. "That we're looking at *two* murderers?"

He was quick, Merry had to grant him that.

Carmichael did not reply; and as if she had come quickly to a decision, Dana Stevens wheeled and made swiftly for the police station. Head down, John Folger moved in her wake. Merry and Carmichael followed, reporters nipping at their heels. Only Tucker Enright was

left alone on the shady grass, his expression thoughtful
and his eyes remote.

"Lunch," Peter said. He put his hands on the edge of
her desk and leaned determinedly above her, his broad
shoulders blocking the light streaming in through her office window. "It's Friday, woman. I sat up all night and ate
the meanest of breakfasts in the solitude of my empty
kitchen."

"Rebecca would never allow such a thing. I don't believe you."

"Rebecca has been gone these five days on a visit to
her daughter in Springfield," Peter said accusingly. "You
have no idea how I've been living. Besides, I know you.
When you skip a meal, you get light-headed."

"I'm starving," Merry conceded. "All those bright
lights and sharp questions can stir up an appetite."

"Then let's go. You're not wandering out of this building alone, so you might as well submit to eating in my
company. How does the Boarding House sound?" Merry,
as he very well knew, was a sucker for their four-cheese
ravioletti with pancetta and Parmesan cream. "The pa-
tio's open," he added.

"I can't justify it, Pete," she said abruptly. "I'll eat a
sandwich right here, and you can stay and watch me consume it, but the last thing we need is some Boston reporter taking a photo op while we chew our pasta and
quaff our wine. Imagine the caption. *Nantucket's hard-
working police force pursues serial killer—or do they?* It's
not going to happen."

"I thought as much." Peter reached down into his canvas workout bag and fished in its depths. "So I stopped by
the Boarding House on the way into town." He held high
a pair of Styrofoam boxes.

"What have you got in those things?" Merry asked sus-
piciously, her hands poised to adjust her half-glasses. "It
wouldn't be something with pancetta and Parmesan,
would it?"

"Maybe," Peter replied unconcernedly as he looked around for a seat. "But you'll have to wrestle 'em from me to find out."

The Suzuki Samurai he had rented at the airport managed to negotiate the rutted track to the house, but Jack Osborne winced with something like pain as the car jostled and jounced its way between the overgrown hedges. In Betsy's day the drive was carefully graded and covered each spring with crushed quahog shells—less practical than paving, perhaps, but a tradition among the grand houses of Siasconset's North Bluff. Now, tall weeds whipped at the car's undercarriage, and storm-tossed branches lay like severed limbs directly in his path. What else had he expected? Eight years was a serious piece of neglect. The decay hurt his eyes, all the same. Betsy had loved this house as she'd loved few things. And where Betsy loved, her money followed. She would have been appalled to see it like this.

He turned the car into the parking area before the separate garage, some hundred yards from the path to the door, and as he killed the motor and engaged the parking brake, he saw how the paint had flaked in ragged white ribbons from the old wooden doors. Salt air. A ruinous substance, insidious, inexorable; curling around the eaves with damp and penetrating fingers. The house could only be worse.

He sat a moment in the stillness that followed the engine's dying, one hand on his knee, the other on the ring of car keys, and listened. A rustle of wind in the dune grass to the house's rear, the tearing cry of a gull. Not the sound he had been listening for. What was it? What had he always heard at this particular moment, in this particular place? *Chopin*—nocturnes? preludes?—drifting across the lawn from the open living-room window, where Betsy—tanned, her shoulders jutting sleekly from a white halter dress, her black hair loose—stroked passionately at the keys.

Was it even worth getting out of the car?

Yes, came a voice in his brain—Betsy's voice, after all. *It is always necessary to name one's fears.* The essential lesson she had taught him, so many years ago.

He eased open the car door and set one foot down, then another. How his students at Harvard would laugh if they could see him now—Osborne the master of Socratic method, Osborne the killer of grades and dreams. He patted his back pocket, reassuring himself that the house key was still there—the same key he had always used, and then never used again in all the time since her disappearance. He had been incapable of returning to this place afterward, had forced all thought of it from his mind. And yet so much time had passed while he'd slaved in Cambridge. Slaved, and healed, and watched class after class of young lawyers graduate; grew old, and grew resigned, finally, that Betsy would never return. The years were written on the house's clapboard facade.

This path to the door, now, and its border of hydrangeas—except for the overgrown grass and the astonishing breadth of the bushes—this at least had not changed. The first round heads of greenish-white incipient flowers poked forth from the wealth of leaves. He remembered them as a deep and deliberate blue, spilling duskily out of oriental bowls in the Marlborough Street library. Betsy used to dry them for the winter.

He paused at the door, seeing the cracks in the slate steps—salt air again—and reached for the key. He had considered returning here only once, when his friend Wade Freer—of the art-gallery Freers, as Wade was fond of saying—persuaded him to sail over from the Vineyard on his forty-two-footer. A summer holiday from their joint labors at the law school. A party of friends. A weekend moored up in the Nantucket boat basin. He had thought he was finally strong enough.

"I actually have a house there, you know," he had said as casually as he could. "Not that it's fit for human habitation."

"One of those inherited monstrosities?" Wade had asked.

And Jack had nodded. A monstrosity.

That was the weekend he'd met Roxie. He'd never even ventured to the Sconset end of the island, as it happened, having learned he was not, indeed, strong enough. Not yet.

But if Betsy had taught him to believe only one thing, Jack thought as he thrust open the door, it was this: that we are *never* strong enough for what we fear will hurt us. We combat it, finally, out of our deepest weakness.

He stepped into the foyer and breathed in the familiar stillness that lived under its high ceiling. The sharp smell of must assailed his nostrils, and the staleness of a house long closed. He peered around, eyes adjusting to the dimness of the rooms, their windows blank behind drawn drapes, the furniture so much humped cordwood under the graying white dustcloths—and then his senses leaped into awareness. The must and the staleness, though present, were nonetheless too faint for eight years' accumulation. There was a movement to the air, a discernible current. Somewhere a window was open.

Jack dashed swiftly through the house, eyes searching for a billowing curtain, a drape pulled wide—and in the pantry, just to the rear of the kitchen, he found what he was looking for.

A pane of glass above the outer door's knob. Smashed first, and the shards pushed inward, so that a gloved hand might reach for the lock. He bent close to peer at the glass on the floor, then studied the window frame. No dust. No markings of weather. A recent break, then.

Jack straightened upright, his mind working swiftly. Was it coincidence? The work of a vandal aware that the house was deserted?

Or a more deliberate rifling—a purposeful search, for something particular that must not be found, now that Elizabeth's bones were recovered?

He turned away from the pantry door and moved with

the sureness of long habit to the phone in Elizabeth's study. It was only as he reached for the receiver that he remembered—the line had been dead for years.

"So what you're saying"—Merry sat back in her desk chair—"is that you've been robbed of a fortune."

"Exactly."

"In valuable Ian Markham sculptures that you've never worried about before, and only now discovered are missing."

"Exactly," Jack Osborne said. "Once I realized I would have to drive into town to report the theft, I took a few moments to look around the house. Other things may be gone as well, but I noticed the loss of the sculptures immediately."

"They just leaped out at you, as it were," Merry said helpfully.

"It was fairly obvious," he retorted, crossing and un-crossing his legs impatiently. "Some of them were mas-sive. Life-size human figures, copper-plated. The cloth covers that had been thrown over them were lying scat-tered on the floor. If you come out to the house, Detec-tive, you can see for yourself. I've left everything just as I found it."

"Everything," Merry repeated.

Osborne frowned. His bearded jaw jutted pugna-ciously. *"Yes."*

Merry leaned across the desk, a pen balanced between her fingers. "What brought you to Nantucket, Professor?"

"What are you suggesting, Detective?"

"I'm just wondering how recently you studied your wife's will."

"Elizabeth's *will*? What on earth does her will have to do with anything?"

"Were the sculptures insured, by any chance?"

"Of course. Though I doubt to their current market value. That would have been done by Betsy some time ago, and I can't tell you whether the policy is up-to-date."

"You can't. A brilliant lawyer can't tell me whether his insurance is current. How charmingly absentminded of you, Professor Osborne. How academically foggy and quaint. Are you aware, by the way, that there's an all-points bulletin out for your arrest? You should have been stopped at Logan."

"I took the ferry from Hyannis," Osborne said. "Arrested for what?"

"Let's just say the FBI wants to question you in connection with the murder of Roxanne Teasdale. They've been hunting for you for two days."

"I left town."

"I know. The question is, *when*. Before Roxanne died, or after? And just how long have you been on the island? Five hours—or five days?"

"Would you mind," Jack Osborne said, "explaining why you find it necessary to be offensive?"

"I'll make a deal with you," Merry offered congenially. "I'll stop being offensive if you tell me why you showed up today. I mean, you haven't actually made Nantucket your second home all these years—though I understand you've visited more than you were prepared to admit during our last conversation."

Osborne measured her words. Then he shrugged delicately. "There's no reason not to tell you. I came to pay my respects to Emily Teasdale."

"To Emily?" Merry's black brows came together dangerously. "But I thought Emily had gone to Boston."

"Emily is about to go," Osborne corrected her, "having waited, by previous arrangement, until after my visit. It was one concession I wrung from her. She categorically refused to let me attend the burial in California."

"Too bad," Merry said, "but think how hard it was for her, discovering that Roxanne had kept her relations with you a secret."

"That," Osborne agreed, "and the fact that I'm old enough to be Roxie's father. I don't mind telling you that Emily took no pains to hide her contempt."

"Why did you come? You can't have expected her to throw open her arms to you."

"No." Osborne's eyes drifted away, and a palpable sadness worked at the corners of his mouth. "I didn't love Roxanne. I'll say that freely. But I was fond of the girl, and I understood how she viewed me. I was her knight, Detective. I was a seductive older man who could show her the ways of the world. Bring her roses, put her up in fine hotels, make her feel sophisticated and accomplished. I never played with Roxie's feelings. I never intended her to be hurt. I assumed that one day she would outgrow me and naturally move on. But when she—when some *animal* destroyed her—" Osborne's fists clenched convulsively and then released. He drew a shuddering breath.

"It's absolutely horrible," Merry interjected quietly, "and there is no sense to be made of it."

"Well—" Osborne looked at her steadily. "I wanted to talk to her grandmother. I wanted her to know that Roxie was simply young, and high-spirited, and terribly alive. That I had tried to make her happy. That however many things caused her sorrow right now, my relationship with her granddaughter should not be one of them."

"You felt *guilty*," Merry said, surprised.

"Oh, probably," Osborne replied with a sheepish look.

"And Emily? Was she convinced? Did she give you absolution for corrupting Roxanne?"

Something flared in Osborne's face—anger, resentment, a bitter self-knowledge—and then died. "I doubt it," he said. "But she was good enough to allow me into the house, though she had a watchdog with her—"

"A dog?"

"Well, an old guy, actually," Osborne replied. "I think it's possible she was afraid I actually *killed* Roxie and had come back to finish her off. Emily made her appointment with me and got this absolute character to stand over me when I came."

"Was he white-haired? With a beard? Bright-blue eyes?"

"Yes! You know him?"

"He's my grandfather," Merry said casually. "Now, let's talk about why you took a ferry from Hyannis instead of flying over from Boston."

Osborne sighed and closed his eyes. "A friend of Roxie's called me Tuesday at the law school. Told me what had happened to her."

"Lily Olszewski?"

"Lily. Yes. I . . . couldn't concentrate for the rest of the day. Couldn't make sense of what I knew was true. I got in the car and drove to Hyannis. Checked into a motel. Called Emily the next morning and persuaded her to see me. She wouldn't make time for me until today."

"So for three days you kicked around Hyannis?"

"It sounds implausible. . . ."

"That's one word. I'm sure the FBI will check it out." Merry stared at Osborne with thinly veiled hostility. "Back to those sculptures. Are you familiar with the provisions of your wife's will?"

"She set up a trust," Osborne supplied, "for some art-therapy group. I wonder if it's even in existence."

"You haven't checked?"

"No. Why?"

"I just wondered," Merry said. "Your wife left them her houses as well. Sconset *and* Back Bay. With all their contents."

There was a pregnant silence. Osborne's face clouded. "So what you're saying," he managed, "is that the sculptures would have gone to the trust, too."

"Yes," Merry agreed, intrigued that he took the loss of the Marlborough Street house so calmly. "It's something of a blow, isn't it?"

"I imagine," he replied. "They're probably quite valuable."

"Don't you think it's odd?" Merry asked him. "That

they should disappear *now*? Once Elizabeth's will comes into effect?"

"I suppose so," Jack Osborne conceded impatiently. "Someone must have decided to move quickly or lose the sculptures forever."

"Exactly, Professor Osborne," Merry replied. "That someone wouldn't be *you*, now, would it?"

Chapter Twenty-one

"That was a figure of a woman." Osborne pointed to a bare space in the corner of the drawing room. "A life-size copper naiad. And over there was the *Couple Embracing*." He waved vaguely toward the drawing room's French doors. Beyond them lay the bluff, and the sweep of springtime Atlantic, and the loneliness of dune grass. Merry half expected to see Nan Markham's bright-red hair pop up from below the bluff, or hear Satchmo's bark; but the view remained empty of both children and dogs.

"More figures, huh? Markham seems to have specialized in them."

"It may have been a phase," Osborne replied, smiling crookedly, "that coincided with his use of my wife as a model. Most of the women were loosely disguised visions of Betsy."

"Even the one of—how did you put it—two figures embracing?"

Jack Osborne declined to answer.

Merry looked up from her notepad. She had agreed to accompany the professor back to Sconset once Dana Stevens and Tucker Enright had finished questioning him. Privately, Stevens had told Merry that Osborne had stuck to his Hyannis story, and she had asked the state police in Barnstable to check out the alibi with his motel. Not that the alibi proved anything; Osborne could easily have flown from Boston to Nantucket the night of Roxie Teasdale's murder, then returned to await Lily's phone call. His time in Hyannis was largely irrelevant. And for the night of Roxie's death he had no alibi at all. He claimed to have been home alone.

Merry's job was to keep an eye on Osborne until the FBI found a plausible basis for arresting him. A visit to his dead wife's Sconset house should reasonably kill most of the afternoon.

"So is that it?" she asked him now. "Six statues altogether?"

"One more, I'm afraid. In Betsy's bedroom. The head of a man. It used to sit on her vanity table."

"Ian's head?"

"Perhaps Ian as he would like to have been seen." A touch of acid in the last remark that Merry could not help but appreciate.

"Clarence," she called over her shoulder toward the pantry, where the crime-scene chief was painstakingly dusting the frame of the broken window for prints, "do the surface of this table by the French doors, okay? It's mahogany. Maybe the thief gripped the underside or something."

"Ayeh, Marradith," Clarence shot back testily. "I'm havin' Nat here dust anythin' that's exposed. You just get on with yahr business, and we'll get on with ours."

Nat Coffin poked his head around the drawing-room doorway and grinned in Merry's direction. "His nose is turned, Detective," he said. "Pining for a post with the FBI."

Merry sighed and followed Jack Osborne slowly up the winding curve of steps to the old house's second floor, glancing minutely around the rooms adjacent to the one he had entered. "And you're sure nothing else was taken?" she said, for perhaps the fifth time that afternoon.

"No," Osborne replied. "I'm not. I'd have to do a complete inventory, and that's likely to take days. Even if I managed to remember what *should* be here in the first place."

"So what we've got, as best you can judge, is seven Ian Markham sculptures of copper-plated ceramic, value unknown." She looked up from her notebook curiously. "Were these things attractive, Professor? I mean—*copper-plated ceramic?*"

Osborne shrugged impatiently. "Betsy certainly thought so. And Betsy had impeccable taste. The copper-plating was a relatively new technique for Ian. He perfected it here, in his studio."

"I've got to ask you," Merry said, setting her notepad down on the dustcloth-covered mattress and pulling off her half glasses to stare Osborne directly in the face. "What in the hell were you thinking? This place is a treasure trove. You simply locked the doors and walked away *eight years ago*, without so much as an agreement with a neighbor to keep an eye on the place from time to time? By rights, you should have been robbed blind in three or four days."

"Not I," Osborne said quietly. "Betsy. Betsy should have been robbed blind. None of this belongs to me. None of it ever did."

"Is that it?" Merry swept a hand expansively around the room. "Indifference to things that were hers?"

"I don't know." The law professor hesitated. "Maybe. I was just angry at first—angry that she had been such a fool as to run off with Ian in *Mood Indigo*. Which is what we all thought had happened, however little we talked about it. I was so angry, I never wanted to come here again." He stopped and looked at the floor, as though the intricate pattern of the rose-colored Chinese carpet might spell out his mysteries. "And then, after a while—a year, eighteen months—it seemed simpler never to think of the place again."

"And yet you stayed in the Marlborough Street house."

Osborne hesitated.

"Despite the memories. Despite Elizabeth's *things*."

"Yes. That will change, of course, now. I'll probably find a place in Cambridge. Avoid the commute."

Merry perched on the edge of the bed. Her weight dislodged a cloud of dust. "Forgive me, Professor, but I find most of what you tell me very difficult to believe. I always have—from the moment we talked in your Back Bay office until you appeared in my doorway this afternoon. Your stories don't entirely work."

"Stories?"

"Well, there *are* several," Merry pointed out. "There's the one you ginned up the night Elizabeth disappeared, about sleeping soundly and thinking nothing the next day of her passport lying on the beach, until you reported it around noon. Then there's the bit about your ignorance of how your wife came by all those broken bones—I can't get *that* one out of my head. And now we have the Sudden Disappearance of a Fortune in Statues—a fortune that, by rights, belongs to Ian Markham's wife. As I'm sure you are perfectly aware. You have a story for every occasion, Professor. We could trade them back and forth long into the evening. And they might just improve in the retelling."

"Are you always this antagonistic toward summer people?" Osborne asked, his color rising. "Or is it just men?"

"Are you always so quick to take offense," Merry rejoined mildly, "or just when you hear the truth?"

"I've had enough of this," he spat out, and reached for the door. "I'll simply report the theft to my insurance company and note that the local police were decidedly uncooperative."

"Like you did when Elizabeth disappeared. Those police. Always asking nasty questions. Never taking anything at face value. I'm sure your insurance will pony up immediately—they're never suspicious, like the police. And that way you can collect twice—once from the chumps who've insured you, and again when you hock the Markham stuff. I guess that's the kind of savvy that gets people tenure at Harvard these days, huh?"

"Go ahead," Markham said savagely. "Search my hotel room. I'm staying at the Harbor House. Search the car, if you like. Search high and low. But you'll find nothing. Because the last thing in the world I'd have wanted to take were those god-awful pieces of kitsch that Elizabeth loved so besottedly. I hated them, do you understand? *Hated* them. I'd have turned them over to poor Julia with the rest of this miserable house in an instant if I could, no matter how much money I'd have gotten. I can't get rid of it all fast enough."

"Because of the memories, Professor?" Merry asked quietly. "Which memories in particular? I confess I'm curious. Because your neglect of this place—your absolute avoidance and abandonment of it, in fact—looks remarkably like the disgust of a guilty man."

"Guilty? Guilty of what?"

Merry shrugged. "Strangling your wife, maybe, in a jealous rage? Burying her body somewhere it should never have been found? Maybe you even sabotaged Markham's boat. It has a nice symmetry to it—because everyone, of course, thought your wife was on *Mood Indigo*. Nobody really looked for her with much gusto, including the grieving husband. I've been wondering why. *Why* it was necessary to keep Elizabeth's body missing for so long."

"And what has your feeble brain come up with?" Osborne asked harshly.

"You handed it to me today," Merry replied. "The

statues. Not worth much, except to Elizabeth, when they were made—but they've skyrocketed in value, so I'm told. If Elizabeth's death had been proved soon after Ian Markham had died, her collection would have gone immediately to Art in Mind. But Elizabeth remained in limbo. Markham's tragedy gave his reputation a boost. The sculptures were suddenly valuable. Why not wait and see? Let Art in Mind die from lack of interest and support, let Markham's pieces become rarer and rarer, and then stage a robbery at a propitious moment. And what moment could be more propitious? You're about to lose your Back Bay house. That's clearly of some value to you, since you've stayed in it for years. And I notice Elizabeth left you absolutely nothing to live on in her will. But those sculptures of Markham's would probably set you up for life, even sold on the black market. And how satisfying, really, to turn a buck behind the backs of those two. Ian and Elizabeth. The ones who betrayed you."

Osborne slumped heavily against the wall, his expression dazed. "You can't possibly be accusing me," he said, "of all these . . . *enormities*."

"No," Merry agreed. "I really can't. I have no proof. And I'm still working on one part of the problem. Somebody moved your wife's bones from wherever they had lain for years and reburied them in January on Sconset beach, where they were found a few weeks ago. For the life of me, I can't come up with a reason why you'd do that. Yet."

"I'm sure you'll invent one, given time," he said, and studied her face. "I didn't take you very seriously, Detective Folger, that day you came to Back Bay."

Merry smiled. "Well, isn't *that* a surprise."

"I take you rather more seriously now."

"Thank you." Had she unsettled Osborne? Or was he merely an excellent actor?

The professor waited for her to lead him from Elizabeth's bedroom, an unconscious gesture of civility Merry bowed to without protest. She could hear Clarence's heavy tread as he mounted the stairs at the end of the hall, bound for Elizabeth's vanity table with his dusting kit.

"Detective," Osborne said tentatively.

"Yes?"

"About those broken bones of Betsy's."

Something quickened along Merry's spine.

Osborne nodded at Clarence as the crime-scene chief shrugged past them, leaving the stairway clear.

"I've been thinking. Perhaps you should talk to Julia Markham. She may know more about Betsy's last year than I could possibly imagine."

"I'm on my way to talk to her now," Merry told him. "Why don't you come along?"

The Markham place was only a few blocks away from Elizabeth Osborne's stately home on Baxter Road, but it might have been a different world.

"My God." Jack Osborne's eyes widened as he took in Codfish Park's abandoned houses, and the empty foundations where several had been moved. "What happened here?"

"Weather," Merry said briefly, and brought her Explorer to a halt in the sandy lane before Julia Markham's door.

Jack got out of the car, followed by a vigilant Howie Seitz, and stood staring at the ravaged beachfront. "That's Ian's studio," he said, pointing to a small fisherman's shack tilted crazily on its foundations. "It's been hit." He walked like a man in a dream across what remained of Codfish Park Road and stopped before the damaged building. Then he passed his hands over his eyes. "I should never have come back here."

Merry pocketed her keys and, after an instant, followed him to the eroding bank. Osborne was right, she thought; the building was like a metaphor for everything that had happened here—destruction, loss, abandonment, decay. The sculptor's studio must have been a charming thing eight years earlier—rose covered, perched on the edge of dunes no longer in evidence, filled with the white glare of sunlight refracting off sand. Now it looked as though a giant hand had plucked it from the earth, tossed it drunkenly in the air a few times, and left it battered and forgotten for the next wave to claim.

"I wouldn't get too close," Merry advised Osborne. "These places are pretty unstable." She shaded her eyes and looked down the road, searching for Mabel Johnson's house, and was reassured to find it still sitting on its small rise above the sand. When all this was over, Merry promised herself mentally, she'd figure out what to do about Mabel. There had to be a way of helping her.

"There's the electroplating vat!" Osborne exclaimed, with something like excitement. "And Markham's tools. His firing oven. I can't believe it—like Sleeping Beauty's castle. Julia's left everything exactly as it was."

"That's what Peter said," Merry replied, half to herself, and joined the law professor by the studio window.

He was leaning forward, hands cupped around his eyes, the better to view the ravaged cottage's interior. "I bet you could still fire up the equipment and gild yourself a lily," he mused. "How bizarre."

"Don't you need an electrical current?" Howie asked. "The fire department will have cut the line by this time, if the Markhams even thought to keep it up."

"Of course," Osborne said. "It's just the appearance that's so deceiving. I bet there's still a pretty toxic soup in that vat, by the way. It's fairly large—it had to be, given the size of Markham's figures—and if it's going to sail out to sea, you might want to get someone to inspect it first."

Merry stood as if turned to stone by his words, her eyes on the studio's battered window frame. "Detective?" Howie reached for her elbow and shook it slightly. "You okay?"

"I'm fine," she snapped. "You're completely right, Professor. We need to get our environmental police over here, and sooner rather than later. But right now we'd better get up to the house. I don't feel completely comfortable about the building's stability."

Jack stepped gingerly away from the studio's broken foundation and glanced past her, toward the Markham house. He whistled. "Looks as neglected as our place. Only it's been lived in."

"Yep," Merry said. "Times have not been good for Julia and the kids."

"I should have talked to her. I should have offered some help," Osborne said, almost inaudibly.

Merry looked at him searchingly as they walked up the path to the front door. "Why didn't you?"

He smiled briefly, bitterly. "It was my wife who ruined her life, remember? We both thought she was on that boat with Ian. Neither of us could really face the other."

But you must have known Julia stood to benefit from Elizabeth's will, Merry argued to herself, *and yet you did nothing to prove your wife was dead. Curious, if indeed you felt some guilt over Julia's state. A case of out of sight, out of mind? Or is the concern for Julia a sham, like everything else you've told me?*

"And yet," Merry said aloud as she knocked lightly on Julia's door, "Elizabeth wasn't on *Mood Indigo* when the boat went down. She may already have been dead. So, tell me, Professor. Who do *you* think killed your wife?"

Julia opened the door on the heels of that question, her eyes wide and staring as she looked from Merry to Osborne. She swayed slightly in the doorway, her mouth open as if to speak; and then, without a word, she crumpled at their feet.

"Lie still," Merry urged, her hand on Julia's forehead. "Don't try to speak."

But the half-conscious woman struggled upright, elbows braced against the floor, her head twisting and mouth working. "You!" she said, pointing a shaking finger at Jack Osborne. "How could you?" She turned imploringly to Merry. "Keep him away from my Nan—please!"

Merry's brows came down over her green eyes, and she studied Julia intently. The woman had curled into a fetal ball, her black hair hanging snakelike over her cheeks, and was crying helplessly. "Stay with them, Howie," she said over her shoulder. "I'll go find the kids." She rose swiftly and headed out the entryway toward the kitchen when an inhuman screech of terror stopped her in her tracks. She looked back at the two men and saw her own astonishment mirrored in their faces.

"No!" Julia screamed, crawling toward Merry. "He'll kill me too! Please! Don't leave me!"

A finger of fear crawled its way along Merry's back. Julia Markham sprang to her feet, a wiry animal, and lunged for Osborne's throat.

"You can't have her! Not my baby! I'll kill you first!"

Howie grasped the woman's frail shoulders, attempting in vain to pull her hands away from Osborne's face. He was bellowing with pain, and as Merry went to help, the professor laid a glancing blow to Julia's head. With a sharp cry she stumbled and fell to the floor. Her skull struck the edge of a metal toy truck one of the children had left lying in the entryway, and as suddenly as a deflating balloon, all struggle went out of her. Howie stared, wordless and appalled.

Jack Osborne, his balance regained, half fell in a crouch by her side, one hand outstretched. "Julie," he murmured, but drew back before he could touch the inert shoulder.

What to do with the man? Merry thought frantically. Julia Markham desperately believed he was a murderer. Should she pull a gun on him? Expect attack at any instant? Merry tensed, her fingers reaching for her service revolver, and waited to see what Osborne would do.

His head came up, and he looked at her beseechingly. "We've got to get help," he said.

Merry nodded. "Howie," she said, "the phone's in the living room. Probably under some clothes or magazines.

You'll have to hunt." Her eyes never left Jack Osborne's face as Howie went.

"Mum," a faint voice said from the doorway. Nan Markham, one finger in her mouth and a doll trailing from her other hand. "What have you done to my mum?"

"So what happens next?" Jack Osborne asked her later, in the emergency room's waiting area.

Merry looked at Nan and Cecil, who were sitting quietly on either side of Peter Mason, their legs swinging a few inches off the floor as he turned the pages of *James and the Giant Peach*. "I'll probably ask my friend to take them home tonight. He lives on a farm—has a dog, some sheep, the whole nine yards. Julia should be up and around tomorrow. Or so the doctor tells me."

Julia Markham had regained consciousness at the arrival of the white-clad ambulance crew, had started screaming again at the sight of Jack Osborne, and was swiftly sedated. She lay now in the splendid isolation created by temporary hospital screens, half-dreaming, half-agonized, amid a ward of new mothers.

"I don't mean the kids," Osborne said quietly. "I mean about me. Julia's act was pretty convincing. And she's accused me of murder."

The law professor's face was marked by exhaustion. Between his meeting with Emily Teasdale and his arrival at Nantucket Cottage Hospital, he'd had a long day. "I could charge you with the murders of Ian Markham and Elizabeth Osborne, based on Julia Markham's accusation," she said, "but someone with your legal background would argue that Julia was deranged. I'd like to talk to her when she's more coherent. So I've asked Howie to take you back to the Harbor House, and to stand guard outside your door. The guard will be changed periodically over the next few days. It would be easier to put you in a cell, of course, but I could keep you there for only twenty-four hours. A small matter of shower rights for the accused under Massachusetts law. But, then, you'd know all about that."

"I see," Jack Osborne said faintly. "I guess I'd better call a lawyer."

"Good idea."

"Sir," Howie said, with a hand on his elbow.

And with only the mildest appearance of chagrin, the professor went. There were worse things, Merry reflected, than being forced to stay at the Harbor House.

Chapter Twenty-two

"It's too late for you to leave," Peter argued as Merry slipped quietly away from the doorway of his guest bedroom. Nan and Cecil Markham were sound asleep beneath the covers of their twin beds, cheeks flushed in the faint glow of the lamp Peter had carefully left burning. If nightmares came, at least they need not be endured in total darkness.

"I've got to go," Merry said gently, and made for the stairs.

Unwillingly, Peter followed her. "I might point out that it's Friday night."

"You might. And then I'd have to tell you that I promised Bill Carmichael I'd look through the serial victims' files today. Or that I told the entire world via television that I had the guy in my sights, and nobody else was going to be hurt. Then Jack Osborne shows up, and *presto!*

I'm back on the Osborne case. It's like a drug. I can't let Elizabeth go."

"Any closer to the answers?"

Merry shook her head and turned to look at him as he descended the last of his steps. The staircase of the two-hundred-year-old house was just high enough, and the ceiling just low enough, that Peter was forced to tilt his head at an angle in order to negotiate his way between the floors. "All I'm finding is more and more questions."

"Maybe you need a break."

"I'll take one when all this stuff is put to bed," she promised.

"Will you? And what if there's another mess that only Meredith Folger can resolve?" Peter's face was un-wontedly sober; and Merry knew that he needed something she was too tired to give. Reassurance, undivided attention—sheer normalcy.

"You're a godsend, Peter, you know that?" she said, de-liberately changing the subject. "I wouldn't want these kids to be left with anyone else."

"Except Ralph."

"Right. But Ralph's got me to contend with tonight."

"Would you do me a favor? Let me call your dad to pick you up? Or Howie? I don't like the thought of your traveling alone."

"I'll be fine. I'll go straight to the station and sit up with my files for company. Really."

"Then at least call Ralph and explain why you're not coming home. We don't want him to lose sleep."

"At least I know *you* won't," Merry teased, "since you're unlikely to camp out in the Rover ten feet from my door tonight. I have Nan and Cecil to thank for *that*."

"How did you know?" he asked her, disappointed. "I thought I was the best of spies. Invisible to all but the eyes of evil."

Merry reached up and touched his cheek briefly with her hand. "I always know when you're near. Consider that a good thing."

"I do," Peter said, his expression lighter now than it had been, and kissed her.

Lights blazed in the Water Street station, and the ubiquitous crowd of newsfolk and cameramen still huddled, spirits unquenched by the descent of darkness or the siren call of Friday-night laughter from the eating establishments that lined the surrounding streets. Merry was more cautious this time, however, and slipped the Explorer into an illegal spot near the war memorial on Federal. Then she moved as quietly as a shade through the shrubbery along Chestnut, thankful for the dense island darkness and the waning moon, and ducked through the station door unnoticed.

She bumped into a harassed Dana Stevens near the stairs.

"Still here?"

"Yes," the FBI agent said shortly. "Not that it's made a damn bit of difference. We're getting nowhere."

"How's Enright holding up?" Merry asked. "I was hoping to talk to him."

"Gone AWOL."

"Probably eating dinner. He's a man who likes his food. You had any yet?"

"Nope. I'm heading out right now. Care to come?"

Merry shook her head and held up a brown paper bag Peter had pressed upon her as she'd left Mason Farms. "I've brought my milk and cookies, thank you very much."

"You stopped at home?" Dana asked, her interest quickening.

"No. I'm staying at my dad's, actually. Why?"

The agent waved a hand dismissively. "Never mind. Just wondered if you'd received another love letter. We're all waiting for one. Your press-conference footage ran, by the way, an hour ago."

"I know," Merry replied. "I watched it at the hospital."

"How's your hysteric?"

"Sedated."

Dana nodded. "That business about to wrap up?"

"I know you'd like it to." Merry paused. Then, "Yes," she said. "I think it's basically over."

"So did Jack the Ripper do it?"

"I'll let you know. Listen, Dana, I'm trying to catch our environmental police. I'll talk to you later, okay?"

But neither Jamie Ferreira, the officer in charge of responding to calls about hazardous waste, nor his assistant, Chris Mancuso, was sitting behind their companionable desks, poring over the materials and newsletters that other members of the force found so tedious. Both had quit at their usual hour and were probably well embarked on some weekend ritual of relaxation. Merry scanned the reference works arranged tidily in alphabetical order on the top shelf of Jamie's cubicle and seized the most promising amid the technical jargon.

She already knew, really, what had happened the night that Elizabeth Osborne died; all she needed now was some sort of confirmation. She found it within seven minutes of sitting down with *Industrial Chemicals: Their Hazards and Uses*, and spent the next fifteen or so staring into space, imagining how it must have been.

Then she turned, somewhat reluctantly, to the mountain of manila folders Bill Carmichael had helpfully left on the corner of her desk.

It was the saddest of plunges into meaningless waste—a compendium of lives full of hope, and lives simply lived. A memory album, of sorts, for five young women, women ten years younger on average than Meredith herself, whose dreams of love or meaningful work or small children running through the sunlit reaches of high-ceilinged houses had been abruptly and brutally extinguished. *Sandy was an accomplished athlete who hoped to ride for the Olympic equestrian team,* one interviewer had noted. *Everyone loved Janine, particularly her theater group of underprivileged kids in Charlestown,* said another. *Melanie's younger brother Buck, a high school junior, is severely affected by her loss and is undergoing counseling recommended by this officer.*

The silent victims, Merry thought. The ones the killer never thinks of—every single person these young women had touched. How did their families come to terms with it? All the years of effort—the struggles with school, the teenage tantrums, the survival of the first driving test and the last late-night prom—the successful navigation of the college years (although one victim, Jennifer Morgan, found on the Charles River bike path, had died in her sophomore year)—and then this. A life eradicated.

The sense of futility was overwhelming.

A smiling snapshot of each victim, taken in life, accompanied each file. Merry arranged the inside front covers in an overlapping pattern, so that the five women were arrayed in a mournful lineup. And realized suddenly what had been nagging at the edge of her consciousness—all of them were blonds. Surely everyone else had noted the fact; it was part of the pattern. And what color was the hair of the girl Manuel Esconvidos had carried off in his trunk?

She shuffled through the disordered reams of paper teetering precariously on every square inch of her desk's surface and found the file marked *Lisa McChesney, Attempted Abduction.* Flipped it open and stared. Another blond.

And Roxanne Teasdale's long, shining hair was a deep auburn.

Merry shoved the last file aside and pulled off her reading glasses, understanding something of Bill Carmichael's anger. Manuel Esconvidos—maverick, misogynist, and former resident of five suspect locales—was free on bail tonight, and there was nothing Bill or Merry could do about it.

A light tap on her half-open door, and Tucker Enright's face peered around the jamb.

"Doctor," Merry said. "The very man I wanted to see. Enjoy your dinner?"

"Immensely," he said. "I highly recommend that place on Federal. Elegant, satisfying, and just steps from the station, too."

"I know it well," Merry said, considering 21 Federal with a hungry pang. "Do you have a minute?"

"Of course." Enright slid through the doorway and bent to shift some files from a chair. He wore jeans tonight, and a cherry-red cable-knit sweater. A lazy, good-natured ease was written into every line of his body; and studying him, Merry felt her own weariness deep in the bone.

"Did you receive another letter?" he asked her.

"No. But there are some things I'd love to talk about. You know Jack Osborne has checked into the Harbor House."

The psychiatrist nodded. "I read over his statement again before dinner. It was a curious feeling, Meredith, to sit in that room with Dana and interrogate a man I've known for years. A man, I'll freely confess, that I have reason to dislike and resent. I've never had to do that. I understood, for a minute, how you must feel every day. Pursuing and accusing your own neighbors."

"And protecting them," Merry countered gravely. "Don't forget the good part. But what do you think, Tucker? Is he our man?"

Enright sat straighter in his chair and steepled his fingers. *This is the way he must look at his Harvard seminars,* Merry thought, watching the concentrated stillness creep over his face. *Like a priest awaiting confession.*

"There's a problem here, Meredith," he began. "You know how I feel about Osborne personally; there's a jealousy because of Betsy that goes way back. Admittedly. That might influence how I view him."

"I know. We'll take that as a given. Just tell me what you think as a psychiatrist."

Enright looked at her and smiled. "Is it that easy?"

"I'm the woman who decides to be happy, remember."

"And you can just *decide* to be objective, too?"

"No," Merry replied, "but I keep my training in the forefront of my mind. Look. You're a professional. Take refuge in that. Forget about who Osborne *is*. Think about him as though he were a stranger. Imagine a glass wall, a one-way mirror, between the two of you. And tell me what you see."

"All right," he said. "Osborne's an utterly contained person. He never reveals his emotion if he believes that emotion is dangerous—only when he thinks it will win him something. Trust, security, affection. He can turn it on at will. He uses his intellectual talents in the same way—throws a curtain of reason over the most implausible actions. He's calculating. He's purposeful. And he does not make mistakes. I think he could quite reasonably have committed these murders."

"But what's his motivation? I can see a reason for killing his wife—jealousy, rage—but why kill Roxie Teasdale?"

"You tell me. You've been focusing on the victims. Why *would* Jack kill that girl? He's supposed to have loved her, after all."

"Not *loved* her. Even he admitted *that*," Merry mused. "He told me today that he was something of a knight in Roxie's eyes. An older man who could show her the world. He felt affection for her, he said, but nothing more."

"Jack, Jack." Enright sounded a little sad. "What did Betsy do to you?"

"Betsy?"

"She must have done something—some deep emotional damage. The guy acts as if he feels powerful only when he's around women half his age. Dependent, trusting, *weak* women. Like the entourage of students who follow him everywhere. He's incapable of equality in a relationship. Is Viet Nam responsible? Or Betsy and her betrayal? I don't know enough to say. Tell me more about Roxanne, Meredith. How long were they involved?"

"About nine months. According to her friend, Roxanne was thinking of taking the LSAT. She wanted to go to Harvard Law."

"Wow. The chicken comes home to roost. If she managed to get in."

"Right," agreed Merry. "It's one thing to have a relationship with a girl who lives thirty-three miles out to sea. Another thing altogether when the girl moves into your backyard. Maybe Osborne decided to end the relationship in a precipitate fashion."

"And simply used the method he knew best. Convenient—he winds up his affair and fits the death into a baffling serial pattern."

Merry's eyes narrowed. "You really think he's responsible for the previous murders?"

"I don't know. Do you?"

"The other victims were blond. Roxie's hair was auburn."

"Huh. Interesting," Enright said. "I hadn't focused on that. It may mean something—or it may mean nothing at all. But that's for the FBI to figure out. With dates, DNA samples, places, means. All the technicalities that make up the noose."

There was a moment's pause.

"And when they do?" Merry asked him. "Will *you* prove that Osborne is sane?"

"He *is*."

"But think of it." Abruptly, the horror of it all swept over Merry. "What he *did* to that poor girl. A girl who was in love with him. It's absolutely *sick*."

"It's revolting," Enright corrected. "It's disturbing, it's tragic, and it's against every norm of civilized behavior. But it is *not* sick. Osborne—or if not Osborne, whoever killed Roxie—knew precisely what he was doing."

"So you're not convinced."

"I hesitate to condemn even Jack Osborne without further evidence."

Merry inclined her head in Enright's direction. "Point taken. You're absolutely right. And in my better moments I think the same way. I just haven't had many of *those* lately."

Peter was wandering deep in the valley of a dream when the screams began. He groped upright, his hands clenched around a sheet. *Who was screaming?* A child.

A child? In *his* house?

He thrust his feet to the floor in the next instant, remembering Cecil and Nan, and reached for a bathrobe. The automatic movements of a somnambulist, while his mind searched for sense. The light switch—and an immediate recoil. He snapped it off again, damning his eyes. Better to find his way in the dark and cling to the illusion of sleep.

He gained the hallway, where a small body hurtled abruptly into his legs. "Whoa, whoa, buddy," he said, reaching for Cecil's thin shoulders. The boy's arms were clenched tight around Peter's waist, his face buried somewhere near the robe's capacious pockets. The shoulders themselves were heaving with sobs. "Had a nightmare?"

An emphatic nod.

"Shhhh," Peter said, brushing tentatively at Cecil's hair. "Shhhh. It's all right."

Another shudder. Good thing the robe was terry. Anything else would be soaked by now. "What about Nan? Is she awake?"

No answer.

Peter disengaged the boy from his legs as gently as possible and, holding his hand, walked the few steps to the guest-room doorway. It was ajar, but he detected no stirring from within; only a faint cough, and then the resumption of a child's even breathing. He pulled the door closed.

"How about we head downstairs for some milk and cookies, and you can tell me all about it?"

Cecil held tightly to his hand as they descended the stairs, like a boy of six rather than nearly eleven, Peter thought, and they exchanged not a word until the comforting light of the kitchen, and the cheerful ticking of the clock over the stove, and the appearance of the promised milk. Real cookies were not to be had with Rebecca still absent in Springfield; but Peter managed to find some peanut butter and crackers, and these proved acceptable.

"So," he said, pouring them both some milk, "was it awful?"

No answer.

"Were you falling? Lost? Or was someone chasing you?"

Cecil sniffed hugely, his eyes on the table surface, his crackers untouched.

Peter looked around for a box of tissues, found them, and offered one to the boy. Then he pulled out a chair and threw himself into it. He was thoroughly awakened now, all his senses alert, and he was not about to let the woebegone figure hunched in his kitchen return to bed unshriven. Every nightmare must be confessed, after all, if it is to be forgotten.

"What's your dad like?" Cecil asked faintly.

"My dad? My dad is dead, I'm afraid. Over ten years ago."

A quick look from the boy. "Longer ago than mine. Were you little?"

"Not really. Not like you."

"I was three."

"I know."

"So you remember yours."

"Very well," Peter replied, handing him a peanut-butter-logged cracker, "and I love him still. That doesn't die. Did you love your dad, Cecil?"

Cecil nodded automatically, then stopped. He took a

bite of cracker, chewed it, and drew a shuddering breath. "No," he said. "No, I didn't love my dad. I was afraid of him. I still am."

"Is that what you dreamed of? Your father?"

There was a silence. Cecil looked at Peter over the rim of his milk glass, his eyes very dark.

"The dream about his drowning?"

"No." Cecil's voice was faint. "When he drowns, it's not a nightmare. The nightmare is when I think he's still alive."

"Cecil—"

"Did your dad ever hit you?"

"He spanked me occasionally."

"I mean *hit* you."

Peter's brow furrowed darkly. "With his fists? No. Yours did?"

Cecil nodded again. "Me and my mum. That's what I was dreaming tonight. He was angry, like always, yelling and hitting my mother, and she was crying and trying to get away from him, and I wanted to kill him—I wanted to—but I was stuck to the ground, like my feet were nailed there, and then Nan was crying too, and he was hitting her. Which is all wrong, because she wasn't even born when he died. Only sometimes dreams are like that. The people and places get all confused."

Peter nodded.

"And when I saw that Nan was there, I knew he'd never really died, and that he'd come back to get us all. I tried to hide, but he found me, and his face was terrible, all puffed and pale like he'd been drowned for a long time, and that was when I started screaming." He drew a shuddering breath. "But I woke up."

Peter said nothing for a moment, his fingers turning the peanut-butter knife for something to do. "You remember things like that happening?"

"I remember."

"And you were only three?" Even as he said it, Peter knew that Cecil's age meant nothing. Scenes of violence could be imprinted on the mind at any age; and when the victim was a toddler—or worse, the toddler's mother—the blows would take on a terrifying significance.

"I remember everything," the boy said softly, with a firmness that tugged at Peter's heart. "The way he used to throw her against walls, and she would slide down to the floor, her knees hunched up and her hands over her face. The crying sounds. The sounds at night. Sometimes I tried to stop him—" Cecil swung his arms wildly, futilely. "I'd punch at his legs—and he'd slap me so hard, my nose would bleed. So finally I just tried not to hear. I'd stuff the blanket into my ears and hum with my head under the pillow. But I always heard. Even on nights when there was nothing *to* hear."

"Have you ever talked to your mother about it?"

"No." A decisive negative.

"Why not?"

"Because it's my fault."

"Your fault?"

"I just made him so mad," Cecil said, low and ashamed. "I'd hear him shouting at Mum—*that bloody brat. He's draining the life out of me. I wish he'd never been born.* I guess I just cost too much."

Peter snorted.

"Anyway—I think Mum blames me. It's different with Nan. She came after. Dad didn't hate her. And she's not a—a coward—like me."

"You're not a coward, Cecil."

"Yes I am! I am!"

"That's ridiculous. Would a coward have set sail for England the other day?"

The boy shrugged. "That's pretend. I'm always brave in pretend. I can be a different person then. When I'm just Cecil, I'm always scared. I was scared when Nan went in the water, you know—and if you hadn't been there, she would have drowned. It's always like that. I go numb. The same way I did with Mum when I was little. I should have done something to save her."

"Your mother?" Peter said, incredulous. "You were three years old!"

Cecil was very pale. "Sometimes I still feel that way. Like I'm three, with my head under a pillow." He looked fully at Peter for the first time. "I think that's why I hate my dad so much, even now when he's dead. Because he's made me hate myself."

Peter sat by Cecil's bedside until the boy fell asleep, and then, its being nearly five o'clock in the morning, he went downstairs and made a pot of coffee. As the first rays of sun lightened the sky, he looked out across the moors, across the backs of his sheep, which were just beginning to stir, toward the faint line on the horizon that meant the sea. He sipped contemplatively from his mug, his face expressionless, his mind turning over all that Cecil had told him.

And at six o'clock he placed a call to Meredith Folger.

Chapter Twenty-three

"Mrs. Markham," Merry said, and tapped lightly on the rolling screen that shielded Julia from her neighbors along the hospital ward.

"What is it?"

Merry stepped around to the bed and found, to her surprise, that Julia was not only sitting up, but was fully dressed. She glanced at her watch. Barely eight A.M.

"You're leaving."

"Of course. You think I can bloody well afford to sit in hospital all day? It costs the earth—and, besides, I've kids need tending to." Julia's black eyes snapped at her. "I can't believe you brought me here in the first place."

"We weren't certain what was wrong. And the children, by the way—"

"—are safe with your holier-than-thou Peter Mason," Julia finished. "I *know*. I've had it from the nurses first thing. Now, if you're satisfied you've done your duty, perhaps you'll bugger off and leave us all alone."

"I can't do that, Julia," Merry said.

"*Bloody* things," the woman said, tearing viciously at a knot in her shoelace. It simply snarled more hopelessly, and with a stifled curse, she tossed it away and put her head in her hands.

"How long has it been since you had a cigarette?"

"A hundred years."

"Come on." Merry reached for the discarded shoe. "I've already talked to Peter. He's bringing the kids to your place in an hour, after they've had breakfast. I'll drive you to Sconset. We can talk on the way."

"You think Jack Osborne strangled his wife, don't you? That's why you lost control yesterday. It was the sight of his face, after all those years." Merry glanced sidelong at the woman in her passenger seat and sighed inwardly. This promised to be a one-way conversation. Julia Markham's head was turned toward the open window, the sole condition under which Merry would allow her to smoke in the Explorer. As Merry watched, she blew a dusty gray cloud into the damp spring air. Heavy fog had rolled in from the Atlantic during the night, and they were crawling steadily enough through a blank wall of shifting mist, the car's headlights picking out a yellow, if poorly defined, sort of path.

"I don't have the slightest idea who offed Betsy," Julia said flatly, "and I bloody well don't care."

"Yes, you do. Elizabeth Osborne's death has dictated your whole life since. Admit it."

No answer. Merry slowed for the right-hand turning into Sparks Avenue, wary of any oncoming vehicle too well hidden in the cloak of fog and, after a moment of anxious peering, spun her wheel. Almost eight long miles in this until they reached Sconset. Never mind; they had a lot to discuss.

"You have a serious habit of professing opinions, Julia,

that are exactly the opposite of what you believe," she observed. "A life of contradictions, I thought, when I first met you. I've been thinking about it ever since."

"You don't know a bloody thing about me or my life," Julia muttered bitterly.

"Maybe not. I certainly don't know you well. But I saw a picture of you once. You were a happy woman, whatever people say about your husband and his infidelities. You were tanned and clear-eyed and smiling for the camera. Looking forward to your second child. Celebrating victory."

No response, not even the flicker of an eyelid.

"And then, suddenly, after Ian's death, you changed. Shut down your business, cut off your friends, posted No Trespassing signs at the end of the drive. Stopped buying new clothes, stopped combing your hair, even. Stopped connecting with your kids. A different woman entirely from the one I saw in that picture."

Merry eased into the rotary, glancing blindly left and right, then spurted for the through lane praying that she was actually clear. "Maybe grief explains it. A period of mourning. But *eight years*? Why don't you have any photographs in your house, Julia? Or even a mirror? Is the contrast between who you were and who you've become too much to face?"

Julia tossed her half-smoked cigarette out the car window and scrabbled desperately at the door handle. "Stop the car. Stop the *car*!"

"Why?" Merry asked calmly as she glided into Milestone Road. "So you can run across the moors until you run out of land? You've been running long enough. Living like an animal gone to ground. It's time you faced things, Julia."

"You and that man of yours," Julia said, her voice thin with spite, "have a platitude for everything, don't you?"

"I've thought about that night quite a bit," Merry continued. "Just as I imagine you have. Neither of us was there, after all. We both have to imagine what happened from the little we know. Ian sent you back to Boston because of Nan, right?"

Julia looked at her then, her face suddenly composed. "I left of my own accord, actually. Couldn't take it anymore—the two of them flaunting their bit on the side, and me as big as a cow. Couldn't take his brass. So much for your *happy woman*." She grabbed for her purse and its salvation of cigarettes. "I should have stayed."

"Because if you had, Jack Osborne might not have murdered Elizabeth?"

Julia's head came up. A glint of hope flashed in her eyes. "You believe it too."

"I'm not sure," Merry said. "But I've been wondering why you do. The mere discovery of Elizabeth's bones a few weeks ago tells us nothing about who killed her, much less incriminating Jack. And then I thought about those contradictions—between the old Julia and the new. Why did you stay here so many years, after all? Why not head back to Cambridge after Ian died, throw yourself into Art in Mind, give your children a wider perspective?"

"I told you, I hadn't any money."

"It's far more expensive to live on an island, Julia— even if you let your house fall into ruin—than in Boston. Believe me, I know." Merry shook her head decisively. She kept her eyes quite steadily on the road, almost afraid to see Julia's face. "No, money had nothing to do with it. You were tied to that house, as though it held you prisoner. You've been living in fear, Julia, haven't you? Fear and a terrible guilt."

The woman beside her sighed shakily and thrust a second cigarette between her lips.

"It was you, after all, who found Elizabeth's body—or what was left of it. In the electroplating vat."

Julia's lighter snapped closed. It fell from her nerveless fingers. "Blast," she said, and crumpled the unlit cigarette viciously in her hand. "You're spinning fairy tales."

"Straight out of the Brothers Grimm," Merry agreed. "But I can't prove it. Or not conclusively. I was hoping you would just go ahead and tell me what it was like. Get it all off your chest."

Julia merely looked out the sightless window.

"I'll help you along, shall I?" A passing truck loomed without warning out of the fog, a careening metal wall fronted by watery headlights, and as abruptly rumbled by. Sounds were sharper, denser, when sight became questionable. "You didn't return to Nantucket immediately after Ian's death. A few months must have passed. Nan would have been—what? Three, four months old?"

"After Christmas," Julia whispered. Her face had gone dead white, intensifying the impression of age, and Merry was afraid she might faint again. *Keep her talking,* she thought. *Keep her focused.*

"After you were settled in the house, you went down to have a look at the studio. Maybe you waited a day or two—the pain of Ian's death would have made it difficult to see his things, I imagine. But eventually you went."

The woman beside her nodded, just once, as though in the grip of a trance.

"I did some reading, last night," Merry mused. "It's toxic stuff, sulfuric acid. But essential for copperplating. You add it to the hydrochloric acid and the copper sulfate in the vat, throw an electric current, and *bingo!* A fine layer of copper is deposited on the surface of the glazed clay. Problem is, the sulfuric acid penetrates any sort of opening. A pinhead-sized gap in the glazing is enough to destroy an entire piece." She slowed momentarily as headlights loomed out of the fog. "It certainly destroyed Elizabeth. Reduced her to a skeleton. And left that curious bleaching on the surface of her bones that the FBI's anthropologist couldn't explain. But you knew, didn't you, Julia? You pulled her bones out of the vat."

"It was . . ." The words came out harshly and with a sudden violence, as though the force of memory propelled Julia's speech. "It was like some sort of ghoul show. I had to drink for days afterward, just to forget what my hands had done. To accept what it meant."

They were both silent for an instant, remembering, envisioning.

"But you didn't forget, did you? Worse—you became afraid."

Julia's eyes squeezed shut.

"Someone had done this to Elizabeth. And now you knew about it. Who was her killer? Who might come back for you and your children? Jack Osborne! *Jack*, who claimed to have slept soundly while Ian prepared his boat, and Elizabeth packed her passport, and the two of them sniggered up their sleeves at the two poor fools they planned to leave behind. They had been planning for months, until your sudden decision to head for the mainland made it so simple. They would leave separately for *Mood Indigo*, under cover of darkness, so that Jack had no reason to suspect.

"Only Jack *did* suspect. He watched Elizabeth take her farewell walk along Sconset beach, her slim summer sandals in one hand and her precious passport in the other; and in a fit of jealous rage he rushed out and strangled her. That's what you thought, right?"

"There's no other possibility, is there?" Julia's voice shook. "You've forgot the telling bit. *Someone* put her body in the studio vat. Who else but Osborne? It was a deliberate attempt to incriminate my Ian. Nobody knew Ian would die that night in his boat. Osborne figured the poor sod would have to face the music. Stand trial for Elizabeth's murder. It's obvious."

"You clearly thought so, Julia. And your suspicion became a kind of prison. *You* had found the bones. And you could never tell the police—they might think it looked as if Ian had strangled Elizabeth and fled in his boat afterward. How would your children feel, with a nasty cloud over their father's memory? All they had was the notion that he was a great artist.

"Elizabeth's body had to disappear, didn't it, Julia? And with it, any investigation into her disappearance."

Julia stared down at her fingers, twisted in her lap.

"You couldn't risk throwing her bones out to sea in the dead of night—you knew the surf is so heavy in winter they might easily be washed back onshore—and if you attempted to move them, you could be seen. So you did what anyone in a panic might do. I don't know for certain, mind," Merry said, downshifting as they approached the outskirts of Sconset, "but I imagine you lifted a floorboard in the studio and stuffed them into the cobwebby dark. Hoping we'd all just forget."

"But *I* didn't," Julia retorted. "I thought of those bones every night. I grew to loathe that studio, hovering like a vulture on the dunes. I couldn't get it out of my sight. It even blocked out the ocean view. And all those tourists! That first summer there were hundreds of them. Poking around the studio, peering through the windows, coming to the house to ask for the loo. It was an abomination! Any of them might have—"

"Might have broken in to take a souvenir and found what they shouldn't," Merry finished implacably. "Yes. Hence the No Trespassing signs. And the imprisonment in your own home. I wonder you could bear to go out for a loaf of bread."

"It makes you funny, living with a nightmare." Julia's voice had turned dreamy. "Living with ghosts. You go strange in the head. Talk to yourself. Avoid people's eyes. I mean, what are they staring at? Do they know? Is it so obvious? Have I screamed it aloud in my sleep?"

They were well into Sconset now. It was a changed village huddled in the shifting clouds of mist, remote as mythical Brigadoon. Merry drove slowly past the tennis club, braking sharply for a wandering dog. Even the animal was dispirited by the weather, eyes staring wildly at her headlights, drooping ears and tail glistening with damp.

"And then the storms began," Merry observed as she headed for Codfish Park. "The hurricanes and the snow, in ninety-two and ninety-four. And now the winter of ninety-six. Which bout knocked the studio off its foundation?"

Julia clenched her fingers together. Her nails were neglected and broken, but she smoothed them with a surprising tenderness, like a child tucking a blanket around a favorite doll. "In December," she said. "Just before Christmas. Everyone bleated on about how lovely the snow was—so perfect for their idiot Christmas Walk, all the bloody *tourists* coming back again to spend their useless money—"

"And your nightmares became real," Merry added quietly. "Elizabeth turned in her grave."

"I couldn't risk the building washing out to sea." Julia made no move to open the car door, though they had pulled up before her home. "I couldn't have some bloke from the fire department declare it condemned and poke around among the wreckage and find what he shouldn't. I thought I would go mad."

"And so you stole out at midnight just before the next big storm hit—Sunday night, January seventh—and retrieved the bones from under the floorboard. A dangerous and frightening prospect, I imagine, with the wind gusting as it always does, in Sconset in winter, and worse that night because of the approaching storm. You were very brave. Or very foolhardy."

"How did you know?"

"You were seen."

Julia gasped. "I never was!"

"Well, not seen well enough to be identified," Merry amended. "But the Lord moves in mysterious ways, so your neighbor tells me, and the Lord told her to get up that night and take a look out the window. She saw someone burying something at a spot on the beach not far from her house. The spot where your children later found Elizabeth."

There was a short and heavy silence.

"How long have you known?" Julia asked numbly.

"That you were the grave digger? Only a little while," Merry replied. "Although it should have been obvious far earlier. How ironic that it should be Nan and Satchmo who dug them up."

"Ironic isn't the half of it," Julia muttered bitterly. "It's Betsy. It's bloody Betsy, never able to leave us alone." She'd still made no move to get out of the car. Merry glanced toward the Markham house, searching for Peter's Rover. No sign of him, or the Markham children. Probably in the midst of eating a well-deserved breakfast, and dreading their return to this unhappy place. She had time enough to deliver her final blow. She devoutly wished that she hadn't.

"If it's any consolation, Julia, I know you've been through hell. I think it would have been preferable, all the same, to have turned the bones over to the authorities the morning you found them. You've been protecting a lie, you know. It may be that Jack Osborne didn't kill his wife. And that Ian did."

"Bullocks!" The wild black hair whipped into Julia's eyes, and she gazed unseeing at the dim outline of the studio, perched drunkenly in its wreath of fog. "Ian loved Betsy!"

"Ian hated control, and Ian had a vicious temper," Merry countered. "I know you felt it for years yourself. Did he stop hitting you once he took up with his psychiatrist?"

The muffled moan of the Sankaty Light foghorn, high on the invisible bluff, filtered down to the sea. Its timbre was relentlessly melancholy. Julia's expression crumpled suddenly, from outrage to defeat.

"Am I right in thinking Ian first met Elizabeth as her patient?"

"The police made him go. After . . . he landed me in hospital while I was pregnant with Cecil."

"She had a habit, didn't she, of falling in love with the wounded?" Merry said gently. "She'd already married one of them. Why not take a lover from among the rest? Only Ian didn't want to be saddled with Elizabeth for the rest of his life. Any more than he could stand the constraints of marriage. He wanted out of everything that seemed to trap him—his affair, his court-ordered treatment, his du-

ties as a father . . ." *And how much better for all of you,*
she finished mentally, *if the bastard hadn't stayed.*

Julia Markham was as remote as the hope of summer.

"Maybe Ian didn't even plan to kill Elizabeth. Maybe it
was an accident—the result of a row. But he put his
hands around her lovely neck, hid her body in the vat,
and ran. No one has known the truth for years, Julia, because he died a few hours later. And you've been covering
for him ever since."

"You've got it all wrong," Julia repeated savagely, her eyes
still fixed on the studio. "*Jack* killed her. He had to have
done. Why else put the body in the studio, if not to throw
the blame on Ian? Ian *himself* had no reason to do that."

"I know," Merry said. "Unless he was desperate to hide
the murder and chose the most immediate and obvious
place for Betsy's body. Trying to drag her across Codfish
Road to your garage and his car—then carry her onto the
boat, and throw her overboard once he was well out at
sea—too risky."

She paused, wondering how much Julia could take,
and steeled herself to go on. "Or there's the possibility,"
she added "that Ian knew exactly what the acid would do,
and thought that by the time the bones were discovered,
he'd be long gone. Think about it, Julia. If revenge was
what Jack Osborne wanted, *why didn't he go after it*?

"Say Jack *did* kill Elizabeth and intended to frame Ian.
Wouldn't he have wondered why the body was never
found? Why the hue and cry died down? And wouldn't he
pursue the investigation into his wife's disappearance? He
could have insisted your home and studio be searched—
or even *told* the police that Ian had attacked Elizabeth
before."

Mutely, Julia shook her head. Merry heard the gravelly
rustle of an approaching car's tires. Peter, and the children with him.

"I'll tell you why not, Julia. Because Jack Osborne believed what everyone did. He thought Elizabeth went
down on *Mood Indigo* with Ian."

The statement hung in the air between them, persuasive and absolute.

"That's why Jack stopped looking. Why he went back to Boston and got on with his life. And why he never showed up at your door to ask what you'd done with those bones."

Chapter Twenty-four

No letter from the killer awaited Meredith on her arrival back at the station, just as there had been none on her pillow the previous evening, or lying on the kitchen table, or folded with Thursday's copy of the *Inky Mirror* that lay forgotten in Ralph Waldo's armchair. A relief, of sorts—and a worry. If the killer wasn't interested in responding to the press conference, what in God's name was he busy doing? The possibilities swirled in her brain with increasing urgency.

But the press conference had spawned its own set of ills. The assembled corps was actually demanding another one, in a noisy effort to feed its insatiable appetite for breaking news. And the motley team of federal, state, and local officials was at a complete loss what to tell them. For there was no progress to report.

"So you're finished, Meredith, with that business in

Sconset?" John Folger asked testily as she stood in his office an hour after depositing Julia at her home in Codfish Park. "Or has it merely gone from murder to petty larceny?"

"Sir?"

"The statues. The ambiguous fortune in art you're professing to investigate along with everything else that's criminal on this island. Why didn't you give that one to Bailey?"

Merry hesitated. The truth was that she dreaded handing *anything* to Matt Bailey; but in the matter of the stolen statues, she actually had an excuse.

"Jack Osborne asked for me personally," she replied. "Mine was the only name he could remember on the local force, I guess. And then once Dana Stevens had his statement, she asked me to keep him busy."

"Along with half the force running relays in front of his bedroom door. Tell me. Did he steal his own statues?"

"If he did, where are they? And I think it's *grand* larceny, Chief, not petty."

"So I've already heard from Patrolman Seitz," her father retorted. "Only Seitz can't be sure, lacking the essential expertise in fine-arts appraisal. He was looking for you earlier—wanted some advice about valuing those things. You have him typing up your reports these days, I see."

"When you're as busy as I am, sir, you learn to delegate." Merry smiled wearily, and then her momentary humor faded. "Of course! What an idiot I've been!"

"I wouldn't go *that* far," her father began, but Merry cut him off with one upraised hand.

"Sylvia Whitehead," she said bitterly.

"Who?"

"Friend of Mom's. Gallery owner."

"Your mother never had a friend by that name."

"Sylvia said you'd say that."

John gestured dismissively. "So this woman will know what the statues are worth?"

"She should," Merry replied. "She's the one who stole them."

Nearly ten A.M., and Sergeant Nat Coffin was still an hour away from the end of his shift in front of Jack Osborne's hotel-room door. He had volunteered to relieve Tim Forrest, who had relieved Howie Seitz; but Nat was frankly yawning as he stood waiting for his release. The professor had been up for some time, moving around the space beyond the hotel door; and Nat had recorded the noises mentally for something to do. A flushing toilet, a shower, the creak of a drawer pulled open—the normal routine of a man getting dressed for the day.

Osborne had ordered room service, which had appeared half an hour later on a white-clothed trolley. He nodded politely to Nat as the waiter pushed his breakfast through the door, and the clink of coffee cup against saucer, the occasional clearing of a throat, had followed like night follows day. Now Osborne was watching a morning talk show. Bright words—inane chatter—seeped relentlessly into the hallway. Nat was half lulled to sleep by the flood of talk. His head dipped low on his chest, and he smiled gently.

The single blow to his head, when it came, took him completely by surprise. He registered shock with a short animal grunt—then collapsed in a heap at the base of his chair. It was there that Tucker Enright found him twenty minutes later, groaning miserably as consciousness returned.

Jack Osborne's room, naturally, was empty.

"I've been an idiot, Howie."
"How so, Detective?"
Merry kept her eyes firmly on the tufts of spring grass as they trudged over the patch of lawn separating the police station from Federal Street and what had been Sylvia Whitehead's gallery. "I handed this woman the temptation of a lifetime when I told her Elizabeth's house and

all its contents had been left to Art in Mind. She *must* have known there were Markham sculptures just sitting all over the Osborne place. Untouched and unseen for years. Appreciating in value left and right. A gold mine. She told me she needed money to reopen her gallery, rents being what they are in town these days. I should have known. I should have given the robbery more than half a thought."

She picked up her pace a bit, though she knew they were slamming the barn door on a long-vanished horse. "She's probably packed them in crates hours ago and sent them out on the morning ferry. God, I'm stupid! Wasting Clare's time on fingerprinting the window frame while the only obvious culprit is swathing the damn goods in bubble wrap!"

Howie maintained a respectful silence that was somehow more depressing than any counterargument he might have made. He clearly agreed with her. She *was* an idiot, and everyone—including Matt Bailey, whose case to bungle this should have been—would soon know it.

They waited for a straggle of cars to creep slowly down Federal, then crossed to the opposite curb. Sylvia's windows above the candy shop looked blankly out on the foggy morning. In such dim light, shouldn't she have turned on a lamp or two? Merry glanced at her watch. Still only ten A.M., and the stores just opening. Merry reached for the apartment's street door—locked. She pressed the buzzer to the side of the doorway, and they waited for long, relentless seconds. No response from above.

"You looking for Sylvia?" A blond-haired girl peered around the candy shop's door and eyed Howie's uniform curiously. "She's sleeping late today. Probably the weather—makes you want to roll over and go back to bed. I was late myself. Is anything wrong? Can *I* help you?"

"No, no—we're just friends of hers. Thanks."

The face disappeared, intrigued and disappointed.

"Looks like she's flown the coop along with the loot," Howie muttered, sounding for all the world like a forties gangster. He pushed his police cap back on his dark curls and squinted up at the dull windows. "Worth tearing the judge from his golf game, you think, to ask for a warrant?"

"What golf game?" Merry retorted. "In this fog he'll be sitting happily over a late breakfast, rereading Thursday's paper. What've we got to lose?"

Forty minutes later they were back in position before Sylvia's stairs, warrant in hand, gazing upward once more at her unlit windows.

"We can be pretty sure she's not sleeping," Howie said reassuringly as he positioned a crowbar beside the locked doorknob. "And I doubt she's out painting. What's there to see, in this murk?"

"She's done studies of fog in the past," Merry replied distractedly. She was mentally questioning the point of their efforts: if Sylvia was indeed gone from the island, she was hardly likely to have left the statues behind her.

Wood groaned, then splintered as Howie forced his metal bar between door and jamb, heaving his six-foot frame against the lever. In seconds the door swung wide.

"And that," Merry said grimly, "has just instructed an admiring public how best to force an illegal entry. Let's get in and out as fast as we can."

"Hey!" called the candy-shop blond. "What're you doing? Is Sylvia all right?"

"It's okay," Merry tossed over her shoulder. "Really. Everything's fine." Crowbar in hand, she followed Howie hurriedly up the stairs.

But it was unnecessary to force Sylvia's interior door. To their surprise it stood wide-open. The thin buzz of a television filtered out into the landing. Howie paused on the threshold, uncertain whether Sylvia herself might not suddenly appear.

"Hello?" Merry called; but only silence replied.

"Maybe she ran out for coffee or something while we were hitting up the judge."

"Why are you whispering?"

He shrugged, looking sheepish.

"If she's still here, so much the better. We've got a warrant. Head through the kitchen and turn right. There's a small storeroom where she keeps her stuff."

They gave only a cursory glance at the living room, although Merry's eyes faltered at the coffee table's half-drunk mug of coffee, cooling by an opened section of the newspaper. Had Sylvia heard them in the street earlier that morning and gone off in a panic? Merry considered this with half her mind, intent on the storeroom and its secrets.

"Wow," Howie gulped, rearing backward as he turned into the kitchen hallway. He had nearly bumped heads with a pugnacious figure, arms upraised in furious salute, and the unexpectedness of the attack had startled him out of his wits.

Merry had forgotten how large some of the Markham pieces were supposed to be. Life-size, Jack Osborne had said, and exaggerated, like modern-day Rodins. They were all there, Merry thought, swiftly running through the inventory in her mind. This one was probably drawn from Osborne himself—the upraised arms a metaphor, perhaps, for his feelings toward the artist. Just beyond were the grappling forms of *Couple Embracing*, the blatantly erotic statue Elizabeth had thoughtfully placed before her drawing room's French doors. Merry craned on tiptoe, looking for Ian Markham's head, the one that had sat on Elizabeth's dressing table. It must be beyond the massive ones, in the storeroom itself.

"How the hell did she get these up here?"

"I don't know," Merry answered, struck by the implausibility of it. "A friend, maybe. She likes to paint with a woman named Irene. But they must've rented a truck, or something. Unless Irene owns one."

"Think of the exposure," Howie argued, picking his

way through the forest of figures toward the storeroom door. "Could she just do a double-park on Federal and off-load this sort of stuff in broad daylight? Right behind the police station?"

"With all the attention the police have given her," Merry commented scornfully, "she probably could." She eased herself down the hall in Howie's wake. "Sylvia *is* an art dealer, after all, whether her gallery is defunct or not. She still acquires stuff for people all the time. Who's likely to think a given piece is stolen? Only someone who'd seen the piece before. And no one's seen these babies since—"

"Mere." Howie's voice was raw and flat. "Get over here."

She looked at him in surprise, her brows knit. "Look, Seitz, I know we're on pretty informal terms, but I'd appreciate it if you didn't call me 'Mere.' You get in the habit of that now, you'll be doing it at the station, and it'll look pretty bad."

"She's dead." Howie raised a hand to his mouth and swallowed.

Merry brushed him aside. "Get in the kitchen."

Sylvia Whitehead lay sprawled against the storeroom's far wall, her sightless eyes bulging, her tongue loose and purple. The sight caused Merry's stomach to convulse, much as Howie's had done, and she turned away, her eyes squeezed tightly shut. The vision of Sylvia—wry, intelligent, lonely Sylvia—in such a state was obscene enough. But what was worse, somehow—a more personal violation—was the torn canvas wedged around her neck. It was a portrait of a girl—eight, maybe nine—with blond hair and straight dark eyebrows, her legs tucked up under a massive book. Merry's portrait, the sharp, bright strokes of the palette knife as familiar as her mother's signature.

Ha, ha, the killer's note said. *Beat you to the punch, I'm afraid. Or to the kill. Your move, Detective, at least for*

*a little while. But I can't give you very much longer. So
many girls, you know, so little time. Although poor Sylvia
was hardly a girl, now, was she? I think I'm starting to find
older women attractive. Remember that.*

John Folger's hands were shaking. He noticed it and
set the letter aside. "It's the same?" he asked futilely.

Merry nodded. "So Stan says." The FBI forensics chief
had compared the letter found next to Sylvia's body with
the one sent two nights before to Merry's apartment.
Same typeface, same paper—though what such statistics
told them, Merry was hard-pressed to say. She felt numb.
If Roxie Teasdale's death had seemed tragic and senseless, Sylvia Whitehead's was an abomination. Merry had
known and liked Sylvia. Had wanted to know her better.
Had thought, even, that she might retrieve something of
the lost Anne Folger in Sylvia's company. And worst of all,
the body was still warm. Sylvia had been dead two hours
at the most, Dr. John Fairborn said. The murderer might
even have been with her while Howie and Merry exchanged pleasantries with the candy-store clerk on the
street below. The girl couldn't remember anyone climb-
ing the stairs to Sylvia's; but she *had* been late that morning. As she'd told them before they left to get their search
warrant.

Merry clenched her fist and punched angrily at her
knee. "Christ, Dad, it makes me angry!"

"It has me absolutely terrified, Meredith," her father
replied in an undertone. "I don't mind saying. I want you
off this case. Hell, I want you off the island."

"No."

"That's a direct order."

"No!" Merry shot to her feet. "You tried to take me off
Del Duarte's murder last year, Dad, because you thought
I was emotionally involved. It was a stupid idea then, and
it's a stupid idea now. I'm sticking with this to the end."

They stared at one another angrily, too much alike for
either to back down, and then John Folger's eyes slid

away. "But will it ever end, Meredith?" he asked wearily. "Not even Enright can predict that one."

"Where is he, by the way?"

"Ran over to the Harbor House. Said he wanted to interview Osborne again."

"But Osborne's got to be out of it. He can't have killed Sylvia."

"Chief," Howie Seitz said, ducking his head into the door. "Dr. Enright just called. Nat Coffin is down. Osborne's nowhere in sight."

Chapter Twenty-five

The fog rolled inexorably up the beach from the Atlantic, a blank wall obscuring the conning tower of the enemy submarine prowling just beyond the edge of sight; but Lord Cecil of Trevarre knew the Nazis were out there, all the same—No, that wasn't right. Could a submarine even get close enough to a beachhead to do any sort of harm? And how could *Lord* Cecil be fighting in World War II anyway?

He'd have to come up with something else.

Lord Cecil of Trevarre peered desperately through the glass, his weary eyes searching in vain for the sight of a friendly ship; and at that very moment, a cannon ball whistled just past his head from the French privateer looming suddenly—

No, that wouldn't work either. If Lord Cecil couldn't

see the Frenchies in the fog, how could the Frenchies aim their cannon?

He kicked disconsolately at a scallop shell and looked down the shoreline toward the Coast Guard compound above Low Beach. Satchmo was just breasting the first line of waves, muzzle high and back legs working. Watching him, Cecil shivered. This morning at Peter Mason's he had dressed in the same pair of shorts he'd worn the day before, having neglected, in all the hurry of their removal to the farm, to bring a change of clothing. Once back at Sconset, he had simply shrugged into a sweatshirt and headed out to the beach, ignoring the lunch his mum and Nan were consuming in the companionable, if silent, confines of the kitchen. Cecil wanted to think; and as with everything Cecil did, he thought best in solitude.

He sat down in the damp sand and dug the heels of his tennis shoes into a shallow pit. Nothing suited him today—neither his play-acting, nor Nan, nor being home once more with his mum. He looked out across the water, hoping for a ship, or perhaps a fin that might signal a wandering shark. But the fog obscured the horizon completely, so that his view of the Atlantic ended abruptly thirty feet from shore. It reminded him of pictures he had seen in books, of medieval maps, with their edges trailing away to nothing. *Here there be dragons.*

His dreams were like that. Clear and limitless by day, an uncharted sea at night.

Peter, at least, hadn't scolded Cecil as his mum would have, or told him that he was too old to scream like a baby—as though the demons were something he could control, and summoned at will when he wanted a bit of attention. Peter had acted as though nightmares were perfectly normal, and in fact, he'd told Cecil about his own. The worst one—the one Peter clearly hated—Cecil perfectly understood. That was when Peter dreamed about his brother, Rusty, who had been murdered at the farm.

"I was very angry with Rusty at the time that he died,

Cecil," Peter had told him. "And so I felt that I had somehow caused his death. That's ridiculous, of course—but I
can't get rid of the feeling, and sometimes it comes back
to haunt me. Maybe you feel the same way about your
dad."

"Like I made him die?"

"Sure. We all *say* that, sometimes, but we don't really
mean it. *I wish so-and-so were dead.* And suddenly he is.
It's enough to make anybody feel terribly guilty. That's
where the nightmares come from."

"So how do I make them stop?" he'd asked.

Peter had shrugged. "I still haven't been able to. But
I'm dreaming about Rusty less and less. Maybe I've
started to forgive myself for what I can't change."

Now, alone on the beach, Cecil heaved a deep sigh
and thought about forgiveness. Had he forgiven himself
yet? What did forgiveness feel like? Lightness, probably;
but he wasn't feeling light at the moment. There was an
ache at his center he couldn't seem to shift. Peter was the
only person he'd ever told about his dad—about the
fights and the fear—and he felt almost disloyal. Why had
he said so much?

*Because I was happy at the farm. Because I liked being
there.*

He liked the new lambs gamboling shakily on the
moors, the wide cranberry beds that seemed to reach to
the island's very limit, the feel of the old saltbox itself. He
liked Peter's sheepdog Ney, a rangy half-breed willing to
chase an endless supply of balls, when he wasn't herding
the children from room to room. He liked sitting around
the dinner table, watching Nan's cheeks turn dusky gold
in the light of the fire; and at bedtime, he liked the way
the sloping eaves of their room seemed to bend down, en-
folding and protective.

"It's a safe place. Like England," Cecil said aloud. The
place he had been trying to reach for most of his life.

The sound of his own words shook him abruptly from
daydreaming, however, and the chill of the damp sand

penetrated his thin shorts. He shivered again, and tucked his chin snugly into the neck of his sweatshirt. A fog horn blared dully from Sankaty Light, punctuated by the harsh calls of gulls. The birds wheeled overhead, grumpy and caustic, at home in the colorless air. With a grunt, he pushed himself to his feet and trudged slowly through the sand toward the Gully Road lot. His bike was propped nearby, on a mound of budding beach plum.

"It's been too long," Merry complained bitterly as she turned into the Milestone Road and sped toward Sconset.

"I know." Tucker Enright's fingers were beating a ceaseless staccato on the dashboard, a frenetic gesture he hardly seemed to notice. He wore a bullet-proof vest and a borrowed service revolver, and from the tightness around his mouth, Merry could tell he was in a high pitch of nerves. She was relieved to see that he handled the gun with confidence—no squeamishness or fumbling fingers. In fact, he told her as he slipped the automatic's magazine expertly from its butt, he'd trained at Quantico for just such an emergency.

They had elected to take the Sconset route, while the rest of the force under John Folger's direction covered the ferry and the airport, the boat basin and the Town Pier. The Coast Guard had been mobilized, and a spotting helicopter was on its way from Hyannis. Not that it would spot much in this fog. But in Merry's heart, she knew Jack Osborne wasn't running for daylight. Osborne was finishing what he had set out to do. Sylvia Whitehead had died at his hands while the police—while *she*—had stood below Sylvia's window that morning. Now Julia Markham was next.

Dear God, let the kids be at the beach.

"It's got to be Julia," Enright said. "She's the only one who can finger him for Betsy's murder. She found the bones and reburied them. He knows it, and he's come back to finish her off. Roxanne Teasdale was just window-dressing—to plant the idea of a serial killer in our heads. But Julia's the real victim."

"What is the man thinking?" Merry burst out. "Say he gets to Julia first—who does he think we'll suspect? Jack Osborne! You don't just hit your keeper over the head for nothing. He's got no alibi to speak of. Why didn't he simply slide out the hotel-room window and leave Nat where he was? He could have been back in bed when we came knocking at the door with two bodies on our hands."

"I'd say he's panicking."

"Let's hope he panics enough to screw up," Merry said viciously, and jabbed her foot to the floor.

Cecil pedaled steadily down the rutted, sandy length of Codfish Park Road, Satchmo barely visible in the fog behind. Past the turning for Beach Street, where the boy glanced at the dim outline of the Schwartzes' house—all quiet, no sign of either Lenny or Ruth on this Saturday morning—and then past Fawcett and Jackson. He had nearly reached the corner of Jefferson, where his own cottage sat forlornly facing the teetering wreck of his father's studio, when a sudden breeze tore the curtain of fog, shifting and billowing in ragged clouds over the roofs of the gray-shingled houses. Cecil looked up from his handlebars and braked abruptly. He had just seen the man.

The man who had scared Mum so badly yesterday.

The figure was creeping surreptitiously along the side of the cottage toward the rear porch and its screened door, ducking his head when he passed by the windows, so as not to be noticed. The impulse to call out died unvoiced in Cecil's throat. He turned, very quietly, and wheeled his bike away through the fog, with a low whistle for Satch. He prayed that he had not been seen, that no pounding of footsteps would follow him back down Codfish Park.

What to do? His thoughts raced as swiftly as his thudding heart. That sneaking man meant to hurt his Mum and Nan; he knew it instinctively. If Cecil tried to walk in on him, he'd probably hurt Cecil too. He swallowed hard, overcome with a rising panic, and pedaled jerkily up the Schwartzes' driveway. *Peter* wouldn't have been afraid. *Peter* would have broken down the door and thrashed the man within an inch of his life. Should Cecil ride over to Mason Farms and find him?

Stupid, he thought bitterly. *Stupid jerk.* Fetching Peter would take too long. He would have to do this himself. He eyed the Schwartzes' dark windows, imagined them laughing together over clam chowder somewhere in town, feeling fortified against the fog in their Shetland sweaters; then he glanced up and down the length of Codfish Park. Most of the small shingled houses were still shuttered. None of the summer people were back yet. One light shone from the place across the street—old Mrs. Johnson's—but she walked with a cane. He couldn't bother her with this.

What he needed was the police. Police who could break down the door and yell *Freeze!,* like they always did on television. And that meant finding a phone. There were some public ones near the shuttle stop at the Sconset rotary. Cecil shoved his hands in his pockets. No change. Would it matter? He could call the police, couldn't he? 911 *must* work, whether you paid for it or not. Tears pricked hotly at his eyes. *Mum and Nan. I'm wasting time.* As he stood motionless in the drive, a cold, moist nose was thrust into his dangling palm. Satch.

"Come on, boy." He grabbed the huge old dog's leather collar and led him around the house to the Schwartzes' backyard. Found the length of clothesline still tied to the deck railing, where it had been so many weeks before, when Satchmo had discovered the bones on the beach. "You've gotta stay here for a while," Cecil said gently as he tied a stout hitch and patted the dog's head. "Don't worry. I promise I'll be back."

The Markham house was silent as Merry and Enright crept toward its tangled garden. They had parked a block away on Codfish—near Jack Osborne's rented Samurai, Merry noted grimly—and proceeded on foot. They had to assume that Osborne was already inside the house, and use extreme caution in their approach. The warm glow of a lamp in the front room suggested that *someone* was at home, but Merry prayed it wasn't the kids.

Enright, crouching low, skittered along the side toward the back door. Merry took the front.

She eased her way up the porch steps, wincing as a warped board creaked in the stillness, and hesitated, not wanting even to breathe. It was then she heard Julia's voice—strained, cracking with tension, but very much alive.

"You run along then, Nannie, and have a good time with Cecil. Stop at the Schwartzes', why don't you, for some cocoa on the way home? I'm sure they'd love to see you."

"But Mum," the child said wonderingly, "you *never* tell me to visit the Schwartzes."

"Just do as I say." Julia's tone was biting. "Run along now before the day's over. And tell Cecil I love him, hear?"

"Tell him *what*?" Nan sounded flabbergasted.

They were moving away from her, Merry thought, toward the back door. Three sets of feet, and only one of them a child's. *Where's Cecil?* Then the whining sound of unoiled hinges. The screen door opening, she guessed—and hoped that Enright was there.

He was. "Hello, Osborne," he said loudly enough for Merry to hear him. "Leaving already?"

Julia Markham screamed. Merry grabbed the front doorknob and felt it move under her hand. Unlocked. She burst into the house, gun leveled.

"Hold it, Osborne! You're under arrest!"

Jack Osborne glanced over his shoulder. At the sight of Merry standing at the far end of the hallway, he looked almost relieved.

"Step away from Mrs. Markham and put your face to the wall!"

Gun trained on Osborne's face, Merry advanced slowly toward him, her eyes never leaving his. Osborne seemed about to protest—to argue—but Tucker Enright seized him by the shoulder and spun him around, pressing his borrowed gun to the lawyer's head. Merry dashed to his side and began patting down Osborne's shirt and trousers. No weapon.

Enright grasped Julia Markham's elbow. Her bewildered black eyes looked from the psychiatrist to Merry and back again. "Tucker Enright, with the police—what's going on? Jack says—"

"Jack says a lot of things," Enright interrupted grimly.

"The *hell* I do." The professor twisted in Merry's grasp. "You've got this all wrong."

"I've got another dead body, Osborne, and I'm not about to find a third. Don't move." Merry cuffed the lawyer's hands behind his back. She eased him to a seat on the floor.

"Did you really think," Enright said, "that you could ever possibly escape?" There was gloating in his voice, an ugly sound; and Merry looked sharply over her shoulder at him. Enright still held the gun trained at Jack Osborne's head.

And as she drew breath to speak, he fired.

In the sandy soil of a vacant lot, Cecil Markham crouched on his hands and knees, dampness seeping through his jeans. He had called 911 from the town phones, glancing fearfully over his shoulder in case The Man should catch him, and a cheerful voice at the other end of the line had assured him his message would get through—and that Detective Folger was already on her way. He'd debated staying where he was, in the hope of intercepting the detective; but a voice whispered that this was cowardice. His place was by his Mum and Nan. And so he had turned resolutely and trudged back toward

Codfish Park, a small but upright figure in the advancing gloom.

A direct approach by the front steps had seemed unwise, however, so Cecil turned up Beach and crept along the grassy alley behind the Codfish Park houses. There he had stalled—afraid he might ruin Merry Folger's plans if he barged in, unwanted, before she arrived. He squinted now as he gazed toward the street, desperate to see through the fog.

And at that moment, the clouds of mist shifted, then broke. Cecil caught a glimpse of the gray Explorer, parked a block from his house. So she was already *here*. Relief flooded through him.

It was amazing how Merry Folger always knew when someone was in trouble. Cecil scrambled to his feet and walked briskly toward his back door.

"So what's the schedule here, Tucker?" Merry asked, with a poor attempt at bravado.

She had never seen a man killed before.

The coldness of the act left her shaking with rage and grief. At the moment of the gun's firing, she had screamed aloud—a futile instant of utter horror. Now part of her mind was struggling for control. She could not afford to be weak.

Another part of her mind had gone on screaming.

He had cuffed her hands behind her back, and bound her ankles with duct tape. The handcuffs were Merry's spares, thoughtfully loaned to Enright before leaving the station. The man's planning—the way he had set her up—infuriated her; and anger at such a time, she knew, would be as fatal as fear.

"What is this? A personal vendetta? Or a bit of on-the-job training?" The same bantering tone, almost condescending; and almost effective, if she could stop herself from trembling.

"Be quiet, Meredith," Enright said. Three words, nothing more; but enough to warn her.

Julia Markham had known, seconds before Enright pulled the trigger, what he intended to do. She had leaped for his gun, although she leaped too late to save Jack Osborne. And after the bullet had gone home, Enright struck her a vicious blow with the butt of the automatic. She lay wan and lifeless now on the cluttered living room floor.

It simplified things, of course.

Merry kept her eyes on Enright.

He pulled at the tape he was wrapping across Nan's mouth, tightening it further, and the little girl's eyes squeezed shut. She was crying relentlessly, her bound hands unable to brush away the tears. Her nose was beginning to run.

"Let Nan go," Merry said suddenly. Her entire body ached with tension and misery. "Let her go. You could do that. And still get away."

"Not a chance, my dear." Enright spoke almost sadly, and when he looked at Merry, all the old gentleness she had come to trust shone out of his eyes. "She'd run for help in a minute."

I've got to keep him talking, Merry thought, *or we're all dead.*

"What do you want? A plane somewhere? Guaranteed safe passage?"

He took his time answering. As though she were irrelevant. As though she had already ceased to exist.

"It's not enough to get away, Meredith. You know that. I have to leave someone behind."

"To take the blame."

"Of course."

Jack Osborne.

"In a few moments," Enright said, "I'll use your cellular to call for backup." He patted Nan absently on the head and crossed to where Merry was propped upright against the sofa. "When the police arrive, I'll show them the bodies. Jack—whom I killed as he attempted to flee—and you, who unfortunately caught a stray bullet. And then the Markhams. Jack had already killed *them* by the time we arrived."

He crouched down next to her. Took a strand of Merry's hair and slid it softly between his fingers. She flinched.

"You're certifiable, Enright," she said. "You're utterly insane."

His grip on the pale strands tightened perceptibly. "What do *you* know about it, Meredith? Does a madman exhibit anything like my precision? Of course not. You know *nothing* about insanity. You're an ignorant child— but a dangerous one, all the same. You nearly ruined my work—and all the good I might do."

"Is that what you did for Roxie Teasdale? Come off it, Tucker. You're a raving lunatic."

His blow struck Merry viciously across the face, and she cried out from the shock of it. "Her death was necessary. A conscious choice."

"A means that served your end." Merry's cheek burned. She tried to ignore it, tried to hold back the tears. "You needed a murder that fit the pattern of deaths around the state, and tied them to Jack Osborne. I see that. But why finger Jack at all? Did you hate him so much?"

"Hate had nothing to do with it." Enright's anger had dissipated. The calm that remained was even more disturbing. "If I tied Jack Osborne to some regrettable murders, Meredith, it was entirely because of you."

"*Me?*"

"You refused to let Betsy die."

Comprehension flashed sharply through Merry's brain. "*You* killed her," she said.

Enright had strangled Elizabeth Osborne; and Enright had labored mightily to divert Merry's attention from that fact. The Teasdale murder, the FBI's descent on the island, the letters sent sickeningly to Merry's home—all designed to pull her off the scent of Betsy Osborne's blood. To frighten her, in fact, into running for cover, into dropping her investigation entirely.

"She was going to leave me. Go with Markham in his boat. I couldn't let that happen." He turned the roll of duct tape mechanically in his hands, his face impassive. "I wanted to plead with her—convince her that we were made for each other—but she wouldn't listen. She actually laughed."

"And so you strangled her to death and put her body in Ian Markham's electroplating vat."

"Yes." Enright's expression darkened. "Ian was such an abusive bastard. Nobody would have believed he was innocent. But the bones were never found. I couldn't understand it. It nearly drove me mad."

"Julia buried them. She was terrified of the police."

"I assumed *that*," he retorted irritably. "I'm not an idiot. But I couldn't exactly inquire." Enright reached in his pocket and withdrew a wadded sock. "And now I'm afraid it's time for your gag."

"Manuel Esconvidos really *is* the Boston killer, isn't he?" Merry persisted. "Bill Carmichael's been right all along. You deliberately derailed *that* investigation too."

Enright smiled faintly. "Do you remember when I first flew over, to look at the Sconset grave? I knew there was a chance the bones were Betsy's. I knew I had to do something. And the pattern of deaths I was currently researching was so conveniently at hand. I couldn't let the murders end, however, while Esconvidos was in jail. I needed another body, and another killer, to keep my case alive. So I moved them right into your backyard."

"There's one thing I don't understand. Why kill Sylvia Whitehead?"

"Sylvia." Enright sat back on his heels and drew a deep breath. "It *has* been a busy day. Sylvia I also owe to you, Detective."

"To me?"

"You told me she had run into me just before Betsy's death."

"Did I?" Merry cast her thoughts back. "She may have said something about it."

"It was just possible she had seen me Labor Day weekend. I've never admitted to having been on the island that September."

"Oh, God." Remorse and guilt swept over Merry. "Sylvia. I'm so sorry."

"You have a tendency to talk too much, you know," Enright observed, "and to trust people too easily. It's your downfall, in fact."

Blood pounded in Cecil's ears. He crouched at the living room window, eyes fixed on the horror within. So much blood came from the man lying slumped in the hallway; and his mum—his mum lay dreadfully still. Was she alive? Nan—*Nan*—He clenched his fists. Even Merry Folger could not help him. He closed his eyes and drew a shaky breath. It ended in a sob.

Lord Cecil of Trevarre stood proudly—

No. *Lord* Cecil was useless. Only *Cecil* could save them now.

And if he failed?

The thought overwhelmed him; he forced it aside. At least he would have failed *trying*.

He skittered noiselessly through the wet grass to the back of the house. Crept up the steps to the porch. Seized the first thing he saw—a snow shovel still propped in the back doorway from months of winter service—and hefted it in his hands. His knees felt weak. He ignored them, and turned the doorknob as quietly as he could.

"One thing confuses me," Merry said, as Enright reached for his roll of tape. It was bright blue, much like the rolls Merry had seen a thousand times on the shelves of the station's supply room. *The mundanity of the details,* she thought, *of the fact of my death.* "Jack Osborne. How'd he get out here?"

"He drove." Enright was getting impatient.

"You know what I mean."

"I allowed him to escape."

"You knocked Nat Coffin on the head?"

"Yes. Jack heard the noise and opened his door to see what was going on. There was nobody there, of course, except the unconscious Nat; and so after a minute, he seized his chance and hightailed it to his car. I gave him twenty minutes, then called the station."

"But why did he head to Sconset?" she said quickly, although she knew the answer. Anything to gain a bit of time. Would anyone care that she hadn't reported in? Would anyone even notice?

"I suppose he'd been thinking things over since our conversation with Dana Stevens yesterday," Enright mused. "Jack's a bright boy. He knew the snare was being set. Someone wanted it to look like he'd killed his wife and Roxie Teasdale. But he knew *he* hadn't killed Betsy. And from Julia's reaction to him yesterday, it was fairly obvious *she* hadn't. So who did?"

Just beyond Enright's head, Merry saw a flash of brown. Then a small face. *Cecil. Oh God, no.* She willed herself not to react. Not to betray. But what if Nan—

Her eyes flicked to the little girl. Her tears done, Nan was staring dully at her mother.

"Who else was on the island *then* who was on the island *now?*" Enright continued. "Bingo. *Me.* Jack was afraid I'd get Julia next."

Before Merry could speak, he leaned over and pried at Merry's jaw. She obliged him, and opened her mouth; and as he stuffed the sock inside—a nauseous wad of parching cotton—she heaved upward with her knees. A sharp blow that caught him full in the stomach.

It barely registered. He grunted, and shoved her legs aside, intent on completing his task. Merry twisted and bent forward, spitting out the sock. If she were going to resist, now was the time; she had run out of conversation. She screamed as loudly as she could.

Enright grabbed her hair with one hand and pulled.

With the other, he reached for his gun.

He'll kill me. Christ, he'll kill me. She lunged away, tearing her hair out of his hands.

A high-pitched yell, and the sickening thud of metal hitting bone.

Cecil.

He was a blurred, furious shape as he battered Enright's head, the shovel as tall as his own body, unwieldy, inaccurate at best; and the psychiatrist let out a roar of rage, his arms flailing. Blinded by pain.

Merry rolled away just as the gun went off.

A bullet fired at random; the whine of a ricochet. Cecil took two steps backward, his eyes enormous with fear, and then, in an instant, lifted his shovel again.

Enright was struggling to his feet. The boy took aim at his bent knees—swung once with sickening force—and the man toppled over. The gun skittered out of his grasp.

Merry saw it go—and saw Enright crawl toward it. *"Cecil!"* she yelled. "Get out of here! Run for help!"

The boy stood rooted to the floor, torn between the imperative to flee and the imperative to stay; and then he dove for the automatic pistol. Hugged it to his body and began to rise.

Enright reached him first. He seized the small hands that held the gun.

Cecil cried out, and let go.

"Freeze! Everybody freeze!"

Merry turned.

John Folger was braced in the doorway, gun leveled and Howie furious at his back.

Chapter Twenty-six

"Is she awake?"

Merry turned to look at Peter from her position by Julia Markham's bedside. " 'Fraid not," she replied, and stood up with a sigh. Julia's skull had been fractured by the impact of Enright's gun, and this morning the doctors were finally admitting she was in a coma. They were on the point of flying her to Boston for treatment.

"She'll wake up soon," Cecil Markham said confidently from his seat at the opposite side of the bed. He flashed Peter a wan grin. "My mum is tough."

"So are you," Peter told him. "You've done more in twenty-four hours than most kids manage in a year."

Cecil shrugged and looked away, embarrassed. "Anybody would have, if it was their mum."

"Nope," Peter said. "Most people would have run. Scared out of their wits."

"But I was!" Cecil protested. "I nearly fell down a couple of times, my legs were shaking so badly!"

"So what? You kept standing. You always do. You're a survivor, Cecil. And in my book, you're a hero. Your mother and Nan owe you their lives."

"Not to mention me," Merry Folger added quietly. "I'll be grateful forever, Cecil, and don't you forget it."

The boy stretched his arms over his head and drew a deep breath. "Guess I'd better wake Nan. She fell asleep in the waiting area."

"You're going over to Boston?"

Cecil nodded. "With the policeman."

"Dad's sending Howie with the kids," Merry explained to Peter. "It seemed the best thing to do."

"We get to fly! In a helicopter!" For the first time in days, Cecil sounded like an eleven-year-old boy. He sounded, in fact, as carefree as the approaching summer. He bent over Julia and kissed her cheek, and with a last look for Peter and Merry, shot out of the room in search of his sister.

"He's pretty happy for a kid who's been through hell," Merry mused.

"You forget. He won."

Merry nodded thoughtfully, her eyes on Julia. "But will she wake up?"

"What do the doctors think?"

"They think they need to hear what Boston thinks."

"Remember Will Starbuck, Merry. These things just take a bit of time." Peter touched her shoulder lightly, his eyes on her face. She was disturbingly pale. "And *when* she wakes up, she's going to need something to turn to. A project of some kind."

"Art in Mind?"

"Why not? She's got a foundation and at least one trustee left standing."

"I'm not sure she'll be willing to restart the center."

"Who knows? Give her the summer to think it over. She and the kids could move into Betsy Osborne's Sconset house for the time being—serve as caretakers—and worry about whether to return to Cambridge in the fall."

"That sounds reasonable. Then maybe Mabel Johnson could take over the Markhams' old place. God knows her house won't be standing for long. It might be *one* good thing to come out of this mess—" She stopped, swallowed hard, and looked down at her fingers.

"I'm sorry about Jack Osborne."

The door swung open, and a gurney rolled into the room, propelled by a very determined Dr. John Fairborn. Noise, more bodies, the gadgetry of life support—and Merry and Peter found themselves abruptly in the hallway.

"The helicopter must be here." Merry looked around for Cecil and Nan.

"In the waiting area, I think," Peter said, and steered her in that direction. She seemed to be almost sleepwalking. "Have you eaten anything?"

"Couple of bags of pretzels. I feel sick to my stomach, Peter—I couldn't touch a thing."

He pulled her gently toward a bank of seats and settled her into one of them. "Stop beating yourself up, Merry. Be thankful you're alive."

"But Jack Osborne *isn't*. Sylvia Whitehead *isn't*. Roxie Teasdale—"

"I know. I know. But that's not your fault."

"Then whose is it?"

"Tucker Enright's."

"If I hadn't been so blind—and so trusting—all of them might be alive today. They died because of *my* stupidity, Peter. Died for no good reason. I should have seen. I should have done something to save them. When I think of how thankful Osborne looked, as I burst into Julia's house—and then—and then—I delivered him up to that *maniac*—"

"Merry." Peter drew her close. She was shuddering with weeping, and this seemed to him a good thing. "Feel bad if you must. Feel terrible. But don't feel like a murderer. You didn't kill Jack Osborne. Or Sylvia White-head. And no one could have saved Roxie Teasdale."

"Someone should have! Don't you see—I have no business being a police officer if innocent people are victimized by my mismanagement! I should turn in my badge today!"

"You didn't make Enright pull that trigger. In fact, Dr. Enright would say those people died because *he* decided they had to. A conscious choice from a sane man. He'd be offended to hear you, Meredith. You make him sound like just another nut."

"I guess I'd better practice, then, for my sworn testimony," she shot back bitterly, "because I want that jury to hear, *from the woman he tried to kill,* that Tucker Enright is completely sane. I want him locked up forever—and I don't mean in a psychiatric ward."

"But how can anyone who takes another person's life be called *sane?*"

"Enright did it every day. For him, it was absolutely vital to make the guilty ones pay. As he had made Elizabeth Osborne pay, years ago, for the crime of leaving him." She mopped at her eyes and drew a deep breath. "I think Enright's work became his absolution for Betsy's murder. He could exonerate himself by making sure the *other* guilty ones never killed again. Does that make sense?"

"In a twisted way, yes," Peter admitted. "But it suggests he's even sicker than I thought."

"Oh, you liberal bleeding heart," Merry said, and gave him a crooked half-smile. "You'd like all the criminals to have a comfy bed and three squares in the nuthouse, wouldn't you?"

"Not Enright," Peter said soberly. "I don't want to wake up in a cold sweat because he's just been paroled for good behavior. If he dies in maximum security, I hope you'll have no regrets."

"None."

"When I think of what might have happened to you—" Peter lifted her chin with his hand, and stared intently into her eyes. "The coda to his serial killer drama. Four bodies at the scene, and Dr. Tucker Enright conducting the conference the morning after, complete with pictures."

"It didn't come to that," Merry said quietly.

"Enright intended it to. You were merely lucky."

"I know. But don't dwell on it." She stood up and walked toward the waiting area.

"But I *do*," Peter objected, keeping pace with her. "I think about it all the time. Not just with Enright. With everything." He pulled her around to face him, the two of them an island in the empty hospital corridor. "I worry about *you*, Merry. About this life you live with guns. Carrying them, firing them, *needing* them to get through your work day. Couldn't you have been an interior designer, or something?"

"You're far better at color swatches than I am, Peter. Look at our respective houses."

"Don't joke, Meredith. I mean it. This business of yours—the danger, the risk—it's too much for me."

He saw the apprehension flood her face, and the way she tried to control it.

"What are you saying?"

"I'm asking you to take some time," Peter said carefully. "Think about what you're doing. What you want."

"And what *you* want, is that it?"

"I would hope that would be part of what you wanted, yes."

"You're asking me to quit. Turn in my badge."

After an instant, he shrugged. "Maybe I am. You brought it up, after all. And I can't say I'd mourn the loss of tension in our lives. Your work is pretty hard to live with."

"Oh, God," she said despairingly, and took two steps backward.

What had he said? Again Peter tried to draw her close, but this time she was rigid, her arms fixed at her sides.

"Don't do this, Peter," she murmured. "Don't let me down gently. I can't stand it."

"It means that much to you?"

"Of course."

"I thought you might be getting tired of it. Looking for a graceful exit."

"From you?" She leaned back and stared at him. "Never."

"Never?" His pulse quickened. "I was talking about your job, but I'll take a declaration of love when I hear it. *Never*, huh? Sounds pretty deathless to me."

"Peter—I meant that I—"

"And there's the matter of that bet we made at the Ritz. About Jack Osborne killing his wife. Heads I win, tails you lose?"

She hesitated a moment, transfixed by his words. Drew a shuddery breath. And then closed her eyes tight, as though making a terrible wish.

"*Heads,*" she told him.

About the Author

FRANCINE MATHEWS has worked as a journalist and a foreign policy analyst. She is the author of four Merry Folger mysteries, including *Death in A Mood Indigo* and the upcoming *Death in a Cold Hard Light*. Under the name Stephanie Barron, she is the author of three best-selling Jane Austen mysteries, *Jane and the Unpleasantness at Scargrave Manor*, *Jane and the Man of the Cloth*, and *Jane and the Wandering Eye*. She lives in Colorado, where she is at work on *Jane and the Genius of the Place*.

If you enjoyed Francine Mathews's
DEATH IN A MOOD INDIGO, you will not want
to miss the next exciting Merry Folger mystery,
DEATH IN A COLD HARD LIGHT.

Look for

Death in a Cold Hard Light

A Merry Folger Mystery
by Francine Mathews

in hardcover at your favorite bookstore in June 1998.